A Story of True Love

The novel shows the times and life of aristocratic English families in the late nineteenth century, when the common mode of transport was horse-driven carriages. It tells the story of a very rich young Englishman, Nevlin Lane, who comes from a highly respected aristocratic family. Family conflicts and harassment drive him from a life of luxury and material comforts to a life of poverty and hard labour in an Austrian gold mine. Even in the state of poverty, Nevlin Lane does not compromise with his basic principles of kindness, truth and generosity towards others. By a remarkable coincidence, he meets Sylvia Bond, a cultured and talented girl whose parents were at one time wealthy and well-respected. Their love for one another blossoms and endures in spite of unforeseen hardships and unexpected events. The story reveals the true love that binds the two. It is full of suspense and heart-warming episodes. It reveals how kindness and good deeds are always rewarded by God. This novel is an English translation of an Urdu novel, *Samrhae Naykie* (Reward of Kindness) written in 1928.

Omesh Govind Mathur was born in Delhi, India. He went to England for higher studies in 1954, and graduated from the University of Durham, in Mechanical Engineering. He immigrated to Canada in 1968 and worked for the Ontario Government till his retirement in 1993. Omesh lives in Toronto.

A Story
of
True Love

A Translation of an Urdu Novel
Samrhae Naykie (Reward of Kindness)

OMESH GOVIND MATHUR

PRESTIGE

PRESTIGE BOOKS
3/28, East Patel Nagar
New Delhi 110 008

ISBN: 81-7551-089-7

Composed by Vivek Mathur, Delhi 110 006 Ph. 3981867
Printed by Chaman Offset Press, New Delhi 110 002

Preface

This book, *A Story of True Love*, is my humble attempt to translate into English, a great novel *Samrhae Naykie*, written in Urdu by my grandfather, Mr. Har Govind Mathur of Delhi. The novel was based essentially on a story in English, probably written earlier in the twentieth century. It is my belief that though the basic theme is taken from that story, my grandfather expanded it into an Urdu novel, inserting his own style and philosophy to create a beautiful love story, *Samrhae Naykie*, which means, Reward of Kindness. *Samrhae Naykie* was his own creation and reflected his way of thinking about life. The present book, *A Story of True Love*, is an English translation of the same.

My grandfather, in his book, has acknowledged gratefully the help given by several persons (including my father Mr. B.G. Mathur, a civil engineer), in translating and proof reading the novel which was published in Lucknow, India, in 1929.

Urdu was the language of the day at the time my grandfather wrote the novel. Several famous poets and writers used the Urdu script for their work. I was afraid that this novel written by my grandfather will eventually be forgotten by my family members as most of them know only Hindi and English. To preserve the legacy for the present and future generations, I decided to translate it into English.

This novel has a deep moral significance. It shows that those who are kind and honest always reap the reward of their noble actions. I hope the readers will not only appreciate and enjoy the beautiful story, but also learn a profound lesson from it. The message of the novel is that God always rewards kindness and good deeds. This is a universal truth, true for all times, past, present and future.

I have attempted to be as close as possible to the original

text in Urdu. However, it is neither possible nor necessary to have a verbatim translation as many words in a language do not have an exact equivalent in the translated language. To maintain readability, I have taken the liberty to convey the overall meaning of a sentence in English. At the start of each chapter, my grandfather wrote a two/four line Urdu couplet. It was difficult to translate these into English without writing detailed explanations. Therefore I have taken the liberty to translate them as close to the Urdu text as possible. I am aware that some of these may not sound appropriate but they convey the essence of the chapter.

I am grateful to my wife Asha Mathur for all her encouragement and faith in my ability to translate this novel and for her patience in editing the book. She and my daughter Niti and son Ashish, inspired me to undertake this very satisfying work of translation. My young grandson, Karan Raj, took great interest in my work and was a great incentive for me to complete this laborious task of translation. I hope his generation and others to follow will find this book interesting.

The love and affection of my two elder brothers, Dr. Tej Govind and Mr. Mahesh Govind, and their respective wives, has been a source of strength and inspiration to me. All my sisters and their spouses have always helped and supported me in times of need. Their love and faith in me has been a source of inspiration at every stage of my life. I gratefully acknowledge their contribution to whatever success I have achieved in my life.

I would like to express my special thanks and gratitude to my sisters, Mrs. Shanti Rani, Mrs. Sushila Rani and Dr. Rama Rani, and my brother-in-law, Mr. C.B. Mathur, for their editorial assistance and valuable comments. Rama was instrumental in getting this novel published. I am indebted to her for her help.

In the end I want to thank very sincerely Dr. R.K. Dhawan, the editors and publishers of this novel. Without their help and guidance I could not have published it.

Toronto, Canada **OMESH GOVIND MATHUR**
January 2000

I dedicate this novel to my parents

My mother, Mrs. Bishan Pyari, died in March 1941 when I was very young. She was love personified and taught me the meaning of justice and fairness. My father, Mr. Brij Govind Mathur, was a very practical and knowledgeable person. He was a civil engineer and retired from his job in 1947 but continued to work with other government organizations till 1962. He died in April 1975. He was a saintly person and had read widely about various religions. His teachings are a rich treasure that one can leave for one's children. His advice and teachings have helped all of us, brothers and sisters, to overcome the most trying times when money or other material things were not of much use. His religious teachings gave us the inner strength to face the most adverse situations courageously.

As I venture on this task of translating the Urdu novel *Samrhae Naykie* into English, I seek the heavenly blessings of my parents in the fulfilment of this work.

Prayer

The novel Samrhae Naykie *begins with a prayer written by my great grandfather, Mr. Bal Gobind Mathur, under his pen name "Gulzar." This prayer is taken from his book of poems titled* Zakhirae Balgobind *(Treasures of Balgobind), probably written in the late nineteenth century.*

Where are You—the Master of the two Worlds
You are the Supreme God

Give my eyes the power
To see Your presence everywhere

The learned praise You
Everyone bows to You

Everywhere I look
I see a new image of You

The rich and the poor, the learned and the illiterate
Amongst all multitude—you are unique

How can one describe you
The tongue and the pen do not have power to do so

Only my heart knows, what You are
Nature reflects Your glory and greatness

Everything reveals Your presence
Every object manifests Your glory

Give me the eyes that I may see You
Give me the understanding to understand You

Gods Brahma and Mahesh
Are constantly worshipping You and are amazed by You

Your Balgobind alias Gulzar
Begs to remain always in your Grace.

Chapter 1

It is essential for a person to remain human
Those with kindness and compassion can motivate others

The Lornehope Camp, in Austria, was known for large deposits of gold in the gold mines. It was also known that people from far and near and from different countries came here to dig the gold mines in the hope of finding gold. A majority of the mine diggers were from poor and low-caste families and some were even robbers. However, it was also known that a few of the young workers were from cultured and rich families. They came to Lornehope Camp to escape personal problems at home or the wrath of their parents. They were digging with the desire to find gold. These workers usually worked under assumed names and their real name and past was neither disclosed nor known to any one in the camp.

In the beginning the Lornehope Camp was a completely deserted place surrounded by wild heath and barren fields all around. The gold mine workers established a sort of make shift colony in the nearby valley by constructing small thatched huts. There were also a few nice bungalow-type houses of mud. At a short distance from this colony of workers was a town, where the rich and the poor lived in brick houses. There were all kinds of shops in this town where people could buy things of daily needs. The majority of the population of this town consisted of farmers.

One year, the summer was so unbearable that people cried

out for relief from the relentless heat. It was said that even the birds got roasted alive by the heat. Though there were some trees around the mine workers' colony, there was absolutely no breeze. Once in a while one could hear a bird chirping but usually the birds just sat on house tops with open beaks. The workers were so exhausted by the heat that they did not have the strength to scare away the birds from their houses. The horses and dogs struggled to stay alive by lying on the banks of the nearby river. They had no flesh left on their bodies and were reduced to bare bones.

In Lornehope Camp, Mr. McGregor had a contract for selling liquor. He was also appointed by the King of Austria to act as the sole contractor for the excavation work at the gold mines at Lornehope Camp. This gentleman allotted a piece of land, after due measurements, to workers who wanted to dig for gold at the camp. No one was allowed to dig at any other place without proper and specific permission from Mr. McGregor. He made the mine workers sign a written contract and every one had to follow the rules and conditions of the contract.

Mr. McGregor had a large office in which many accountants, clerks and security personnel worked. The security staff was visible everywhere and looked after the mine workers and their property. The local church, the post office and the hospital were also under the supervision of Mr. McGregor. He was also responsible for the welfare and well-being of all the workers and other people living in Lornehope Camp. Any worker who found a gold piece was paid at the rate of $5 per ounce by the office of Mr. McGregor. However, it was very difficult to find gold and the workers had difficulty in earning enough money to buy food for two daily meals. In spite of this the workers had hopes of striking rich some day and they worked with great diligence and perseverance in digging at the gold mines. Everyday they hoped of finding a large piece of gold which would make them rich and with this hope they spent all their time in digging at the mines.

Near Mr. McGregor's office, and at some distance from the huts of other workers, there was a neat little house. In this house lived an English gentleman Nevlin Lane. He was a polite, kind-hearted and a handsome young man who treated every one with respect. He came from a good family and was a victim of unjust persecution by his father and brother and was forced to leave his home. Physically he was very strong with a tall, muscular body. He had assumed the name of Ian in the camp. As Ian, he mingled freely with all the workers, and worked at the gold mine. He employed an old woman of the Camp, by the name of Mathula, as a servant and provided her with food and clothing. She lived in the same house. She was responsible for getting all the groceries from the market and cooking and cleaning the house. She ensured that everything was provided to Ian at the right time. She was kind hearted, good natured, hard working and honest. She devoted all her time in looking after her master's comfort and well being. Since Ian also belonged to a decent family, the two of them got along well and lived a content life.

Ian's real name, Nevlin Lane, was not known to any one in the Camp. Everyone knew him as Ian and addressed him as such. Ian had started feeling a bit frustrated with his fruitless search for gold for two years. Whenever he thought of leaving the camp, the hope of finding gold and becoming rich kept him working. He consoled himself with the thought that one day he will find gold and his hard work will be rewarded. He, therefore, kept on working with great determination and courage.

Though outwardly Ian looked like the other workers, his robust health, polite manners, kindness, gentlemanly behaviour and style of living suggested that he was from a noble family. People said that this Englishman was working as a labourer due to some personal problems and though he was poor and frustrated, he was always there to help the sick and the needy. For this reason all the workers treated him with respect and admiration.

Nevlin Lane did not develop any close social relationship with the people at the Camp and except for formal greetings, kept a distance from them. He rarely went to the town market place. Though he knew everyone he did not socialize with them. However, if he heard of anyone being sick or in need of help, he went out of his way to help them. He considered it his duty and treated everyone with kindness and respect.

He spent carefully whatever he earned with his hard work. One day the strenuous work made him sweat profusely and all his clothes became wet with perspiration. In addition to this the memory of his home made him very sad. For relief he started pacing the verandah of his house. At the usual time, the cook Mathula rang the bell for dinner. On hearing the bell, he went inside the house. After finishing his dinner, he lit his cigarette and went for a stroll outside the house. He saw a man wearing simple clothes coming towards his house. When this man came nearer, he recognized him as the Camp doctor. Nevlin Lane greeted him with enthusiasm and walked with him to his house, talking about the doctor's work and his general welfare. Once inside the house he requested him to be seated on a chair.

The doctor, besides treating patients in the local hospital, also worked as the lawyer and the priest for the community. He knew that this Englishman worked at the mines, but because of his noble behaviour he was sure that this person had not revealed his real name and was working under the assumed name of Ian. He thought there was surely some secret in his life. The doctor wiped his face with a handkerchief and with his eyes lowered looked at the bright face of Nevlin Lane. After a few minutes he raised his head and asked Ian, "Mr. Ian did you have any luck in making any money during the last year?" In response to this question, Nevlin Lane looked at the doctor and said that he had not made any worthwhile gain. He then opened his beautiful leather tobacco case and offered it to the doctor with respect.

The doctor took some tobacco from the case. He lit his pipe and returned the tobacco case thanking Ian and said with a concern in his voice, "There is a great increase in the cases of fever these days and I have to travel all over the town to look after the patients. Thank God you appear to be in good health. In addition you appear to be an experienced person. It is good that you do not socialize with these dirty workers and keep away from their filthy huts. This is why you are unaware of the problems of the general public. The condition of the workers here is getting worse. It is unfortunate that in search of gold they neglect their health completely to the extent that even medicines have little effect. Instead of finding gold pieces they waste their life in digging the hard rocks."

Nevlin Lane agreed and said, "Sir, poverty and illness naturally go together."

The doctor said, "But in spite of limited means you appear to be in good health and your face indicates robust health."

Nevlin Lane thanked God for his good health and replied, "I am satisfied with my position. I do not worry unnecessarily about the problems of the world and live a happy life. I eat fresh food of my liking and make my cook work as hard in cooking the food as you do in preparing your medicines."

The doctor asked, "Probably you also do not drink?"

Ian replied, "I do not drink every day but once in a while I take a little drink as medicine."

The doctor said, "The real reason for my coming to your place at this time is that about a furlong away from your house on the west side, an old man has become very sick. He has lived here for the last six months and is probably one of the workers. I have to say with regret that in this Lornehope Camp, there is no regulation or law that requires a worker to tell his real name or the country he comes from. There are no official records or information about these workers. People from different countries come here under assumed names and like sheep, get lost in the multitude of workers here. We are unable to find their real name and background. This old sick man, like you, appears to be well educated and comes from a good family. He speaks good English. From his general disposition and the way he conducts himself it appears that he is from a cultured family and comes from a big city. With him is a young girl. She reads and writes fluently. She is a very cultured and soft spoken person. There is a certain sweetness in her voice. However, she is so slender that it will be appropriate if I call her an innocent little child. Just now, I have come from their place. The patient seems to be close to death. In my opinion if a few drops of brandy are given to him, he may revive. In the hospital there is no liquor of any kind and I never take a drink myself.

I am sure that because of your kind nature, you will give some brandy for the sake of this sick man. The old man is having convulsions because of cold and weakness. If some brandy is given to him as medicine, his condition may improve."

Hearing this, Nevlin Lane said with his head down, "Sir, I am not worthy of your praise and it is not suitable for an elderly and greatly respected person like you to compare me with any other person. I am sorry that I have only a little brandy left in the bottle and if it can be of any benefit to any person then I have absolutely no hesitation in giving it to you. It is necessary that we help each other in whatever way we can."

With these words he opened his trunk, took out the bottle and handed it to the doctor. The latter said a few words of thanks and left for the hut of the sick man.

On reaching the hut, the doctor found the patient lying flat on the ground with his eyes closed. There was sadness on his face and his pulse was slow. There were a few white hair on his head. However, from his face and eyes, he appeared to be no more than forty years. By the side of the patient, a girl sat in old, dirty clothes. There was great anxiety on her face. Her slim body appeared radiant under her worn out clothes, like the moon shining behind a thin layer of clouds. Her face was pale and showed sadness but she was not sick. Her body was very lean and thin. There appeared to be no other reason for this except starvation and malnutrition.

The doctor, after regaining his breath, studied the patient's pulse for sometime. He poured a little brandy from the bottle in a cup and mixed it with a measured amount of water. With great care he poured a little of this mixture into the mouth of the patient. The quantity and the angle of pouring was just right and the patient gulped it down. After giving brandy to the patient, the doctor asked the girl who the patient was.

The girl replied in a very soft and sweet voice, "Sir, he is my respected father. I am entirely dependent on him. Except for my father there is no one else in this world whom I know and who would care for me."

Hearing this the doctor tried to support the patient to a sitting posture. It required all his physical strength and a great deal of effort to do so. He started to fan the patient's face with his cap. In about fifteen minutes, the patient regained consciousness. The old man first looked at the girl who was standing by his side and then at the doctor. He motioned to the doctor with his hand to go outside. The doctor understood his meaning and said to the patient, "Probably you want to talk to your daughter in private and that's alright." He said to the girl that he will be at the hospital and at the slightest deterioration in her father's condition, she should come to the hospital and inform him. After giving these instructions, the doctor left the house. The girl drew the outside verandah curtain as per her father's wishes and sat down beside him.

The sick man looked at his daughter with loving eyes and said with a sigh, "My darling daughter, my delicate child who has been brought up with great love and affection, you are the joy of my life. The end of my life has come. I am here for only a few more minutes. Look at me and please do not weep. I am saddened by your crying. It is written in the Holy Book that you should not weep for the dead. Please pray for the salvation of my soul so that I may face God peacefully. The children who pray with a sincere heart for the salvation of their parents' soul help them to find peace after death. Please listen to my advice carefully and promise me that you will act on it, so that I may depart from this world in peace. Listen, death is inevitable. No one's parents live for ever. Everyone has to leave this world one day. I too am a humble man subject to this truth. Always remember that this world is full of problems. Those who face the problems with courage, determination and calm, fear God and thank Him for His merciful nature, and consider it to be one's duty to follow the teachings of the Holy Book, do well in the end. I am leaving you in this world without any friends or resources, but if you follow my advice, you may receive help from unknown sources. Circumstances will be created that would end all your misery and poverty and provide means for your comfortable living. Under my shirt you will find a locket wrapped and stitched securely in a cloth pouch. Take it off my neck and wear it. Consider this locket more precious than your own life. Do not part with it even for a minute. You are now fifteen years old. After three years you will be eighteen. On the completion of three years from today, open this locket with your own hands. Inside the locket there is a paper along with the certificate of my marriage and also a certificate of your birth duly signed by the priest. The paper has a complete account of your background. It may help you and change your fate to a life of happiness."

He had hardly finished the sentence when he had a violent coughing spasm. The girl left her father to fetch water and saw a tall, mean and frightening looking man near the curtain, carefully listening to her father's conversation with her. He left as he saw her approaching the curtain. In her haste to get water for her father she forgot to ask him about this man. With great haste she poured some drops of water and brandy several times in her father's mouth. On drinking this, the sick man felt some strength and once again started to breathe properly. He said to the girl, "I have given you the necessary education and have made you read books that teach you about this world, its history and its geography. I have also taught you cooking, sewing, and music, which should be a part of every girl's education. I have made you aware of all the teachings in the religious books which show the right way to live in this world. You should follow the teachings of these books. Always remember that God is watching you. Do not discuss anything that is against God. Consider God to be just and always near you. Never entertain thoughts of hatred and revenge. Serve your husband or benefactor with all your heart and sincerity, because by true devotion you get respect and love. Treat everyone with civility and kindness. Judge a person with the wisdom that your training has provided you, whether he is a friend or a foe. Never get involved with cheating and deceitful behaviour. Face the problems of the world with patience. What did I want to say—oh I am forgetting—yes—yes, I remember. Tell me, have you worn the locket around your neck—do you promise to act on my advice?"

The girl showed her father the locket round her neck and said in a sad voice, "I shall always keep this necklace next to my heart and would never take it off my body. Three years from today I shall open the locket with my own hands and find out what is in my fate. I thank you from the bottom of my heart for giving me excellent education. With the help of the training that you have given me, I shall work to earn my living. I will not be a party to anyone's fraud or cheating. I will not say or do anything without due thought. I will never, under any circumstances, deviate from the path of righteousness. I will always follow your advice. I will pray everyday to the all merciful God to give you peace and salvation."

On hearing this the old man kissed his daughter several times on the forehead and said in a low voice, "My darling daughter, because of your upbringing and education, I have great expectations from you. May Almighty God protect you from the dangers of this world and be with you in all your troubles. I leave you in the hands of the God. Goodbye . . . Goodbye . . . Goodb . . ."

He could hardly finish the last word. His breath stuck in his throat and he died. The girl fainted on her father's body.

Hardly had five minutes elapsed when the doctor came to the house to inquire about the patient and also brought a bottle of medicine. He lifted the curtain and went inside. He found the girl unconscious and the patient dead.

He immediately came out and saw an ugly, evil looking man standing outside the door. The doctor recognized him by his face as he had come to the dispensary two or three times to get medicine. The doctor took him to be another worker and did not know anything about his character. He welcomed the presence of another person in such a situation and said with an urgency in his voice, "The old sick man is dead and his daughter is unconscious. At such a time you should help her. Please go as fast as you can and summon help from neighbourhood. I am also going to send a couple of women to look after the girl and provide some assurance to her. On your way, inform the neighbours and the nearby workers of the death of the sick man so that they may prepare him for the coffin and the grave."

After giving these instructions, the doctor went inside the house to revive the girl. He saw that she had regained consciousness and was immersed in grief and crying. The doctor said a few words of sympathy and encouragement. When an old woman from the neighbourhood arrived, the doctor left for his home. The old woman sat down beside the girl and began to console her. That mean looking man whom the town people knew by the name of Lewryk, pulled up a chair and sat down in front of the house.

Chapter 2

No one may know the secret love
Though the heart may burn

My heart moves around you like a potter's wheel
Like a person who prays always facing the holy place

More than two days had passed since Nevlin Lane had last met the doctor. He was so busy with his work that he did not find enough time to go out and inquire about the condition of the sick man or to go to the doctor to find out as to how the sick man was doing. Except eating his meals at the regular time and spending a few minutes with Mathula, the cook, to make sure that she had money for the necessary groceries and food items, he did not have time for anything else. Every morning, he picked up his shovel and his meal of boiled rice and went to work. One day he came home for lunch at noon and found flies all over the table. He fanned with his cap and scared away the flies from the table and ate his lunch. With the intention of taking some rest, he lay on the bed and tried to take a nap. However, the scenes of his country and home in London danced before his eyes. He could clearly see his luxurious house in Devonshire in front of his eyes. He could hear the laughter of his childhood friends and was lost in the memories of the past. He recalled the days of learning at school and the games he used to play with his friends. All this made him very restless and he kept tossing and turning. He wondered to himself, "Oh God, what should I do! It is over two years that I have been digging in the mines; the loneliness is unbearable; because of poverty my condition is worthless. To go to London in this situation and to meet acquaintances would not only be foolish but very shameful. The doctor was right in belying expectations of finding gold here. It is simply wasting one's life breaking stones and starvation can lead to all kinds of disease." Then he said to himself, "Even if I go, where can I go! How can I show my face to my friends and relatives without any money in my hand. It is better to die here than to go and beg in London. I cannot expect any help of any kind from my cunning and selfish relatives; they will laugh at me. To live with my friends will be disgraceful."

He was engrossed in such thoughts when he heard the cook calling him, "Ian, Ian." Startled by the shouts, he got up and went to her. Mathula told him that there were no groceries in the house for the evening meal. On hearing this, Nevlin Lane went to his room and took out his silver purse from the box. He turned the purse upside down and counted all the money. Twelve shillings in all! Looking at this paltry sum of money, he had a big laugh. He thought to himself that the days of good living were now over as this money was just enough for two days and with that thought he gave all that money to Mathula and asked her to get the essential groceries from the market. Mathula left for the market. Nevlin Lane picked up his shovel and meal of boiled rice and with courage, determination and full faith in God, he slowly went to his place of work.

He stood near the hole that he had made in the past two years and with a sincere heart he promised himself that today he was not going to dig the hole any more than six strikes. If he did not find gold in sufficient quantity, then he was going to bid goodbye to Lornehope Camp for good. The doctor was right in saying that digging for gold was nothing but fighting with stones and dying without a coffin or grave. With the firm determination of not striking more than six times, he lifted his pickaxe above the head and with full force struck at the hole and started counting, one, two, three, four, five. At the fifth strike, the usual reddish colour sand started to come out of the hole. But Nevlin Lane did not get disheartened and with his full force he made the sixth strike. The sixth strike split open the big stone and from underneath a heavy slab of gold fell near his feet. Nevlin Lane stood in wonder for a few seconds. The disappointments of the past years did not let the full impact of finding the gold slab register for sometime. After he got over the initial shock and recovered his senses, he could see the gold clearly. He lifted the slab with both hands to estimate its weight. It was so heavy that his hands started shaking. He estimated the value of the slab based on its weight to be not less one thousand pounds and cried out:

> (God) You fulfill prayers
> The hopeful is never disappointed by you

Nevlin Lane kept the gold slab in front of his eyes and raised both his hands towards the sky and prayed, "Oh God, God! it did not take You long to change my luck. The money that I brought with me also finished today, and without Your Grace now, I would have starved to death. I would have rotted in a foreign country without a grave and my enemies in London would have rejoiced at my fate. God, You are present everywhere and You look after your devotees every second. It is true that no one can harm anyone who is under Your protection."

With such thoughts, he said to himself, that with this money he should return to London. Though with this money no one will count him as rich but he would not be considered as a poor beggar either. After reaching London, he planned to buy a farm in his home town, Devonshire, and do farming. This way he could live the rest of his life in peace and comfort. Nevlin Lane felt a strange feeling of joy inside him. He felt strong, confident and full of hope.

He kissed the gold slab and wrapped it in his shawl. Walking at a brisk pace he reached his home before Mathula returned from the market. He kept the gold slab inside the box and while he was locking it, Mathula returned from the market with the groceries.

She stood at the door of Nevlin Lane's room and shouted, "Ian, Ian. Sir, in the town's market all the things are very costly. After spending the money I could barely buy groceries for two days and no money was left to buy wine. My body is aching all over and I feel absolutely tired and exhausted. You used to have some liquor in the bottle but have given the whole bottle to the doctor. If there was some liquor I would have taken a couple of sips and would feel better. Now it is very difficult to buy any more from the shop. Even if you wanted to get some for me from the market, you cannot, as you do not have a cent left with you."

Ian said, "Yes Mathula, you are right, everything has become very costly. But do not worry and have patience. God is great—He can never tolerate to see His devotees in trouble. You will feel better in a little while without the drink. Why do you lament for the little quantity of liquor. How could you have benefitted from it? I will get you a barrel of wine."

With these words he started to lock the box but with the movement of the hand, the gold slab struck the inside seam of the box. The cook heard the sound caused by the impact of the slab and she jumped with joy. She laid her hand on Ian's head and said, "Ian, did you find enough gold to lock in the box? I heard the sound of gold slab. Please tell me the truth—do you really have a gold slab in the box?"

Nevlin Lane had never told a lie in his life, either in joke or in reality. In fact he used to dislike people who lied and used to keep far away from such persons. He smiled and said, "You have guessed right. The all merciful God, in His Grace, blessed me with a gold slab today. Jump and dance with joy but do not speak loudly about the gold slab, remember even the walls have ears. There are many robbers and muggers here. They keep a tab on every mine digger's house. They may hear you and come and rob us. The robbers can take away our hard-earned money and people will blame us for being foolish in not safeguarding our possessions and we will regret it all our life. Mathula, listen to me carefully. With the finding of this gold slab, all my life's dreams are realized. Today is 16th. This is the day of the town fair and assembly when Mr. McGregor will come to his office. Today, till late in the night, he will take the workers's gold and pay them money in proportion to the quantity of gold they have produced. There will be a big gathering of the workers. In addition to the workers, the town's people will also come to see the fun and buy sundry items at the fair. Every two weeks this fair and assembly is held till midnight and all the workers enjoy a big party. Today I will also participate and enjoy the fair and then . . ."

Mathula interrupted him and said, "And then you will run away from here?"

Ian replied, "You are right again. You know very well that I am most anxious to return to my country. As soon as I get the money for the slab, I will go to London. You have a share in my happiness. I will give you a part of the money I get for the slab. It is not my nature to be greedy. Please get me some tea quickly so that I may reach the fair as soon as possible. It is getting nearer the time when Mr. McGregor will be coming to his office."

Mathula replied, "Tea alone will not be enough. Ian, listen to me. You should take two cups of tea and soup with bread. I will get all this ready in ten minutes. Without bread in your stomach you will get very tired carrying the weighty gold slab all the way."

Ian said, "What you are saying makes sense." He kept his hand on her chin and pushed back her hair from her face and said to her in a kind voice, "You are tired from the shopping. Let me light the fire and wash the dishes. You can then make me some tea."

Mathula said with a smile, "It is not right. I am here to cook meals and I am quite used to it. I do not feel tired at all in cooking as it is my job. I will take no time in cooking the meals. You go ahead and change into clean clothes and I will have the dinner ready in a few minutes."

With this she got busy in working and within a short time she laid the table. While eating dinner, Nevlin Lane said to Mathula, "From today's earnings, I will give you an award of fifty pounds. Please consider that as your share and accept it."

Mathula laughed without control and her jaws became visible

in her soft face. She lowered her face with shyness and looked at Ian's face with wonder and very innocently asked: "Would you really give me fifty pounds?" In response Ian said, "Certainly I will give you fifty pounds. What's there to doubt or wonder? An honest man always does what he says. You have given me great comfort. Because of you, for the past two years, I have been free of problems of running the house and cooking meals. The time that I would have spent in doing house chores, I spent in digging. Without any worry I have been getting my breakfast and cooked meals on time. An honest and loyal person like you, in all fairness, deserves fifty pounds. I will certainly give you fifty pounds."

Mathula thanked Ian from her heart for his kindness and generosity. When he finished eating, Mathula said to him, "Do not delay any further as the time for the assembly is getting close. God is the absolute sustainer. In His Grace, he has bestowed upon you the reward of your hard work. May God always increase your earnings. Your kindness and generosity is not hidden from the laws of Nature. May God always give you happiness and good health. May God always look after you."

With the blessings of his kind and God-fearing cook, Nevlin Lane wrapped the gold slab in his shawl and left for the fair.

It was a beautiful evening and the moon was coming out of the clouds. With the gold slab close to his chest and sparkle in his eyes, Nevlin Lane walked like a newly married man carrying his beautiful bride in his arms. He felt very happy and lucky.

Nevlin Lane walked through the narrow and difficult valleys which passed through the huts of the workers and reached the camp of Mr. McGregor safely. His tent office was much bigger in size than the tents of other officers on his staff. It was well lighted with lamps and chandeliers. The voices of several people in the camp could be heard from a distance. Before entering the tent, Nevlin Lane had decided that he will ask that money for the gold slab be paid in Pound Sterling, the British currency. He had also decided that he will leave for London within a couple of days and after reaching London he would make plans for his future life.

It was generally seen that the foreigners were anxious to return back to their country. They could not stop thinking of their home and friends. At the slightest excuse, the foreigners were ready to return to their country. Nevlin Lane also entertained such thoughts and he entered the big tent of the contractor in a cheerful mood. In the middle of the tent, near a table, Mr. McGregor and the doctor were standing. The tent seemed to be full of local people and mine workers. On the floor of the tent, all kinds of people were sitting on a rug close to each other. The tent was absolutely jam packed with practically no room left anywhere. Even at the doors, men, women, old people and children were standing. Nevlin Lane found some space near the door next to the table; he went and stood beside that door. Several people including Mr. McGregor and the doctor saw him and greeted him. He acknowledged everyone's greetings by bowing his head. His acquaintances looked at the bright face of Nevlin Lane. However, because of shortage of space nobody dared to call him to come and sit beside them.

Ten minutes after Nevlin Lane had reached, Mr. Loket, the chief clerk of Mr. McGregor, got up from his seat and said in a loud voice: "Ladies and gentlemen, about six months back this year, an unknown old man, whose real name and country we have been unable to find and have no hope of finding in spite of all our efforts, came to Lornehope camp. Two weeks back he passed away. In this place people of various religions and countries come to dig for gold but I regret to say they do not tell us their real name or country. In our books of registration, they give false names. If they die here, our kind hearted and respected contractor Mr. McGregor has to provide all assistance in arranging for their last rites. He considers this as the only human thing to do and he does it gladly. This old man seemingly had no friends and no possessions. However, my friend the doctor treated him with great care. Yet he died. You are all aware that death is not a disease but a command from the ultimate Supreme Power and no one, neither king nor beggar, can escape His Will. Neither medicine nor prayers can change His command." The crowd looked at the doctor and thanked him.

Mr. Loket continued: "This person has left a daughter.

Though at this time she is in great shock and full of grief, she can be restored back to good health in a few days. Ladies and gentlemen, you are well aware that it is not possible to find servants in Lornehope Camp. Everyone is busy, day and night, in digging for gold and some do not even have time to cook their meals. If one of you, from the kindness of your heart, would take this orphan girl in your care and look after her, then this poor girl would prove to be very useful as a servant. Ladies and gentlemen, look in the direction of my finger at the south side of the tent, the innocent helpless poor girl is sitting amongst four kind women beside the very religious and pious woman in the black dress."

At this everyone's eyes rivetted on the girl. Nevlin Lane also looked at her from head to foot and thought her to be a cultured and noble person. He noticed that her hands and feet were very thin and her eyes were full of tears. Her face reflected great anxiety and grief. She appeared restless amongst those women and moaned ever so often. One of the women sitting next to her, moved with both hands her glamorous beautiful long hair from her face and tied them at the back and kissed her forehead. People also noticed that this innocent beautiful young girl, with lowered eyes, continuously looked at Nevlin Lane who was standing near the main gate. Her beautiful eyes were fixed in his direction. From her expression and behaviour it appeared that she considered Nevlin Lane to be a real gentleman. He also noticed that this innocent lovable girl was looking at him and he felt a natural wave of love towards her. He felt sad for the helpless girl and looked at her with loving eyes.

The doctor looked at Nevlin Lane and whispered to Mr. McGregor, "Look, the person standing by the gate seems to be the only person who knows the true worth of this girl. This educated and cultured English gentleman is looking at the helpless girl with compassion and sympathy." The contractor responded in a low voice, "You are right—only a king or a jeweller can evaluate a diamond's worth." He wanted to say more but a loud voice from one corner of the camp proclaimed that the girl should be given to him, "I will look after her safety and welfare." Another voice came from the south side of the camp, "I need a servant badly and the girl should be given to me." Several persons shouted from the west side that they will take responsibility for the upbringing of the girl. Two people shouted from the north side, "We are farmers and we shall take care of this girl. She will be very comfortable at our place."

At this moment, Mr. Loket said, "Listen, we cannot give precedence to one person's claim over the other. We suggest that the few elders of this community put their heads together and recommend how to handle this situation."

One farmer from the crowd got up and said in a loud voice, "This orphan girl should be auctioned to the highest bidder. One who can give maximum cash on the spot should be considered the rightful owner of the girl. This way no one will have any grounds for a complaint." This suggestion appeared to be acceptable to everyone. On direction from the contractor, Mr. Loket said in a loud voice, "There can be no better suggestion than this. Everyone is free to bid." The girl looked very frightened and grief showed all over her face. She clung to the woman looking after her and looked all around with anxious eyes. All the four women, sitting by her side tried to console her by gently patting her back. Mr. McGregor seemed agitated. He smoked a pipe and concentrated on the procedure for auction. He had visions of auctions in olden times. Everyone in the tent was thinking of the auction and were waiting with abated breath for its result.

Mr. Loket, after consulting the doctor, stood up and addressed the crowd again: "Ladies and gentlemen, this helpless orphan girl is now being auctioned. Listen very carefully to the conditions of the auction. The first condition is that the person who calls a bid must have either cash or gold to pay straightaway. No one will be allowed to send for money from home or make a promise to pay later. So make a bid according to what you have on your person now. The second condition is that whosoever bids the highest will get the girl. The third condition is that the maximum time limit to increase a bid will be five minutes. If no one comes forward with a higher bid in five minutes then the last highest bid will be accepted. No one is allowed to speak during the bidding process. There will be no deviations from these rules. Now whosoever wants to start bidding may begin."

A voice came from the east side, "Before starting the auction, it should be decided that who will keep this money and how it will be spent." A farmer from the south side said that it was obvious that this girl was public property and no particular person should benefit from the proceeds of the auction and therefore the person who would be incharge of this money should be selected by the general concurrence of the public. On hearing this, Mr. Loket said, "I think the doctor should be responsible for keeping an account of the money and he should decide how best to spend the money in getting medicines for the welfare of the workers working at digging mines, and get other essential items necessary for the comfort of workers." One person said jokingly that the money should be spent in establishing a garden. Another person said the money should be used in getting more wine and liquor. A third person said, "Establish a rest house." A fourth person said, "Establish a mental hospital." An elderly person said that the money should be used to build a church. Several suggestions were made. It was agreed that the doctor should get more medicines in the hospital and spend the funds for the welfare of the workers.

Mr. Loket asked the bidding to start. Every one kept quiet and looked at each other. Several monied people wanted to start bidding but did not find courage to start the bidding process. At this Mr. Loket took out all the change in his pocket and said, "I will start the bidding with one shilling. Anyone may increase this bid."

From the crowd, a voice came: "Two shillings." Another person said, "Three shillings." So on and so forth. Someone said, "Six shillings." After the silence of a couple of minutes, Lewryk, the evil and ugly looking man standing by the curtain at the time of the death of the old man, came forward, stood next to the girl and shouted, "One pound." Several people in the crowd knew the character of this man. Some had seen him committing daring robberies and snatching valuables from the travellers. However, no one was prepared to waste his time in reporting to police and be a witness. That's why he was never arrested by the police. Moreover, the farmers used to think that he was just another worker. They had seen him fighting and creating trouble and were afraid of him. At Lewryk's bid of one pound, a silence fell over the crowd. However, some farmers carried the bid forward to two pounds six shillings. But when Lewryk bid two pounds seven shillings, then even the farmers became quiet.

The public knew Lewryk to be a person of bad character and used to hate him. Nevlin Lane also knew Lewryk to be a thief and had seen him being beaten up with shoes by a farmer. The sight of this wicked man bypassing all the farmers and standing by the side of the girl made Nevlin Lane angry. His face became red with anger. With a concern for safety, Nevlin Lane sat on the gold slab. He looked at the girl who looked very worried. He found the girl staring at him with pleading eyes.

Mr. Loket said in loud voice, "Gentlemen, don't be greedy. Do not place money over humans. Two pounds seven shillings is too little a bid for this girl. Let not this golden opportunity slip from your hands." At this some rich farmers and shopkeepers increased the bid to two pounds eighteen shillings. Lewryk looked at the locket around the girl's neck and shouted in a loud voice, "Three pounds." There was silence for two minutes. Mr. Loket said, "Look gentlemen, it is getting late and now the bid may be increased in pounds only." Nevlin Lane, who was so far just watching the process and feeling jealous of wicked Lewryk, got up from his place and said in a quiet but determined voice, "Four pounds."

Wicked Lewryk looked surprised and astonished. He looked at Nevlin Lane with disgust and annoyance. People next to Lewryk heard him muttering to himself as to how this poor worker dared to bid against him. How can an ordinary person be so bold as to face him. In an anxious voice he shouted, "Five pounds."

Nevlin Lane immediately said in a shy voice, "Six pounds."

Everyone became quiet. No one could increase the bid above six pounds. Only Lewryk and Nevlin Lane seemed capable of continuing the bidding process. Everyone looked at them. Only the helpless girl's eyes were focused on Nevlin Lane and it looked as if she was thanking Nevlin Lane. Lewryk said "Seven pounds." Nevlin Lane raised it to eight pounds. When Lewryk bid nine pounds, Nevlin Lane at once raised it to twenty pounds. Lewryk without any hesitation said, "Thirty pounds." Nevlin Lane at once said, "Fifty pounds." Lewryk did not relent and said, "One hundred pounds." Nevlin Lane also did not back out and started to bid in increments of hundred pounds. When Lewryk said, "Eight hundred pounds," Nevlin Lane, without any hesitation whatsoever, said, "Nine hundred pounds."

At this bid, Lewryk got worried and started to think as to what he should do. Because of this hesitation, he lost the momentum. He thought that this man was just a worker. He was very poor. Only yesterday his informants had told him that he had spent the last of his money that he brought from home. He gave it to Mathula for groceries. It was certain that he was planning a secret move against him. He may have seen him robbing people and now, here, he wanted to accuse him as a robber and get him arrested. That way he would take the girl away for free. It was best for him to keep quiet now and let Ian's bid stand, otherwise he may create trouble for him. If he was an educated and clever person, why would he spend his life digging for gold? He did not have money to buy food beyond two days. Let the bid finish in his favour. It is obvious he did not have this kind of money and after the bid, when he was unable to produce ready cash, he would blame him for the robberies. He would then beat Ian up in public and take the girl away for his last bid of eight hundred pounds. He was quite familiar with the secret of the locket around the girl's neck. Because of her, he could get upto one hundred thousand pounds. With this girl in his hands, he could become very rich. He would go to London and meet his darling daughter Rachel. He would get her married in grand style with a boy from a rich family. Money can hide all faults. His daughter Rachel was young and beautiful. Several boys from good families would be interested in marrying her. After her marriage, he would bid goodbye to the profession of robbery and spend the rest of his life in peace and quiet.

He would settle in some city where people did not know him. Thinking thus, Lewryk stopped bidding. Mr. Loket started to call, "Nine hundred pounds once, twice—" and then he stopped and looked at the audience and with a certain style, said again, "Nine hundred pounds twice," and finally said, "Nine hundred pounds thrice."

Nevlin Lane, without any hesitation or delay took the gold slab from his shawl and kept it on the table in front of Mr. McGregor. The contractor weighed the slab himself and after a careful evaluation, ordered that one thousand pounds be paid to Nevlin Lane. He ordered Mr. Loket to deposit nine hundred pounds in the treasury and give the balance one hundred pounds to Nevlin Lane. Nevlin Lane said, "Sir, at this time I am not able to understand the calculations and carry the hundred pounds with me. Please arrange to send one hundred pounds to my house in the morning."

Nevlin Lane shook the girl's hand with great warmth and expressed his sincere sorrow and promised to look after her. He escorted her out of the tent with care and affection. The crowd shouted, "Ian, congratulations, well done, well done." But the wicked Lewryk was very upset. He came in front of Nevlin Lane and said, "Ian, you cannot take this girl. She belongs to me. You can make one hundred pounds profit and hand over the girl to me right now. Here take one thousand pounds and get away from this girl."

In response Nevlin Lane said in a brave and determined voice, "For me, money does not have any value, it is not even worth the value of stones. This orphan girl is dearer to me than even my life. I consider my money to be far less important than this girl. Though I am poor right now, I have a big heart. Humanity and justice is in my blood. I am not scared by anyone's threat. I keep away from wicked and selfish persons. However, I am not afraid to face them if such circumstances arise. I have spent my life helping the helpless and orphans. I am well aware of your character. I warn you not to cross my path." With this he pulled a revolver from his pocket and said in an angry tone, "Get out of my sight. Now!" As he finished this sentence several farmers and people came and gathered around Nevlin Lane. With so many people around, Lewryk did not have the courage to say anything further and went away. Nevlin Lane looked at the girl and found her scared. He hauled her on his back and said goodbye to the people around and started walking at a fast pace towards his house.

Chapter 3

This poor disciple of God
Started with only faith in God

Whatever happens is God's will
Man is helpless before Him

The cold night breeze and the beautiful star lit night refreshed Nevlin Lane's mind. His worries and tension seemed to disappear as he walked with the girl on his back through lonely valleys, towards his sweet smelling, thatched house. Suddenly a thought came to his mind and he started to talk to himself, "How come that my heart controlled my actions? Without any consideration for the future life, I spent all my hard-earned money. What can I possibly gain by the purchase of this girl? Who knows who are the parents of this girl, which family she belongs to, what kind of temperament she has, what kind of character she has? What shall I do with her? I spent nine hundred pounds for nothing. The balance one hundred pounds will not be enough even for her clothes and food." At this stage his thoughts changed and his better judgement prevailed. He started thinking, "Whatever had to happen has happened and I did what I had to do. There is no point in feeling sorry once the arrow has left the bow. Negative thoughts is a crime against God. To help and assist the helpless people without any motive is the duty of every human being. My elders have taught me that good deeds once done should be forgotten." With such positive thoughts, Nevlin Lane felt very happy inside. In a charitable frame of mind, he said to himself, "I did the right thing to take this orphan and helpless girl under my care and protection. God is all merciful and kind. It is His Will that I take care of this girl, look after her safety and share her problems. Without God's orders even a leaf cannot move—nothing happens without God's Will. God knows that He created this wave of love in me towards this girl. It was His order that I free this girl from the clutches of the evil-minded and wicked Lewryk. He created this desire in me to help this girl and take her under my care. I spent my money for a noble cause. Only God knows what future holds for me. Maybe it is all for my own good."

While Nevlin Lane was engrossed in such thoughts, the girl sat motionless on Nevlin Lane's back with her eyes closed. She said to herself, "Oh great God, You are Omnipresent, You are the Provider of our daily bread, You look after the orphans and the helpless. It is beyond comprehension for us mortals to understand Your wisdom. By Your Grace and kindness You made this kind and an angel-like man to be the protector of this poor and helpless girl. This man is surely from some rich family and God, You sent him in this jungle to help me and be the caretaker and protector of a helpless person like me. Oh God, this young man's hands, feet and back seem to be hard and strong like steel. I wonder why my heart is attracted to this kind hearted man. His strong built and handsome features are fixed in my eyes."

As the girl was engrossed in such thoughts, the thatched little house began to appear in the distance and the cook Mathula could be seen waiting at the door with a lantern in her hand. As Ian approached the house, she came forward and said in an anxious voice, "Ian, is that you approaching? Thank God that He has brought you back safely. I have been worried about you for a very long time. What is this on your back? Did you purchase a sack of wheat?" She lifted the lantern higher and said, "Oh this is a woman but she appears to be dead. What made you bring a dead woman's body to the house?"

Nevlin Lane said with a smile, "No she is neither a sack of

wheat nor a dead woman's body. She is a helpless and orphan girl without any friends or relatives. She is exhausted because of grief and fear. Let us hurry and go inside the house and please cook some food and feed this girl."

Mathula said, "Alright, but please tell me what money did you get for the gold slab?"

Nevlin Lane faced her and said, "Everything is alright. You will get your share tomorrow." With this he eased the girl's hands from his back and put her gently on the ground. The girl sat down in a corner, keeping her head down with shyness. Nevlin Lane sat down on the chair and took off his watch and looked at the time and said in a happy voice to Mathula, "It is not too late in the night—let us quickly have whatever you have cooked and then we can talk."

Mathula, after getting a firm reply from Ian, did not consider it prudent to carry on the conversation. She got the tea kettle from the stove and poured a cup of tea and kept it on the table. Nevlin Lane addressed the girl and said, "My little one, how are you feeling now? You should not have any fear. You are perfectly safe here. You are now in my house. Do not lament or grieve. Come here and drink tea. Consider this house as your own."

The girl appreciated the kind words of Nevlin Lane and felt grateful. She looked at Nevlin Lane with shy eyes and said in a soft voice, "Sir, I thank you from my heart for your kindness and generosity. At this time I am not hungry at all and do not feel like eating or drinking anything." She said this in such a sweet and soft tone that Nevlin Lane was very much surprised. He thought to himself, "A person who speaks in such soft and polished way can never be the daughter of an ordinary mine worker. The rough and uneducated workers here do not speak in this civilized manner. It is certain that this shaken girl with winning manners is from a rich family and educated and civilized parents." Nevlin Lane felt very happy with these thoughts. The girl saw the surprised look on Nevlin Lane's face and guessed what Nevlin Lane was thinking and to add to his happiness she looked at him with friendly eyes and smiled and kept quiet. When Nevlin Lane saw that she was quiet and not saying anything, he said to her, "Please tell me why you refuse to drink tea. Anyway, dear little girl, tell me what is your name—oh no, no, I should not be bothering you with useless questions at this time in the night and aggravating your already tired and worried mind. It is not the time to chat or discuss, but time for you to rest."

On hearing this, the girl looked at Nevlin Lane and smiled sweetly and said in a meek voice, "My late father used to call me Sylvia. My name is Sylvia Bond."

Nevlin Lane said, "Oh, Oh. Sylvia is indeed a very beautiful name. There was a famous queen of England by the same name. Dear, tell me, are you still upset and worried?"

Sylvia glanced all around the house and said in a calm voice, "No, I am not worried at all."

Nevlin Lane said, "That is good. Now you eat some food and then go and rest. A good sleep will help ease your mental anxiety and tiredness due to the journey."

On hearing this, the girl got up and sat beside the lighted stove and started to straighten her crumpled dress with her small hands. Nevlin Lane pushed the cushioned chair towards the girl and said in a low voice, "I will be sitting outside in the courtyard and you rest here." He asked Mathula to feed the girl and not to talk unnecessarily. As Nevlin Lane got up to go outside, the girl got up also as a sign of respect to him and to bid him good night. Nevlin Lane put his hand on her head and said, "Dear little one, you sleep peacefully. Do not have any concern or fear—sleep with a peaceful mind." Sylvia respectfully took Nevlin Lane's hand from her head and kissed it and then sat down again beside the fire.

Nevlin Lane, with a feeling of satisfaction, went outside. He lighted his pipe and paced the courtyard for nearly an hour. The scene of auction was fresh in his mind and he said to himself, "I wonder what that super power was under whose influence I spent nine hundred pounds in the purchase of this girl. Earlier I had firmly decided that on finding the gold slab I will be very happy to return to my home town London, and to buy a farm in my native place Devonshire and also buy cattle, horses etc. and spend the life in the company of my friends. All my plans are now burned to ashes."

He was lost in his thoughts when suddenly a thought crossed his mind and he felt ashamed and started to perspire. He solemnly promised himself not to have such thoughts. "My thoughts are making me a criminal. Money is made to be spent on good things and not on luxury and comfort. The greed of money can drive one to hell right in this world itself. Money is the root cause of all evil. One should keep away from the desire to accumulate money. Money should be spent on the needs of children and in helping the orphans and the helpless. Spending money in charity and in helping people in need is the real source of happiness and true humanity. The auction was a dream—whatever I saw and heard was a story—so I should forget it once and forever."

With this thought he went inside the house after coughing a couple of times as a sign of his entering the house. He saw Mathula sitting near the stove while Sylvia Bond had gone inside the room. With lantern in hand, he entered the room with Mathula and found Sylvia asleep. As Nevlin Lane was going out, Mathula said to him, "Ian, is it true that you bought Sylvia with the money realized from the gold slab?" Ian replied in a careless tone, "Mathula, do not worry about it. God has given money to man to help the helpless. Remember, I value money just like stones. I have been taught to respect humanity and help the poor and the helpless. I am a man of my words and rest assured that latest by day after tomorrow, I shall give you fifty pounds as promised."

Mathula said, "I am not concerned about my share. But I cannot help telling you that you completely ignored your present and future life and spent the hard-earned money for the girl. In my opinion it was very foolish."

Ian replied, "In your opinion I wasted the money but this is not how I see it. I am not in the least sorry for spending the money. You are old and wise and I can never be angry with you for saying this to me. But I must make you understand that decent and honest people never regret spending money on a good cause. In fact it makes them happy. It is written in the holy book that a person should never shy away from doing good. God is pleased with those who help and assist the helpless and less fortunate and only such a person can climb the ladder of spirituality. Also you should never use the word 'bought,' it demeans a noble action and if you will abstain from using this word I shall be thankful to you. Any way, leave this topic and tell me what Sylvia told you and how you learned about the buying part."

Mathula replied, "As per your instructions I did not start any conversation with Sylvia nor did I ask her any questions. She told me herself that Mr. Ian paid nine hundred pounds from the value of gold slab to get the auction declared in his favour. Except for this we did not talk about anything else. In my opinion this girl belongs to London. She has a certain sweetness and charm in her voice. In your absence she told me some amusing incidents."

Nevlin Lane said in a shy voice, "It is my opinion also that this girl belongs to my country."

Mathula asked, "What are you going to do with this little girl? So far, we two have managed to live with difficulty. With the blessings of elders, you found the gold slab after all this time. You spent all that in the purchase of this girl. You may find another gold slab in the mines in future. Right now it appears that it is not impossible but certainly very difficult for us to feed ourselves and it is likely that we may have to face starvation."

Nevlin Lane said in an angry tone, "Never say the word 'difficult.' Only the weak and foolish use this word. And to use the word 'impossible' is a sin. Persons who are wise and have faith in Almighty God, pass away the difficult days of life with a smile on their face. However, the fools pass their time by complaining and crying. Who knows what God has in store for the future. Even the great saints cannot see the future, so what can men like us say about it. God takes care of everyone. Whatever will be—will be. We can only try. Remember those who fear God and do the right deeds and are satisfied with whatever they have and do their work with complete dedication, are, by the Grace of God, successful in whatever they do—even breaking the mountain down. Hard work is never wasted. It is only human perception that one is fortunate or unfortunate. The Sun and Moon shine the same on a hut or a palace. Similarly, God, who is the supreme judge, treats everyone alike. He looks after those who do kind and good deeds. The laws of Nature are firm. Those who are selfish and act against nature, suffer. You should not worry about money already spent and the future. You do your work as usual with diligence and look after the comfort and safety of this girl without selfishness. Look Mathula, I wonder how this girl happened to be in this deserted jungle. She appears to be from a rich and cultured family. She is certainly not the daughter of any poor mine worker."

Mathula replied, "From her actions and face, she does not appear to be the daughter of any low caste, uncivilized person. I noticed that she is wearing some round thing around her neck and she appears to treasure it very much. Even a rich man does not protect his treasure so much. She would not even let my hand come near her chest. Probably this locket has some invaluable thing inside, which is more precious to her than her life."

Nevlin Lane said in a stern voice, "Listen Mathula, you and I have absolutely no interest in the girl's belongings. No person should try to probe into anyone else's secrets. A wise person is one who takes care of his own problems rather than worrying about everyone else's. Leave the girl alone. Please take care that you do not probe the past of the girl. Keep yourself busy with your work. Pray to the Great God for everyone's welfare. Unnecessary interference in other's affairs is not only a waste of time but it can bring misery and grief."

Mathula said, " I have nothing to do with the girl. I am your servant. I carry out your instructions and would keep on doing so in the future also. I know from experience that you are very wise and whatever you say makes sense. It is written in the olden books that we women folk should listen to men and keep them happy. This is their prime duty. We should ignore the bad habits of men because they will be answerable for their own actions. We should not interfere but just do our duty."

Nevlin Lane thanked Mathula and raised the filament of the lantern and looked at the girl. She was fast asleep with a hand on her chest. Mathula said quietly, "Oh Ian, it is the first time that I really have a good look at the face of the girl. She is very beautiful. I admire her fair skin, slim body and long silky hair. Within a few days, with proper nourishment and carefree life, she will put on some weight. Her cheeks will bloom like a flower. The fact is that in my life I have never seen such a beautiful girl before."

Nevlin Lane replied quietly, "We should not talk, the girl may wake up." He asked Mathula to sleep in his room and he went outside with his revolver and slept inside the house compound, on the grass. He forgot all his dreams of going to London and buying the farm. He felt very proud and pleased with his decision to purchase the girl at the Lornehope Camp auction and slept in a happy frame of mind.

Chapter 4

Those who are really courageous are not afraid of taking action
Helping the needy is the right thing and is the duty of man

So now hear friends time has come for very hard labour
Thousands have even lost their lives on this common path

Nevlin Lane got up in the morning feeling happy and fresh. As usual after taking his bath, he picked up his pick and shovel and left for his place of work that he had bid goodbye to yesterday, for ever. At lunch when he came home, he saw Sylvia laying the table neatly and Mathula cleaning the utensils. As he was in a hurry to get back to his work he sat down at the table and started to drink his tea. The colour and taste of the tea was very good. He looked at Sylvia and said, "It seems that you have made the tea today. Do you know how to cook also? I have not taken such a nice cup of tea in the last two years." Sylvia smiled and kept quiet. Nevlin Lane finished his meals in a hurry and left for work.

In the evening when he was returning from his work, he came across Mr. Loket near his house. After greetings, Mr. Loket gave Nevlin Lane one hundred pounds, the balance of the money from the gold slab sale. He said in a low voice, "Mr. Ian, every one at the office is saying that Mr. Ian is a very lucky man. He got away with an excellent deal. Listen, I just remembered that a man by the name of Lewryk came to see me today. He wants to take the girl from you by giving one thousand pounds. He wants to send her to a school in London and would like to adopt her. For this reason he has requested with great respect and humility that you return back the girl to him. If you are agreeable to this proposal then I will bring you one thousand pounds from this man. You will make a profit of one hundred pounds and he will get his wish. Moreover, your money from the auction, on the advice of administrators of the Camp, is being distributed to the needy and poor. You will earn their gratitude and this will be with you in this world and in heaven. The blessings and prayers of the poor are sincere. You will certainly reap good from the kind deed that you have done with pure heart. A person with such a kind heart deserves to go to heaven."

Nevlin Lane kept the money inside his coat pocket and said with a frown, "Sir, I do not need to know how you gentlemen spend my money. Whichever way you officers decide to spend the money is fine with me. I have done my duty and do not worry about its outcome. I try hard to follow the book of correct teachings, the Bible. I never think about the conflict of hell or heaven. 'We know the reality of heaven but for satisfaction of mind this thought is good.' I am not a greedy man and do not care about profit or loss. Please give my regards to Lewryk and tell him that he has no right on the girl. He should abandon the thought of getting her. He should spend his money in some other noble cause like helping the poor relatives in his family and adopt a poor girl among his relatives. I reject his proposal. I have bought the girl by proper and fair method in the auction with the public as a witness. She is now under my protection. You may tell him that Ian is not miserly and selfish. He is also not scared of anyone's threats. He sleeps outside the house with a loaded gun to protect the girl and no robber dare come near him. I may be a worker but I am a man of principles and have courage to carry them out."

Mr. Loket said, "I will go just now and tell him what you have said and would also advise him that in future he should not utter a single word about acquiring this girl."

Mr. Loket said goodbye and left. Nevlin Lane came to his

house. He found Sylvia standing by the side of the front door. From her face it was obvious that she had overheard the entire conversation he had with Mr. Loket. As Nevlin Lane entered the door his eyes met Sylvia's and she respectfully greeted him. Mathula was not in the house. She had gone to get groceries for the house. However, the dinner was very neatly laid on the table. Nevlin Lane washed his hands and face and sat down on the dining chair. Sylvia stood beside his chair to serve him. She said in a soft and sweet voice, "Sir, why do you make that man angry by not accepting his proposal. You can hand me over to him and make a profit."

On hearing this Nevlin Lane was much surprised. He said in a dry tone, "What do you think I am—a money merchant? Or do you, from your heart, wish to go to Lewryk. Your statement creates a doubt in my mind. There is some mystery in this." Nevlin Lane looked up at Sylvia's face. Her face was red and big tears were in her eyes. He felt ashamed and said in a sympathetic tone, "Listen dear Sylvia, it is not in my nature to say things to hurt and upset anyone or to separate someone from me whom I have taken under my protection of my own free will with happiness. I am not a greedy person. I will serve you with whatever I have and protect you. I neither like to taunt or reproach anyone nor do I like to listen to the same. I never keep any grudge in my heart. I promise you with a sincere heart that I shall not step outside the limits of proper behaviour and your happiness will be my utmost priority. It will be my duty to protect you. I would not do anything which is not to your liking. As long as you wish to stay with me, you can be sure that no outside person dare harm you. Now please discard useless thoughts from your mind. Come and have dinner with me."

Sylvia looked at Nevlin Lane and said, "Please Sir, you eat your dinner and I shall also eat in a little while." She said with a smile, "Last night I overheard all the conversation you were having with Mathula. You were probably thinking that I was asleep. I want to hear from you only one thing. Did you really spend all your hard-earned money to buy a useless person like me."

Nevlin Lane felt very embarrassed with this question and said with his head down, "Listen Sylvia, you do not worry about this at all. I feel ashamed to answer your question. Listen, in future we shall not utter the word purchase or talk about the money spent. You should not be least concerned about my labour and hard work. Man should spend the money for good and noble cause and to help the helpless. Hard work and perseverance keeps this world going and provides relief from pain and troubles. I try to imbibe in me the teachings of the holy book. Under my protection you should not have any worry or concern. Spend your time in carefree way and enjoy yourself. If sometimes you do get disturbed by any such thoughts, just look at me and smile. That will be repayment for everything and you would feel better." On hearing this, Sylvia laughed.

Nevlin Lane went to sleep after finishing his dinner. When Mathula returned from the market, after grocery shopping, Sylvia had her dinner and went to sleep in her room. When she got up after a sound sleep, it was already morning and Nevlin Lane had left for his work.

After a wash, Sylvia prepared the tea herself. She neatly arranged some biscuits on a plate and poured soup in a bowl. With the tea kettle and a cup in one hand and the plate in her other hand, she left for the place of Nevlin Lane's work, inquiring from the pedestrians about the place where Nevlin Lane was digging. She neatly arranged the tea and the snacks that she had brought and respectfully said to Nevlin Lane, "Sir your breakfast is served, please come and eat it." Nevlin Lane kept his pick and shovel on one side, cleaned the dirt from his hand and face and started eating with great enjoyment. Sylvia sat beside him. She asked with a smile, "Sir, what is your name?"

Nevlin Lane was aware that no body had called him by his name in the presence of Sylvia. After some hesitation he said, "You may call me Jack. Any name is alright as long as there is a name, good or bad."

Sylvia said, "Why did you call your name with sadness. Jack is the name of a beautiful flower. No other name can be better than this."

On hearing this Nevlin Lane looked at Sylvia with surprise and said, "You have just quoted a sentence from a book by a famous writer. How did you learn about this famous poet at this young age? Who taught you Shakespeare?"

Tears came to Sylvia's eyes but she wiped them away and said, "Sir, my respected father taught me many books. In addition to studies he also taught me housework and many things about this world. Now please finish your tea—there is still some left in the cup."

Nevlin Lane said: "No, I will not leave any tea. I am puzzled by your talk and I also feel very happy. You should not take the trouble of bringing tea here. It is very hot these days and there is no need for you to travel back and forth and inconvenience yourself. For this work I have kept Mathula as servant."

Sylvia said, "Why Sir, I am not troubled at all. I enjoy housework. How can there be any botheration in doing your work. You are my master. You purchased me and I should do all your work."

Nevlin Lane replied, "Look, in spite of my specific request, you have used the word purchase again. This thought is demeaning. Please wipe out such thoughts from your mind. If you feel grateful to me, then please agree to be my sister. I have no sister. From today I will treat you as a sister and you treat me as a brother."

Sylvia turned her happy and radiant face towards Nevlin Lane and looked at him with loving eyes and said in an innocent tone, "Very well Sir, I will be your sister."

Nevlin Lane said with a tone of satisfaction, "You call me brother Jack and I will call you sister Sylvia or Sil (Gold Slab). I hope you have no objection to my calling you Sil." In reply she said, "My father also used to call me Sil. Please do call me by this name. Do you work like this every day at digging? This is very hard work."

Nevlin Lane replied, "Yes dear Sil, I work here like this everyday. It is from this spot that I got the gold slab last week. Digging is very hard work but now I will not feel it because, you my sister, will get me tea and snacks and will be there to talk with me. In fact I think I will begin to love this work."

Sil asked, "Do you not have any brother either?"

Nevlin Lane said with a sigh, "Yes I have a brother."

Sil asked, "Does he also work at digging mines?"

Jack replied, "No, No. He is a very rich man. He is highly respected and comes from a cultured and well known family in London."

Sil asked, "Then you are also from a cultured and rich family from London?"

Jack laughed and said, "If you are rich and respected, then it is worthwhile to mention that you are from a highly cultured and civilized family. Otherwise to keep on saying that you are from a civilized and cultured family is giving your family a bad name. You do not understand all this. Listen, in this world, a father may consider one of his sons to be talented and honest and bestow upon him all his property and belongings. He may consider his other son to be of bad character and turn him out of the house and tell him to go and find a job and live his own life. Such a child goes wherever his luck takes him and works at whatever work he can find to sustain himself."

Sil said, "I get it that you left your country because of family conflict and have reached this state of poverty. You have taken the job of digging to earn a living."

Jack said, "That is right. In addition there are a few other reasons that I do not wish to discuss."

Sil replied, "Oh my God! In such a state of poverty you took pity on me and bought me for nine hundred pounds, thus spending all your hard-earned money on me. Is this not a very respectable thing to do? Would a wicked person do such a noble act? I have to say with regret that you unnecessarily spent your hard-earned money on a useless girl like me."

Jack said in an angry voice, "It does not behove an educated and civilized person like you to talk like this. You look at it like this. Suppose I had a sister like you who was away from friends and relatives and she faced trouble in a foreign country. If I came to know of it, would I not spend all my money to help and assist her? Do you think I would value money over my sister's trouble. I will be guilty all my life. What greater work can there be for me here? We are now brother and sister and you should get this thought of 'buy' out of your mind completely."

Sylvia took Jack's hands in her hands and looked at them from all angles and then she looked at the hole from where the gold slab was discovered. She gathered the utensils and left for the house without saying anything.

Chapter 5

What is the purpose of acquiring education
What is the outcome of any argument

Pray for devotion and loyalty
You can find God, with sincerity

The next morning at the parliament in London, there was a major session to discuss the agricultural and social reforms. In this session, there were several very learned and able gentlemen and quite a few of them spoke on the topic. However, the most brilliant speech was made by Sir Jordan Lane. The members of the parliament as well as the public liked his speech. The members agreed that his proposal was the best for the country and voted in its favour. There were two members of the parliament who were sitting in the balcony and one of them was staring at the tall, thin figure of Sir Jordan Lane. After the speech, he laughed and said to the member sitting beside him that today this man had established his great ability in the parliament.

Second member replied, "Indeed his speech is brilliant and shows thorough understanding of the issues facing the country. Do you know him well?"

First member said: "Yes, once he and I had a chance to stay at the same hotel in Rugby for a few days. Also I have met him several times at different places and have had conversation with him. In the times of his father, we used to meet at his country palace in Devonshire. However, I cannot say that I really know him and I do not think anyone in this parliament really knows him."

Second Member said with a smile, "I understand what you mean when you say you do not know him well. Sir Jordan Lane is like a black horse, whose mane has to be carefully examined before determining whether the horse is good or bad—you have to live with him for a long time to know him. Tell me how long has he had this title of Sir?"

First member replied, "Not too long. He acquired this title of 'Sir' eighteen months back. His father, Sir Gravlin Lane died eighteen months back. Since this title is bestowed on his family on a hereditary basis, he acquired the title after his father's death. There is gossip amongst friends about the great wealth and jewellery that his father has left behind."

As the parliament session ended, the two gentlemen started to walk towards their home. The second member asked, "I remember some friend telling me about the father of Sir Jordan Lane, but right now I do not recall any specific thing that gave him a bad reputation. Please tell me about him."

First member said, "I know very well all the past background of Sir Jordan Lane. To tell everything will take a long time. However, let me give you a brief resume. Sir Gravlin Lane was a spoiled aristocrat with a fickle mind. In his youth he got attracted to the daughter of a neighbour. This girl belonged to a very rich and highly cultured family, but due to certain turn of worldly events her parents became poor. Sir Gravlin Lane liked that girl very much and wanted to get her in his clutches. This girl was well aware of Sir Gravlin Lane's aristocratic habits and his cunning mind and for this reason, in spite of all kinds of pressures and his constant attention, she ignored him. She fell in love with a highly educated and civilized gentleman. She got engaged to him. In spite of her engagement, Sir Gravlin Lane tried to entice her with promises of riches and jewellery. He simply would not let go of her. The girl stood firm and ignored all his advances and false promises. She married the simple and kind hearted person and said goodbye to

Sir Gravlin Lane. After the marriage, Sir Gravlin Lane created trouble for the young couple and constantly harassed them. He became their bitter enemy and vowed to ruin the lives of the young couple. In fact he left them alone only when their lives were completely destroyed."

Second member asked, "What means did Sir Gravlin Lane adopt to destroy them?"

First member replied, "I have seen it and have heard from other officers of the city that twice he lodged false complaints against the husband and got him fired from his job. Twice he conspired with robbers and wicked persons to break into their house and rob them of all their belongings. In short, whenever he heard of their settling down with a job, he ensured that he was fired from the job and made their life very miserable. The girl could not endure all this misery and constant harassment and passed away. The husband, tired of all this harassment, went to a far away country about twelve years ago. That person was very pious and courageous. He considered it a sin to fight another person. That is why he bore all the misery himself and did not retaliate or fight his enemy."

Second member said, "I heard that they were blessed with a child."

First member replied, "About twelve years back, on harassment from the police, this couple left London. At that time I saw a two or three years old, very beautiful girl in the mother's lap. Since then I am completely out of touch."

Second member said, "I feel so sorry that Sir Gravlin Lane harassed and tortured this kind and pious girl so much. He deserves the most severe punishment."

First member replied, "From a religious point of view, Sir Gravlin Lane should have received the worst punishment from the highest court of God. In fact he lived a very luxurious life and amassed considerable wealth before he died."

Second member asked. "Did Sir Gravlin Lane ever get married or did he just spend all his life in aristocratic pursuits?"

First member replied, "Not once but twice he married. Sir

Jordan Lane is from the first wife. The second wife was very beautiful, simple, kind-hearted. She was a pious woman from a highly respected family. She was much worried about her husband's character and fickle mind and was angry with him for leading such a life. She got very sick due to constant worry and eventually died. She left a son by the name Nevlin Lane. He was a very kind and handsome boy."

Second member said, "I have not seen the boy. Where does he live?"

First member replied, "I learned from a reliable source that due to the ill treatment and harassment by his step brother Sir Jordan Lane, Nevlin Lane went to a far away country. Sir Gravlin Lane dearly loved his second son, Nevlin Lane. He sent him to the best schools and gave him excellent education. He used to dote on him very much. Jordan Lane did not like this at all. With a view to discredit Nevlin Lane, he used to make false accusations against him to their father and harass him constantly. In spite of all this, the love of his father for Nevlin Lane remained the same and he sided with Nevlin Lane all the time. Jordan Lane became a bitter enemy of the kind hearted Nevlin Lane. He made it a point to put him down at every opportunity. He would criticize him for every thing and nagged him everyday. This kind boy lived a miserable life and put up with his brother's constant harassment for sometime. Then Jordan Lane played a very dirty trick. With false accusations he framed his brother and proved him guilty in front of their father. He kept up this charade of dirty tricks and created a major confrontation between Nevlin Lane and his father. In a fit of anger Sir Gravlin Lane asked Nevlin Lane to leave the house. Who knows where this kind, highly educated and clever boy is living and in what condition."

Second member said, "Goodness gracious, Heaven forbid! I do not want to hear about such a wicked and evil minded person. In future I shall never praise the ability of Sir Jordan Lane. I would not like to even see his face. It is difficult to understand why God has given such a person so much wealth and fame."

First member said, "Jordan Lane, whom people respect and

admire because of his wealth, is really a crook who got his father and brother in serious confrontation and made his father turn his honest and gentle son out of the house. Money does not remain with one person always. Sir Gravlin Lane had left, in addition to money, lots of expensive jewellery and valuable property. The real justice is done in God's highest court and a day will come when Sir Jordan Lane will have to bear the punishment for his deeds. He will not get even a decent burial. All the money and wealth will be of no avail. He should have renounced his evil path and adopted a path appropriate to his position. He should have given the rightful half share of the property to his brother Nevlin Lane. On the contrary he has forgotten about his brother and has made no effort to trace him. He wants to grab the whole inheritance."

Second member said, "I think that amongst all my friends and acquaintances in London, Sir Jordan Lane is the wealthiest person. Today, his speech in the parliament was so brilliant and well presented that I will not be surprised if he is appointed as the minister of agriculture."

First member said, "Please be quiet, someone is coming this way."

When they looked at the main road, they saw Sir Jordan Lane coming in a carriage. When he saw two close friends standing on the sidewalk, he waved his hand. When the carriage got to some distance, the first member said to his friend, "Did you notice how sad Sir Jordan Lane was looking sitting in the carriage? He is just the opposite of his step brother, Nevlin Lane, in facial features and body built. He is tall and thin with a long face, depressed chest, thin lips, angular eyebrows and his sideburns extend upto his chin like two straight lines. Due to constant trimming they have become dark like ink. The eyes are somewhat watery blue but he has broad shoulders. However, the head is little bigger in proportion to the rest of the body. By looking at him one can say that he is an able person, highly educated and rich but at the same time he appears to be selfish and self-centred. Another point about him is that he has long hands with small fingers like that of a midget. At the time of his speech in the parliament, whenever he raised his hands, all eyes turned to them. People made fun of his fingers. Every person's face and voice are the introduction to his character. Whenever Sir Jordan Lane talks to a learned and wise person, he changes his style of conversation accordingly. While giving speech in the parliament he speaks with a loud and determined voice. Sir Jordan Lane is a master at changing his voice according to the situation. Whenever he goes to any party as a guest, he talks to anyone who wants to talk to him whether man or woman, young or old. He changes his style, tone and facial expressions according to the subject of conversation. He should be considered a master in gossiping and lies. Often innocent boys and girls and people eager to please him, are fooled by his flattery and sweet talk. After the death of his father, he got a chance to participate in discussions on social welfare and agriculture. To gain popularity, he started to attend meetings of clergymen. He started lecturing on the welfare and safety of workers. He started to show great sympathy for the poor class and in his speeches, he started to ask for funds to assist the poor. Though he does not drink himself, he has in his cellar the finest wines so that people may consider him to be a rich and fun loving person. With a desire to gain more popularity, he has started donating large sums of money to charity. Often in the list of donations by the members of the parliament, the name of Sir Jordan Lane is at the top. Whenever his close friends and colleagues tell him that he should not make promises that he has no intentions of keeping, he recites to them the following verse;

> You need a house filled with artificial things
> People of the world watching are fickle minded like air

In fact Sir Jordan Lane is a man who has created an outward image of splendour. To show the world he has adopted very sophisticated manners with the result that men and women in even the highest circles of the society consider him an aristocrat. People not aware of his true nature, respect him and feel proud to meet him and know him. He has a big ego and pride but his artificial smile and flattery never make others suspect his true nature. His acquaintances have often noticed a certain anxiety on his face and have wondered that in spite of having everything, good education, wealth and fame, what is the cause of his worry and anxiety. However persons, who know him well, know that he is worried about his step brother Nevlin Lane returning some day, and claiming his share of the property. He is also concerned about his father's friends knowing about his past. He knew that old servants were completely loyal to Nevlin Lane and liked him very much. They all used to admire his honesty, outgoing nature and courage. Because of this, Sir Jordan Lane fired several of the old servants and the remaining few keep quiet out of respect." Both the members left for their respective houses.

Sir Jordan Lane also reached his father's big and magnificent palace in Devonshire. It was in a place called Fort Greenwich. He sat down in the library and got busy in reading. Though he had a book in his hand, the scene in front of his eyes was that of the parliament. The loud clapping of the members and public and their congratulatory comments at his speech were still fresh in his ears and he felt happy. The attention of the public from the galleries and the positive comments from all sides were still resounding in his mind. At the same time, he also recalled the gaze of some members of the public sitting on the upper steps of the galleries, who were aware of his background and past deeds. The thought of such friends suddenly made him nervous and his face looked tired and he became restless. To get rid of the thoughts of his friends he closed the book and went to the table to attend to some correspondence. On the table he saw an invitation card for a party given by Lady Marlow. He rang the bell for the servant and instructed him to get his carriage ready. He had a wash and dressed up in expensive clothes. He put some perfume on his handkerchief and went outside and sat down in the carriage. He ordered the coachman to drive to Lady Marlow's house. As his coach passed through the streets, the pedestrians, the shoppers, the shopkeepers, vendors on the sidewalks, all saluted Sir Jordan Lane. A few pedestrians wondered as to where Sir Jordan Lane was going all dressed up in fine clothes at 11 o'clock in the night. One of the pedestrians said,

"There is a big party at Lady Marlow's place tonight. The coaches of several rich persons of the country were seen going in that direction. Probably this well dressed gentleman is also going there."

Chapter 6

Counsellor your advice is of no use
My heart is restless even in heaven

I am with you but my heart is not
Heaven may be heaven, it is not the party of my friend

Yes today I would say in front of your picture
Yes, it is no comparison to your face.

The parties of Lady Marlow generally started at 11 p.m. and went on till two o'clock in the morning and sometimes even the next day was spent in entertaining the guests. Lady Marlow was the wife of a rich, good-natured landlord. She was a jolly, kind-hearted and disciplined person. She was very popular in several high class families. Many young boys and girls admired her while their parents spent the time in entertaining Lady Marlow. They all respected her. At her parties, several boys and girls found partners of their choice and got married. Her house became famous as a match making place. Recently Lady Marlow got acquainted with a very rich young, delicate and beautiful girl. Today's party was in her honour.

The hostesses of the parties, in the rich families of London, did not get any time to relax at all. They were busy from morning till night. They had to work harder than the labourer, the railway worker or the postman because they had to go personally in the morning for shopping, then supervise the servants laying the table properly, write invitations for the party, and thus spend the whole day in one chore or the other. In the evening they had to entertain the guests and arrange for the dinner. They also organized the band and dances. All this used to exhaust them completely.

Today, since she got up in the morning, Lady Marlow was busy till noon in attending to correspondence. After lunch, she went for shopping for the things required for the party and comfort of the guests and this kept her busy till the evening. It was 10 o'clock by the time she finished supervising the servants laying the tables. At 11 p.m. she was at the door to greet the guests and escort them to their seats as per their status.

The coach of Sir Jordan Lane came to a halt inside the compound of Lady Marlow's elegant mansion. Sir Jordan Lane got down and climbed the steps leading to the front door. Lady Marlow shook his hands and said, "The material in your speech, that you read in today's parliament session, was presented with great ability. Every one at the party is talking about your speech. I have been waiting for you for a long time. Thank you for coming." She guided him to the place where all the guests were assembled. She then returned to the front door to greet other guests. Sir Jordan Lane, pleased with the comments appreciating his speech, entered the room where all the guests got up one by one and greeted him. After greeting everyone, as he was going towards his chair, a tall slim eighteen-year-old girl, Audrey Hope, happened to pass by that side on some errand. Sir Jordan Lane called her and this beautiful girl shook his hands and inquired about his welfare.

Audrey Hope was fabulously rich. In London proper, she had a big mansion and in Fort Greenwich, Devonshire, next to the property of Sir Jordan Lane, she had a huge mansion and some property. In addition she had property in the city of Eaton and Yorkshire. She inherited all this property from her parents. Her father, in addition, also left her considerable money in cash. Audrey Hope was a kind hearted, well educated girl. Her mother died a year earlier than her father. Two months before his death, her father, in his despair of any chance of living, appointed his very rich and close friend of exemplary reputation, Lord Marlow and his disciplined, educated and good humoured wife, Lady Marlow as the guardians of his daughter. In his will he appointed Lady Marlow as the custodian of his daughter and at the time of his death he placed the hand of his beloved daughter in the hands of Lady Marlow and said to his daughter, "From today, you are in Lady Marlow's care and protection." His will, which was read in public, stated that Lady Marlow will be the adviser to his daughter for all matters concerning property and money. Audrey Hope was to keep a proper written account of her money and show it to Lord Marlow on a regular basis for review and advice. This arrangement was to continue till such time that Audrey Hope got married.

Audrey Hope considered the Marlows as her sincere well-wishers and never did anything without consulting them or against their wish. She did not spend any money without their permission. She used to keep a record of all expenses, and every fourth day showed it to Lord Marlow and made him initial the account. Lord Marlow had no children of his own and used to treat Audrey Hope as his daughter.

Audrey Hope had come to Lord and Lady Marlow's house in summer after an inspection of her properties at Eaton and Yorkshire and review of accounts of several landlords. Today's party was in her honour. Audrey Hope's property at Fort Greenwich in Devonshire was very large. It was located next to the property of Sir Jordan Lane's father Sir Gravlin Lane. He and Audrey Hope's parents were neighbours when they used to live at their property in Fort Greenwich. Their mansions were on adjacent properties. Audrey Hope was born here in her ancestral home. Upto the age of fourteen she used to play all day long with Nevlin Lane, the step brother of Jordan Lane. Sir Jordan Lane was twenty years older than Audrey Hope and that is why she did not socialize with him. She was also aware, since her childhood days, of his narrow-mindedness, short temper and selfish nature. For this reason even when she happened to come face to face with him, she found an excuse to get away and if forced into a situation where she had to talk to him, she would politely inquire about his health and move away.

But she spent all her time in the company of Nevlin Lane. They did everything together, eating meals, reading, writing, playing. Audrey Hope was quite good natured and would mix with everyone. Several boys and girls of rich families of her age group used to come to her place from the city and she was nice and friendly towards all of them. They all loved her and were always very happy to meet her.

In this party, when Audrey Hope came to Sir Jordan Lane on his calling her, she politely inquired about his welfare. Meanwhile, several girls of highly placed and rich families got up from their chairs and came over to meet Audrey Hope and chat with her. They warmly shook hands with Audrey Hope. She also greeted them with great warmth and inquired about the welfare of the children and elders in their families. She wanted to go with her friends and entertain them but Sir Jordan Lane, with a serious expression on his face, stood before her. Audrey Hope was much offended by this rude and impolite act of Sir Jordan Lane. The happiness she felt in meeting her friends disappeared from her face and she felt uneasy and embarrassed. However, in consideration of Sir Jordan Lane being a neighbour and her elder, she did not express her displeasure at his behaviour. She faced Sir Jordan Lane and inquired if he was feeling alright. She said that she thought that due to the research of books for the material of his speech, he may not find time to come to the party. She said that she was happy that he could come.

In response Sir Jordan Lane said, "Today the parliament was in session and when I was free from there, I came to my house and saw the invitation from Lady Marlow on my table. I came at once to meet my friends and especially you."

He continued, "I have seen you after a long time. Have you finished your tour? Which properties did you visit? Tell me all about your trip." The two of them started talking about their properties and sat down in a secluded corner. Several rich and handsome young men were also interested in hearing Audrey Hope's conversation. They came to the place where Audrey Hope was sitting and quietly listened to her conversation. After briefly telling Sir Jordan

Lane about her trip, she asked him if he had received any news about her sincere friend, Nevlin Lane, and whether he had received any letter from him. On hearing this he looked sad and said with a sigh that a long time back he had heard from one of his friends. In his letter the friend mentioned about Nevlin being alive and well but since then he had not received any information from any source at all. He said that he was very worried about Nevlin Lane and sorry that he did not send him any letter. He said that he had not been able to find out anything about his whereabouts.

Audrey Hope felt disappointed on hearing this statement and with tears in her eyes she said, "You may remember that from infancy till I was fourteen years old, Nevlin Lane and I used to be together all the time at your house in Greenwich. We used to do everything together. Even when my mother used to send for me again and again, I did not feel like leaving your place to go to my house that was only a few steps away. I am constantly reminded of Nevlin Lane's courage, honesty, straight talk and his very humorous and pleasant nature. He never compromised on justice. He used to tell right then and there, on the face, if someone said something wrong. He never kept anything in his heart. It was not in his nature to be mean. He was very tender, kind-hearted and social. He could make a crying person laugh. He was very powerful and handsome. Till today I have not come across anyone like him. Beside the bedroom of your late respected father there is a huge oak tree. We used to play polo under this tree. Whenever he won, he would insist on riding on my back to the agreed spot. Even when I said I was tired he would say that rules were rules. He was a stickler for playing by the rules. And whenever he lost, he would carry me on his back to the agreed spot. His innocent face and his very sweet talk is always with me and I remember him constantly."

Sir Jordan Lane got confused on hearing such praise of Nevlin from Audrey Hope. However, keeping in mind the occasion and the atmosphere, he said to her, "Good persons do not forget their childhood friends. Studying the laws of nature, it is obvious that every one has inside him/her a desire to love. In your nature you have an abundance of sympathy and kindness for others and it is because you are pure at heart. That is why you remember Nevlin Lane so much even though he ran away from home. You consider even the evil person to be good." On hearing this she looked at Sir Jordan Lane with a suspicious look and realizing that he had no love at all for Nevlin, she wisely ignored his comments and asked him if his friend, in his letter, had written anything else about Nevlin Lane.

The coward and wicked Sir Jordan Lane thought to himself that it seems Audrey Hope is very determined to find out about Nevlin and he should say something that would turn her off from him and attract her towards him. With this thought, he paused for a while and then said, "Yes, my friend also wrote that Nevlin Lane started to work in some factory of a rich man in America. However, he did something very wrong and his life was in great danger. On hearing this I immediately sent a couple of my very reliable men with money to help save his life and I also wrote to my friend to help Nevlin in any way he could and get him out of this danger and send him back to me. However, before my men could reach him, Nevlin Lane escaped and ran away to some other far away country. My friend holds a very high position in America but in spite of his resources and extensive search, he also could not trace him. Ultimately my men were forced to return back, helpless to do anything further."

It is interesting to note how Jordan Lane fabricated a complete lie. Such type of selfish persons become blind to reality and are only concerned with their personal gain. They think that they are very clever and the others are fools and cannot see through their game. He did not realize that Audrey Hope was a very clever girl and could get to the bottom of things straightaway. On hearing Jordan Lane's statement of lies about Nevlin Lane, her face became tense and she said with gravity in her voice, "I cannot understand how a kind-natured, highly disciplined, very clever and far-sighted person like Nevlin Lane could do anything wrong. I do not trust what your men said." She continued, "If your friend or your men made up this story, then they are guilty of the biggest fraud. I believe they never met Nevlin Lane or knew him. They have just fabricated the whole thing to earn your gratitude. I do not think you have made any efforts so far to inform Nevlin Lane of your father, Sir Gravlin Lane's death?"

The selfish Sir Jordan Lane realized that his statement did not have the slightest effect on Audrey Hope in diminishing Nevlin Lane's stature. On the contrary she was accusing him of false information. He felt very humiliated. However, he was determined to make an impression on her for his benefit. He ignored the harsh attitude and admonishing conversation of Audrey Hope and in order to gain her favour, said in a sad tone, "You probably heard that my respected father did not even mention the name of Nevlin Lane in his will and what is more, he specifically wished that not even a penny is to be given to Nevlin. In spite of my advice and persuasion, he did not agree to leave anything to Nevlin Lane. Anyway, my father's thinking is gone with him. It is my heart's desire now to leave no stone unturned in finding him. You will soon learn the results of my efforts. I will search for him and when I find out as to where he is, I will go personally and bring him back with me, even though by nature he is stubborn and also very carefree. If somehow he learns about the contents of the will, he will not come back and may even refuse to talk with me. I will never let him know the contents of the will. With love and care, I will keep him at the Greenwich house. I will make him owner of half the share of the inheritance. I am very restless without him. I do not enjoy life without him."

Audrey Hope could see that he did not mean a word of what he was saying. However, she did not consider it appropriate to get into a disagreeable argument with him and spoil relations. She relaxed her expression and said that of course all his restlessness was understandable. Who could really enjoy life and comfort with his only brother missing? She said that it was desirable for a person of his status and position to make all efforts to find his kind and honest brother and give him his share of the inheritance. Both the brothers should live together in peace. She further said that in all the books she has read, the writers have placed true love above all and God is pleased with persons who have true love in their heart. Such a person is blessed on earth and in heaven. She said, "In fact the truth is that you can realize God with true love."

Audrey Hope continued, "I pray to God that Nevlin Lane may soon return back to his country and home and I may see with my own eyes, both of you living in peace and loving harmony. I will be grateful if you can kindly tell me about the plans and arrangements you are thinking of to find him."

With a view to please Audrey Hope, the cunning Sir Jordan Lane replied, "To find Nevlin, I have published posters in America and adjoining countries. I have also placed notices in all the prominent newspapers expressing my restlessness and depression at being separated from him. I am sure if Nevlin Lane happens to see and read anyone of these notices, he will at once come back to me from wherever he is. Out of sheer necessity he will be forced to write to me and inform me of his full address. As soon as I receive his letter, I will inform you of his condition and whereabouts."

Audrey Hope expressed happiness on hearing this and said, "Please do inform me as soon as you hear from him. If I happen to be away from London on some work then please send me a telegram at once. Do not forget your promise."

In response the ill-intentioned Jordan Lane said, "Do not worry. On receipt of Nevlin Lane's letter, whether you are here or away from London, I shall inform you by telegram of his whereabouts." With an intention to change the subject he asked her as to when she will visit her property at Greenwich. He said that she should visit her ancestral home more often as this can be a source of much happiness. On hearing this Audrey Hope replied in a carefree manner, "I think it will not be possible for another ten weeks as Lord and Lady Marlow are planning to go with me. We propose to celebrate Christmas there."

Sir Jordan Lane said, "When you reach there, I will also plan to come to my ancestral home. Our properties are adjacent and we will have an opportunity to meet each other everyday."

Audrey Hope carried on the conversation as long as the topic was Nevlin Lane. But when he changed the subject, she lost all interest and said with a dry expression on her face that her going to the Greenwich house is really dependent on Lord and Lady Marlow's programme. With this she got up from her chair and said, "Oh no! look at the time, I have not seen Lady Marlow for a long time. I got busy here and she must be waiting for me in the garden."

She had hardly finished this sentence, when she saw a handsome, good natured, highly educated and rich young man coming towards her with his head bent down. Audrey Hope jumped a couple of steps forward and said in a loud voice, "Oh, Lord Lorimor, where are you going at this time when all the fun is starting? Can you please tell me where can I find Lady Marlow? I have not seen her for a long time."

Lord Lorimor looked at Sir Jordan Lane with contempt and took Audrey Hope's hand in his hands and said, "Lady Marlow sent me to look for you. Please walk fast as she has some very important work for you."Audrey Hope smiled and pressed the hand of Lord Lorimor and started to walk by his side. During the conversation Lord Lorimor asked her as to what she was talking about with Sir Jordan Lane. At this Audrey Hope smiled bravely and said, "What right have you to ask me such a question?"

Lord Lorimor replied, "When one is in love one does not think of rights."

Audrey Hope wanted to free her hand but he held her hand tightly and said, "My dear, what have I said to invite your anger?"

Audrey Hope looked at Lord Lorimor and said in a terse voice, "Probably you forgot your promise never to use the word 'love' in my presence."

Lord Lorimor said, "I certainly promised that. However, whenever you ask me a question so sweetly, I have to express my right to love you. By nature I am a straightforward and honest person." Audrey Hope said, "This is not a proper reply to my question and your argument is meaningless. Anyway tell me why do you hate Sir Jordan Lane. Don't you know he is our neighbour and we know each other's families for generations. In childhood I used to play at his house."

Lord Lorimor said, "Yes I am aware of all this. However,

I have never liked Sir Jordan Lane and I resent his talking to you. I certainly hate him."

Miss Hope smiled and said, "I can talk to anyone I like. In future I will not like to listen to any sentimental talk of love from you. If I was a man and some orphaned helpless girl admonished me in very strong words, I would be ashamed to make fun of her and tease her."

Lord Lorimor said, "If you consider sincere words expressed from the heart as teasing, then please forgive me. I plead guilty. But I am grateful to you that you have neither asked me to stop loving you nor admonished me for loving you nor have you said that you will not make an effort to love me. Just a few minutes ago, during your conversation with Sir Jordan Lane, you said that 'The truth is you can realize God with true love.' This statement proves that you like a person who sincerely loves. In this situation I have no hesitation in saying:

> We will also develop the habit of greeting you with love
> Though ignoring us may be your habit."

Miss Hope raised her head and looked at Lord Lorimor and said with shyness in her eyes, "You will not abstain. I would like to know what you expect to gain from such talk of love."

Lord Lorimor said, "As long as you are not officially engaged. I will continue with my sincere efforts to win your heart. The world may go upside down but my determination will not falter."

Miss Hope said with mischief in her eyes, "In this situation, it is in my best interest to get married."

Lord Lorimor replied, "The condition is that the person has true and sincere love for you. Look at me, I think no one deserves it more than myself."

Miss Hope said, "Is it not possible that Sir Jordan Lane or some other lost stranger in this God's world have similar views?"

Lord Lorimor said, "I know that you are wise, clever and far-sighted. It is beyond me to comprehend that a person like you would ever think of marrying a person like Sir Jordan Lane. It is a sin to even dream of such a thing happening."

Miss Hope replied, "Well, well, Sir! What a statement! Is he not rich and very popular? It is likely that he may soon become a minister in the cabinet. Does he not have all these qualities?"

Lord Lorimor said, "Agreed that he is popular and also very rich. However, I am sure you will never think of marriage with a useless person like him."

Miss Hope said with a smile, "What kind of a word is 'useless'?"

Lord Lorimor said, "This is a word from your childhood vocabulary. Don't you remember you yourself said to me that you will not marry any useless person whom you do not like?"

Miss Hope smiled and said, "You keep teasing me. Well Sir, I suppose tonight is not where we girls are in control. There will be another day for us to win."

Lord Lorimor said, "We are not fighting. Even if you try to fight with me, your heart will not allow it."

On this Miss Hope looked with a sly look at Lord Lorimor and said, "I tried hard just now to pick up a fight with you and was hoping you will be offended by my remarks. However, you are such a nice person that you carried on the conversation by finding loopholes in what I said. Why do you not consider me to be a dumb, ill tempered and selfish girl who is not worthy of your attention at all. In London there are several well educated, highly cultured girls who will be proud of your attention and would appreciate your loving sentiments. I hope you will no longer think of me as your beloved and would treat me just like any other friend."

Lord Lorimor replied, "As long as I am alive, such a thought towards you is impossible. Such thinking is for persons who are not serious and sincere. I have your picture etched in my heart. You are the only one for me. To think of anyone else is beyond me. Enough . . ."

Audrey Hope cut him short and said with a frowned look, "Enough now. Get lost. Lady Marlow is coming looking for me."

Lady Marlow was very familiar with the friendship of these two young persons. She considered Lord Lorimor having true love for Audrey Hope for the last two years. When she saw Miss Hope with a frown on her face, she figured that they must have had some argument. She returned their greetings and asked Lord Lorimor, "Has this girl been tiring you with her non-stop talk and caused you grief with a frown on her face."

Lord Lorimor said respectfully, "You may say what you like but this humble person would not have the arrogance to say anything."

He then said to Miss Hope, "If you are tired then lean on me." He took her hand and walked four steps. Miss Hope freed her hand with a jerk. Lady Marlow who was standing behind them exclaimed, "Poor Lord Lorimor."

Audrey Hope interjected and said, "Aunty dear, do not pity Lord Lorimor. I am the one who should have your pity as I have been listening to his rubbish all this time and am tired of it. Wouldn't you be tired of listening to his intriguing talk?"

Lady Marlow turned her face slightly to one side and said in a low voice to Audrey Hope, "If I was unmarried, I would be very flattered!"

Chapter 7

There was expectation of love and kindness from you
but you turned out to be cruel

Thought your heart was soft like wax
but it turned out to be a stone.

After Audrey Hope left, Sir Jordan Lane remained at the party for a few more minutes. Though he was looking at the other guests at the party, his thoughts were elsewhere. He was thinking about ways to put down Audrey Hope and take control of her property and money. He was reminded of the incident when the general of an army asked Napoleon if he was thinking about winning the battle. Napoleon replied that he was not only thinking, but had already determined to win it. Like Napoleon, Sir Jordan Lane had made up his mind to marry Audrey Hope.

Sir Jordan Lane was an experienced person in the art of fraud and deceit. He did not love Audrey Hope. For him money was supreme. Audrey Hope was not only beautiful but owned considerable property also. Her property at Greenwich ran parallel to Sir Jordan Lane's property. To amalgamate Audrey Hope's property with his property and to grab all her wealth, Sir Jordan Lane had made a firm decision to marry her. The thought of grabbing her money made him blind to the fact that he was nearly forty years old, much older to eighteen-year-old Audrey Hope. He did not realize that Audrey Hope was very clever. During the conversation she had insulted him and literally called him a liar in front of the servants and friends and had brushed him aside by walking away and talking warmly with Lord Lorimor, without even once looking back at him.

Sir Jordan Lane had been eyeing at Audrey Hope's property for a long time. He knew that she loved his step brother Nevlin. He thought that if she married Nevlin Lane, the latter would inherit not only half of their father's property but also all the property of Audrey Hope. He became a bitter enemy of Nevlin Lane and plotted to frame him on false charges to put him down in front of his father. He constantly complained to his father about Nevlin and eventually managed to convince him that Nevlin Lane would squander all his wealth in gambling and aristocratic pursuits. One day, he fabricated such a serious charge that his father lost his temper and asked his beloved son, Nevlin Lane, to leave the house straightaway.

The fraud and lies do not last for ever. Persons who indulge in fraud and tell lies cannot carry on their act for long. The person who frames innocent people eventually lives a life of suffering and misery. A few days after throwing Nevlin Lane out of the house, Sir Gravlin Lane found out about his innocence, kindness and truthfulness. His mind was completely cleared of all misgivings about Nevlin Lane. How he made amends and compensated Nevlin Lane at the time of his death will be known later.

When Nevlin Lane left the house after a fight with his father, Audrey Hope was not at her ancestral home at Greenwich. Her parents had passed away and she was living with Lady Marlow. The day Nevlin Lane disappeared from the house, Audrey Hope had gone to America in connection with her properties. That is why she never found out the truth behind Nevlin Lane's leaving his house. However, she was very sad at being parted. After his father's death, Sir Jordan Lane tried hard to win over Audrey Hope but she disliked him from her heart.

The way Audrey Hope left Sir Jordan Lane abruptly and went away with Lord Lorimor, happily laughing and talking to him, made him mad with jealousy. He vowed then and there to teach her a lesson. He started making plans to bring her under his complete control. Sir Jordan Lane was well aware that for the past two years, Lord Lorimor was deeply in love with Audrey Hope but there had been no formal engagement. He tried to find out the reason for this and was told that Audrey Hope was lost in her love for Nevlin Lane. She did not let any of the handsome and rich boys to express their love for her. With a smile she disarmed everyone. Knowing this, Sir Jordan Lane attempted to get Audrey Hope to forget the love for Nevlin Lane and to distance herself from Lord Lorimor. He befriended Lord Lorimor and went out of his way to be nice to him. Even if Lord Lorimor sometimes said something unpleasant, he used to ignore it and never showed his anger. He generally agreed with whatever Lord Lorimor said. If sometime they had a confrontation, he would leave with some excuse and start talking to someone else. At the party, when Audrey Hope left with Lord Lorimor, ignoring him completely, he found her behaviour unacceptable. He left the party from a side door and started to walk to his house.

It was early dawn. A few stars were visible in the sky and the moonlight was gradually fading. There was a pleasant breeze. Sir Jordan Lane was walking at a fast pace when someone from behind placed a hand on his shoulder. He was startled and looked back and saw a sad looking, very worried and thin woman. She was young but due to worry and hardships, she looked pale and aged. Her face reflected patience and calmness. Her clothes were old and dirty but looked well on her slim body. She said in a sweet and soft voice, "Jordan, Jordan."

On recognizing the voice, Sir Jordan Lane said in an irritated voice, "Oh, it is you Rachel! Why did you come here at this time?"

Rachel replied, "Oh, Oh Jordan, your neglect and unconcerned attitude has made my condition miserable. I cannot live anywhere. You have become so unkind that you did not even send a proper reply to my letter. I have walked miles to come here at this time. Due to starvation I feel as if I am dying. In desperation, I have come to meet you so that I can talk with you face to face.

I was on my way to your house when per chance I saw you walking here. It is so sad that instead of appreciating my love for you, you appear to be embarrassed to see me. Have you forgotten all the promises you made to me. I was expecting you to embrace me with love and give me some consolation. But you appear to be irritated and angry. You seduced me by making thousands of sweet promises and you ruined me."

Sir Jordan Lane held her hand tightly and pushed her to a side, away from the main walkway. To avoid being recognized, he partly covered his face with a silken handkerchief. He said in an angry voice, "Listen Rachel, stop all this rubbish. Did you not get the letter that I sent you day before yesterday?"

Rachel said, "You are a cruel person. It is because of that heart-breaking letter that I decided to meet you at once. What do you think I am, a toy that you play with, and once you get bored with it, you break it and throw it away, or a sheet of paper that you can throw in the garbage when you do not like what you have written on it? If you really care for your reputation, then you should keep your promise and marry me. Did you not promise to marry me after the death of your father? You made sweet promises and seduced me. Now you want to forget me. This cunning behaviour is no good. Your letter was full of wicked statements. It killed all the expectations I had built over the last two years. You know very well that my mother is not alive and I have no one else in this world. My father came from a rich family, but unfortunately, he got in bad company and became a robber. I do not want to see his face. There was a time when you used to call me the most beautiful girl in the world and praise me all the time. You used to spend hours in my company and now you do not want to see me. I never thought that you would be so deceitful. I considered you to be in true love with me. Since your father's death, I have been waiting every day to hear about the date of our marriage. It is sad that instead of the letter of marriage, you sent a letter threatening me. If you want to be respected by your acquaintances, listen to me carefully. Come with me right now without a minute's delay to the nearest church and marry me otherwise you will be disgraced by the scandal."

Sir Jordan Lane, instead of consoling the poor and destitute woman, said in a threatening voice, "Listen Rachel, you are standing on the public road and if you do not stop your meaningless talk, I will get you arrested by the police officer who is standing on duty at the corner of this road. Because of your foul language to me, you will be sent to prison and would spend the rest of your life with your father in jail. Nothing will happen to me but your reputation will be destroyed for ever. When we were studying at the school, we were immature and it is best to forget the past. You are clever. Put your education and intelligence to good use. Just think, how can a person of my stature ever marry a lowly like you. It is impossible. As I mentioned in my letter, if you promise to remain quiet and behave yourself I will give a regular allowance which will be enough for your living. You should find a nice person and marry him and settle down. Return all my letters that I wrote to you. I neither loved you before nor do I love you now nor should you have any expectations of the same in future."

On hearing this, Rachel started to cry, "Oh you heartless person. You have no kindness in your heart. I wish I had understood your false pretence of love. I would have died of starvation than fall for your sweet talk of love. Is there no law under which you can be punished for such a horrendous crime? It is amazing that the highly educated and clever politicians in London and the publishers of the big newspapers who can get to the bottom of things, are fooled by your insincere talk and are lobbying for your getting a cabinet post. Oh, what should I do. I am so ashamed of myself that I suffer in silence. Your talk today has completely broken my heart and I have no expectations from you. But remember, the laws of God are eternal. Right now you are drunk with power and wealth. You have brought misery and suffering to a helpless woman like me and for this you will have to pay as per God's laws. No one in this world can live in peace by breaking the laws of nature."

As she finished, she fell to the ground and cried out loud, "There was expectation of love and kindness from you but you turned out to be cruel. I thought your heart was soft like wax but it turned out to be a stone."

Sir Jordan Lane looked with contempt at the fallen helpless figure of the girl and quietly walked away. The police man who was on duty at the corner of the street was watching these two people talking to each other, but was not able to hear any word because of the distance. When he saw Sir Jordan Lane, walking by his side, he saluted him with respect and asked him if that beggar woman was harassing him. When Sir Jordan Lane saw the policeman, he suppressed his anger and nervousness and returned his salute. He took out a gold sovereign from his pocket and gave it to the policeman and said, "She is not a beggar but the daughter of one of my retired servants. When she was young she adopted the life of a street girl and I was trying to counsel her to give up her street life and lead a respectable life. But she is shameless and it appears she may not follow my advice. Instead of being grateful she was talking rudely. By false sighs of pain and anguish, she wants to harass and threaten respectable gentlemen. Listen officer, if you ever see her again near me or any other gentleman, arrest her on the charge of soliciting."

The constable, under the influence of the bribe, respectfully saluted Sir Jordan Lane and promised that she would never bother him again and that he would carry out his orders.

Rachel heard the entire conversation that Sir Jordan Lane had with the policeman on duty. She was convinced that the cruel and wicked Jordan Lane will never show any kindness. She decided to work as a nurse to survive but not to take a penny from him.

This incident of Sir Jordan Lane's unbecoming behaviour towards poor and helpless Rachel happened the same night that his step brother, Nevlin Lane, purchased the helpless girl Sylvia Bond at the auction and adopted her as his sister. He had given away all his hard-earned money to help an orphaned, friendless girl at the cost of his future plans and happiness. He promised her that her happiness will be his happiness.

There indeed is a world of difference between a cruel and a kind man!

Chapter 8

It is love no one can know
The heart is burning but soul does not know

Sylvia Bond, under the care of Nevlin Lane, started to mature and bloom at a remarkable pace. Her red face blossomed like a rose flower. The love and affection of her adopted young brother, Jack, helped her to gradually forget the sadness and depression of her father's death and she was happy and cheerful all the time. Her hands and feet became strong and she put on some weight. She looked very charming. She started to assist Mathula in the kitchen in cooking and cleaning utensils. However, when Jack learned this, he admonished Mathula, "Sylvia Bond is my adopted sister and she will not do any work in the kitchen." He told Sylvia that she could bring breakfast for him at his place of work and do minor repairs on their clothes. He gave her several books on religion, philosophy and fiction, to read. He said, "You read these books yourself and read them to me also." Sylvia happily took the books from him and started carrying out the work assigned to her cheerfully. She spent the whole day with Jack reading him humorous stories and telling jokes.

Jack was very fond of Sylvia's voice. Her voice and tone were very soothing. From breakfast till noon, Sylvia used to narrate the text of various books to him. Her laughing at small things was very relaxing for Jack. Sylvia also looked at Jack with love. If any day he was late in returning from his work, she would impatiently wait for him at the front door, and when she saw Jack coming, she burst with happiness like a flower. The other people of the town were envious of their relationship and several merchants and farmers regretted at having missed Sylvia at the auction. The other workers, digging for gold, considered Sylvia to be a goddess, because the workers working by the side of the route that she took for going to Jack's place of work, found gold in much larger quantity, and for once were able to live comfortably and also save some money after getting all the essentials. That is why they called Sylvia the goddess of money and considered Jack to be very lucky. They respected both of them, and were happy to see them.

Due to Sylvia's presence, Nevlin Lane did not feel the work of digging as hard or unpalatable. He was working much harder at digging now, compared to his previous pace. One day Nevlin Lane was so engrossed in digging that after breakfast, he ignored Sylvia and did not respond to her. Sylvia got bored of sitting quietly with no one to talk to. To pass the time, she started singing a song in a soft voice. Jack dropped his pickaxe and listened to the song in complete amazement. He enjoyed the song quietly, without saying a word so as not to embarrass Sylvia. When the song finished, he looked at Sylvia with wonder and appreciation and said, "Oh God, what a touching and beautiful song. Your singing beats the top and famous singers of London. The girls of aristocratic families in London do sing, but they do not have the charm and sweetness that you have in your singing. Have you ever been to London in your memory? Where did you learn to sing so nicely?"

Sylvia looked at Jack with shyness and said in a modest voice, "Did you really like my song? I thought you were too busy digging and would not hear my muttering. You must know music yourself to understand and appreciate singing. This song was my respected mother's song; she taught it to my father and he taught it to me. It was his favourite song and he often used to ask me to sing it for him. He taught me several other songs too. I do not know any city by the name of London. However, on hearing this name from you I recall faintly that there was a huge city where my mother used to take me and we would pass through a street to come to a big marketplace. There were broad sidewalks on either side of the road, where merchants sold all kinds of eatables and other goods. There were elegant and huge shops on either side. There used to be a big crowd of all kinds of people—men, women, both young and old and children. I also recall that in the early morning hours my parents used to take me for a ride on a beautiful pony in a huge park. On one side of the pony my father used to walk and on the other side my mother used to walk, keeping pace with the pony. They both used to hold me at my waist from either side. Oh, I am forgetting the details of the park and this marketplace. Let me think, I may remember some more details of this huge city."

Jack said, "Let go, do not strain your mind. I can guess that you were in London for a short time and lived under the loving care of your parents in your childhood."

Sylvia replied, "I think you are right. Sometimes I remember the childhood play and toys as told by my parents. But I do not remember other details or incidents of my childhood and that is why I do not try to recall them. Anyway let's not talk of these things. Tell me, did you really like my song?"

Jack replied "I liked it very much. I remember hearing this song before. It was sung by someone else."

Sylvia said, "Yes you may have heard it somewhere or read it in some book. My father was very fond of this song. He also taught me several hymns, sung by priests."

Jack said, "Please sing me one of the religious songs."

Sylvia asked, "Have you never heard religious songs?"

Jack replied, "No."

Sylvia appreciated his honest reply and looked at him and said, "If you did not hear them from someone then you must have read them in books."

Jack said with embarrassment, "You can be sure that I never pretend to know something about which I have no knowledge."

With a view to learn about his nature, Sylvia said, "When you do not know anything about a thing then how can you learn anything about it. You will remain ignorant. A strong house cannot be constructed on weak foundation."

Jack smiled and said, "You are right. If a list is made of the things about which I am ignorant, it will be a voluminous book. Look, if I was not so dumb why would I be wasting my time here digging mountains?"

Sylvia asked, "What else would you have done?"

Jack said, "I had an excellent opportunity to join the army as I knew a very senior officer. I was dumb to let the opportunity go."

Sylvia said, "I feel sorry for you."

Jack said, "I do not deserve any pity. There are numerous other men, better than me, who lost everything and became so poor that they could not afford to have two square meals a day. Books are full of such people."

Sylvia said, "Why look at the books. Your and my case is a proof that what you just said, is correct."

Jack said, "I do not want to waste our time in discussing hypothetical cases. There is a secret reason for my being here."

Sylvia said politely, "I have no need to know of your secret reason. I am grateful to God that you were here to look after me. If you were not here to save me, God knows where I would be, maybe with some uncivilised and rough person. This place is full of such people."

Jack laughed and looked at Sylvia lovingly and said, "Sil, how about singing a religious song. To talk of past things and listen to tales of bygone days is like reciting stories. It does not help things. A good religious song can be uplifting and better than just talking of things which have no meaning. A good hymn sung in a soft and sweet voice can be very soothing. It can help one to bear the troubles of life."

As per Jack's request, Sylvia sang a beautiful hymn in French. She sang it with such feeling that Jack was ecstatic. Jack appreciated the song very much and asked Sylvia who taught her to speak French so fluently.

Sylvia said in a modest voice, "As I have mentioned several times, all that I know, I have learned from my late father. My father used to say that good education is an immense power for a person who acquires it and knows how to use it properly. However, from my experience, I know that my father was highly educated and lived by principles. He always lived in a state of poverty and died as a poor man."

On hearing Sylvia speak in such a refined language of her education and family, it struck Nevlin Lane that Sylvia must be from a rich civilized family of London. He thought that if she had any relatives in London from her mother or father's side, they will recognize her and would take her away from him. To find out if she had any recollection of her relatives, he asked her, "Dear Sil, do you remember anything about your mother?"

Sylvia replied, "No Sir. She left for her heavenly abode when I was only ten years old. However, my father often used to talk to me about her. I heard my father say that uptill the time of her death, she always stood with my father in spite of great sufferings and they both lived very happily in a rich style. My father's nature, by God's Grace, was such that the worldly problems and sufferings never disheartened him and he did not worry about them. Whenever my mother used to get frustrated with problems and sufferings, my father would say, 'Worry and frustration never solve any thing. I am never frustrated because when I look at you all my problems disappear and I find solace in your company. It is my constant endeavour to lighten our problems and make you happy.' In addition, my father used to say that my mother was very charming, clever and a remarkable person. He said that they belonged to such a city where the star of good luck hardly ever remains constant. He explained this to me to mean that my parents's luck changed like the weather and their condition never remained the same."

Jack said, "They probably belonged to England. There, people of different countries live and the star of good luck never shines constantly. There the luck of every one changes. Even the villages devastated by draught, are inhabited once again and regain their economy due to rain and sunshine."

Sylvia said, "Oh yes, I recall my father mentioning that they belonged to England and that's where they became victims of unfortunate sufferings."

Jack asked, "What kind of troubles did they face?"

Sylvia replied, "My father used to say that a very rich man with a big title became his enemy. With the resources available to him he troubled my father a lot. Whenever my father got a job, this man, by means of his position and money, got my father fired from the job. He had vowed to destroy my mother completely. My mother became very sick with various diseases caused by constant stress and hardships created by this rich enemy of my parents. She succumbed to her illness. After her death, my father left the country and brought me to France, where he became the headmaster of a school. Everyone at the school was very pleased with him because of his high ability, humorous nature, polite manners and kind heart. As the remuneration was generous, for two years, we had a fairly happy and carefree life. My father used to take me for a walk to the various parts of the city. He bought me expensive dresses of the latest design. We used to eat delicious meals and lived in a spacious house. My father arranged for me to learn good cooking, stitching and sewing and several other arts from experienced teachers. He took me to various parks and botanical gardens to show me different kinds of flowers and how to grow them. He also taught me how to read and write."

She continued, "One day he came from the college looking sad and very disturbed. He said to me that his eternal enemy had come here also. He was telling lies and framing false charges against him to his superiors. He was a religious person and did not wish to confront him and take revenge. He said that taking revenge is a crime in itself. He had trust in God and felt that he should not take a stand against his enemy. He said that it was best for them to run away from France. So we ran away from France to save my father from defamation. My father was very sensitive to his reputation and principles. He could never go to the police or to courts and fight in courts for his rights. It was not in his nature to bribe lawyers and run after various officers to get his job done. No matter what the consequences, he would never twist facts or tell lies. He considered it an insult to stand in front of police and court officials. It was his belief that man suffers because he violates laws of God. Since his adversary was very rich with high connections, my father knew that he did not have any chance of facing him to resolve the issues in courts and he would lose all his reputation and his good name. Therefore he silently suffered all cruelties and kept running from him. He took up all kinds of jobs with railways, post office, banks, schools etc. but wherever he went, his enemy made sure that he was fired from the job. Due to constant stress, harassment and travelling across sea, he became very weak. He came to Austria after leaving the college in France to get away from his enemy. He was under great pressure and in a very troubled state of mind. He wanted to take up a job where the hands of his enemy could not touch him and influence anyone by his money. He was planning to move from Austria in search of such a job when he became seriously sick. He did not survive this ordeal and died here."

On hearing this very sad tale, Nevlin Lane had tears in his eyes and he asked Sylvia in a very sympathetic voice, "What was the name of your father's enemy?"

Sylvia replied, "I asked my father several times the name of his enemy but he neither told me the name nor the reason for his enmity."

Jack said, "I am very sorry. I wish to know the name of your father's enemy because I want to whip him with infinite lashes."

Sylvia hugged Jack and said, "I am very grateful to you for your sympathy. Indeed your love for me is greater than the love for a sister."

She looked at the strong arms and body of Nevlin with loving eyes and kissed him on his cheek. She looked at the hole where Jack used to dig everyday and looked at him and said, "Jack I am confident that by Grace of God, you will find another gold slab here. Where God can create one, He can certainly create another one also."

Jack said, "I have the same hope. Mathula also thinks so." With this he once again started striking at the hole.

Sylvia said, "Mathula told me that you gave her fifty pounds as a reward."

Jack said, "A man's promise is a promise to be kept. Mathula worked very hard and served me with honesty and loyalty. I could work with a free mind and get my proper meals at the right time. She works cheerfully."

Sylvia said, "You are a very decent person, true to your promise."

Jack said, "Dear sister, please be quiet. I do not like to hear praise. Now let me work."

With this, he once again started to strike at the hole in the mountain. The red sand started to fall from the hole in the similar way as it did the first time he found the gold slab. He would pick up the sand and show it to Sylvia again and again. He kept striking at the hole with his pickaxe.

Sylvia looked at Jack and said in her sweet voice, "The entire money from the first gold slab you spent in buying me and the daily food and groceries. The rest you gave to Mathula as a reward. It will be good to find another similar gold slab."

Jack said, "This is my wish also. I am more eagerly looking forward to finding the second slab than the first one."

Sylvia asked, "If you find the second gold slab, how will you spend the proceeds from its sale?"

Jack kept the pickaxe to one side and came and sat down beside Sylvia and said, "If I find another gold slab, I will use the money to buy you expensive dresses that will fill twelve boxes. Then I will send you to London and get you admitted in one of the finest schools of London, where girls from rich and good families come for education, so that you too may get the best possible education. It is best if you leave this jungle town for London as soon as possible after I find the gold slab. This town is not fit for girls of good families like you. I will send you to London where you will be safe and well looked after by decent families, whom I know well. I will spend all the money from the sale of gold slab for your things. I will continue to labour here and live economically to save money. Once I save enough money for the fare, I will also come to London and see in which branches of art and education you have excelled. Looking at the present trend in the world, sometimes I feel that after you have acquired good education and are part of the life in London, you may not wish to see me at all, because I will be poor and shabbily dressed. You may feel ashamed to call me your brother. Oh God, what am I saying! Why did such thoughts come to my mind. No one should ever entertain such demeaning thoughts. I know very well you are not one of those selfish and proud girls. During your education you will never make friends with such foolish girls and they will not influence you. As your father said, 'education is a great power. By education a person becomes wise and able. By acting on what education has taught him, he can be like an angel.' Well Sylvia, tell me if I am wrong?"

He found Sylvia's head resting on his knee. Her eyes were down and closed. She was crying softly. Since Nevlin Lane was not familiar with the way the girls express themselves, he could not understand Sylvia's emotions. On the contrary, he thought that probably due to heat and sitting at one spot, she is exhausted and tired. With this thought, he said to Sylvia, "You probably dozed off. Get up and go back straight to the house and rest. It is very hot here. The thatched houses are slightly cooler in the sun. You go and rest there. With some sleep and rest you will feel refreshed."

After saying this, he stood up and started to dig hard at the hole in the mountain. The red sand started to fall from the hole and he shouted to Sylvia, "Sylvia, look at the red sand." But in spite of his repeated shouts, Sylvia did not look at him but with her head down, kept on walking straight towards the house.

Chapter 9

Oh, what a horrible tantrum in this young age
God has filled her nature to the brim with mischief

Nevlin Lane was sorry to see Sylvia in a bad temper, ignoring him and leaving for the house. Probably she did not like something that he had said, though he could not recall any thing that may have offended her. He thought that she might be angry because of his mentioning about her going to England, but who would not love to leave this jungle and go to an interesting place like London and live a life of comfort and luxury. He remembered that sometimes Audrey Hope also used to get angry with him in the same manner on insignificant things like this. She must be a grown up young lady now. He felt like teasing her. It used to be so much fun with her. He remembered his childhood days with his friends and forgot the anger of Sylvia Bond. He picked up his pickaxe and got busy with digging. When he saw Mathula bringing the lunch, instead of Sylvia, he got concerned and asked Mathula why Sylvia did not bring the lunch today.

Mathula said, "Your Sil has become very proud and arrogant. She asked me to take the lunch. She went and sat in her room. Ian, I am telling you the truth. Today, I did not say a single word to annoy her. Who knows why she is so upset. I just followed her instructions and brought the lunch."

Ian said, "You did well not to say anything to her. Girls at this age are temperamental and get upset for no particular reason.

The only remedy is to leave her alone. Please do not mind her being upset. Also please do not interfere with her affairs."

Mathula said with frustration. "What to talk of interfering in her affairs, I do not even like to talk to her. I only write the daily account in the book. You can do that too. I am good for nothing."

Ian said, "No, No. Do not even think of such things. I only want to say that, like me, you also look after Sylvia's welfare and safety."

Mathula said, "You are the one who is constantly looking after her and entertaining her. You are concerned about her safety all the time. However, she does not care one bit for you."

Nevlin Lane did not say anything to Mathula because he did not like to get into discussion with the servants. He ate his meal in silence and after his meal he got busy with his work. Mathula picked up the utensils and went back to the house.

Striking with great force repeatedly, Nevlin Lane noticed that gold dust, mixed with red sand, begin to fall from the hole. In the evening, he gathered the gold dust mixed with sand in a small bundle and came home. He saw Sylvia sitting in her room but he did not call her. As per his routine, he sat down at the dinner table. On hearing Jack, Sylvia came out of the room with a long face and still looked very upset. Her face was swollen as if she had been crying. She came and stood beside the dining table, but did not look at the small parcel of gold dust that Jack had spread on the table to please her. She quietly laid the dinner in two plates, in one corner of the table and stood on one side with her back towards Jack. Jack looked at Sylvia with concern and said, "Dear Sil, I do not recall saying anything to annoy you. I do not know why you appear to be so angry today. Please come and eat with me."

Sylvia replied, "Please Sir, excuse me. I do not feel like eating."

With this, she started walking towards her room. Mathula shouted from the kitchen, "Please Sylvia before you go, tell me if I have said anything to annoy you today and made you sit all day in your room with an angry face. You have become very rude and arrogant. Ian, see how she does not even reply to us with a straight face."

Jack said with a smile, "You cannot understand the girls of these days. I have often seen young girls getting angry like this. The only remedy is to leave them alone."

After finishing his dinner, Nevlin Lane looked in Sylvia's room through the side of the door. He did not see anyone. He pushed the door and went inside. He did not see Sylvia anywhere. He got very concerned about Sylvia. He saw the open door leading towards the jungle on the north side. He ran through the door outside, towards the jungle. This part of Austria was known for pitch dark nights. One could hardly see one's own hand in front. Nevlin Lane started shouting, "Sylvia, Sylvia!" At the same time he looked all around the house. He heard a faint muffed sound in the north direction. He ran in that direction and in the dim light of stars, he could make out the face of wicked Lewryk standing under a tree. He was threatening Sylvia and she was shivering with fear. She was shouting to let go of her. Nevlin Lane in a mad rage jumped on the wicked Lewryk and with all his force he pushed him to the ground and sat on his chest. He pressed his throat with both his hands and pulled his dagger and said, "Tell me why did you come this side? Tell me quickly otherwise I am going to strangle you right now and finish you off right here."

Sylvia, fearing a bloody slaying, said in a frightened voice, "Please dear Jack, let him go. Spare his life. Do not endanger your life for my sake."

On hearing Sylvia's request, he kept his dagger back in its case and got up from Lewryk's chest. Due to the pressure of Jack's hands, Lewryk's throat was paining and he started massaging his neck. Fearing arrest, he started to say things to please Nevlin Lane. Nevlin Lane indicated to Sylvia, with the motion of his hand, to go back to the house. As per Jack's instructions, she moved away from the scene, but rather than returning to the house, she just sat down under a tree closer to the house.

The wicked Lewryk breathed deeply and addressed Nevlin

Lane in a respectful tone, "Ian, you take all the money that I have and give me Sylvia Bond. This way you will benefit a lot and I will realize my wish. For God's sake, Ian, I request you to please accept my offer."

Nevlin Lane admonished him and said, "Just now I spared your life on the recommendation of Sylvia Bond. After this moment, you should never even think about taking Sylvia. I have adopted her as my sister. I will never part with her under any circumstances. If, in future, I ever see you anywhere near my house, I will shoot you without any hesitation. You are aware of my power today. You cannot fight with me. You stupid man, you should be ashamed to tempt me with the offer of money. I am very well aware of your character. I know your intentions are not good towards Sylvia. You want to make profit from her person. Look at me and listen carefully. In spite of the fact that I am fully aware of your various robberies and break-ins, I have never informed the police of the same and got you arrested. Since you do not stop your wicked pursuits, I have decided to deal with you myself and will shoot you with my gun. Instead of getting Sylvia, you will lose your life."

On hearing this, Lewryk started shivering with fear. He was afraid that Nevlin Lane would shoot him right there and started apologizing. He promised that he will not have anything to do with the girl in future. He begged for forgiveness.

On hearing Lewryk speak like this, Nevlin Lane said, "Alright I forgive you. I follow the saying;

If one bows before you, bow back
If one stops for you, you stop too.

Your character and occupation of robbery is not my concern. Everyone is responsible for his own actions. One reaps what one sows. You will be punished for your actions by God. I do not want to harm you. I am a religious person. Go away, I forgive you this time. Never again come towards this side or cross my path!"

After the wicked Lewryk left, Nevlin Lane checked his gun

and dagger and returned to the house. Sylvia had already returned to the house a few minutes earlier. She was waiting at the door for Jack. She admired Jack for his courage and strength. Seeing Jack coming back, her face lightened up like a lily flower. She took his hand and escorted him inside the house.

She addressed Jack in a quiet voice and said. "Dear Jack, today you beat up that wicked robber thoroughly and conveyed to him the message in very strong terms. I am convinced he will never dare to come this side again. Once again you risked your life for my sake. I thank God a million times that the enemy was suppressed. I am still shaking from the experience."

Jack said, "Please do not be scared. I am well aware of the weakness of that wicked person. The robbers are always scared of arrests. He will never bother you again. Anyway, tell me why did you recommend that I spare his life? Did you meet him before in this Lornehope Camp?"

Sylvia said, "No Jack, no. God forbid, I am not at all familiar with this very wicked robber. The first time I had the misfortune to see his ugly face was the day my father died. He was standing at the door behind the curtain and listening to my father's advice to me. The second time I saw him was at the auction. Both the times, I got very scared of his ugly face. The reason I requested you to let go of him was that I did not want you to be hurt by him. The robbers do not hesitate to use weapons to hurt others. They have concealed weapons on their body to harm others. By God's Grace and your bravery, he had to admit defeat. Now he will not even look in this direction."

After this conversation, she started to assist Jack in taking off his jacket and brushing off the dust from his jacket. While cleaning the sleeve of the coat, she noticed a blood stain. She got worried as she realized that Jack must have hurt his arm. She hurried and got warm water from the kettle and a bandage. She asked Jack to take off his shirt. Jack protested that he did not feel any pain. He said that the sharp edge of a stone struck his arm when he was fighting Lewryk on the ground and it was just a small scratch and there was no need to clean it or bandage it. But Sylvia ignored his protests and got him to take off his shirt. She cleaned his wound on the arm with soap and warm water and bandaged it with a broad bandage in a professional manner.

Jack smiled and said, "Aha, Sylvia you are an expert doctor too. You have bandaged my hand very professionally. With your touch, my whole body feels relaxed. I thank you very much. Listen Sylvia, please do not mention about my fight with wicked Lewryk and the scratch on the arm to Mathula. She will again call me a fool."

He had hardly finished this sentence when Mathula returned from the market with the groceries and refreshments. Jack immediately picked up his coat from the chair and wore it and said to Sylvia, "I will be outside on guard. You and Mathula rest now and have a good sleep." He said, "Good night," and as he was going out, both Sylvia and Mathula told him, in a persuasive tone, that it was very cold outside. It was better for him to rest inside. On their joint persuasion, he agreed and went and lay down on the bed in his room. He was very tired and the moment he covered himself with the blanket, he fell fast asleep. When Mathula was busy in other things, Sylvia took the opportunity to go to Jack's room quietly. She sat beside his bed and gently stroked his face with her soft hands. When Jack turned in his bed, she quietly came out and went to her room. Soon she was fast asleep.

Nevlin Lane got up early in the morning. Instead of going to his place of work, he went to the office of Mr. McGregor, the contractor. Except for the clerk Mr. Loket, there did not appear to be anyone else in the office. He went to Mr. Loket and said, "Tell me where is wicked Lewryk. I have come to ask him as to how he dared to come to my house last night. Who sent him there? You know Lewryk well. On the third day after the auction, you came to me with a request from him and you also know his intentions. Understand clearly that if you do not find him and make adequate arrangements to keep him away from my house, I shall have to call the police and take legal action so that he will stop harassing and robbing decent people here. I shall also write to the high officers of the King of Austria about Lewryk's character and his profession of robbing people here."

The clerk, Mr. Loket, was taken by surprise and immediately called the few employees in the office and his security staff and asked them if they knew the whereabouts of Lewryk. They said that Lewryk had not been to his house since last night and he had not been seen at the usual places also. They further said, "All of us in the security staff keep a track on his movements. However, since last night we have no information about him. He has left his place and gone somewhere. We do not know where he has gone. He has run away from here. We, in the security department are here to protect the public from thieves and thugs and do not send them to harass decent people. Mr. Ian, please be assured that all of us in the security department have absolutely nothing to do with him. We will arrest him. We shall make all efforts to find him. The moment we locate him, we shall take appropriate measures to ensure that he never comes near your house nor harasses any other citizen of this town."

On hearing this, Nevlin Lane felt satisfied. Mr. Loket offered him breakfast with wine. He said to Nevlin, "All the employees in this office consider you to be a very decent person and they are all keen to assist you in any manner."

Nevlin Lane felt quite reassured and happy. He thanked Mr. Loket and left for his house.

Chapter 10

Persons who flatter have no loyalty
Like paper flowers have no fragrance

After his meeting with the woman named Rachel, Sir Jordan Lane did not go out of his house for a few days. None of the servants saw Rachel around the house during this period. The constable, to whom Sir Jordan Lane had given a gold sovereign as a bribe, had also not seen Rachel harassing anyone in the neighbourhood. After one week of this incident, Sir Jordan Lane read a speech at the Exeter Town Hall regarding the measures needed to be taken for the economic welfare of the people. The audience comprised several members of the parliament and publishers of several powerful newspapers. In his speech he outlined proposals for changes in the legislation for social and economic reforms. The public very much appreciated his speech. The newspapers supported his proposals. Their editorials recommended that Sir Jordan Lane be given a cabinet position.

The winter season was over and the spring season had started. The rich people and the members of the cabinet started to go from London to their respective country estates. Lord and Lady Marlow also came to Fort Greenwich with Audrey Hope. To make her happy, they promised to stay at the elegant mansion of Audrey Hope till the beginning of the New Year. After a few days of their stay as per her usual practice, Lady Marlow, in consultation with Audrey Hope, fixed up a date for a big party. All the close friends and relatives were sent invitations. Lady Marlow personally delivered invitations to several rich and distinguished people. She also went to the mansion of Lord Lorimor. When she gave him the invitation, he replied with a sigh that he will not be able to come to the party and apologised for the same. On repeated insistence from Lady Marlow, Lord Lorimor asked if Audrey Hope also wished him to come to the party.

Lady Marlow smiled and said, "Well Sir, what a question! The party is for the enjoyment and fun of Audrey Hope at her ancestral mansion and she particularly asked me to invite you. You must believe this."

Lord Lorimor replied, "Very well, I will come and join the party, provided there is no hunting expedition after the party. I have to be back by the eleventh to go to a distant place."

Lady Marlow said with a smile, "Except for Audrey Hope, there is no one else who will be interested in going on a hunting trip."

Lord Lorimor did not grasp the underlying meaning of this sentence. His mind was diverted to something else when Lady Marlow was speaking. So he kept silent. Lady Marlow returned back home and told Audrey Hope the details of her visit and the conversation she had with Lord Lorimor. Audrey Hope laughed and said, "You unnecessarily troubled him to come to the party. He always teases me with his worthless conversation."

Lady Marlow asked, "Are you really bothered by Lord Lorimor's talk?"

Miss Hope replied, "Aunty, how come you do not believe me? Allow me to write to Lord Lorimor and tell him to do me a favour by not coming to the party."

Lady Marlow said, "Please do not do such a terrible thing. If you write such a letter, he will never ever come to our house for years to come and we will all be deprived of his pleasant company. In this part, Lord Lorimor is the only fun-loving, wise and brave person. He is a very jolly and likable person, who socializes with everyone."

Miss Hope said, "It is better to keep away from such a person.

O.K. let him come. However, I will make sure that in the party he does not do anything that is uncivilized or bother me in any way. Hopefully he will fall in love with some beautiful girl at the party. My friend Miss Chester is beautiful. If I were a man I am sure I would be enchanted by a charming girl like her."

Lady Marlow said with a smile, "I doubt if Lord Lorimor would be attracted to any other girl. Pardon me but in my opinion he will not even look at any one else except you. He only loves you and you say that is bothering you!"

Miss Hope said, "You may say whatever you wish. I do not wish to argue with you."

Lady Marlow also thought it appropriate to change the subject and took Audrey Hope for a stroll towards the front courtyard.

The property of Sir Jordan Lane, known as Court Lane, was near the High Road from the village of Greenwich. At the bend in the road, the property of Audrey Hope started and continued in a straight line for a long distance and eventually joined the property of Court Lane. There was a thin fence between the two properties. A thin fence starting at the side from the front courtyard of Court Lane was visible above the oak tree. Looking at it, Lady Marlow remembered Sir Jordan Lane and said to Audrey Hope, "He is probably due to come here at this time."

Miss Hope looked surprised and said, "Who do you mean? Is Lord Lorimor coming here?"

Lady Marlow replied, "No, not him. I mean Sir Jordan Lane. See the smoke coming from the chimney of his mansion."

Miss Hope said, "Yes I think so too. Before our coming here, he mentioned to me that he will also be coming to his ancestral home."

Lady Marlow said, "It appears that Sir Jordan Lane is not much interested in his house, Court Lane."

Miss Hope replied, "How can he have any interest here? There is no one to keep him company."

Lady Marlow said, "I am very surprised that there has been no party at Court Lane since the death of Sir Gravlin Lane. Oh well, it is none of our business and we should not worry about it. We shall definitely invite him to our party. I have not had much opportunity to correspond with Sir Jordan Lane and I do not know him that well. It is likely he may not care to come if I invite him. On the other hand you know his nature and habits well as you have known him for a long time. Maybe I can ask you to send the invitation."

Miss Hope said, "There is no doubt that I know him from my childhood days though he is much older to me in age. My conversations with him have been brief and to the point."

Lady Marlow was a woman with high ambitions. Since she regarded Audrey Hope as her own daughter, she wanted her to marry a rich and famous person. Lord Lorimor had lots of property, but compared to Sir Jordan Lane, his wealth and property was less and he was not as popular as Sir Jordan Lane amongst the members of the parliament. Lady Marlow was convinced that Sir Jordan Lane would soon be appointed a cabinet minister and would become famous. Because of this it was her heart's desire to get Audrey Hope engaged to Sir Jordan Lane. She had been waiting for the proper time to bring up the subject. With this in mind she said to Audrey Hope, "What do you mean Sir Jordan Lane is much older. He may be older than you in age but he cannot be called old."

Miss Hope said, "I meant that he is older than Nevlin Lane. Dear Aunty, how can I tell you that I badly miss the honest and sincere talk of Nevlin Lane? He used to teach me while we played. Poor Nevlin Lane, I do not know where he has gone. If he was here, he would teach me hundreds of kind and sensible things about life."

Lady Marlow said, "No doubt if Nevlin Lane was here you would have immensely enjoyed his talk. But what can be done? He is not here. In fact I have no hope of his ever returning back. Sir Jordan Lane was telling me that he has made great efforts to find him but there was no information from anywhere about him."

Miss Hope said in a low voice, "Yes that is my information too. However, my dear uncle said that this world is not a small place to find a lost person. He will return back on his own. My heart tells me that he will soon return, alive and well."

When they reached the house, they sat down on the chairs. Lady Marlow continued the conversation, "You should not believe all that your uncle says. He just likes to make light of things. He has no knowledge of family matters. Since you always flatter him and agree to everything that he says, he likes to make you happy and say things to please you. He is however, absolutely ignorant of family problems and his ability to look at and plan for the future is nil."

Audrey Hope said, "This may be your opinion of him. I regard him as wise and very planned in his approach for the future. He loves me like a daughter. There would hardly be another four or five people like him in the world who are so highly disciplined and so kind."

She had hardly finished the sentence when Lord Marlow walked in and asked Audrey Hope, "My dear, whom are you talking about?"

Lord Marlow was a tall and handsome person with a very pleasant disposition. He belonged to London proper. He was very rich. People living under his jurisdiction were very pleased with his fair and straightforward dealings. They lived happily, free of undue financial worries. Lord Marlow was a member of the House of Lords and was also appointed by the British Government as the chief magistrate for his county. Being young at heart and easy going, both husband and wife used to live happily in London. He used to discharge his duties as chief magistrate with great diligence and as per law. He was known to be fair and never compromised justice in reaching his decisions. Both the husband and the wife did their respective work and carried out their duties without any interference from the other. They trusted each other and lived a happy and blissful married life. They faced the worldly problems with patience. Though they had no children, they never expressed any regret or grieved about it. Lady Marlow's hobby was to throw big parties and attend parties given by others. Lord Marlow's hobby was to spend time in the library or in the living room talking with his peers, visiting places and going to theatres. He was always ready to help needy persons. He was very famous in London and was liked both by rich and poor. They used to consider him an honest and decent gentleman and respected him. Both the husband and the wife were fond of hunting. They had undertaken the full responsibility of Audrey Hope's welfare and treated her like their own daughter. She was the daughter of their deceased close and dear friend. They were very sincere advisers to her and considered her happiness to be their main concern.

On hearing her uncle's voice, Audrey Hope let go of the cute little dog sitting on her lap. She ran and hugged Lord Marlow and said, "Such a nice person can only be you and no one else." She put her arms round the neck of Lord Marlow and said with a smile, "Uncle, today is a beautiful day. Let us race our horses to the Greenwich town and go for hunting. I shall beat you in the race. Tell me how soon you will be ready for the hunt."

Lord Marlow said, "Today I am very busy and do not have even five minutes for taking rest. The accounts of the mines need to be finalized. The accountant will be coming soon to the house with the books."

Audrey Hope replied, "Oh no. Today I am definitely going to take you for the hunt. A beautiful sunny day like this is not meant to be spent with the books. I will not allow the accountant to get you involved with the books today."

She rang the bell and summoned the servant. She instructed him to go to the accountant and tell him that Lord Marlow is very busy today, and that he will look at the books some other day.

Lord Marlow said with a smile, "No dear daughter. Sometimes you insist too much. Just think yourself how disappointed the accountant will be with your message. Tell him to come tomorrow."

Miss Hope said to the servant, "Alright, ask him to come tomorrow."

After instructing the servant, Audrey Hope requested her uncle to get ready for the hunt. She said, "I will take only five minutes. I think we are going to have a lot of fun today."

Audrey Hope was very pleased with herself for getting her way with her uncle and she went to her room to dress up, humming a tune from a popular song.

Lady Marlow said to her husband, "Your loving care has made Audrey Hope very stubborn. You immediately agree to anything she insists on. To develop such habits is not good for her."

Lord Marlow replied, "You are no less to blame in spoiling her. If you ask me, it is because of you that I had to postpone my urgent work. If I did not agree to her request, you would have consoled her and forced me to agree anyway."

Lord Marlow had hardly finished his sentence when Audrey Hope came out of the room dressed for hunting. Lord and Lady Marlow and Audrey Hope got on their horses and had only gone a short distance when they saw the accountant coming from the front.

Lord Marlow said, "Look Audrey, the accountant is coming here. He is so dedicated to his work."

Lady Marlow said, "The fact is that Jack is very conscious of his responsibility. If he does not get clear directions, he gets very uncomfortable and will not even listen to the angels. He never allows his work to be postponed."

Lord Marlow said, "There is no doubt about it. He is very determined and punctual. However, I am sure that this time Audrey Hope will make him understand and not let him get upset."

Audrey Hope took the hint and trotted her horse in front of the others. She stopped near Jack and said with a smile, "Good morning Mr. Jack. Look what a lovely day it is today. I am forcing my uncle to come for a hunt. This time it is my fault and I am responsible for the delay caused in your work."

On hearing Audrey Hope, Lord Marlow laughed and addressed the accountant, "Today it is Audrey Hope's pleasure that we do not work. We will work tomorrow and get it all done. Anyway, what is the news about Sir Jordan Lane? You also visited him and you would know of his programme. Is he going to come here today and by what time? Where are you coming from just now? Did you not meet Audrey Hope's servant? We sent him by carriage to inform you that I shall not be working today."

The accountant replied, "Sir, no servant came to me or met

me on the way here. He probably went by the regular route. I took a short cut by the side of the church to come here. I have met Sir Jordan Lane. He will be coming here for sure by this evening."

Lord Marlow said, "Well Audrey, what do you say? Shall we invite Sir Jordan Lane for dinner tonight?"

Audrey Hope pretended that she did not care and said, "Whatever you decide is alright with me."

She spurred her horse forward and they all passed through Fort Greenwich and reached the road. There, at the gate, the old grand security guard of Audrey Hope was standing at his post. Near the gate, five boys and girls, the children of the old security guard, were playing. They ranged in ages from two to fourteen years. When they saw their Mistress approaching, they all stood in a line respectfully, on one side of the road and saluted her in a military style. One of the boys came forward from the line and stood near Audrey Hope's horse. He lifted both his hands up and tried to say something that sounded like, "Please, please."

Audrey Hope said, "Oh this is Tommy. I nearly forgot!" With this she bent down and picked up Tommy and seated him in front of her on the horse. She said to Lord Marlow, "When Tommy was just a small child, I always gave him a ride on my horse whenever I used to pass this side. He has not forgotten that."

Lord Marlow said, "The children and horses have remarkable memory. They never forget a person who is kind to them."

Audrey Hope said, "I suppose they also do not forget the person who has been a bully to them like they do not forget the person who has been kind to them."

She picked up Tommy and gently stood him on the ground and said with a smile, "You are now a big sensible boy. Bye, bye Tommy, I have to go now."

Tommy respectfully stood on one side of the road. Audrey Hope quietly put a shilling in his hand and spurred her horse forward. They all moved on further down the road and passed the main gate of Court Lane. An old guard was sitting at the gate, dozing. The very elegant mansion of Court Lane looked very deserted and desolate. All the doors of the house were closed and deadly silence prevailed. Lord Marlow remarked that the building looked very lonely. He said, "In fact a building becomes lively only when children and people live in it. This building, in comparison to other buildings in the area, is very elegant, beautiful and tall. Sir Gravlin Lane was especially very proud of this building amongst his other mansions and rightly so. It was constructed on a very solid foundation with the finest material and a great attention to details. The outside windows were designed to be tall to let the air and light in. Listen Audrey, look after my horse, I will tie him to a tree and go inside to ask the servant to inform Sir Jordan Lane to come to our place for dinner tonight."

As he was alighting from his horse, a servant in old dirty clothes came from the house towards their side. Lord Marlow asked the servant, "Is your master at home? I want to meet him."

The servant replied, "Respected Sir, my master is not there right now but I have received information that he will be coming by the evening train."

On hearing this, Lord Marlow asked Audrey Hope for a piece of paper to write a note for Sir Jordan Lane. Audrey Hope had a paper in her pocket, but it had her name printed on top and she thought that if the invitation was written on her letterhead, it will appear that the invitation was from her side. With this in mind, she said, "I am sorry, I do not have a spare paper." Lady Marlow had one of the invitation cards with her; she took it out and gave it to her husband. Lord Marlow jotted down a couple of lines on the back of the card with pencil, inviting Sir Jordan Lane to the dinner and gave it to the servant. He instructed him to give this card to his master as soon as he arrived. The servant saluted respectfully and took the card.

Lord Marlow turned his horse and said, "Come on. Let us go through the town towards the jungle and start the hunt."

Audrey Hope said, "No Sir, do not go this way. This road leads to a dead end at a short distance from here. Turn right from here."

Everyone turned right and as they passed the adjoining building, her face suddenly became sad. She said with a sigh, "Uncle this is the place where Nevlin Lane and I used to play for hours. You see that chestnut tree. He used to challenge me to climb that tree. I would try to climb it and fall down."

Lord Marlow said, "Was Nevlin Lane not afraid that you may be badly hurt by the fall?"

Audrey Hope said, "Sir, how could I be hurt? As soon as I would begin to slip, he would hold me tightly by both hands. He was never afraid. He used to laugh loudly at my being scared and would call me a coward. He used to say, that exercise made the body strong from head to foot. He had so much power in his eyes that for several minutes he could hold his gaze without blinking. He kept a sharp eye on me and anytime I used to start slipping from the tree, he would lift me up like a ball. He never knew the meaning of the word 'scare.' If any time I got angry with him, instead of feeling sorry, he would make funny faces and console me and soon I would forget all my anger. He used to treat me with great love and kindness."

Lord Marlow said, "The entrance door of this mansion is very magnificent."

Audrey Hope said, "Oh Sir, the stairs just inside the door, end near the bedroom of late Sir Gravlin Lane. He died in that room."

Lord Marlow said, "But how would one enter the bedroom? By jumping from the stairs?"

Audrey Hope laughed and said, "No Sir, why would one jump? The stairs are circular and there is a landing at the end of the stairs. On the right hand side is the door to his room. I used to go to his room every day through this door."

Lord Marlow said, "I have heard from several friends that late Sir Gravlin Lane was a very ill-tempered person."

Audrey Hope said, "Ever since I remember, I had always seen him sad and depressed. Sometimes he was so depressed that visitors were sorry to see him and would leave with a sad feeling also."

Lord Marlow said, "Our elders have said that a person who seeks revenge can never be happy. I have also heard that whenever he decided to take revenge on anyone, he would go all out and make life utterly miserable for that person. However, I also know that two years before his death, his attitude changed and he became very fair and just. He became religious and pious."

Audrey Hope said, "I have seen him preaching good behaviour and kindness. For the last two years of his life there was a remarkable change in him and a lot of good qualities manifested in his behaviour. After a few days of the incident, when he turned Nevlin Lane out of the house, he became a very religious man. Nevlin Lane's nanny told me that he used to cry for hours for his beloved son Nevlin Lane. The real cause of Nevlin Lane being turned out of the house is known only to Sir Jordan Lane. Just two days before his death, I met Sir Gravlin Lane. He greeted me with great warmth and love. He gave me such valuable advice that even after spending hours with him I did not feel like leaving. In the end he also advised me as a sort of hint, and said, 'My dear daughter Audrey, if ever someone says something bad about one of your close relatives or friends, think and analyze the whole accusation carefully and never take any action on the accusation till you have investigated the whole thing yourself. My experience tells me that the best way to resolve such a situation is to bring the person being accused and the person accusing face to face and get to the bottom of the accusation and find the truth. By such an action, the truth would come out and the facts would be known. By getting angry and keeping it to yourself, the mind cracks like a glass, and can never be repaired. Your eyes get blinded by anger. The consequences of your decision can ruin you with sad remorse and it is never rectified even by your death. One has to then repent every second of one's life.'"

Lord Marlow said, "This advice of his is very practical. When Sir Gravlin Lane turned Nevlin Lane out of the house in a fit of anger, did he also tell him about his will that he will not inherit any thing?"

Audrey Hope said, "I have no information on this subject. Sir Gravlin Lane died a year after Nevlin Lane left the house. When I was here, there was no fight of any kind and Nevlin Lane was living very happily when I last saw him. I left my house here to live with you and afterwards I had gone to inspect my property at Eaton. If I were here at the time of their fight, Nevlin Lane would have confided in me. He never kept any secrets from me. I would have known the real facts and would not have allowed him, under any circumstances, to go away. When I came back here after visiting my properties and went to see Sir Gravlin Lane, he did not tell me anything clearly but gave me a general idea. After meeting him and listening to his advice, I again left for some work in America. I was not here at the time of his death. When I returned a few days after his death, the nanny told me that Sir Jordan Lane had not allowed anyone to even clean the room of Sir Gravlin Lane since his death and had instructed all his servants not to go to that room. Oh I feel sick. Uncle, let's go from here. This house looks very scary. I do not want to look in the direction of his room. It makes me sad."

Lord Marlow said, "You should not believe everything that the servants tell you. When servants get together they generally gossip and distort the facts. Think yourself. How is it possible that Sir Jordan Lane would forbid the servants to clean his father's room. Servants generally are not able to understand the directions of their master and interpret them differently and sometimes they fabricate things on their own."

At this time they galloped their horses and stopped only after reaching the city market centre. The brisk galloping of the horses wiped the sadness Audrey Hope felt by looking at the house of Court Lane and she once again felt happy. Lord Marlow told Audrey Hope, "You and your aunt shop around and buy things that you like. In the meanwhile I will go and visit a friend who lives round the corner. I will not be more than fifteen minutes."

Audrey Hope said, "I know your fifteen minutes mean an hour. When you get engrossed in talking to your friends you lose control of time. What shall we do standing here aimlessly as I do not like to buy from the shops here. If you allow me I will go to London and buy all the things I need from there. In this town, first of all I do not get the things of my liking and if I do find something that I like, it is very expensive here."

Lord Marlow said, "For such things you should really get permission from your aunt. You should do whatever she says."

Lady Marlow said, "You may go wherever you have to go but please come back soon."

Lord Marlow promised to come back soon and left. The two ladies waited on one side, on their horses, under a tree near the corner shop on the street. They entertained themselves by looking at the buildings all around and watching the different people shopping in the marketplace. In front, on a tall building, they noticed the picture of a man. This was the picture of a dacoit about whom they had both heard and had seen his picture in the newspapers. The dacoit was sentenced to life imprisonment for several robberies and fraud but he escaped from the prison. The police department had posted an award of one hundred pounds to anyone who would help them capture this man. As the two ladies were discussing about this dacoit, the chief of police, Mr. Trail, passed that side. He was tall and good looking. He carried out his police duties with great diligence, honesty and integrity. All the people working under him were happy with him because of his fairness and just treatment. Men and women from all walks of life had great respect for him. Mr. Trail belonged to the city of Greenwich itself. In his childhood, he used to play with Nevlin Lane and Audrey Hope at Court Lane and they were good friends. The elders of Mr. Trail had long standing relations with the elders of Nevlin Lane and Audrey Hope. Mr. Trail used to love Nevlin Lane like a brother from the days of their childhood. When he saw Audrey Hope and Lady Marlow standing under the tree, he came over with a big smile and saluted Lady Marlow and shook hands with Audrey Hope. After inquiring about their welfare he asked if he could be of any service to them.

Audrey Hope joked, "You only know how to lock me up—what else are you good for."

Trail replied, "Ah ha. Sister Audrey, I get the meaning of what you are saying. Your memory of the childhood play is still fresh. One day while playing the game of four corners, you got very upset and started shouting and I locked you up in one of the rooms at Court Lane. You remember that incident. That was when we were both children. Now your brother is grown up and wise. Come on, get down from your horse. I am going to order some refreshments and would not let you go without you joining me for the same."

Audrey Hope said, "Brother, you were going somewhere on a mission. So you go ahead. I do not want to disturb your official work. At this time I do not feel like having anything. We are waiting here for Lord Marlow's return and were looking at that picture on the tall building. I read about him in the papers. Is this the picture of the same dacoit?"

Trail replied, "This dacoit is very cunning and also clever. He escaped from the maximum security prison. The senior officers in the police department are much troubled by his escape and that is why I have to devote a lot of my time and effort in finding him. His name is Banks and he belongs to this city of Greenwich. His arrest warrant was issued from my police station and he was given life imprisonment. This wicked dacoit tore up his blanket at the prison into small strips and made a rope out of it. With the help of this rope he jumped from the window towards the jungle. He disappeared two years back and to date we have no trace of him. My superiors are pressurizing me to find him as soon as possible. If he ever comes here, he will not go back alive from my jurisdiction."

Audrey Hope said, "This type of dacoits are generally very fearless and bold. They cannot keep away from their country for long and sooner or later visit their hometown in some form of disguise."

Trail replied, "What you are saying is absolutely correct. On the third day after his escape, one of my constables informed me that he had seen Banks, sitting under a tree in the Court Lane compound. When he saw the constable, he disappeared behind the tree in such a way that to this day we have been unable to find him. Another policeman saw Banks in the room of Sir Gravlin Lane. On receiving this information, I immediately went there to investigate. I met Sir Jordan Lane who informed me that his father had just passed away. In such circumstances, I did not consider it fit to question Sir Jordan Lane and the other servants about Banks, as I thought it was not possible for Banks to enter the deceased's room with so many people present. Since that day there has been no news about this scoundrel."

Trail had hardly finished his sentence, when Lord Marlow returned after visiting his friend. Lord Marlow wanted to talk to Mr. Trail but he noticed that Audrey Hope was looking very sad and pale. He simply greeted Mr. Trail and turned his horse to go back. Audrey Hope and Lady Marlow followed him. When Audrey Hope caught up with Lord Marlow's horse, he asked her, "About which dacoit you were talking to Mr. Trail?"

Audrey Hope said, "Both my aunt and I are not going to talk to you, till you take us to the horse racing show at the park. It is now too late to go to the jungle for the hunt as there is not much time left."

Lord Marlow said, "The horse racing in the park is not today but tomorrow. I promise to take you to the horse racing. But first tell me what reward I will get for taking you to the horse racing."

Audrey Hope said with a mischievous smile, "I will arrange for you to kiss my aunt's smiling face."

At this comment all the three laughed, galloped their horses and reached the house.

Chapter 11

Even if someone dies, won't the work will still be done
Even if one is unpopular, the name is still known.

Sir Jordan Lane reached Greenwich station by the evening train. The station master and two porters on duty saluted him. However, several other men and women, who had come to the railway station, completely ignored him. When Audrey Hope had arrived at the station a few days earlier, several rich and famous landlords and tenants, common men and women, her young friends, servants and the station employees who were even off duty, came to welcome her and greeted her with warmth and affection. The people of Greenwich, old and young, rich and poor, admired Audrey Hope's amiable and kind nature. But they considered Sir Jordan Lane to be proud and dishonest. Even his servants were weary of his short temper, rude and unfair behaviour. When he arrived at the station that evening, two porters carried his baggage to a carriage, driven by two black horses, which was waiting outside and he left for his mansion. The servants as per instructions, had lighted the main rooms used by their master. The butler, the cook and the guard were there to greet him but were looking tired and disinterested. Half-heartedly they carried his luggage to his room upstairs. Sir Jordan Lane also looked tired and sad. As he entered the room, his personal valet came and helped him to take off his coat. Sir Jordan Lane complained of a cold and lay down on his bed. The servant presented the invitation card of Lord Marlow. On reading the card, there was a trace of joy on his face and he got up from the bed and looked himself in the mirror. There were wrinkles and sadness on his face. He thought, "If I go in this condition then Audrey Hope will truly think of me as being much older than her. After a good night's rest, I will feel better and the tiredness of the journey will be gone. When I am fresh in the morning, I shall visit them." With this resolution, he sat down on the table and wrote the following note in response to the invitation:

My dear Sir,

I have just come from London. I have to write several important and significant papers regarding the country's affairs. For this reason I very much regret, I cannot come this evening. However, I shall come and meet you all sometime tomorrow. Please excuse me for not being able to come this evening.

With kind regards,
Jordan Lane

He sealed the note in an envelope and instructed his servant to deliver it to Lord Marlow right away. He instructed the cook to lay the dinner on the table. On the front wall of the dining room, he saw the pictures of his father and step brother, Nevlin Lane, who looked very handsome in the picture. There was brightness on his face. His father looked rather sad in the picture. By looking at these pictures, Sir Jordan Lane's face became sad. The cook had cooked very delicious dinner but Sir Jordan Lane did not enjoy the food. He never felt happy about anything in the house. Whenever he came to the house, the mental stress and agony appeared to surround him. The house looked very depressing. The servants appeared to be on duty with miserable faces. Sir Jordan Lane himself was feeling down with worry and anxiety. He went and sat down on the bed. He rang the bell and summoned all the servants to his room. He asked them about the general news of the city and happenings there. In particular he asked them if a woman, by the name of Rachel, had come to the house. They all said with one voice that not a single man or woman came to the house, except today, when Lord Marlow along with Miss Audrey Hope had visited the house before they left for hunting. They further informed him that after they left, farmer Kieals had come to see him. He wanted to know the reply to his application that he had sent by mail, a few days earlier. He promised to come back the next morning. His accountant had also come and he had left the books on his table for his review, concerning accounts of the mines. Except for these people, no one else had come and there were no telegrams or mail worth mentioning.

Sir Jordan Lane said, "If farmer Kieals comes tomorrow morning, please tell him that no money is granted for the cultivation of the farms. Keep the accounts book on the table near my bed, I will review them tonight." He further instructed the guard that if a woman by the name of Rachel came, she should not be allowed in the house without his permission. With such instructions he dismissed the servants and lay down in the bed.

Sir Jordan Lane could not sleep due to worry and anxiety. He got up from the bed, took the bunch of keys from his pocket and picked up a lighted candle. He went through several rooms inside the house and came to a room on the south side of the house. He quietly opened the cupboard lock with the key and took out a briefcase. He used to keep this hidden from the eyes of all his servants. Whenever he used to get very restless, he opened this briefcase and carefully looked at all the papers inside. Tonight also he did so and looked for a particular piece of paper that he had been searching for the last two years. When he did not find the paper, he went to the room where his father Sir Gravlin Lane had died. He climbed the winding staircase to reach his father's room. The deceased father's bed, pillows, the lamps, chairs and furniture were all covered with thick dust. The wall clock and his father's pocket watch had stopped working. He found everything in the room exactly as it was at the time of his father's death.

If Sir Jordan Lane was even a little bit saddened by his father's death and had some respect for his father, he would have adopted his father's study and bedroom for his use. He would have kept the place clean and tidy. He would have learned from his father's life and experience and followed his advice. From his father's inheritance, he would have helped the poor and needy and spent money for charity. He would have given a due share of the property to his step brother Nevlin Lane and to his other relatives as per his father's wishes and developed their goodwill towards his father. He would have set up some kind of trust or charity by which everyone would remember his father kindly. However, the cunning Sir Jordan Lane wished his brother dead and treated all his father's friends and close relatives with rudeness and contempt. He had established the sole ownership to all his father's wealth and property. He was even after the wealth of his other friends and neighbours.

He had forbidden anyone to enter or clean his father's room. The reason behind his instruction was that from the pocket of Sir Jordan Lane, an important paper, with his father's signatures, had fallen on the floor at the time of his death. He searched for this paper as soon as his father breathed his last but did not find it. Sir Jordan Lane was afraid that it could get into the hands of someone who could force him to share his inheritance with others. The person who is greedy and selfish, is blinded to God's ways and ignores all God's laws. He forgets Nature's law, "What you sow is what you reap."

Sir Jordan Lane had previously searched his father's room four times for this piece of paper. Today also he came in its search. After entering the room, he lighted a second candle. With shaky hands, he opened the brass cabinet which used to be near the headboard of his father's bed. He searched for the paper inside the cabinet but did not find it. With his hands, he dusted the chair and the bed and searched every nook and corner of the room. When he lifted the side of the bed to look for the paper, he heard a loud flapping sound. He started shaking with fear and his face became tense. He braced himself up and realized that the sound made was by the birds flying from the nest that they had made in the roof. He came out of the room, saddened that he had not found the paper. He came back to his room and lay on the bed. As he was very tired, he fell asleep.

Chapter 12

I remember your face though forgetting your glance
The arrow is pulled out, its head remains stuck in the heart

On the eleventh day of the month, at the party of Lady Marlow, all the ladies and gentlemen who were invited, gathered at the beautiful mansion of Audrey Hope. The house was richly decorated for the party. It dazzled with colourful chandeliers. Audrey Hope's youthful grace and beauty radiated from all her body. Everyone was enchanted by the magic in her eyes and her graceful manners. She wore a dress of the latest design which made her look all the more beautiful and charming. With a smile on her face, she attended all her guests. A great variety of delicious food was laid on the tables. Several varieties of costly wines, filled in glasses, were on the table. When the bell rang for the dinner, the guests got busy in eating. Audrey Hope went from one table to the other and in a pleasant manner, offered wine and various dishes of food to her guests. The guests expressed their sincere appreciation for the lovely party and her attention to them. After dinner, everyone got busy.

In this gathering Lord Chester was also present. He was a tall, handsome and a kind young man. His wife had died while he was still young and he remained a widower. He was on the look out for a suitable match for his daughter, a beautiful, kind and highly accomplished girl.

The room was full of young beautiful girls but the centre of attraction was Audrey Hope. But her true admirer, Lord Lorimor, sat quietly like a statue, and admired her great beauty in his heart. Several other beautiful girls from rich families tried to win him with their sly looks. However, Lord Lorimor did not pay any attention to them and was mesmerized by Audrey Hope. Since a long time, he had eyes only for Audrey Hope and did not look at any other girl.

Lady Marlow considered only two persons worthy of Audrey Hope, Sir Jordan Lane and Lord Lorimor. She recommended them to Audrey Hope in one context or the other. When she noticed Lord Lorimor lost in thoughts of Audrey Hope, she could not resist herself and whispered to Audrey Hope, "Take pity on your true lover, Lord Lorimor. Go and entertain him also. During the dinner time also, you did not go to his table though you visited adjoining tables. This is against the etiquettes of a good hostess. At this time he is burning with your love like an insect burns itself at the candle."

Audrey Hope made an excuse to Lady Marlow and whispered, "My heart is hard like a stone and is not easily melted."

Audrey Hope said this just for outwardly show. In reality she had already surrendered her heart to him because of the true love she saw in his eyes and his charismatic personality. But she wanted to test his true love. She had, on purpose, adopted this careless attitude towards him to find out if Lord Lorimor truly considered her worthy of his love and had patience to bear with her and whether she could trust him to be her partner. With this in mind she sometimes talked very nicely to other persons and ignored him.

The party at Audrey Hope's house was a week long affair. All the things required for a week were there and the hostess had ensured that her guests did not experience any kind of inconvenience. A hunting party was arranged on the fourteenth, and another party at the hunting lodge. Audrey Hope thought that the week long party would give her a chance to judge the true love of Lord Lorimor.

For two days, Sir Jordan Lane had not gone out of the house because of disturbing and sad thoughts. In these two days he tried his best to recuperate his spirits and look cheerful. It did not help much. On the third day, which was fourteenth, he put aside his melancholy thoughts and dressed up in expensive clothes to go to the party of Lady Marlow. He knew that Lord Lorimor would not give him much opportunity to win over Audrey Hope. However, he was proud of his ability to outsmart people and use his sly tactics to fool others. He felt confident that Lord Lorimor was no match for him. With this thought, he renewed his determination to woo Audrey Hope. He reached Lady Marlow's party in a very cheerful mood. Everyone present at the party, except for Lord Lorimor was aware of his past. He looked at him with contempt and made an excuse to go from there. He started looking at the flower planters. Audrey Hope came to Sir Jordan Lane and greeted him. She said that she had heard that he was not well for the past few days and inquired as to how he was feeling now.

Sir Jordan Lane replied, "As you probably know, I have to write important papers concerning the country's affairs and this requires concentration. For the last two days I have been busy writing these and could not come to your party on the eleventh. A week-long party must have meant a lot of work for you and you must be tired. In fact, today I have come only for your sake. How are you?"

Audrey Hope said, "Sir, with the blessings of my elders, I am always happy. There is no reason for me to be tired. I do not have to sit in the parliament for hours or write speeches. To look after guests is a daily routine for girls in my position."

As Audrey Hope completed her sentence, Lady Marlow came there. Sir Jordan Lane stepped forward and greeted her very warmly. He then got busy in talking with persons who had gathered round him.

Sir Jordan Lane was a master of artful deceit. Like a stage actor, he could change his facial expression according to the occasion. He could adjust his way of talking according to the ability of the person. He was also very good at talking to girls like a true admirer and thus making them believe that he cared for them and they would fall for him. After making all kinds of excuses, he consented to join them for lunch on great insistence from Lady Marlow. They all walked towards the dining table.

Though Lady Marlow was very close to Audrey Hope, she had not been able to judge as to whom Audrey Hope had given her heart. She had observed that Lord Lorimor often expressed his love to Audrey Hope but she also knew that Audrey Hope got irritated by his attention and expression of love. She therefore eliminated Lord Lorimor from her list. Today she decided to concentrate on Sir Jordan Lane as the only person worthy of Audrey Hope. She sat next to Sir Jordan Lane and asked Audrey Hope to sit next to her. She started to make small talk with Sir Jordan Lane. Lord Lorimor also came and stood by the side of Audrey Hope. Just as an insect is attracted to a light, he was attracted to Audrey Hope. Sir Jordan Lane was very happy to get Audrey Hope's attention and he was all smiles answering her questions. In this gathering, in addition to several other persons, Lord Chester was also aware of Sir Jordan Lane's background and his mean and selfish nature. He got up from his chair and stood by the table of Sir Jordan Lane. To tease him, he offered him a glass of wine. Everyone knew that Sir Jordan Lane neither drank himself nor offered drinks to anyone. Instead of making some excuse, Sir Jordan Lane started to give a lecture on the evils of drinking and the guests gathered around him to listen. Some of them began to make fun of him. One of them said that a good wine clears one's head and makes one happy. It was not an evil but a blessing. The second person said, "One who drinks has to offer the drinks to others also, and this costs money. A wise man never spends his money on useless things and Sir Jordan Lane is at the top of the list of wise persons." He believed:

> The pleasure in wine is more than the pleasure of paradise
> The eyes light up when you take a sip of wine.

Another person spoke up with a view to silence Sir Jordan Lane, "Every wise and educated person, whether he is a man or a woman, old or young, knows that anything which makes you drunk is bad. It applies not only to liquor but to anything that leads to forming a bad habit. The substance that dulls your senses not only makes you lose money but also creates many kinds of illnesses and destroys your family." Another person cut him short and said, "Ladies and gentlemen, let us have some good music now." Every one applauded the suggestion and requested Audrey Hope to sing a song. She went to the piano and sat down on the chair. Sir Jordan Lane followed her and to please her, wiped the piano with his handkerchief, even though the piano was sparklingly and spotlessly clean. He then whispered a song in Audrey Hope's ear and requested her to sing that song. Audrey Hope did not consider it appropriate in this situation to refuse his request. She started to sing the song in a very sweet and captivating voice.

Sir Jordan Lane, who had absolutely decided on his wicked plans, got bold and looked at Lord Lorimor with contempt in his eyes. With a smile on his face he started to make provocative gestures to him. But Lord Lorimor stood in his place quietly. He was admiring in his heart the sweet voice of Audrey Hope and at times would say, "Very good, very good." However, whenever he noticed the rude gestures of Sir Jordan Lane, his expression changed to frustration. Audrey Hope did not notice all this. She knew that Sir Jordan Lane's smile was artificial and he was not sincere. She also knew that Lord Lorimor's appreciation was sincere and she looked at Lord Lorimor several times with loving eyes and throughout the song addressed her attention towards him. To continue to enjoy her sweet voice and song, Lord Lorimor suggested that Sir Jordan Lane request Audrey Hope for another song. Instead of requesting her for another song, he went and sat down on a chair and started to analyze the meaning of Audrey Hope's loving looks towards Lord Lorimor during the singing. Lady Marlow was looking at them and the expression on their faces. To defuse tension, she said in a loud voice, "Ladies and gentlemen, it is time to get ready for the hunting party. Let us hurry up."

At this announcement, everyone got up. Sir Jordan Lane suppressed his emotions and said to Lady Marlow, "Please give me permission to go to my house and change clothes for hunting. It will take only fifteen minutes. Please do not leave in a hurry. Do wait for me. As your neighbour, I would like to accompany your guests."

Lady Marlow replied, "We shall certainly wait for you. Please come back soon."

Chapter 13

By continuously expanding our horizon of search
We shall find you wherever you may be.

Sir Jordan Lane, duly equipped with a gun and a sword and riding a fast horse, returned back before the departure of the guests. Lord Lorimor also came back riding a beautiful fast horse. All the guests gathered together and left for the hunting grounds in a group. Sir Jordan Lane rode beside Audrey Hope's horse. Lord Lorimor followed close by and kept an eye on them.

After they had gone some distance, Sir Jordan Lane asked Audrey Hope, "Please tell me your conditions for the hunt."

Audrey Hope said, "What conditions can I suggest except that the gentlemen go hunting for rabbits and the ladies make arrangements for the dinner. If there is any spare time, we shall watch the hunt."

To embarrass Jordan Lane and to stop him from further conversation, she said to him, "Sir, the gun that you are carrying is probably not yours. I have seen it with Nevlin Lane."

Sir Jordan Lane replied, "No, No. This gun is mine. I bought it myself and it was very expensive. I hunt with great ease with this gun. It never misses the target."

Audrey Hope said, "Today we shall know the quality of your gun. I always thought that in my close acquaintances, there is no one as clever as Nevlin Lane in shooting. Once I went with him to the grounds near the railway station. I vividly remember that with one shot he grounded thirteen rabbits and even then I did not congratulate him on his bravery and excellent shooting. I called him a coward and he laughed loudly."

On hearing this Sir Jordan Lane heaved a big sigh. Lord Lorimor asked him, "Who is this Nevlin Lane. I am sorry I have never met him."

Sir Jordan Lane said, "Sir, he is my step brother. I regret that he left the house. I have tried hard to find him."

Lord Lorimor said, "It appears that Audrey Hope knows your step brother Nevlin Lane from childhood. It is very surprising that your efforts in finding him have not been successful. It should not be too difficult to find a lost person provided the search is done properly."

Sir Jordan Lane said, "I have done everything possible. Now it is in God's hands."

With a view to change the subject, he looked at Audrey Hope and asked her. "Where have the arrangements been made for snacks and refreshments?"

Audrey Hope said, "At a place called Cole. The same place where Nevlin Lane used to take me for morning strolls."

Sir Jordan Lane pretended to take a deep sigh and with the intention of closing the discussion on Nevlin Lane, he galloped on his horse. Everyone else followed him and soon they reached Cole.

Audrey Hope said, "Oh! This place reminds me of Nevlin Lane. Look at that tree with a huge trunk, right in front. The shadow from leaves of this tree covers a circumference of almost one furlong. There used to be a thick shrubbery around this tree. We used to enjoy racing around this shrubbery. The thick shrubs grew within the round area and we used to race our horses around it. People gathered to watch us. From the parapet round the tree, the rider at the distance is clearly visible. Everything is still the same."

Sir Jordan Lane looked frustrated at this description, and with a view to change the subject, he turned round and pointed his finger at another tree. Before he could say a word, Lord Lorimor said to him, "Sir Jordan Lane, let us race our horses around the tree and see who comes out ahead."

Sir Jordan Lane thought it embarrassing to refuse the challenge. So he said to Lord Lorimor, "I will be agreeable if Audrey Hope rewards the winner with a prize."

Audrey Hope had a lovely flower in her jacket buttonhole which was given to her in the morning by Lord Lorimor. She showed it to her guests and said, "The person who wins the race will be rewarded with this flower."

To watch the horse race, all the ladies and gentlemen gathered on the parapet round the tree. Sir Jordan Lane and Lord Lorimor started their race on the periphery of the shrubberies around the tree. The audience cheered them on. They laughed when one of them slipped a little from his saddle. Sir Jordan Lane did not hesitate to adopt unfair means even in a friendly race like this. By design, he suddenly slowed down and fell a few lengths behind. Lord Lorimor looked back to see what had happened and in that instant, because his concentration was disturbed, his foot slipped from the stirrup. Sir Jordan Lane at once galloped his horse at full pace and passed Lord Lorimor while he was trying to regain his balance and get his feet back in the stirrup. By the time Lord Lorimor resumed his full pace, Sir Jordan Lane completed the round ahead of Lord Lorimor and won the race. The crowd shouted, "Congratulations, congratulations!" and clapped loudly.

Audrey Hope forgot all about the reward with the crowds clapping and the commotion all around and got busy in making arrangements for the dinner. However, Sir Jordan Lane was not the one to forget his reward and in front of all the guests he asked Audrey Hope for the promised reward. She said in a careless tone, "I proposed the reward of flower to add excitement to the race and for the crowd to cheer. It really does not mean anything. However, if you are keen to have your reward, here is the flower. It is all crumpled now, but since you insist, you can have it." She detached the flower from her jacket lapel and gave it to him.

Sir Jordan Lane ignored her words and stepped forward to accept the flower. He pinned the flower on the buttonhole of his shirt near his chest and said with a big smile, "I value this flower a thousand times more then a diamond."

Lord Lorimor burned with envy and, avoiding the gaze of the guests, went and sat down on a chair in the corner. He began to think that he should plan some other game with this flower as the prize so that he may win the flower back from Sir Jordan Lane and give it back to his beloved Audrey Hope. He thought that if the flower remained with Sir Jordan Lane then it was likely that he would also be successful in winning the heart of Audrey Hope and Lord Lorimor would have to remain a bachelor for the rest of his life. His chain of thought was interrupted by the ringing of the bell for the refreshments. Lady Marlow requested the guests to take their seats at the dinner table. By chance, Lord Lorimor's seat was directly across from Sir Jordan Lane's seat in the opposite row and Audrey Hope's seat was next to Sir Jordan Lane's. Sir Jordan Lane felt very happy with this arrangement. He started to talk with Audrey Hope and asked her about the status of her properties. He frequently looked at Lord Lorimor and smiled which greatly saddened Lord Lorimor, but he sat quietly.

After the refreshments, everyone prepared for the hunt. Lord Lorimor raced his horse behind a rabbit which suddenly turned right instead of left. The brave Sir Jordan Lane fired a single shot at the running rabbit and wounded it. Lord Lorimor shouted, "Well Sir, a good shot."

Sir Jordan Lane replied with great pride, "Yes, no doubt. No big deal to kill this rabbit. Even if it was a lion, he would have died."

Lord Lorimor said, "You are indeed a wonderful gunner."

As he completed his sentence, an eagle-like bird flew out of its nest inside the tree. Lord Lorimor took aim and fired and the bird fell to the ground.

Sir Jordan Lane said, "Well done, indeed an excellent shot."

Lord Lorimor said, "You have probably not heard the praise I got in Mexico for my marksmanship. Did you ever go there for sightseeing? That place is the main centre for hunting. People of that place are known for their archery and marksmanship. They know of several ways to shoot from a gun. I had an opportunity to live in Mexico for a long time and learned several tricks of the gun there. Even now I practice every day."

Sir Jordan Lane replied, "I have never been to Mexico but I have heard great things about their marksmanship. Why don't you show me some skill of the gun that you learned there."

Lord Lorimor took Sir Jordan Lane near a tall tree and took out the invitation card for the party from his pocket. In the centre of the card, he carved a big circle with his knife and plunged it in the branch of the tree in such a way that the upper edge of the knife became a peg. He then asked Sir Jordan Lane, "Can you make the bullet go through the hole in the centre of the card in one shot?"

Sir Jordan Lane replied, "Very funny. This seems like a game for children. There is no expertise required in shooting the bullet through the hole. It is not at all difficult. Let us make a bet on this."

Lord Lorimor said, "Since morning you have started the bet based on flowers. One bet has already been made on Audrey Hope's flower. I bet on it a second time. If you are not able to shoot through the hole in one shot and I succeed, I will take this flower from you. I got it especially for her this morning from my garden. However, if your bullet goes through the hole in one shot then once and for all, I will not only give up the thought of this flower but also the thought of its owner."

Sir Jordan Lane disagreed, "No Sir. I have already won this flower as a reward from her. I cannot part with a thing given by Audrey Hope; it is very precious to me. I do not accept your proposal."

He wanted to say something more but at that moment Audrey Hope came there. She was troubled by the heat from the sun and came to that very tree for shade and rest where these two were having a heated argument. She said to them in carefree voice, "Why are you not hunting for rabbits? What are you watching here? The delicious dinner that Lady Marlow has planned for tonight is dependent on a good supply of rabbits. If you do not hunt any rabbits for tonight's dinner, then all you can expect is bread and butter."

Sir Jordan Lane said in response, "We were discussing a proposal for target shooting."

Audrey Hope said, "I have come here often times with Nevlin Lane to watch and enjoy hunting but except for racing the horses after the hunt, I have never seen any one making any proposals regarding target shooting. Under this very tree we used to sit down for the refreshments and snacks." She uttered a deep sigh and said, "I am sorry."

Her deep sigh got Sir Jordan Lane thinking and alarmed Lord Lorimor, but they both stood there without saying a word. Audrey Hope gathered her gown and stepped forward to go. She expected them to walk with her. But when she saw them standing where they were without any intention of moving, she turned back.

To defuse the tension and divert their attention, she said, "Gentlemen, what proposal do you have in mind for target shooting? Why don't you follow Nevlin Lane's example. I never saw his shot missing its target. One day he killed several rabbits in one shot."

Sir Jordan Lane said, "I admire your memory. You remember all your childhood things in vivid detail and they are always at the tip of your tongue."

Audrey Hope said, "Sir, I remember Nevlin Lane's utmost honesty, his habit of always telling the truth and strong determination. All these memories come back to me and I cannot help reciting them."

After Audrey Hope left, Lord Lorimor said in an angry voice, "Sir, are you willing to accept the bet of the flower for shooting the bullet through that hole in one shot or not?"

Sir Jordan Lane thought if he did not agree to his proposal, then he would always consider him to be a coward. So he agreed to the bet on the flower. He straightened his shoulders and carefully aimed the gun to shoot the bullet through the hole and fired. The bullet, instead of going through the hole, passed it by and went into the jungle. He felt very ashamed and said with a dejected face to Lord Lorimor, "Show your ability now."

Lord Lorimor, with true love in his heart and with all his concentration, took the aim carefully and fired with such expertise that his bullet passed right through the centre of the hole. Sir Jordan Lane, reluctantly, conceded defeat. As per the agreement of the bet, he took the flower from his coat's buttonhole and gave it to Lord Lorimor who was ecstatic at getting the flower back. He immediately climbed his horse and galloped in the direction Audrey Hope had gone. At a distance of approximately one furlong, he saw his beloved Audrey Hope walking leisurely. He stopped his horse and got down and stood beside her. With great flair and happiness, he presented the flower to her and said, "'Please accept your flower back. I was successful in the competition for marksmanship with Sir Jordan Lane and won the flower from him."

Audrey Hope took the flower, threw it on the ground and crushed it with her shoes. She said in a very angry tone and with anguish on her face, "To fight over an insignificant flower does not befit a person of your stature and wisdom. I never expected an honest and kind person like you to act in such an immature way."

Lord Lorimor said, "Do not forget that when you took this flower from me, you put it in your jacket's buttonhole. How could I bear to see it with anyone else? I wanted this flower back and I got it back. There was no fight about this."

Audrey Hope said with a frown on her face, "I saw with my own eyes the signs of anger on your faces. It does not take long for a fight to erupt and tempers to flare. I am sorry that sometimes menfolk act in such a foolish manner and they put their life in jeopardy for insignificant things."

Lord Lorimor said, "This flower has great significance. It concerned the woman whom I love with all my heart and she is dearer to me than my life."

Audrey Hope said, "Was it for me that you had bets on marksmanship like uncivilized hooligans and were determined to fight it out?"

Lord Lorimor said, "Instead of saying uncivilized hooligans, say brave persons prepared to lose their life for a cause. I was determined not to allow your flower to be with someone else."

Audrey Hope said, "Well Sir, do you think I will be pleased with such a senseless act? Do you think I am so mean and selfish?"

Lord Lorimor said, "There is no act of bravery that I will hesitate to carry out to prove my love for you. Why, even if this flower was dropped in the sea, I . . . "

Audrey Hope said, "You would have jumped in the sea to retrieve this flower."

Lord Lorimor replied, "Without any doubt. Dear Audrey, do you think I lack courage and am a coward. For your love I can do things that others cannot do. You may put me to test anytime."

When Audrey Hope heard Lord Lorimor call her by her first name, she thought that he was so lost in her love that he was already considering her to be his wife. She told him with a careless attitude, "What a nice speech! It is very pleasing to hear all this. Let me see what difficult task I can ask you to carry out."

Lord Lorimor said, "Order me to do anything. I am determined to complete it successfully."

When Audrey Hope heard Lord Lorimor's words of courage and masculine determination, the face of Nevlin Lane came in front of her eyes and suddenly, without thinking, she said, "Can you bring to me a lost person. I am restless because of a person who is not traceable, and am not at peace with myself. Without finding him out, I can never be happy."

These words came out without her realizing what she was saying. She clasped her neck and sat down on the ground. She said in a very soft voice, "I am very sorry I made a request that is utterly unwise. If someone hears it, he will laugh at me and call me foolish."

Lord Lorimor did not give Audrey Hope time to regret her request and asked her, "Who is this lost person? I consider it my duty to carry out your orders."

Audrey Hope looked into his eyes and said, "Nevlin Lane."

Lord Lorimor looked surprised and asked with anxiety in his voice, "Is he the same Nevlin Lane who is the step brother of Sir Jordan Lane? Has he not been able to trace him? Why are you so concerned about his whereabouts. Are you in love with him?"

Audrey Hope hit the ground hard with her foot and raised her eyes to look at him directly and said, "What you have just said has no meaning. Is it not the duty of a human being to be concerned about his friend and still love someone else. Is it a crime to have pure love for someone. Do you not know that Nevlin Lane has been my friend since childhood. For a long time we lived together, played together, studied together, ate together and talked and entertained each other. It is strange that while I live in comfort and luxury, my childhood friend roams I know not where and no one cares to find him out."

Lord Lorimor said with great sympathy, "I will go right this moment and search in all cities and villages, and God willing, I will find your childhood friend and bring him to you. My dear, promise that after I find him, you will be mine?"

Audrey Hope said shyly, "What do you mean I will be yours! O.K. I will remain single for two years and will wait for you."

Lord Lorimor said with immense joy, "Please give me permission to start the search."

Audrey Hope said, "I solemnly promise to wait for your return for two years."

Audrey Hope gave her hand to Lord Lorimor. He knelt on the ground and gently kissed it. Without saying a single word, he left and soon was out of sight.

Audrey Hope felt very sad at the departure of her true lover. She thought of the long separation from him and the inconvenience and trouble he would have to face on his journey. She leaned against a tree and cried uncontrollably and shouted again and again, "Lord Lorimor, Lord Lorimor."

To carry out the wishes of his beloved, like a true gentleman, Lord Lorimor braced himself up and went straight to his house. The first thing he did was to write a letter to Lady Marlow and summon his old reliable servant and instruct him to deliver it to the addressee right away.

At the party, Lady Marlow made sure that the food was properly laid on the tables and rang the bell for dinner. All the guests sat down and as they were about to start, the messenger came and gave Lord Lorimor's letter to Lady Marlow. After reading the letter, she said, "Lord Lorimor had to go to London on a very urgent business and he has already left Greenwich."

Sir Jordan Lane said in a concerned tone, "Where is Audrey Hope. She is nowhere to be seen."

Lady Marlow looked all around and said, "Look she is quietly walking towards her tent."

Lord Lorimor also sent a letter to Audrey Hope which read thus:

> My dear, I will go to the railway station after making all the necessary arrangements at my house and would leave for London by the evening train to start the search for our friend. Please do not forget your solemn promise of two years. I will not spare any effort to search your friend. If he is alive, I will definitely bring him back with me.
>
> Your admirer and well wisher
> Lorimor

Chapter 14

The eyes of a devotee like to see the face of God
I like to see her face that is very bright

I have no motive or concern to pray to God
I like the delicate amorous glances of the proud figure

I read the account of my own life night and day
How to tell her that I like the little grains of her attention.

No person has escaped the effect of changes and revlutions in this world. Not only man, even inorganic things, birds and beasts, do not escape changes. A man's childhood, youth and old age, all three stages are influenced by changes and life passes in grief, worries and joy. In one's lifetime one experiences the wonderful events and incredible happenings. People who think about these happenings are convinced of the instability of the world. Such persons try to achieve lasting happiness by seeking supreme God. The rivers change their course, mountains shift and new places are created. The habitations are buried and deserted and new habitations spring up in deserts and gradually develop into villages, cities and countries.

Lornehope Camp, where gold slabs were mined, was on a flat and barren plateau. There was a thick forest all around it. Nevlin Lane and Sylvia Bond, during their stay there, saw that this sleepy and deserted place mushroomed into a lively and bustling city. Day by day, the city became more lively. Skilled and respectable people started to settle at this place. The senior officials of the Emperor of Austria started to visit the place more often. The laws for administration, protection and safety of public were put in place. Proper buildings were erected for a police station, post office, telegraph office and hospital. With the assistance of a religious society, a very polite, able and knowledgeable priest, with his young daughter, also came to Lornehope Camp church from London. The people started paying more attention to religion due to the sermons delivered by this priest. Some public servants also called their families to live there. Several skilled artisans and merchants also set up their shops there. The marketplace now had an appearance of liveliness and bustling activity. The hospital was equipped with all kinds of medicines. Provisions were made for the comfort and convenience of the patients. The local doctor, who also acted as a lawyer and a priest, got good increment in his salary and he no longer had to depend on various households.

The contractor for liquor Mr McGregor carefully planned for everything, published the new laws and regulations and distributed the same to everyone by means of pamphlets. Proper laws were established for carrying arms. A licence was issued by Mr. McGregor if, in his opinion, the person was responsible enough and needed a gun or revolver. Plans were drawn and work started to replace the huts of workers with proper houses. The small habitation of Lornehope Camp was transformed into a bustling, colourful big village.

Nevlin Lane's house was of thatched straw, but it was comfortable. His desire to return back to his country had become less intense. Sylvia Bond, who was very lean and thin when she first met him, was now a strong and a very beautiful woman. Her walk was quite intoxicating. She was lost in the love of her companion and protector, Nevlin Lane. On Sundays, she used to go to the market for a stroll with him. They both lived happily and comfortably, like a brother and sister, without any fear or problems.

Nevlin Lane used to go for a walk in various directions. Since he had some knowledge of geology, he would pick up the sand at various locations and smell it to find out if there was gold under the surface. One day he said to Sylvia Bond in a loving tone, "Dear Sil, you have not reminded me for a few days about going for a walk. Probably you do not like going for a stroll in the jungle."

Sylvia Bond said, "How could I ask you because so far I have been under the impression that you are happy going alone and do not wish me to accompany you. If I knew that you wanted me to go with you, I would have walked two steps ahead of you every day. In spite of my best efforts, I have not been able to know what you like. I have noticed that your mind is not constant. You are a very private person and therefore no one can find out as to what you like and what you do not like."

Nevlin Lane smiled and said, "Alright, now I ask you to accompany me for the walk. Do not delay, get ready quickly and let us go."

Sylvia Bond cheerfully put on her coat and hat and happily accompanied Nevlin Lane. He silently admired the fast and easy manner of Sylvia Bond's walking and also the way she was dressed. He thought that this was the way young girls in London used to dress up and go to school. But generally those girls did not have such a sophisticated and pleasant way of walking as Sylvia. Her way of walking and the way she looked at him shyly, were the characteristics of a civilized lady. He recalled that he had read that the girls who were brought up with the love and affection of their parents and brothers, grew up fast and soon became mature. Though Sylvia Bond had been at his place for only a short period, she had matured fast. Because of her slightly shorter height, she looked young but in fact she acted and behaved like a grown up woman.

To test how fast she could walk, Nevlin Lane quickened his pace. But she was always a couple of steps ahead of him. Nevlin Lane admired her way of walking and said, "Look, there is forest all around us. This forest is there because plants and trees in the jungle extract the moisture from the morning dew and the environment, thus creating a green jungle. With the melodious chirping of birds and the sounds of animals, the whole jungle is filled with heart-warming sounds. The religious persons derive peace and happiness from such an enchanting atmosphere. Why Sil, do you also enjoy this?"

Sil was so happy to be walking with her hand in the hand of Nevlin Lane that she did not want to hear anything. She smiled in response to the question and said, "Every human being, every second, should be thankful to the Almighty God for His creation and His loving care of everyone. However, it is very difficult for a human being to devote all the time in His prayer and follow His teachings all the time. On every Sunday, I control my wandering mind and devote sometime to His prayers which I have memorized. I express my eternal gratitude for everything He has given me. I do not ask Him for anything. I simply thank Him for His kindness and care in looking after me."

Nevlin Lane said, "What you have said just now is worldly wise and applies to every person in this world. My teacher told me to admire this workshop of God and thank Him for everything. We must feel content with whatever God has given us. This way life becomes better and such persons acquire peace and salvation. God has given every human being a sense to know when he is doing wrong and is going against Nature. When this happens, He issues a warning. One should practice to listen to these warnings."

Sylvia Bond listened quietly and Nevlin Lane continued, "Your mention of Sunday reminds me of London. On Sundays, more than any other day, there was a bigger crowd and much more activity in London's market place. Thousands of people with new and fancy dresses ate and drank at various eating places. All kinds of delicious food and liquor was available and people enjoyed and got a lot of time for socializing. Men and women, young and old, bought various items of luxury. Very few people went to church with a sincere heart for prayer. However, first of all, London did not have the melodious chirping of the colourful birds, nor the abundance of lushgreen fields, nor the fresh spring water which nourishes the plants, nor the fresh and refreshing outdoor breeze, that manifests the wonderful work of God. All these things are enough to lure the mind away from the city. In London, all you hear is the ringing of church bells. However, people are busy in their own activities and it is very unlikely that they even care to hear the sound of church bells. London's bustling activity and liveliness presents a very interesting scene."

Sylvia Bond smiled and said, "Sir, your entire discourse has proved that you are at present missing London very much and it is making you restless. Do you want to go back to London?"

Nevlin Lane said, "Yes, I am keen to go back. But knowing the limitations and facts of my present situation, I try and forget about it. I consider it an insult to go to London in this condition of poverty. To go to my relatives and close friends and depend on their kindness and generosity is not the way to fulfil my desire to go to London. Anyway, whether I go or not is immaterial. I have saved enough money to send you to London and provide you with a comfortable life. I have, by careful budgeting, saved enough amount for you to go to London and get admission in a good school. I will regularly send you enough money to live comfortably until you finish your education."

After finishing this sentence, he unbuckled his belt and took out a beautiful leather pouch and said to Sylvia, "Look dear Sylvia, see how much money I have saved. This is enough to send you to London. Who knows some day if I am lucky enough, I too will be able to go to London."

Sylvia turned her face away and with tears in her eyes, she said, "I do not want to go to London and leave you alone here. Without you, London would look worse to me than a deserted and scary forest."

Nevlin Lane said, "You are very innocent and immature. You do not know what is in your best interest and what will benefit you."

On hearing this, Sylvia did not say anything but stood by the side of Nevlin Lane and started to laugh as if to tell him that she was not immature or a child any longer. She said, "Look, I come upto your shoulders." However, Nevlin Lane did not understand the meaning of her behaviour. His mind was busy planning her trip to London. To get his mind off from sending her to London, she jumped in front of him and said, "Jack, you were telling me that a lot of new people have come to Lornehope Camp from London. Do you know any one of them?"

Nevlin Lane said, "I have heard that a few officers with their families have come in different departments. As you see, I am so busy with my work of digging that I have no spare time to go and meet any of them to find out to which families they belong."

Sylvia Bond said, "Mathula mentioned to me that a new priest has come with his young daughter and that he has set up a tent here. He has also arranged for his lodgings at the church itself and would start his sermons from next Sunday."

Nevlin Lane said, "Oh yes, Mathula has told you the truth. Two days back, when I was returning from my work, I saw a beautiful girl passing that side. I will not be surprised if she turns out to be the daughter of the priest."

Sylvia Bond said, "You must have seen some other new arrival. From the description that Mathula gave, the daughter of the priest is ugly looking, there is no charm in her face and she is a fully grown up woman."

Nevlin Lane said, "The girls can be considered grown up when they have the maturity to know a man by just one look, whether his intentions are good or bad. Besides, when they have the ability to think on their own and know what is right and what is wrong, a girl can be considered a grown up woman. A woman can be called ugly if she has some defect in her body. For example, if her head is too big in proportion to her body, or her nose is flat or her lips are too thick or her teeth protrude out or her eyes are small and pushed back in the forehead. If none of these defects is there, then a woman may be considered as charming and beautiful. Whether the complexion is white like a bag or whether the eyes have shyness, is immaterial. Whereas girls who have a blooming complexion, soft hair, playful eyes, are bold and their walk is light, are considered young. You may compare any girl."

Sylvia said, "I am often at a loss to understand you. What you are saying is funny. I do not understand what you mean by saying 'compare.' Where am I going to find a young girl and bring her here to compare with the criteria given by you. Is beauty the same as what you have defined? Anyway, I do not want to get into a discussion of what is beautiful and what is ugly at this time. Please tell me who is this girl who has caught your attention and what purpose has she in coming to this jungle? Is she going to open a shop?"

Nevlin Lane said, "I just finished telling you that I am so busy with my work of digging that I have no time for meeting other people and socializing. I cannot tell you who this girl is and what is the purpose of her coming here. On my way I happened to look at her because she was looking at me and was coming right in front of me. As per etiquette, I lifted my hat and she said 'Good morning' and passed me by."

Sylvia teased him, "Ah ha! From what you have told me, it is not very difficult for me to infer her intentions. Her staring at you and saying good morning to you has a lot of meaning behind it. Why Sir, is it the custom of your London, that young men remove their hat for young girls who are strangers to them?"

Jack said innocently, "I never had an opportunity to greet or talk to young ladies. Nor have I passed time in the company of young girls. Thus, I am not familiar with the etiquette and customs of London. However, whenever I meet a friend, man or woman, I always greet him with civility. Also from the very childhood I like to talk to anyone who likes to have a good time, whether he is a man or a woman, young, old or child. London is a thickly populated city, where you can find such men and women. In Lornehope Camp, people are dull with no liveliness in their heart. If by chance, I find anyone from my country here, I cannot be uncivil to him. I have always enjoyed teasing young girls, especially the stubborn and ill-tempered ones who are full of ego and selfishness. I also enjoy the company of decent and well mannered girls."

Sylvia said, "As far as I know, priests are very religious and pious persons. They can look into future. I am very surprised that this priest allows his young daughter to roam around on her own and does not keep her busy in the house."

Nevlin Lane did not reply to Sylvia's comments because he did not like to find faults with others and also did not enjoy commenting on other people's private affairs. He quietly started to walk fast and reached the banks of the river. Sylvia Bond, who was keeping pace with Nevlin Lane came and stood beside him. He looked at her and said: "I want to go on the other side of the river. I am fully convinced that the sand on the other side of the river has gold in it. Last Sunday, I had a chance to climb that hill that you see in the front, on the side of the river. From the top of the mountain I saw a long beautiful valley on the north side where several boys were playing while tending to their herd of cows and sheep. I saw very shiny sand in their hands. I wanted to go there but suddenly the sky became dark with thick clouds and I anticipated heavy rain. So I walked fast and returned home. I realized that the sand must have gold dust otherwise it would not shine so brightly in the rays of sun."

Sylvia said, "Test your knowledge and the inference you reached. I will come and assist you in your search."

Nevlin Lane smiled and said, "You appear to be very young but when I hear you speak like this, I feel that a very brave, highly educated, wise and experienced woman is speaking. You may not have the stamina to cross this river with me. Though the river is shallow, it has a very fast current and the flow is treacherous. I do not think you will be able to walk in this fast flowing water."

Sylvia said, "Wherever you can go, I can also go!"

On hearing Sylvia speak with such confidence, Nevlin Lane felt very happy. Her attitude was comparable to that of Audrey Hope. When Nevlin Lane used to play with Audrey Hope, she used to make such brave statements too. The face of Audrey Hope came in front of him and with the thoughts of their childhood games, he stepped into the water to cross the river. Sylvia followed him. A few times Sylvia stopped to steady her feet. When she stopped, Jack said to her in a loving tone, "Sylvia, for God's sake, return back to the bank of the river. What if you slip?"

Sylvia kept smiling and crossed the river keeping hardly a yard behind Jack. He said several times, "Well done, well done." And started to climb the hill. Sylvia also walked along side of Jack through the narrow and difficult passage and covered the distance to the top of the mountain with courage and a smiling face. Jack very much admired the courage and stamina of Sylvia.

After a while they reached a place where the hill separated into two parts. Between the two parts, an approximately nine to ten feet wide river was flowing. The flow of the water was not only very fast but also very turbulent. Jack said to Sylvia: "Why Sil, I asked you several times to return back when we crossed the last river but you did not listen to me. How are you going to cross this very fast flowing water and reach the other side of the hill. The flow of the water is very fast and I do not know how deep it is. I think it is best for both of us to return."

Sylvia said, "If you had come alone, would you have turned back from here?"

Nevlin Lane said, "No, I would have crossed this river with one big jump and reached the other side of the hill and looked for the gold. However, now you are with me and it will not be possible for you to cross this fast flowing and turbulenter water. Therefore, I cannot think of any other alternative but to return."

On hearing Jack speak like this, Sylvia carefully lowered both her legs in the water to test its depth. Jack shouted with concern, "Dear Sil, please listen to me and do not dare to go even a step further. The water is very deep."

Sylvia ignored Jack's request and proceeded to cross the river. She had just gone a little further when her feet lost control and she went under the water and began to drown. Jack at once jumped into the water and pulled Sylvia out by holding her long hair and eased her on his back. He carefully made an attempt to cross the river. Sylvia was somewhat disorientated by her ordeal, but when she found herself riding Jack's back, she felt very ashamed. She shyly requested Jack to put her down and promised that she would be more careful now and would take steps more firmly. Jack ignored her request and asked her not to try to get down and to sit very still, otherwise they would both go under the current and drown. On hearing this, Sylvia became very quiet. Jack tightly held both her hands which Sylvia had put around his neck. He balanced her evenly on his shoulders and very carefully started to cross the river. In mid river, the water came upto Jack's shoulders but he did not lose courage and reached the other side of the river safely. He gently put her down on the ground. He laughed and said to Sylvia, "Dear Sil, you are completely drenched. You must have been very scared seeing the water come upto my shoulders. But I admire your courage. You kept sitting on my back with a strong heart and determination."

Sylvia was savouring the close contact with Jack. In response to Jack's question, she gave Jack a big smile and said, "Why Jack, how can I be scared with you. No, I was not at all scared. In fact I enjoyed the up and down motion of the water."

Jack said, "That's good. I am grateful to God that he kept you safe. However, it was very scary for me when I saw you go under the water. My heart jumped up high and I was very worried."

Sylvia said, "Ah ha. Now I know you are the one who gets scared. Why should I be scared. I am neither made of sugar nor am I a merchant of sugar that I would get scared with the thought of the goods getting destroyed by melting in the water. That daughter of the priest may be scared whose face is white like sugar. She is the one who roams around alone in this jungle like white sugar toys. She is the one who will be scared of water."

Jack turned his face to one side as if he did not care and smiled quietly and said, "Oh my God. What you have said is really funny. This subject of sugar seems to be your favourite. In your opinion, persons with white complexion are made of sugar? No Sil, that girl is the daughter of the priest with muscles and bones like us. If there is any sweetness in her, it is not in her body, it is in her voice."

To dry their drenched clothes, they both stood facing the sun and soon the clothes dried on their bodies. They once again started to climb the mountain. Sylvia walked right behind Nevlin Lane with the same pace. Nevlin Lane would stop every now and then and pick up sand and smell it. They walked quite a long distance and came to a small cave.

Nevlin Lane picked up the sand near the cave entrance and smelled it and shouted with joy: "Look Sil, it is impossible that there is no gold in this cave. Be happy because now you will be rich. But speak in a low voice so that no passerby may get a wind of our secret discovery. This cave certainly has gold. My guess cannot be wrong. I have learned this art from very able teachers. I will put a mark here and tomorrow morning I will bring my tools and start the work here. I will dig till I find gold. You remain at the house all the time. If the detectives from Mr. McGregor's office come to inquire about me, tell them that I have gone for hunting. The contractor's detectives would certainly come to the house to find out my whereabouts. I think I will have to dig here for just four days. Sil, as a precaution let me warn you now that in this world there are very few people who like to see others succeed. Usually the people here are of a very jealous nature. They do not work diligently at digging gold as per their assigned task. They are always out to cheat others of their gold and harm them. Such people are everywhere."

Jack took out the parcel of bread and meat from his pocket and asked Sylvia to sit beside him and they both started to eat their meal.

Sylvia said, "Jack, do you really want to go to London? Are you still determined to return back to London? I notice that you often remember your friends, relatives and childhood playmates. Sometimes in your sleep you murmur of your past experiences in London."

Jack said, "Before I found the slab of gold I was really very keen to go back to London. But now I am keen to send you to London."

Sylvia said, "Please do not think of such a thing. Look Jack . . ."

She had hardly spoken these words when Jack cut her short and said, "Listen, I am thinking of your future and it is for your betterment. I want you to be more educated and skilled than the girls of my acquaintances in London. This is not the right time for me to go to London. But I will instruct Mathula to buy you a direct ticket for London. This way no one will suspect anything here."

Sylvia said, "I do not want to go to London without you."

Jack got up without discussing the subject further and went to one side behind the trees to answer the call of nature. Sylvia just sat on the stones and, to take her mind away from the subject of London and ease her tension, began to turn the small stones around her.

Jack returned and stood beside a tree to light his pipe. Sylvia came running to him and opening the closed fists of both her hands, said very excitedly, "Look Jack, I have found all this gold under the stones on the west side of the cave."

Jack examined the gold and went with Sylvia to the side of the cave. He lifted some stones and found plenty of gold under each one of them. He said to Sylvia, "I guessed correctly that there is gold here. With the force of water the gold from the mountains got crushed into gold sand and embedded itself under the stones. There is gold under all these stones. Perchance you discovered this gold dust now, otherwise this gold dust would become dry and get mixed with the other sand all around and acquire the same colour. It would have been very difficult then to trace it. Your star of luck is shining. You must go to London and live proudly in the company of rich girls there. Please give me your handkerchief."

Jack filled his and her handkerchiefs with gold dust from underneath the stones. They filled their waist belts with gold dust. Jack shouted with happiness: "Now let us go home. On the way please do not mention a word about finding this gold. No one is allowed to take gold out of here to any other city or country. The secret agents of Mr. McGregor keep a constant eye, day and night, on the houses of all the workers here. The price that Mr. McGregor gives us for gold is very low. In other cities, we can get six times the price. Very early tomorrow morning I will come here with my tools and bring back a substantial quantity of gold to the house."

He started to walk back to the house with Sylvia by his side. When they came to the fast flowing river between the mountains, they found that the river level had gone down considerably and it had become like a small canal. Sylvia was very surprised to see this and asked Jack the reason for the same.

Jack said, "When the water starts flowing from the top of

the mountains, its flow becomes very fast by the time it reaches the lower plains. When the water spreads into flat fields further down, the flow becomes less and the turbulence is gone. It is our good luck that the flow and force of water is much less otherwise it would have been very difficult to cross the river with all the gold in our pockets, belts and handkerchiefs. This has made us heavy."

The two of them covered the distance continuing their talk. Jack's face was radiant with joy and happiness but Sylvia's face was sad. Jack asked her the reason for her sadness. Sylvia did not want to keep on repeating her reluctance to go to London and to change the subject she said, "Let us not talk too much because it is quite likely that the discussion of gold may prop up during our conversation and if someone hears it, then he will rob us."

Jack was not satisfied with this answer. To know what was really bothering her, he said, "Sil, all the gold that we have found from this place is your property. You are the one who discovered it under the stones. On reaching London, all this gold will come in very handy. You will live luxuriously and enjoy the lively atmosphere on Sundays."

Sylvia said, "Oh no. I nearly forgot that today is Sunday. I remember well, that once you said that if one finds anything valuable of gold on a Sunday, then it is bad luck and is a cause of great loss. Today is Sunday and we have found gold. This is not good for us."

Jack said, "No doubt I said that. What I really meant by finding something valuable of gold was that to wear expensive gold jewellery or new clothes on a Sunday is bad luck and also if someone finds some lost expensive gold jewellery on a Sunday, then it is not good for him. This gold does not belong to anyone. It is given to you by the Almighty God who took pity on us and showed you the place where Nature's treasure is in abundance. He wants you to benefit from it."

Sylvia did not consider it appropriate to carry on a discussion on this subject and she walked in silence and reached the banks of the first river. This time the river water level was much higher and the flow of water was also much faster and turbulent. Jack made Sylvia understand the danger and scared her with the possibility of her being swept by the water flow. He persuaded her to sit on his back. He then started crossing the river very carefully. The depth of water was upto Jack's waist level. He walked with firm footing. When the river bank was very close, to scare Sylvia, he joked by jumping up and down. Sylvia was very scared by his jumping but she maintained her cool by sitting firmly and bravely on his back. When Jack turned his face to look at Sylvia, she smiled back. Seeing Sylvia smiling quietly, Jack said to her with a big smile, "Dear Sil, your hair looks very beautiful to me. Your hair is long, soft and shining. With the wind it constantly covers my face and I am not able to see ahead and look at potholes on the river bed. Could you please brush aside your hair from my face?"

Sylvia was happy to hear Jack admiring her hair. Whenever the wind blew her hair on Jack's face, she gently pulled it aside from his face with both her hands and said with a smile, "My hair is long like a horse's tail and my wrists are getting tired by constantly removing them from your face."

Jack looked at Sylvia's face and noticed that she appeared to be very happy and the sadness from her face had disappeared. Seeing her happy Jack said, "Why compare your hair with a horse's tail? Your hair is softer and shinier than silk." After this he walked fast and crossed the river and reached the bank. He eased Sylvia from his back and stood her on the banks of the river. He held Sylvia's hand and started walking towards their house. In a very low voice, he murmured to himself but he could be heard saying, "The health of my dear Sil is, by God's Grace, very good. Her beauty is unparalleled and unique and her voice is so sweet. She is of a jolly nature and is very brave and she has a strong heart. She is very methodical and well groomed. She is kind hearted. There would hardly be any girl like her in the whole of London."

Sylvia heard every word of Jack's low murmur. She felt very happy. With a joyous heart she entered the outer boundary of the house. She noticed two persons sitting in the outside verandah of the house but due to the distance she could not make out their faces. She gently squeezed Jack's hand and said in a low voice, "Look Jack, who are these two strange people sitting in our verandah?"

Jack put his hand on his gun and got ready to face them. However, when he reached nearer, he noticed that one of the persons was dressed as a priest and of course he had seen the girl before. He said to Sylvia, "This girl is the same girl I met the other day. I had mentioned to you about meeting her. Now this establishes without a doubt that she is the daughter of the priest and this gentleman is the new priest here."

Jack and Sylvia stepped on the verandah. The priest and his daughter were busy talking and did not see them coming. However, when they both stepped on the verandah, the priest looked at Nevlin Lane. Nevlin Lane stepped forward, took off his cap and bowed his head in respect to the priest. Both the priest and his daughter got up from their chairs. The priest removed his hat and shook Nevlin Lane's hand and said, "Before I ask you anything about where you went for a walk, please tell me your name."

Nevlin Lane did not consider it appropriate to tell his real name and said with a smile, "All the people here call me Ian."

The priest did not quite catch the name and thought he heard the name as Iain. On this understanding, before talking of anything else, he excitedly said, "A ha. Your name is Iain Herringdon. I know the elders of your family in London. I have no words to express my admiration of your family. Your family is very highly educated, well respected amongst friends. They are the rich landlords of London and they are thorough gentlemen. My coming here is just a coincidence. I was going for a walk towards the jungle and on the way I saw your very nice looking thatched house. From its general neat and clean appearance, I guessed someone from London must be living here and my daughter, Miss Brown, suggested that we come over and make the acquaintance. When we came to your verandah, we learned from your cook that you had gone for a walk and will return before sunset. Thanks to you, we did not have to wait for long."

The priest asked her daughter to shake hands with Nevlin

Lane. She stepped forward and with a happy face she shook Nevlin Lane's hand warmly. She thought that he was Iain Herringdon, belonging to a very rich family from London as per her father's comments. Ian also shook her hand warmly and said to the priest, "Father, I am very grateful to you and Miss Brown for visiting us. Come, let us go inside the house."

Now the priest had been advised by the local security and police department that it was not wise to go inside the house of any worker who did the work of digging. The reason was that most of the workers were very poor and had only a few old utensils and broken crockery in the house. Their clothing and meagre furniture was old and dirty and when a respectable rich person or an officer of the administration visited them, they felt very ashamed and frustrated and this reflected on their quality of work. Therefore the priest declined to go inside by saying that it was so pleasant and fresh outside in the verandah. He pointed towards Sylvia and asked, "Who is this young lady?"

Ian said, "She is my sister."

On hearing this, the priest extended his hand to shake her hand as well and Sylvia warmly shook his hand and said a few words of thanks to him. However, Miss Brown did not get up from her chair and Sylvia also did not try to shake her hand. She simply stared at Miss Brown with curiosity with her beautiful big eyes. She noticed the clean and fresh look of Miss Brown and her well fitting expensive clothes. She became very conscious of her old, dirty cap and gown. She figured that this was the reason why Miss Brown did not shake hands with her as she considered her to be inferior. However, she was wrong. Because, both the priest and his daughter were admiring Sylvia's beauty, her sweet voice, her very civilized and kind manners, her slim body and very charming face. Miss Brown looked at Sylvia again and again and admired her silky smooth long hair and bright big eyes and wondered why there was no similarity in the features of Ian and his sister. In her heart she envied Sylvia. Her mind could not resist talking to Sylvia and she asked her, "Did you also go with your brother for a walk?"

Sylvia said, "Yes Madam. Every day I go for a walk with

my brother Jack." She said this sentence in a sweet voice with great eloquence. Miss Brown became an instant fan of hers, but was startled to hear the name Jack. She looked at Ian with innocent and inquiring eyes and said, "This place is a jungle, very deserted and lonely. How do you keep yourself entertained here?" Sylvia had seen Miss Brown looking at Jack with innocent eyes and she guessed the intentions of Miss Brown. She said in a mischievous and envious tone, "This depends on how you look at it. It may be a jungle in your eyes and then it would certainly look deserted and lonely but to my eyes, there is hardly any other place so green and full of natural beauty. We two live here very happily and comfortably and we thank God, that so far we have lived here happily in peace and harmony. I sincerely pray to the Supreme Power that nothing comes between us to cause us grief and pain."

On hearing Sylvia speak like this, Miss Brown thought that Sylvia did not like their coming here. She looked at her father and signalled that they should leave. The priest got up from his chair and said to Ian, "Both myself and my daughter are very glad to meet you. I do hope that a nice person like you would come to our tent at the church whenever you have some spare time and would also join us for the sermon and prayers."

Nevlin Lane also thanked the priest for their kind visit and for the invitation to visit their tent. He stepped forward to accompany them as they left the house. Jack was totally unaware of the unpleasantness that the couple of sentences had created between Sylvia and Miss Brown, as at that time he was busy talking to the priest. He neither listened to their talk nor realized that Miss Brown was offended by what Sylvia said to her and that Sylvia felt very upset by Miss Brown's behaviour and her manner of speaking. He was totally engrossed in his conversation with the priest.

When the priest and Miss Brown stepped down from the verandah to leave, Nevlin Lane removed his cap and bowed with respect and joined them to walk upto the boundary of the house. Sylvia also walked behind them but she stopped when Jack kept on walking with them. She did not like Jack going like this. She returned back to the house with a sad face and sat down on a chair covering her face with both her hands. After walking a little distance, Jack looked back and realized that Sylvia was not behind them. It was getting dark also. Jack stopped and shook hands with Miss Brown and the priest once again and said, "Please excuse me for not accompanying you further but I must return to the house. My sister would be waiting for me. In this jungle I cannot leave her alone for too long."

Miss Brown said, " Please do not trouble yourself by walking too long a distance with us. May God keep you safe. Please do not forget to come to the church next Sunday to listen to the sermon." She smiled once again and said with a certain style, "Please do remember and do not forget. You must also bring your sister with you. I am very happy to meet her. Your sister is exceedingly beautiful. May God keep her happy."

Nevlin Lane returned home after saying good bye to the priest and his daughter. After some time the priest said to his daughter, "Iain Herringdon comes from a very respectable family of London. I wonder why he is living in this desolate jungle. There is surely some secret for his adopting this place for his living." His daughter agreed with him and said, "I am more surprised than you are. Iain Herringdon is very handsome. He appears to be very kind. He is well educated and well mannered and interesting to talk to. It is a great mystery to me that a person of his status would live a lonely life in this jungle and dig for gold."

The father and daughter reached their house talking about Ian and the reason for his living there. Miss Brown had fallen in love with Ian. She could not sleep all night thinking and remembering Ian.

As soon as Nevlin Lane reached his house, he called Sylvia and said, "Dear Sil, did you see how the people are from London, my country? They are so nice and civilized. The moment I shook his hand, I knew that the priest was from London. His daughter also, I think she will be good friend for you. It's a coincidence that such nice people have come to this jungle. Dear Sil, I have promised them that I will attend the sermon at the church next

Sunday. Both of us will go." Sylvia said in a very low voice with shyness, "You go alone but I, I——." She said the word "I" and then looked at her clothes. She left and got busy in serving the dinner.

Nevlin Lane understood Sylvia's hesitation. He looked lovingly at the beautiful face of Sylvia and sighed. He did not say anything but sat down to eat his dinner quietly. After dinner he got busy in planning mentally about how he would bring the gold from across the river. He went to his room to sleep and forgot to talk to Sylvia about the type of fabric and the estimated requirements for her dress. Sylvia said to herself before sleeping, "I do not like to go and visit other people and socialize for no reason. Except for Jack, I do not consider anyone else to be beautiful and worthy. I am happy with my life and do not like to hear comments of others."

Chapter 15

Heart is trapped in the beauty of friend
Look the hunter is trapped in his own trap

Nevlin Lane got up early in the morning before dawn and after his morning routine, left in a hurry to look for the gold, without talking to Sylvia. He left with his pickaxe and shovel for the same hill in the expectation of finding gold. On his way back, he went to the market. He bought fabric for a dress, with a matching cap and shoes and other essential accessories. In his mind he tried to match everything with what Miss Brown was wearing the previous evening. He also bought scissors, thread reels, both white and coloured, needles etc. required for stitching a dress. He returned to the house after buying all this material. When he reached the house, he put the bundle of purchases in Sylvia's hands and said, "In spite of an extensive search I could not find ready made dresses in the market here. Moreover I forgot to ask you for your measurements. Therefore, I have bought the cloth for a full dress as per my own estimation. I am sure you know sewing and stitching. Please make a dress for yourself as per your liking."

Sylvia happily took the bundle from Nevlin Lane and thanked him very much. She wanted to say more, but Jack did not allow her to say anything in appreciation of his gesture and with a shy look went for a wash. Sylvia took the bundle of clothes and kept it in her room. She then very neatly laid the dinner on the table.

After finishing the dinner, Nevlin Lane said to Sylvia, "Tomorrow morning I will go to the same mountain again to dig for gold. I also went there today making sure the people here did not see me. Tomorrow I will go there by the jungle route. If any one comes to the house and asks for me after I have left, please tell them that Jack has gone out hunting for the day. I will come back to the house after the sun has set and it is dark. You will be all alone in the house most of the day as Mathula has to go for grocery shopping to the market. But don't be afraid, especially of wicked Lewryk. I have made sure that he does not come his side at all and I have also written to the senior officials of the department about him. Mr. McGregor has also taken steps to ensure that no robbers come anywhere near this place. So do not worry. Have no fear in your mind and relax."

Sylvia said, "Now I am not afraid of anyone. When I was weak, I was helpless. Now I am in good health. Even fear will be scared to come near me. Please leave your gun with me. I can guard the house better than the police."

On hearing Sylvia speak with such confidence, Nevlin Lane put his fully loaded gun in Sylvia's hands. Sylvia carefully handled the gun and aimed at a tree. Nevlin Lane asked her not to fire and said with a happy face, "Sil, I have not seen a brave and courageous girl, like you, even in London."

Sylvia smiled and said, "Do I have more ability than Miss Brown in anything? Am I stronger and more courageous than her?"

Nevlin Lane said, "Oh. Miss Brown does not compare with you in any thing. She appears to me to be very timid. I heard her yesterday requesting her father to walk fast as she was very scared of the darkness. I think she will be scared even if she heard a little sound from a mouse. I do not think she even knows how to hold a gun."

Sylvia said, "Look at my marksmanship." She aimed at a stone that was lying near the boundary of the house and fired. The bullet hit the mark and broke the stone into two pieces and disappeared in the jungle.

Nevlin Lane said, "Well done! Very good! You have an excellent aim, my brave Sil. I have complete trust in you."

Next day, Nevlin Lane left early in the morning and went in the direction of the mountain. Sylvia kept herself busy the whole day in cutting the cloth and sewing her dress. With great effort, she managed to finish by evening. Mathula returned in the evening after doing the grocery shopping. She saw the completed dress and examined it carefully from all sides, admiring its various cloth lapels and its design. To her, the dress appeared to be more beautiful and finely stitched than the dress of Miss Brown. She said in a happy tone, "Sylvia, God knows I am telling the truth. You have stitched this dress better than even an expert tailor. Even a tailor cannot cut and design such a perfect dress without some help and guidance. You are a very clever girl. You are very proficient in all the housework. I get completely enchanted by your songs. Today, after seeing how neatly and ably you stitch, I feel very happy."

Sylvia said, "From a very young age I have been stitching both gents and ladies clothing. My father arranged for me to be trained by expert teachers who taught me how to measure and stitch clothing and also how to knit and do embroidery. In my father's time, I used to stitch his clothes and my dresses from very fine material. Today I spent the whole day, and with some effort managed to complete this dress so that Jack may know that I very much appreciate and love the cloth that he brought for my dress. I hope he will be convinced that instead of ruining the cloth I have managed to stitch a good dress. I trust he will also like this dress." She bowed to Mathula and saluted her for her appreciation of the dress and her stitching.

Mathula said, "My blessings are with you. May this dress prove to be very auspicious and lucky for you. May you succeed in everything you do in your life." After giving her blessings, Mathula said to her, "Sylvia Bond, you must have seen by now that Jack is a very honest, unassuming and a simple person. He spends all his time in digging. Obviously when one does not even look at a thing, how can he admire and appreciate the workmanship. You can test what I am trying to say this evening and see whether I am right or not. Let us see if he admires the very fine stitching and design of your dress when he sees it this evening. Sure, he will say it is very nice and looks good because he generally likes everything that you do and say. I have noticed that he quietly, in his heart, admires you and says that you are a remarkable girl."

Jack returned to the house after it was dark. He was very tired from the hard labour and strain of digging. However, from the expression on his face he looked happy and there was joy in his eyes. As he came to the verandah, he started calling, "Sylvia, Sylvia!" When he entered the house, he saw Sylvia standing and looking like a bride. She had had a bath, her hair was well groomed and soft like silk and her face was radiant like a rose flower. She was wearing a very well designed dress, finely stitched and of a perfect fitting. The dress looked gorgeous! Her whole appearance had changed completely. She was standing in a unique captivating pose like a new bride. Jack said in a very happy voice, "Sylvia is this you or has some angel of heaven descended from the sky above? It is a thing of great joy and pride that you completed the whole dress in only one day. You are a very accomplished and clever girl."

On hearing Jack speak like this, Sylvia felt a strange sensation, like an electric charge, in all parts of her body. She felt very happy and her eyes became wet.

Sylvia said hesitatingly, "Thank you very much. Do you like the way I have stitched this dress?"

Jack said, "I like it with all my heart."

Sylvia asked, "Can my stitching be better than that of Miss Brown?"

Jack replied, "I do not know why you keep bringing the name of Miss Brown in our conversation? If you are the sun then she is a moon."

Sylvia said shyly, "I thank you very much for comparing me to the sun but some people prefer the moon."

Since Nevlin Lane enjoyed teasing young girls from his childhood, he said in response to her comment, "In their proper place both the sun and the moon can be attractive. During the day time the sun and in the night, the moon, are benevolent. You look at me and let me admire the workmanship of the beautiful dress you have made. He looked at the design of both the dress and the gown carefully from all sides and kept on saying, "Marvellous, absolutely marvellous. What fine and neat stitching. It's not only me, but anyone who will look at this dress will say the same. Wear this dress on Sunday for the sermon at the church. The eyes of hundreds of people all around will be on your dress and they will admire it. You are a source of great pride and joy to me."

On hearing Jack admiring her, tears of happiness came to Sylvia's eyes. Nevlin Lane gently kissed her cheek.

Nature has given women a unique power that when any part of the woman's body touches a part of a man's body, a special kind of phenomenon takes place which can create the sensation of faintness. All the religious books and big saints, therefore, forbid any contact between man and woman, whether they are relatives or friends. Many rich and famous people and saints have lost all that they had by falling in love with women other than their wives. This privilege is only for a husband and wife. The wise people never allow their emotions to override their sense of right behaviour and they at once reject the desires of sin and improper behaviour.

Both Sylvia and Jack were persons of excellent character and very wise. As soon as Sylvia felt a feeling of faintness by repeated kisses of Jack, she forcibly pushed Jack's face away from her. Jack also came to his senses at once and because of his discipline and wisdom he went and stood on one side. He said, "All right sister, let me not examine your dress so closely but I cannot help admiring the excellent job you have done in stitching this dress. Look here, you are going to get dinner, but please do not change your dress yet. You may change after we eat and before going to bed."

Sylvia said in response, "I will be back shortly. Let me adjust the buttons on the dress properly." She went to her room. She did not change the dress, but sat down on the chair to calm the strange pounding of her heart. She started to think about what happened to her to make her lose her senses. For ten minutes she just sat quietly and when she could not find an answer she got up and straightened her dress with her hands and checked the locket around her neck that her father had given to her at the time of his death. It was hanging from her neck and she felt satisfied. She came out and laid the dinner on the table. She asked Jack to sit down for dinner and she stood beside him to serve him. After serving him, she stood near his chair.

Jack said, "The food tastes so delicious today. I do not think that even the King of England was ever served such delicious food." Jack ate his food, laughing and joking all the time. After dinner he asked Sylvia, "Where is Mathula?"

Sylvia said, "She did return from the market before you came back. But she forgot to pick up the packet of tea and went back for the same."

On hearing this, Jack took off his coat and opened his belt and took out a heavy, long piece of gold and kept it on the table. He said to Sylvia, "Look, today I found this very costly piece of gold, not by digging at the cave, but from underneath the stones. There is a lot of gold under those stones. However, it is mixed with sand. If we go and gather this gold, we can go to London together and live like rich people. To go to London even this piece of gold is enough."

First, on looking at the gold piece, Sylvia became pale. But when she realized that Jack is talking about both of them going together, her face lit up with joy. She said excitedly, "I fully agree and accept the proposal of going to London with you. To go there without you will make me sad. Tell me, do you really mean that you will take me to London with you?"

Nevlin Lane said, "Yes Sylvia, we shall both go together. On reaching London, I shall continue to look after you and your safety. If, in London, some near and close relative of yours claims guardianship, then I will take steps to legally let them take care of you, provided you so desire. In a couple of days I will go and see Mr. McGregor and get the money due to me for the work I have done. After that I will go to my old place of work and dig as usual for a few days, so that no one will suspect us of planning to run away. In the meanwhile I shall firm up our plans for reaching London and I would inform you of the same. Now tell me, after reaching London, would you like to buy a farm in Devonshire or would you rather buy it at some other location. You should buy cattle, horses, ducks in large quantities so that from the income generated by them, you would be able to live a life of comfort and luxury."

They both spent the evening talking of such subjects and felt very happy with the unexpected find of gold and congratulated each other on their good luck. They speculated on prospects of buying a farm and other things. They both felt tired and sleepy by the time Mathula returned and retired to their respective rooms and went to sleep.

Next day, very early in the morning, Nevlin Lane went to the office of Mr. McGregor to resolve something that he had decided in his mind overnight. On the way, he saw a new beautiful tent by the side of the road. On the side of the tent was a nice little garden. All around the garden was a colourful fence with one central gate for the entrance. The gate was closed. About ten steps from the gate a young girl was taking a stroll in the garden. Nevlin Lane wanted to go inside the garden and rest for a few minutes, but when he saw the girl all alone, he decided not to go in and just took a quick glimpse of the neat and clean curtains of beautiful lacework inside the tent, and coloured bamboo curtains in the front. He went straight to the office of Mr. McGregor. There, as usual, the employees were working at their desks doing their routine work. Mr. McGregor, his assistant and clerk, Mr. Loket, and the doctor, were discussing something in Mr. McGregor's office. When they saw Ian entering the office, all three of them stood up from their chairs and greeted him. Mr. Loket, after shaking hands with Nevlin Lane, asked him if everything was alright and what was his purpose of coming to their office. He said, "I hope no wicked person is troubling you."

Ian said, "I thank you from my heart for your nice arrangements. These days I have no problem of any kind."

Mr. Loket asked, "Have you noticed that Lornehope Camp is much more lively these days compared to before?"

Before Ian could answer, Mr. McGregor interjected and said,

"Why young men, the liveliness now will be nothing compared to what I propose. This place will glitter and become lively like London and Paris."

The Doctor said, "Tell us Mr. Ian, did you derive any benefit as yet from your hard labour and did you find more gold as a result of your digging or are you still living hand to mouth?"

On hearing the doctor speak like this, Nevlin Lane thought that all these people say what the contractor, Mr. McGregor, likes to hear and he has complete control over everything here. The laws do not allow any one to keep any gold with him. Every little gold found must be handed over to the contractor for cash right away. No one is allowed to take, even an ounce of gold, out of this city. If anyone is found to break these laws, he is immediately arrested and put behind bars. Here, they only give five shillings per ounce. If anyone of them comes to know of the gold he had found, he will immediately take steps to make sure that he does not go outside the boundaries of this city and will not give him more than five shillings per ounce for the gold. With these thoughts in his mind, Nevlin Lane said in a carefree tone, "Doctor, in spite of the hard labour I have not been successful in finding enough gold that would enable me to lead a comfortable life. I have been working here for several years now and all that I found was that gold slab. As you all know, I spent all the money from the gold slab to take care of the helpless girl. Since that day I have not found any gold at this place. In fact the purpose of my visit to the office of the respected contractor is to request him to allot me another piece of land where I can try my luck."

After listening to Nevlin Lane, Mr. Loket, on a cue from the contractor, said to him, "In our opinion and to the best of our knowledge there is no other piece of land around here from where there is a possibility of finding gold. Wherever there is a probability of finding gold, the digging is already in progress. As per rules and the laws we cannot remove any one from the land assigned to him."

The contractor, Mr McGregor also joined Mr Loket in expressing his views and said to Nevlin Lane, "Mr. Ian, as you can see for yourself, Lornehope Camp is climbing the ladder of success and we are constantly implementing several new plans to improve things here for everyone. We are informing everyone of our plans and improvements made, by publishing posters. We are inviting skilled tradesmen, good administrators, people with expertise in special areas and skills, to come and settle here. We are strictly enforcing laws. Under these circumstances how can we ourselves go against the rules."

Mr Loket interjected and said, "We are not satisfied with the progress so far. We shall soon be building a church here for prayers and for educating people in religion and moral teachings. Religious teachings will be given to persons so that they can improve their life."

Ian asked, "Is a regular big building of church with bricks and mortar being constructed for prayers?"

Mr. Loket informed, "After distributing some money to the needy and the poor, a large sum of money is left from your gold slab. After the auction that day when you purchased the helpless poor Sylvia Bond, the general consensus of the public was to spend the money in the construction of a church. However, soon after, there was an epidemic and we spent part of the auction money in improving the lot of the poor. Still a large sum was left over. The public also donated money with the result that now there are two thousand pounds in the fund. We shall see what we can build for the church, from this money. Since your amount is the largest, your name will be engraved on a stone and placed in the church building." He continued, "I think it is also important to let you know at this time that we have made foolproof arrangements to take care of robbers. Since the day you lodged a complaint with our office regarding Lewryk, we started process to permanently deal with the matter. Lewryk, along with his twelve comrades, has been driven out of the boundaries of Lornehope Camp."

On hearing this, one of the clerks sitting in the office said, "The way Lewryk and his twelve comrades were driven out has created a lot of discontent amongst the public and I am also against it."

Mr. Loket said, "I do not see any harm in this."

The second clerk said, "When wicked Lewryk and his comrades were living at Lornehope Camp, they were under our constant surveillance and did not dare to commit any robbery or fraud. Lewryk was fearful and scared of the police and there was generally peace and quiet. Now it is impossible to keep an eye on him. He and his fellow robbers now sit and hide in the surrounding hills. Unfortunately, he has made friends with the people living in the mountains and robs the travellers. Two days back these persons attacked the treasurer of the bank. Because the treasurer was well armed, he was saved from being robbed. Otherwise he would have lost his life and all the money. Moreover, according to the new laws, only special persons and the police officers are allowed to carry guns and the public is not allowed to have guns. For this reason the common man is likely to be robbed by these robbers."

Nevlin Lane said, "I consider it my duty to let you know that I agree with the sentiments expressed by this dissenting clerk. It is obvious that the public is now more afraid of these wicked persons. In my opinion, to take away arms and guns from the citizens, the farmers, the landlords and the persons working outside the boundaries of the city, is a mistake. To take away guns is to put their lives and property in danger and to make them scared. It is not enough to let the police shoulder the whole responsibility. Can you tell me how many persons have been murdered in the last year in encounters with these robbers against the ones in domestic quarrels? How many have been prosecuted in the courts on murder charges? Moreover, if a common man is found guilty of a murder by the courts, he will be punished as per the laws. To make the people afraid of the government and take away their arms and guns is to put their lives in danger and make them cowards. The public can never rise against a government that has a huge army, arms and ammunition. If any one does act against the government, he will get due punishment."

After expressing his views on the subject in this manner, Nevlin Lane asked that he be excused so that he may return back to his house. Mr. Loket offered him wine and breakfast. Nevlin

Lane ate the breakfast and after thanking everyone, he left for his house. As he was passing the tent of the priest, he saw Miss Brown strolling near the gate of their tent. It appeared she was waiting for some one because she was facing the road. She was walking so that she could see everyone passing that side.

When Nevlin Lane was on his way to the contractor's office, Miss Brown had seen him. However, she did not consider it appropriate to shout for him. Now this young lady was eagerly waiting for his return. The truth was that Miss Brown liked the young Iain Herringdon very much. She had fallen in love with him. She was restless to meet him. She was planning, in her mind, various strategies to trap Nevlin Lane so that he may fall in love with her. She knew that Nevlin Lane knew nothing about love. He never liked to talk to young girls when they were alone or at a lonely place. He was naive and unable to grasp the various indications that young girls offered to express their love. In London, whenever he had an occasion to talk to young girls and women in his neighbourhood, he made sure that either their parents or husbands were present. Since childhood he was very naughty and liked teasing the girls. He always said things to tease them irrespective as to who was around. He enjoyed their getting angry and making faces. Since everyone knew Nevlin Lane to be a thorough gentleman and very disciplined, no one took offence at his jokes. Nevlin Lane never got angry or took offence to other's comments. He was never uncivilized towards anyone. At this time, as Nevlin Lane was passing by the garden of the priest's house, he noticed Miss Brown standing by the side of the fence. As Nevlin Lane began to take off his cap to greet Miss Brown, she smiled and said, "Please do come in and see how much work I have done to make this flower bed and plant the flower seeds.." She picked up a small shovel and said, "I have been digging with this shovel but the earth is so hard that my wrists are now sore."

The fence was very low and he was standing by the fence. He laughed at the small shovel. Miss Brown also laughed with him and she invited him to come inside and look at her garden. Nevlin Lane jumped over the fence and stood beside Miss Brown. A big shovel was lying near the flower bed. Nevlin Lane picked up this shovel.

Miss Brown said, "Sir, two of our gardeners take the whole day to dig one flower bed with this heavy shovel. This shovel is very heavy. Please keep it down. Come and look at the buds which are just coming out in these trees. Can you tell me how big and of what colour the flowers will be from these buds?"

Nevlin Lane said, "First let me make a flower bed out of this land here. Your wrists got sore by digging on this land."

Without waiting for a reply, Nevlin Lane picked up the shovel and struck hard six or seven times at the land near the other flower beds. In no time he dug a foot deep bed and with his hands sorted the loose earth to make a flower bed. He was just getting ready to dig a second bed when Miss Brown came running and held his hand. She admired in her heart his powerful hands and strong wrists. She insisted on him not doing any more digging and holding his hand, led him to the living room inside the house. She asked him to sit on the fine sofa. She fetched grape wine from the cupboard and filled up a cup and offered it to Nevlin Lane. She admired his well built body and thought how handsome he was. She came and sat beside him, touching his knee with her body. She held the cup in both her hands and insisted he drank the wine from her hands. Now, if there was anyone else in place of Nevlin Lane, he would have guessed her intentions and would have fallen for her. However, Nevlin Lane controlled himself and smiled. He moved to the far corner of the sofa so that Miss Brown's legs did not touch his knee. He took the cup from her and drank it himself. After finishing the drink, he got up and thanked her and left for his house.

As soon as he entered the house, Sylvia asked him, "Where did you go so early in the morning without eating your breakfast as per your usual habit? Did you go to meet someone?"

Nevlin Lane said, "I went to the office of Mr. McGregor, the contractor, so that he may remain under the impression that I am still digging at my usual site. As I was returning back, after my discussion with him, Miss Brown saw me walking on the road and invited me inside to look at her garden and flowers. Her garden was very green and neat and the living room in the house was also well furnished and tastefully decorated."

Sylvia felt very envious on hearing this and said, "So you even went inside and saw her house? Did she herself take you inside the house?"

Nevlin Lane said, "First she was trying to dig a flower bed with a little shovel. I had a hearty laugh. With the big shovel I dug up the hard ground in no time and made a beautiful flower bed for her. She then took my hand and led me inside the house. She offered me some wine and talked to me for some time, laughing all the time."

Sylvia said, "I hate her because of her outlandish manners and bold behaviour."

Nevlin Lane said, "Why do you hate her? Just sitting at home you call her behaviour bold? I am surprised at this. You cannot judge a person and know his or her good and bad points without spending sometime together in his or her company. She came to your place with her father only once and you talked to her very briefly. Then she left with her father. How can anyone judge the character of another person in such a brief meeting. I do not understand what habits you saw in her that made you decide that you do not like her and started to hate her. On the contrary she admires you very much and wants to be your friend. She seemed very keen to meet you and get to know you. I think she is worthy of your friendship and you should try and be her friend."

Sylvia made a grim face and laughed and said in a sarcastic tone, "She is definitely not my type and not worthy of my friendship but she may be fit to be your friend."

From the very early days, Nevlin Lane was dogmatic and if anyone made fun of his comments without due and justified reason, he took this up as a challenge. Consequently when Sylvia laughed and spoke to him in a sarcastic tone, he decided to stick to his argument and said, "Alright, if you consider her fit for my friendship then let it be so and I will become her friend. In my opinion she is not ill-tempered nor does she have any bad intentions in her heart."

Seeing Nevlin Lane so determined, Sylvia suddenly remembered the advice given by her elders that under no circumstances should the women continue a domestic argument. In the heat of argument people say and do all kinds of things which can lead to serious consequences and even destroy a relationship. If women doubt something or believe that the person they love is not telling the truth, it is best to keep quiet. With a smiling face they should bring up a subject which may make him feel that he was right rather than to escalate the argument. This way the worst of men would feel ashamed and calm down. They may even realise that they were wrong and apologise. The anger of a man is like the boiling of milk in a pan. As soon as it starts boiling, it also starts to calm down. The wise and clever women know how to control their men. Sylvia remembering such teachings of her elders did not reply back and kept quiet. She did not say a single word about Miss Brown. She smiled sweetly and said, "Look at me, I almost forgot to lay the table for lunch."

With this she served the lunch and rang the bell. When Nevlin Lane sat down, she stood beside his chair to look after him.

Chapter 16

Crowd has numerous faces but following the direction of heart
God willing, I will find that person

To carry out the request of his beloved Audrey Hope, Lord Lorimor, without the slightest hesitation, left for his home in London to make arrangements for the running of his estate and financial matters. It was necessary for him to make these arrangements as he was leaving to search for Nevlin Lane. He wanted to plan for his estate from a long term point of view because he did not know when he would return or whether he would come back alive. He was not at all sorry for leaving his home and his life of comfort and luxury. On the contrary he was very happy to get this opportunity to carry out the wishes of his beloved. He firmly believed that when he returned to London with the childhood friend of Audrey Hope, she would marry him. Lord Lorimor was a true lover of Audrey Hope.

Soon after reaching London, Lord Lorimor invited his long time friend and adviser, Mr. Peterson, whose firm had acted as lawyers to his family for generations. He informed him of his intent to travel. He made him responsible for looking after his house and estate and all financial and business matters in his absence. With foresight and planning, he also wrote his will in his own hand writing in clear words and specified that after he was gone, Miss Audrey Hope would be the sole beneficiary of his property worth millions. The will was to be executed by Mr. Peterson. Once he was free of these matters he instructed the servants to prepare for his travels.

The lawyer, Mr. Peterson asked in a sympathetic voice, the reason for his travel. Since the family lawyers are also privy to the family secrets, people generally do not hide things of personal nature from them, nor do they doubt the lawyer's discretion in private matters. Lord Lorimor told the lawyer that he was deeply in love with Audrey Hope and that she was faithful and sincere. She had promised not to marry anyone else provided he could find her lost childhood friend and bring him to London with him. He told him that he was undertaking this journey to fulfil her request. He further said to the lawyer, "If I come back alive I will meet you again. Otherwise please execute my will as per my instructions and transfer all my estate to Audrey Hope legally."

The lawyer was taken aback by this confusing talk. He asked, "Are you familiar with Nevlin Lane's face and features? Do you have any idea as to where he might be living?"

Lord Lorimor said, "Neither Audrey Hope nor myself have any information as to where he might be. In my memory, I have never met him nor am I familiar with his face and features."

The lawyer said, "I have never heard or seen any woman making such an unreasonable and senseless request. Where and how would you find a person whom you have never seen or met. I think this is the most foolish thing."

Lord Lorimor said, "What you are saying is correct. However, I am so much in love with her that I cannot think as to what is right or wrong. The countries, cities, mountains, rivers, I will search them all. Also, wherever I will find someone resembling Sir Jordan Lane, I will inquire from him about Nevlin Lane. If on the basis of my love I am successful in my search, I can look forward to spend the rest of my life in luxury and comfort."

The lawyer said, "Leave such thoughts alone. The person who lives in this world knowing all the time that all this is just a dream, and can get along with both foolish and wise persons and does the kind and right deeds, is considered fit to realize God. Instead of facing the hardships of travel, you should publish posters. Place advertisements in all the newspapers of the various places and distribute posters. Nothing can work better than these to find a lost person."

Lord Lorimor said, "I have heard, that to find him, Sir Jordan Lane placed advertisements in the various newspapers in America. But I do not trust him. After reaching there, I will find out whether this is true or false. If the advertisements placed by him are not to my satisfaction, I will publish new advertisements. I will also search for him in all the factories and other places in America, Australia and Austria. I am determined to carry out the wishes of my beloved. You probably do not realize that if she wanted the search to be made through posters and advertisements, she would have done so herself and would not have asked me to undertake the search."

The lawyer said, "The women are generally unsuspecting and are unaware of the worldly ways and fraud. They have no idea of the problems and hardships involved in travelling. Please take advantage of my experience and advice. I will tell you a solution that will both meet the request of your beloved and will probably help you to realize the goal you desire. In America, Austria and several places in Australia, I have some friends who are very rich and are in high positions. Some of my friends in these places hold senior positions in the police department. Just now, in your presence, I will write letters to all my friends. They will search all over for the person named Nevlin Lane. They will inform me immediately on finding out about his whereabouts. Then we can go and bring him here to your beloved."

Lord Lorimor said, "If you have friends in America, Austria and other countries, there is no doubt that they would search for him. Please write letters to your friends and give them to me. I will personally deliver these letters and request them for their assistance in searching for Nevlin Lane. The old saying of elders is true, No one else can do your job the way you would do it yourself. Because of your integrity and responsible ways, I am confident that in my absence you will look after my estate, business and house with care and due attention. I am also sure that I can trust you to keep the purpose of my trip strictly confidential, even from your wife and children. Under any circumstances, please do not utter a word about my trip to Sir Jordan Lane."

The lawyer said, "I cannot help admiring your determination and devotion to your goal and I hope you will come back after the successful completion of your mission. I know your sincerity and believe there is no power in the world that can make you change your mind. The elders and saints say that a person who single-mindedly, with faith and determination, pursues a goal, is invariably successful in realizing it. Rest assured about your estate, business and house because I will look after these as my own and will take care of all your affairs here. I would also ask you to inform me, once every week, about your travels, welfare and full address. I also solemnly promise that I shall not speak a word about your travel and whereabouts to Sir Jordan Lane or anyone else, even to my closest and dearest friends or relatives. I will guard, with my life, your will and the letters that you send me."

Lord Lorimor expressed his thanks and satisfaction at his lawyer's loyalty. As per his advice, he took some cash, a large amount of currency notes and a few bank drafts that could be deposited in government banks in other countries. He wrapped part of it in a pouch tied to his belt and hid some in the layers and pockets of his clothes in his different suitcases. He did this to ensure that if he lost some luggage in the journey, he would still have money available. On a piece of paper, he wrote with his pen the three letters, A, B, C, and told the lawyer that whenever he needed more money in a foreign country, he would wire him for money and if in the telegram he wrote the code words A, B, and C, to then send him three thousand pounds. If he needed more, he would send separate telegrams with that many alphabets. "Please consider every alphabet to mean that I require one thousand pounds and immediately send me the same amount by telegram or by whichever means you consider most appropriate." He then took leave of all his employees and with his luggage, boarded the ship for New York.

On the ship, Lord Lorimor met persons of different temperaments, coming from different walks of life and going to different destinations. He met several children, elderly and young people in a cordial manner. He enjoyed their company.

He toured famous sites of each city he visited in America, ate delicious food and dressed every day in well designed clothes. At night he slept thinking of his beloved. This was his normal daily routine. However, he never talked to anyone about the real purpose of his visit. In every city he visited, he went to the factories and offices and talked to both the rich and poor workers and met senior officers in the offices. He visited various hotels, hospitals, gambling casinos, theatres and churches, looked for anyone resembling Sir Jordan Lane and inquired about Nevlin Lane. He searched America and the neighbouring countries. He obtained several copies of papers of previous years from various publishers at a considerable expense and browsed through all of them for advertisements. When he did not find a single advertisement given by Sir Jordan Lane in any of the newspapers, he spoke with the publishers of the papers to find out if they had received any letter from Sir Jordan Lane. None of them had heard from him. He then placed several advertisements in the various newspapers on Sir Jordan Lane's behalf. In short he did every conceivable thing to search Nevlin Lane and explored all possible avenues. The various letters that he had taken from his family lawyer, Mr. Peterson, were personally presented by him to the party concerned. He met the senior police officers and the other rich and influential persons who were friends of his lawyer. They were most obliging and assisted him in every possible manner. They, in turn, introduced him to several other very rich gentlemen in their cities. However, it was of no avail. He still could not get any information about Nevlin Lane.

One day, by chance, he met one of his old friends, Lord Gilmour, on a street in the marketplace. Lord Gilmour was a well known landlord of America. He had been to London several times for vacations and used to stay at the mansion of Lord Lorimor. He was thankful to Lord Lorimor for his excellent hospitality and for looking after him so well. He was familiar with not only America but also Austria and the surrounding countries. Because of his cordial nature and as a part of his business, he knew all the senior government and industry officers. He was very kind and always ready to help others. He was also very fond of travelling and hunting. He was very happy to meet Lord Lorimor at the marketplace. He implored Lord Lorimor to come to his house and got his baggage from the hotel. For several days he showed him round America and took him to shows at the various theatres at his own expense. One day he noticed that Lord Lorimor looked sad and in a sympathetic voice he asked him the reason for the same. Lord Lorimor was well aware of the kind nature and true friendship of Lord Gilmour and disclosed to him the secret of his heart. He told him about his love for Audrey Hope and her request to search for Nevlin Lane. He told him the whole story from the beginning. Lord Gilmour listened to his friend's description with great attention and after he had finished, Lord Gilmour suggested to Lord Lorimor that he should search for Nevlin Lane in Austria and its various cities. He also expressed his desire to accompany Lord Lorimor to Austria and assist him with his search. He also told him that he knew that the majority of young men, when they left home in anger, went to Austria and adopted the occupation of digging for gold to maintain themselves. Lord Lorimor liked this suggestion. Accordingly it was agreed that they would both leave for Austria.

Lord Gilmour selected twelve of his strong and loyal young employees to go with them and arranged for all the things required for travelling. They all left America for Austria. They visited several cities in Austria and met senior officers and rich landlords, inquiring from everyone about Nevlin Lane. They finally reached the city Fairfeld. Here Lord Gilmour knew two rich persons. These friends told them that at a distance of twenty miles from Fairfeld, there was Lornehope Camp, where gold mines were located. They suggested that they visit Lornehope Camp and inquire about Nevlin Lane and it was quite likely that they would be successful in their mission. Since it was already late in the evening, it was decided that they would leave early in the morning. Lord Gilmour instructed his employees to be ready to start at 3 a.m. and his employees made arrangements accordingly. After packing their bags they all went to bed, but Lord Lorimor could not sleep. In the light of the lamp, he wrote a long letter to his beloved Audrey Hope and described all his travels and also mentioned that the next day, he would be going to Lornehope Camp, which was twenty miles from there. He finished the letter and sealed it in an envelope and kept it in his pocket with the intention of mailing it at the post office on his way in the morning. He then went to sleep.

Chapter 17

She only remembered the outwardly injustice and oppression
She forgot the good times, the fun days and kind deeds

Nevlin Lane went for three consecutive days to dig up and gather the gold behind the hill, under the stones. With great effort and hard work, he gathered and stashed all the gold in a safe place. On the fourth day he took Sylvia with him and they both, little by little, filled up their waist belts and pockets with gold dust and started the task of bringing it back to their house and storing it. In three days they transported the entire gold dust to the house. Nevlin Lane was very happy at finding all this gold. However, Sylvia's face showed a certain sadness. She was jealous of Miss Brown's friendship with Nevlin Lane.

Nevlin Lane was not able to go to the church for two weeks to listen to the sermon by the priest. On the third Sunday, remembering his promise to the priest, he went to the church with Sylvia. Several men and women were gathered at the church. As soon as Sylvia reached there, all the women folk gathered around her and expressed their happiness at meeting her. Both the priest and his daughter Miss Brown were also happy at her coming to the church. Several persons in the crowd admired Sylvia's dress and her charming and radiant looks. After the sermon and the church ceremonies, the priest escorted Sylvia and Nevlin Lane to his camp. Miss Brown entertained Sylvia, assuming she was the sister of Iain Herringdon. However, Sylvia remained aloof and unappreciative of Miss

Brown's attention. Miss Brown, on the other hand, ignored Sylvia's indifference. She cordially took Sylvia's hand and escorted her to her room. She showed Sylvia her jewellery, different dresses and the embroidery done by her. However, Sylvia persisted in her indifference towards Miss Brown and did not show any interest in her things. Nevlin Lane noticed Sylvia's indifference and fearing that this may lead to some unpleasantness, he got up and begged leave of the priest and her daughter. He started walking with Sylvia towards their house. On the way he said to Sylvia, "I am unable to understand why you look at Miss Brown with hate in your eyes. She wants to be your friend and you keep her at a distance. She showed you all her jewellery and clothes and served you such delicious dishes, but you did not show any interest. You were rude and arrogant to her. I felt ashamed and embarrassed because of your attitude. I guess it is not entirely your fault. My attention and love have spoiled you and I feel like asking you to go away from here."

On hearing this, Sylvia kept her hand on Jack's shoulder and said sweetly with great joy and innocence, "Yes Jack, you are right. We should go away from this place as soon as possible. It is in our best interest that we leave for London without any further delay. We have enough gold for a reasonably comfortable life in London. As you said, let us get out of here."

Sylvia turned around Jack's last sentence in such an innocent and sweet way that Jack laughed. He said in a loving voice, "Dear Sil, you do not know how much money is required to live comfortably in London. The gold dust that you and I have brought from the valley has three parts sand and one part gold. Because of great expense in separating the gold from sand, we will get very little gold out of it."

Sylvia did not talk any further about the journey or going to London. In silence she walked with him till they reached the house. She had her dinner and then retired to her room for the night. As she laid on the bed, she began to analyze the meaning of Miss Brown's comments and actions. The way she showed off and danced around Jack and the way she looked at Jack and smiled at him had made her very jealous. She kept turning and tossing all night and did not sleep well.

Next day, as per his routine, Nevlin Lane got up early in the morning and went to his old place of work to dig. He pretended to work for a while and returned back early to the house. He took a bath, combed his hair, brushed his clothes and went out again. When Jack left the house, Sylvia started thinking that Jack must have gone to see Miss Brown, otherwise why would he dress up so nicely. She was right. Jack indeed had gone towards the camp of the priest and as he reached near their house, he saw Miss Brown standing at the door of their house. As she saw Nevlin Lane passing her house, she ran and cordially took his arm and escorted him to their living room. She thanked him for coming.

Miss Brown picked up the bouquet of flowers from the centre table. Sometimes she pluck a couple of leaves from the bouquet while talking to Nevlin Lane and at other times she rearranged the flowers. Watching her, Nevlin Lane laughed and said, "You seem to be very fond of flowers."

Miss Brown said, "All women like flowers. Why, is your sister not fond of flowers?"

Nevlin Lane did not know whether Sylvia liked flowers. He simply said, "My sister is too busy with various household chores and does not have time for flowers. I can bring very beautiful flowers for you, more beautiful than the ones in the bouquet. I know which flowers match and are the right colour for a bouquet."

On hearing Nevlin Lane speak this way, Miss Brown felt very happy and her eyes lighted up. To hide her playing with the flowers, she said with a smile, "I do not wish to trouble you for flowers. This would mean unnecessary botheration for you."

Nevlin Lane said, "There is no trouble in this. On the other side of the mountain, by the valley, the trees are laden with lovely flowers of all colours."

After another few minutes of conversation, Nevlin Lane returned to his house and after eating dinner, he went to sleep. He did not have an opportunity to talk to Sylvia about Miss Brown.

Next day Nevlin Lane, as usual, went to his old place of work.

On his way back for breakfast, he detoured and went to the valley where he had previously seen all the lovely flowers growing. Within an hour, he gathered a bunch of beautiful flowers of different colours that he thought would make a lovely flower bouquet. When Sylvia saw Jack with the basket full of lovely flowers, she smiled in a captivating fashion and innocently said, "Jack I admire your excellent choice of flowers and thank you from my heart for this lovely gift of flowers that you have brought for me."

She transferred all the flowers from the basket in her handkerchief and said in a very happy voice, "I feel like keeping these flowers next to my heart. Though I wonder how I can keep all these flowers. Oh yes, I know what I can do. I will make a bouquet with the same happy spirit with which you have brought these. I am sure you will like the way I match the different flowers and colours in the bouquet."

Nevlin Lane did not know what to say. If he had known that Sylvia liked flowers so much he would have brought flowers for her every day. He looked at Sylvia with an embarrassed look and said, "Sil, I did not know that you will adore the flowers brought by me."

Sylvia smiled and said, "What made you think that I may not like and admire flowers? The flowers brought by you are just the right ones for a bouquet and I like them very much. The person who can select such beautiful flowers shows his own inclination towards fine things in life."

Nevlin Lane said, "Alright. I will definitely bring similar flowers for you tomorrow. I brought these flowers for Miss Brown. I had promised to bring her flowers today. Please do not mind what I have said. You keep these flowers. I will make another round of the valley and get more flowers for her."

On hearing this, Sylvia lost her temper and was consumed by the fire of jealousy. She said with a frown on her face, "Please forgive me but I do not want a share of things meant for Miss Brown." With this she threw all the flowers from her handkerchief on the floor.

On seeing Sylvia so angry, Nevlin Lane laughed and said in

a calm voice, "The young girls are generally very insolent and unnecessarily get angry at very insignificant things. If you consider these flowers, which are growing in abundance in the valley, to be her property, then very well, I will go and give her these very flowers." Considering Sylvia's anger to be a sign of her young age, he picked up the flowers from the floor and went to Miss Brown's house. He kept the basket full of flowers in front of her. On seeing such lovely flowers, Miss Brown thanked Nevlin Lane and looked at him with lustful and inviting eyes. Anyone else in place of Nevlin Lane would have fallen for her invitation and kissed her but Nevlin Lane was different.

Nevlin Lane was a person with good intentions. He was not going to fall for any foolish girl without considering all the implications. He ignored all the signs and actions of Miss Brown and quoted a passage from a book. He wanted to discuss the same but Miss Brown interjected, "Sir, the flowers that you have brought for me are lovely and I like them very much. There is a world of difference in these flowers and the flowers in London. I have never seen such freshness and natural beauty in the flowers of London. In the beginning I used to feel very lonely here but now I like it here. In comparison, now I think London to be too artificial and desolate." She kept a few flowers in her blouse pocket.

Nevlin Lane listened quietly while sitting with her on the sofa. Miss Brown got up and took the tea kettle from the cupboard and said to Nevlin Lane in a very pleasant voice, "I shall be grateful if you stay for a cup of tea." She held the cup to his lips and also gave him a cigarette. Nevlin Lane lit the cigarette and got up to go home. She said, "I do not know where my respected father has gone. I have been waiting for him for a very long time. I want to see him."

Nevlin Lane said, "If I meet your father, I will ask him to hurry back home. I will also tell him not to leave you alone but to take you with him if he has to go far. Now there are two alternatives. Either I go alone and look for him or you may also come along."

Miss Brown liked the idea of walking with Nevlin Lane. She

wanted to spend as much time as possible with him.

Generally men look for an opportunity to lure the girls to lonely places to express their love and try to get them in their control. However, Nevlin Lane had no love for Miss Brown and he never looked at her with such intention. He was a thorough gentleman and out of courtesy, whenever he saw Miss Brown, he stopped and greeted her. Even the other day when he dressed up and went out, he had gone to the house of the doctor. He asked him to request the contractor, Mr. McGregor, to allot him a new plot for digging. On the way he happened to meet Miss Brown and went to her place. Today also he had gone to deliver the flowers to her to show his skill in making a bouquet, so that she may consider him a decent civilized person and not just an ordinary worker. Moreover, in the couple of meetings, Nevlin Lane had figured out that her knowledge was shallow. Most of the time she talked foolish. That is why he did not pay much attention to what she said. Rather he was thinking that the gold pieces and gold dust that they had found so far was not enough and he needed to double the amount of gold to be able to go back to London.

Miss Brown noticed that Nevlin Lane was lost in his thoughts and asked him, "You seem to be engrossed in some deep worry. Please do me a favour and share your thoughts with me. Are you anxious to go to London?"

Nevlin Lane said, "Your question indicates that you are also thinking of going to London. Often when a person makes a remark like that, it is a reflection of what is in one's own mind and the remark shows what that person is thinking."

On hearing this Miss Brown was startled. She controlled herself and said, "I am not missing London at this time nor do I have any desire to return to London. In comparison, this place looks more promising to make me happy."

Nevlin Lane said, "There is no doubt that this place is getting much more lively now. But there is hardly a person who does not miss his homeland. All foreigners count the days and as soon as they have enough money, they are ready to go back."

Miss Brown said, "I know now that you are very anxious

to return to your homeland. Do you really want to go back to London?"

Nevlin Lane answered, "You are right. I propose to go to London in the near future and I . . ."

As he completed the sentence, they saw the priest coming from the front. The priest asked what they were discussing and if he could share their conversation.

Nevlin Lane said, "Yes Sir. I was saying just now that I am going back to London and I will miss all the people here. I will be especially sorry to leave my kind friends like you and Miss Brown. But such is this world that some day we have to go our own way leaving behind all friends and relatives. All foreigners look for an opportunity to return to their homeland. One who gets a chance, takes advantage of it without any delay. Why Miss Brown, is this not right?"

Miss Brown's face became very sad on listening to Nevlin Lane's plan to return to London. She replied in a nervous voice, "What you are saying is right. But must you return to London? In how many days do you propose to go?"

Nevlin Lane said, "I have not mentioned to any one else about my plans. Considering you to be my fellow countrymen, I have mentioned this to you in confidence. Please do not reveal my plans to anyone else. Sylvia Bond and I will be leaving for London soon."

On hearing this Miss Brown felt devastated. Her face lost its colour and her legs began to shake. However, Nevlin Lane ignored her condition and turned his face away from her. He began talking to the priest. After a while, the priest left the two of them standing and went and sat down on a nearby stone. After he left, Miss Brown said to Nevlin Lane in an incoherent voice, "You seem to be very happy about your plans to go back to London. In my opinion, the people here are much more friendly and helpful than in London."

She wanted to say something more but her whole body started to shake and she began to fall. Nevlin Lane caught her just in time. Seeing her condition he guessed that she was very upset and saddened about his going to London. But to tease her, he asked, "Miss Brown how are you feeling? Are you feeling dizzy?"

Miss Brown was shaking all over but she straightened up and said, "Oh no, I do not have any dizzy spell. I just slipped because the ground was uneven."

Nevlin Lane could see that she was pretending but to humour her, he said in a concerned tone, "I am sorry. Let me check if you are hurt."

Miss Brown said, "Thank God, I have not sprained my ankle. My foot slipped and I would have definitely fallen to the ground if you did not so kindly support me." She looked around and said, "My father has gone far away. Please call him. I do not wish to go any further. I want to return to my home now."

Nevlin Lane said, "Please wait. You still seem to be shaky and unstable on your feet. Sit down on this stone for a few minutes and rest for a while." Miss Brown did not accept his advice but took a step in the direction of her father. When Nevlin Lane saw her walking, he took her hand and put it on his shoulder. Miss Brown started to walk slowly. Nevlin Lane could feel her heart still beating fast and her body shaking all over. She was moaning and uttering sighs. Nevlin Lane asked her, "Surely you do not feel well, your ankle seems to be hurt? If you were not hurt, your face would not be so pale."

On receiving such attention and hearing sympathetic words from Nevlin Lane, Miss Brown could not control herself and tears came to her eyes. She put her head on Nevlin Lane's shoulder. He thought that she was about to fall and he grasped her and held her close to himself. Miss Brown clung to him. A strange sensation went through their bodies. Nevlin Lane realized straightaway that it was all an act by her to get close to him and he regretted his lapse of judgement. He realized that she was deeply in love with him and wished that he had made it clear to her at their very first meeting that he was not the right person for her and not worthy of her love. Now she was unnecessarily suffering because he was leaving. With this thought and realization, he removed her hand from his shoulder and gently pushed her away from his body. He said to her in a kind voice, "Please sit down on this stone. I can see your father from here. Look, he is standing twenty yards away under that tree looking at something. I will go to the office of Mr. McGregor, the contractor, and send his horsedrawn carriage for you. On my way I will ask your father to come to you. You can go to your house in the carriage."

On hearing this, Miss Brown got very upset and said in an irritated tone, "Please forgive me. Do not take the trouble to get the carriage for me. I can walk to the house on my own feet. You need not accompany me. You go ahead with your work. There is a short cut to our house from the side. I will meet my father on the way and we will go home."

Nevlin Lane was sensitive to sarcastic comments and he could not tolerate her tone of voice. He took leave from her and left straight for his house. After walking just a few steps, he saw some flowers lying on the road. He recognized these flowers to be the same that he had picked from the valley and given to Miss Brown. These were the flowers that Sylvia had treasured like diamonds earlier. He gathered these flowers and guessed that these must have fallen from Miss Brown's pocket when she feigned dizziness. With a view to return these flowers, he turned back and raced to Miss Brown. He said with a smile to her, "These flowers, that you liked so much, were lying on the road. They must have fallen from your pocket. I picked them up. Please keep them in your handkerchief and take them to your home."

Miss Brown, rather than accepting the flowers and thanking Nevlin Lane, stared at his face with a peculiar look.

Nevlin Lane said, "Why are you hesitating to accept the flowers? Please take these flowers otherwise I will think that you are angry with me."

Miss Brown frowned and said, "It was not necessary for you to come back and take the trouble of returning these flowers. I am not angry. I just want your goodwill. What shall I do with all these flowers? For your sake I will just take one flower and this will remind me of you once you have left for London."

She carelessly took one flower and turned away resuming her

walk. Nevlin Lane threw the rest of the flowers towards the jungle, away from the main road. As it was getting dark he took a short cut by the side of the jungle and reached his home before dark.

Miss Brown was sweating as she reached the place where her father was sitting. The priest asked her in a surprised tone, "Where is Iain Herringdon and why has he not come with you? I was just admiring God's magnificent creation and was lost in its splendour. Tell me why have you come back alone?"

To hide her emotions from her father, Miss Brown fabricated a story and said, "Mr. Herringdon had to go to the office of Mr. McGregor. He was walking fast and passed by your side in front of me. He went this very way but probably you did not see him. I am sorry he did not tell you about my following behind and coming here." Conversing like this, both father and daughter reached their home.

Miss Brown said that she did not want to eat dinner as she had a headache and retired to her room and went to bed. She did not sleep all night thinking about the going away of her friend. In her mind she was saying, "Iain Herringdon, why did you come in my life and treat me with such kindness and attention? Why did you meet me four or five times? Why did you steal my heart and make me fall in love with you? Why did you come to tell me about your going away? Why do you want to torture me? Why did you forget all my kindness in a moment? Why?"

After Miss Brown and the priest left the place, the clerk Mr. Loket happened to walk past the place where Nevlin Lane had offered the flowers back to Miss Brown and thrown the rest of them towards the jungle. He saw the flowers lying on the ground. He picked them up in his handkerchief and took them to his home.

After saying goodbye to Miss Brown, Nevlin Lane reached home just before dark. He saw Sylvia lying on the chair with her face turned and lost in deep thought. As Nevlin Lane was very tired and exhausted, he just ate his dinner and went to his room without any conversation with Sylvia. He laid down on his bed and started to make plans for going to London. Late in the night he dozed off.

Next day he got up early and went to the place where he and Sylvia had found the gold. He had gone without any tools, just to survey the site. He was taken aback to see a tent pitched there and several dozen workers working on the site. The noise from the digging by pick and shovel was deafening and no other sound could be heard. He realized that his secret was out and hundreds of other people would take advantage of his discovery. As these thoughts were going through his mind, Mr. Loket came out of the camp. He saw Nevlin Lane and motioned him to come near him.

Mr. Loket shook Nevlin Lane's hand and asked about his welfare, "What are you looking at? It is because of your goodwill that we have found this new gold mine here. Yesterday when you were talking to the daughter of the priest at the road side, I happened to be passing that way. I saw you throw some flowers towards the jungle. When you walked away, I picked up those flowers. I called you several times but you did not hear and soon you were out of sight. I looked at those flowers carefully and realized that these were from the valley by the mountain. I have known you for a long time, to be an educated gentleman and I figured that you would not go to the valley by the mountain without any specific reason, nor would you go all that way just to pick up flowers. I guessed that you must have reason to believe that there was gold there and I was aware of the fact that you had also approached us for an alternative site for digging gold. Putting all this together we came to the decision that there must be gold here and Mr. McGregor ordered that digging be started on this site. I am sure our thinking is not wrong. Therefore you should take the credit and also start digging at this site. In addition to your wages for the labour, you will get ten percent bonus for all the gold that you dig. Accordingly Mr. McGregor has issued these orders for your benefit."

Nevlin Lane looked surprised and said in a soft voice, "Thank you. You go ahead and organize digging as per your plans. It is likely that you will find gold here. Regarding my starting work here, please give me a couple of days to think about this. If I decide to dig here, I will let you know. I will start the digging at any spot that you would assign to me. It is possible that I may profit from this new site. I will go back now."

Mr. Loket took him inside his tent and offered him breakfast and wine. Nevlin Lane thanked him and finished the breakfast and glass of wine. He begged leave of Mr. Loket and came straight to his house. Sylvia asked him the reason for coming back so early.

Jack said, "I am sorry that our secret of the valley, on the other side of the river, is out. Mr. Loket and Mr. McGregor have several dozen workers working there. They have also asked me to dig there and try my luck."

Sylvia said, "I regret very much that other people are taking advantage and benefitting from your research and discovery. Now you have lost the opportunity of deriving any profit from that site. If you start digging at the mountain site, I am sure that Mr. McGregor will not give you anything more than your wages for the hard labour. These people are interested only in making money and do not care about any one else's welfare. Are you going to dig at the mountain site?"

Jack said, "The time for working is now over. As you said there is no more hope of gaining anything further from here. We should now leave for London."

Sylvia asked, "Is Miss Brown also going to come with us to London?"

Nevlin Lane said with a frustrated tone, "Why do you start talking about Miss Brown every time? I am a person of very high morals. Unfortunately, you do not understand my nature after all this time. Why should I be concerned about Miss Brown? As far as I am concerned I have nothing to do with her. I do not care about her—she can go where she wants. I am not related to her in any way. If there were hundred girls like Miss Brown in this place, I would sacrifice all of them for you."

Sylvia's sad face livened up like a rose and she felt very ecstatic. Her eyes began to sparkle with joy. She kissed Nevlin Lane's hand and asked, "When would we leave for London?"

Jack said, "We shall leave today as soon as it is dark. I have planned everything. Do not mention even a word about our plans to Mathula. Send her to the market on some pretext early in the evening. In her absence, as soon as it gets dark, we shall go from this place. Pack your clothes in a small bundle and wear your new dress. I will wear my coat that I wear when I go to work. I will put a blanket on my shoulder and hold the pouch of gold under my arm. Travelling all night we should reach Fairfeld in the morning. We shall sell the gold there and get a bank draft made. We shall also get some cash and travel with other travellers to Blaird." He jumped with joy and said, "At Blaird, we shall buy train tickets for London and reach next day. Sing with joy and let's say three cheers to London. Let us pray to God that we reach London safely."

Sylvia said, "Amen! Amen!"

Both Sylvia and Jack sang happily and prayed for a safe journey to London.

When Mathula returned from the neighbourhood where she had gone for some work, Sylvia sent her to the market to get a packet of tea. After she left, Sylvia took a bath and put on her new dress. Jack also wore his work coat and put the gold bar and gold pieces in the coat pockets and tied the sand mixed with gold in a pouch which he hung from his shoulder strap. He put the blanket on his shoulder and took the fully loaded gun. He took Sylvia's hand and they both left the house. At the gate, Sylvia turned her head and said in an emotional tone, "Our dear house, accept our last salute as we are leaving now and good bye!"

She started walking at a fast pace alongside Jack. On the way they talked in very soft voices about life in London. In the midst of the jungle when it got late in the night and the night air became a little cooler, Sylvia said with a very happy voice, "Jack, see how wonderful God has made this moonlit night. The heart seems light and the eyes feel fresh. Everything appears twice as wonderful. The moonlight seems so pure. I am feeling very happy."

Jack said, "May God help us to reach our destination safely. You should see the beauty of moonlit night at the London park. Let us pray to God and ask for His guidance in the journey. Please walk very softly so that there is no sound. The sound echoes in these mountains and the robbers hiding in the mountains can hear it and come to rob us. For the fear of these robbers I did not rent horses and decided to walk."

Sylvia was ecstatic walking with her hand in Jack's hand. She could not help singing a song. Her charismatic sweet voice sounded very good in this quiet jungle and Jack admired it. However, with foresight, he said to Sylvia, "Dear Sil, in this desolate jungle and in this moonlit night, I like your sweet voice and song very much. But this is not the time and place to sing because in this quiet jungle even when you speak very softly, the sound can be heard from far away."

Sylvia said, "Oh, I will not sing. When we reach London, we shall sing together every day."

Jack said, "Why are you talking of London—we have hardly covered a quarter distance to Fairfeld. London is hundreds of miles away." He took out a cigarette from his pocket but after some hesitation he put it back in his pocket.

Sylvia said, "Why did you not smoke the cigarette?"

Jack replied, "One should not smoke in the jungle. It is night time. The smell of the smoke, mixed with the night air, can be smelled even from far away. The robbers would know of our location and come to rob us. Dear Sil, listening to my talk of caution and hypothetical situations, please do not take me to be a superstitious person. A person should think of all possible consequences. While travelling, one should be very careful and cautious. Foresight and planning can make things right. A man should do whatever he can to plan properly. Rest is in God's Hand. His Will, will be done. The destined fate cannot be postponed or changed. Look at me, what sort of a subject I have started. You yourself are very wise. What I want to say is that you must be tired. If so, let us stop for a while and rest."

Sylvia said, "I am not tired at all. Walking beside you and listening to your voice has made this walk in the night very enjoyable. I can walk hundred miles like this without any trouble at all. I am not as delicate as Miss Brown. I do not like even one thing about her. That's why I became sad whenever I met her. Now it is not even worthwhile to talk about her. She can go where she likes. Just now I feel so very happy walking with you in this moon-lit night that I cannot describe my feelings in words."

She had hardly finished this sentence when they heard the sound of horses galloping from behind. Seeing Jack surprised and worried, Sylvia clasped him tightly. Her whole body touched Jack's body like the way Miss Brown's leg had touched Jack's while they were sitting on the sofa at her house. Seeing Sylvia so frightened, he picked her up in his arms and seated her under the protection of a dense tree. He whispered in her ear very softly, "Do not breathe hard. Who knows whose horses these are that we hear. Please do not speak till they have passed by this side."

For a few minutes, they both sat very quietly under the tree. After sometime Jack looked all around and said to Sylvia with a happy voice, "Sil, God has been merciful. It seems from the sound that the riders on the horses have gone towards the south. However, you keep your gun ready."

Sil said, "My gun is not here. You have only brought one gun with you. You left the other gun at the house."

Jack said, "That is alright—do not worry. That gun was given to me by the contractor. My own precious gun is with me."

He wanted to say some more but they heard voices of men from the north side. Jack's face lost all its colour when he heard the voices. Sylvia started to tremble. They heard one person saying with authority in his voice, "Young men be alert. Act with great care. This young man is very brave and strong. Make sure he does not run away. Immediately hold his arms tightly and surround the girl from all sides by making a circle round her so that we can capture her alive." On hearing this, both Jack and Sylvia got very frightened and clung close to the tree trunk. They looked in the direction of the voices to see if they could recognize anyone of them. Jack took the gun in his hand and they both got ready to face them with courage.

Chapter 18

Look at the irony of fate where the ladder broke
Only a couple of steps were left to reach the destination

Both Sylvia and Jack were very frightened and held on tightly to the trunk of the tree. Due to the constant vigil, they realized that the wicked Lewryk was coming towards the tree on a horse and he was followed by twelve other robbers, all mounted on horses. Jack kept the loaded gun on the ground and opened the gold pouch with both the hands and transferred all the gold sand from the pouch to his coat pockets. After transferring all the gold sand to the pockets, he held the gun in one hand and with the other hand held Sylvia's waist tightly and whispered very quietly in her ear, "Lewryk must have somehow learned of our departure. He has come here to rob us. Just watch my strength and see with what courage and cleverness I face the robbers. Under no circumstances will I allow the robbers to come near us."

Sil wanted to get up and take a closer look but Jack tightened his grip on her waist and kept her down. The horse riders passed in front of the tree and went towards the other side. Jack moved away from the trunk of the tree and whispered in Sylvia's ear, "The wicked Lewryk is searching for you everywhere. It is good that I did not light the cigarette otherwise he would have known our location and stopped near this tree."

Sylvia said, "Oh my God! Was he the wicked Lewryk? Was

he the one telling his comrades to hold me tightly and form a ring around me. May God punish him for his deeds. Jack, can you tell me why Lewryk is after me?"

Jack said, "Have you ever analyzed his talk? Twice or thrice he has tried to take you under his control so that he may take undue advantage of you. His intentions are bad. He is also very greedy. To accumulate money, he has become a dacoit. He constantly watches the travellers coming and going this way. Surely he must have come to know that we are travelling this way with the gold, and he wants to rob us."

Sylvia said, "He cannot suspect me of carrying the gold because there was no discussion of the gold upto the time we were leaving the house. Neither did Mathula know anything about this. How did he then come to know of our plans? Mathula returned me a change of eight shillings from the grocery money and certainly this change is in my pocket. Assuming he gets his information about us from Mathula, he would only know that we have eight shillings. How could he ever know about the gold pieces? Mathula is a very sincere and loyal person. She never talks to such persons. To suspect her of saying anything is a sin."

Sylvia then looked for her locket and it was, as usual, safely hanging around her neck. She wanted to tell Jack all about the locket. Then she remembered the advice given by her late father. She thought to herself, "My respected father asked me to guard this locket with my life and not to open or mention a word about this to anyone till the age of eighteen. I guess my father advised me so, with a long term view, that no greedy or selfish person may take advantage of this and harm me. I wonder if it applies to Jack, my benefactor, a person who protects me and looks after my safety and who is absolutely honest. Jack is kindness personified. He took pity on me and bought me at the auction. He protects me in every way and treats me with great love and care. He has even adopted me as his sister. He is so sincere in what he says that his behaviour towards me is like his real sister. He puts his life in danger to protect me and is doing so even now. He always places my happiness before anything else. I do not think I want to keep anything secret from him." She was convinced that this was the right thing to do. She looked at the handsome face of Jack and looked into his eyes and said, "Dear Jack, I want to tell you a secret."

Jack turned away his face and said in a careless tone, "Dear Sil, please be very quiet. You do not know that at this time I am very concerned about another matter. I do not want to hear about anything now. Once we reach Fairfeld safely, you may tell me all that you want."

On hearing this, Sylvia kept quiet and the golden opportunity was lost.

For sometime, Jack kept thinking about something and then suddenly he roused from his deep thinking and said to Sylvia, "It's a pity that you left the other gun at the house at Lornehope camp. But you should not fear anything. I know wicked Lewryk very well. He is a coward. He is also well aware of my strength. Twice I have put him down and challenged him. I would have finished him the day he met you outside the house and was threatening you in the darkness of the night. But on your request I let him go. Thank God that he passed this side without seeing us and went further away. Hopefully he and his comrades will not come back to this side again. He must have received information about our travelling this way, that's why he was instructing his men to capture you. The travellers coming from Fairfeld have many more valuables as compared to us and he must have gone to rob them. Listen Sil, once you got Lewryk freed from my grip. However, please do not ever ask me again to spare his life. If he crosses my path here I will fight him with all my strength. As long as I am alive I will not let him capture you. God willing, I will kill him without any mercy."

Sylvia did not reply back but clung to Jack's waist and started to breathe deeply with fear. Jack listened very carefully for any sound coming from the jungle. When he did not hear any sound of any kind for fifteen minutes, he said to Sylvia, "How long can we stay here? Our destination is far away and we must reach there as quickly as possible. It is better if we move from here. But walk very softly without making any sound and keep your eyes open. Please cover yourself with this blanket so that you are protected from the cold air of the night."

Sylvia laughed and said, "Walking beside you and listening to your loving concern has made me feel warm all inside me. In fact, I feel hot even in these clothes that I am wearing. However, you may be cold, so why not take the blanket off your shoulders and wrap it around your body to warm yourself."

Jack was too engrossed with the graveness of the situation to understand Sylvia's comments or give them any thought. He simply held Sylvia's hand and urged her to walk. Sylvia placed her beautiful, delicate hands in the smooth and strong hands of Jack and said, "Jack your hand is so long that my hand can be easily hidden inside it."

Jack said, "You are still a child. Your whole body can be easily covered by my chest."

Sylvia responded with a smile, "You mean you are old? If according to you I am a child, how come I am nearly as tall as your shoulders. You have a big built, that's why I look small before you."

Jack said, "Alright. You are not a small child but a grown up woman. However, at this time please walk very quietly. In the night, the sound travels for miles in the jungle. There is a fear of attack from our enemy. For God's sake, let us be quiet. You can discuss everything once we reach Fairfeld. At this time my mind is preoccupied in planning for your safety. I also find your presence to be of solace to my heart. I am sincerely praying to God that in this moonlit night, no evil eyes fall on you."

On hearing this Sylvia smiled and kept quiet. She walked beside Jack at the same fast pace that he was walking. In the silence of the jungle the moonlit night was very refreshing. The sound made by the leaves of the tall trees was sweet and enchanting and sounded like heavenly music for the travellers. Sylvia and Jack, the two travellers, occasionally looked at each other and kept on walking at a steady pace, engrossed in their thoughts of London. After travelling for five or six miles they saw very thick bushes and between the bushes was a very narrow straight path. Nevlin Lane feared that there may be some wild animal hiding in the thick bushes or there may be robbers hiding and awaiting travellers. In addition there was also the possibility of clothes getting torn by the thorns in the bushes. For these reasons he considered it unwise to travel on the narrow path. Sylvia also concurred. They decided to take rest for the night under the tall tree which was near the thick bushes and continue their journey at dawn, thus protecting themselves from all dangers. Once they agreed on this plan, Jack said to Sylvia, "Dear Sil, you rest under the tree in the front without any fear so that you are fresh in the morning for the journey." Sylvia did as instructed by Jack. Jack covered her with his blanket. Twice Sylvia said that she did not need it and that she was not feeling cold. Jack said softly, "Dear Sil, please do not argue and cover yourself with the blanket and think of sleep. I do not want you to catch a cold due to the cold night air. It will be difficult to travel with a cold." Sylvia covered herself, just keeping her face uncovered and went to sleep straightaway.

Sylvia's face was aglow in the moonlit night. It looked as if someone had placed a rose on a slab of ice. Nevlin Lane, feeling satisfied, laid down under the adjacent tree. He was, in his heart, admiring the lovely and glowing face of Sylvia. He said to himself that children go to sleep as soon as they lie down. Look how peacefully Sylvia is sleeping, in this jungle, unaware of anything. After sometime Sylvia turned in her sleep and the blanket came off her body. Nevlin Lane got up from his place and covered her with the blanket again and gently patted her to sleep like a father or elder brother. Thinking that she is asleep, he came back to his place and sat down. He looked at Sylvia's glowing face and promised to himself that soon after reaching London, he shall admit her in one of the finest schools of London and provide her the best of education. This would mean separation from her because men were not allowed in women's schools. His thinking changed again and he thought that it did not matter whether he admitted her in school as a day student or make arrangements for her to stay with some friends. In either case it will mean separation from her. It will be impossible to look after her personally on a continuous basis, the way he was able to do here. The thought of separation from her caused a funny feeling of jealousy in him. He wanted to embrace her but resisted and began to think as to why the thought of separation from her made him so depressed and uneasy. He said to himself that these thoughts were not right because he would like to have the best for his sister. While he was thinking like this, Sylvia laughed in her sleep and called, "Jack, dear Jack." On hearing her voice, Jack came to her side and found her fast asleep and snoring. Jack thought that oh, oh—she loves me truly. Even in her sleep and dreams, she is only thinking of me. Nevlin Lane patted her gently and said in a soft whisper, "My dear Sil, my little one, your love for me is true. Even in your sleep you take my name. How can you think of anyone else? I am the only one close to you and you think of me as your protector, your well wisher and as your brother. Under the circumstances I will not tolerate separating from you ever, even for a moment. Dear Sil, rest assured that without you all the money and wealth is meaningless." He just carried on talking like this. Sylvia was awakened when Nevlin Lane began to pat her and just kept lying. She listened to all that he whispered. Sylvia got up to respond to Jack's loving sentiments.

Before she could speak they heard a movement in the bushes behind them and someone struck a hard blow on Jack's back from behind. Nevlin Lane immediately controlled his gun and just as he was getting ready to confront, a second person struck another blow on Jack's head and a third person tied his arms strongly with a rope. Nevlin Lane turned back to look carefully and saw twelve strong persons on horses behind him. Sylvia wanted to run and get close to Jack, but one of the riders caught her and dragged her by her leg towards the front. Sylvia shouted, "Jack, Jack, Jack!" Her shrieks hurt him like an arrow piercing his heart. Like a mad man, with all his strength, he got up and exerted great effort to break the rope round his arms. When he looked at Sylvia, he saw that she was biting and clawing with her nails, the legs of the robber who was dragging her away. She looked as angry as a lioness trying to protect her cub. She did not allow the robber to go more than ten steps. She attacked him with great force and anger. Shortly afterwards, he saw wicked Lewryk, the dacoit, standing next to Sylvia. He said to his companions in a loud voice, "Do not drag the girl. I shall take charge of her. You go and kill this man named Ian. Do not let him get free. See, he is breaking away the rope in pieces. If he gets free he will create problems."

Nevlin Lane heard this. Within a couple of seconds, one of the dacoits hit him hard on the head. With the trauma of the blow, Nevlin Lane fell to the ground. Sylvia shouted loudly, "Oh, you cruel persons, do not kill my Jack. Set him free now and I will quietly and willingly go with you wherever you want to take me." Lewryk pointed his gun and shouted at Sylvia, "Keep quiet. If you utter another word your life, too, will be in danger."

Sylvia said, "You cruel damned dacoit, go ahead and kill me. I shall be happy to die. But for God's sake, please do not kill Jack." She kept her head at the foot of the horse and pleaded, "Please take all our gold but spare Jack and let him go."

Lewryk said, "Yes we will take all the gold and also kill your Jack. We will also take you to our house. It is best if you keep quiet." He ordered his companions to take all the gold from Jack and shoot him. After giving the order, he dismounted from his horse and picked up Sylvia with both his hands and hauled her in his lap. Sylvia started to shake with fear and fainted. He lifted Sylvia and mounted his horse. He laid Sylvia in front of him on the horse as if she were a dead body. He shouted at his comrades in a loud voice, "I have got the girl now, let's all go."

Nevlin Lane heard all this talk of Lewryk with his companions and the conversation between Sylvia and Lewryk. He was full of anger and tried with all his strength to free himself from the rope. As dacoits were very loyal to their leader, they all mounted their horses and followed their leader as per his instructions, leaving Jack tied up in ropes and without killing him. Only the dacoit, Tommy, stayed behind as per his leader's instructions and sat on the chest of Nevlin Lane with the intention of robbing him of all the gold. To save the trouble of emptying out all Nevlin Lane's pockets, he took his coat and wore it himself and threw his own coat on Nevlin Lane. Nevlin Lane so far was lying motionless. But when he heard Lewryk shouting for his companions to follow him and saw Lewryk mounting his horse with Sylvia in his lap and running away, he shook himself violently. The rope broke in pieces and the dacoit Tommy fell to the ground. Nevlin Lane picked up his gun and shot Tommy dead. At the sound of the shot, Sylvia at once came to her senses and thought that Tommy had shot Jack. At this thought she fainted again. The wicked Lewryk saw Tommy falling to the ground. He aimed at Nevlin Lane while sitting on the horse and fired the gun. Due to the strong wind, the bullet deflected downward and by the Grace of God, bruised Nevlin Lane near the ankle. Nevlin Lane experienced intense pain and leaned on the trunk of the tree. He began to shout loudly, "Dear Sylvia, my dear Sylvia!" Hearing Jack call her name, Sylvia once again became conscious and wanted to jump from the horse and run towards Jack, but Lewryk took his foot out of the stirrup and held Sylvia tightly by his knee and foot. To frighten Sylvia, he shot the last bullet from his double barrelled gun and galloped away. After a few seconds, Sylvia could not hear Jack's voice. She listened hard but could hear nothing and assumed that Tommy had killed Jack. She began to cry and screamed at the top of her voice, "Jack, oh Jack, oh Jack." The whole jungle began to echo with her cries. Nevlin Lane also heard her voice and he became exceedingly restless. To save Sylvia from Lewryk, he summoned all his strength and took a few steps forward, but due to the intense pain, he lost his balance and fell to the ground and fainted.

Chapter 19

Do not know how you passed the night of separation
Heart suffered great pain whenever it remembered you

Lord Lorimor and his very dear friend Lord Gilmour, left Fairfeld at two o'clock in the morning for Lornehope Camp with their twelve strong riders. They reached that spot in the jungle at the very same time when the dacoit Lewryk was running away on the horse towards Fairfeld, holding Sylvia tightly with his knee. His comrades were following right behind him and Sylvia was crying loudly and shouting, "Oh Jack, oh Jack!" Her shouts were heard by Lord Lorimor and he galloped on his horse, in the direction from where the sound of the woman's cry was coming. When Lewryk saw someone galloping at a very fast pace towards him, he turned his horse around and began galloping towards Lornehope Camp. Lord Lorimor also turned his horse in the same direction and followed him with full speed. When Lord Gilmour saw his friend galloping in another direction, he also followed him with his twelve companions and overtook the other dacoits who were with Lewryk. A fierce gun battle ensued between these two groups. While Lord Gilmour and his friends were fighting the other dacoits, Lord Lorimor took an aim at Lewryk and fired. The bullet hit Lewryk and he fell off the horse. Sylvia also fell off the horse. When Lord Lorimor saw her, he stopped his horse and got down. He picked up Sylvia in his arms and climbed back on his horse and galloped away from the scene without looking to see whether the dacoit Lewryk was alive or dead. After sometime Lord Lorimor looked at the girl. He had laid Sylvia on the horse in front of him and was holding her head with his left hand and supporting her legs with his right leg. He saw that Sylvia was crying constantly and breathing deeply. Lord Lorimor stopped the horse and very gently helped Sylvia to get down and laid her down under a tree. He said, "Please have no anxiety. I will soon take you to a safe place."

On hearing this Sylvia could not help saying:

"I have just barely got out alive from one danger
Oh my God, in what new trouble am I now!"

When Lord Lorimor heard the very appropriate words said in a very sweet voice, he was overcome with pity and concern for the girl. When he looked at her face, it was white like the moonlight. Involuntarily, he clasped her hand and patted it and asked her to open her eyes. She appeared to be unconscious. He shouted in panic, "Lord Gilmour, Lord Gilmour." He saw Lord Gilmour coming along with his companions. Lord Lorimor shouted again. Lord Gilmour came closer and dismounted from his horse. He saw a young beautiful girl lying on the ground near Lord Lorimor's knees. He smiled and asked Lord Lorimor as to how, in this dense jungle, he found this very beautiful girl. In response, Lord Lorimor addressed his friend and all the other companions, "Gentlemen, if any one of you have some water with you, please let me have it so that we may pour it in her mouth. I have rescued this girl from the clutches of a dacoit. Splashing water on her face and pouring it in her mouth may help revive her."

On hearing this all the riders dismounted from their horses. One of them took out a bottle of water and poured some water in a glass and gave it to Lord Lorimor. He placed the head of the girl on his thighs and gently splashed her face and forehead with water. This did not revive her but she breathed a little easier. Her pulse got better and this indicated that she was alive. It was agreed that the best thing would be to make a stretcher and carry the girl to the hospital in Lornehope Camp. The stretcher would protect her from the jolts of travelling and also get her some fresh jungle air. One of the riders said that approximately three miles from there a very experienced doctor from London had established a camp. He had met him when he was travelling by train to his home in London and the doctor was on his way here to establish this camp. He suggested that they should get the girl treated by this doctor. Both Lord Lorimor and Lord Gilmour accepted the offer. Lord Gilmour ordered his young and strong men to act accordingly. Six of his loyal riders, who were in his employment for a long time, went in the jungle and cut some tree branches. They brought these to where everyone was gathered. They joined togeher the tree logs and branches with the reins of the horses to make a strong, sling type stretcher. They took out the blankets from underneath the saddles and made a soft and comfortable bed. Three strong riders gently lifted Sylvia and very carefully laid her on the stretcher. Four strong riders lifted the stretcher by the side poles and placed them on their shoulders and started to walk towards Lornehope Camp. All the riders were familiar with the short route and took turns in carrying the stretcher. They all slowly walked towards Lornehope Camp.

Lord Lorimor said to his friend Lord Gilmour, "I aimed my gun at the dacoit who was carrying this girl away and fired the shot. He fell off the horse from the shock of the shot. I am confident of my aim and I am sure that dacoit is no longer alive. Tell me how your encounter was with the other dacoits? With God's Grace I hope none of our people were hurt."

Lord Gilmour said, "When we saw you suddenly racing away in one direction, we all followed you with a view to provide you protection. However, we were confronted by a group of dacoits who blocked our path. Our companions fought with great courage and soon overpowered them. Since the dacoits were not organized, five of their men were killed right there. Another four of them were badly wounded and fell to the ground, and two of them abandoned their horses and hid in the bushes. All their horses were seen running away without control, towards Lornehope Camp. We thought it was a waste of time to search for the two dacoits who had run away. We were more concerned about your safety. I heard you shouting my name and we all raced and came here."

One of the two dacoits who ran away, came to the location where his leader Lewryk was lying unconscious on the ground after he was wounded by Lord Lorimor. The bullet had hit him on his thigh. His companion lifted him and took him to a nearby place. After a few days of nursing the wound with medicines and bandages, Lewryk was well enough to return to his house.

After learning the details of the encounter from his friend Lord Gilmour, Lord Lorimor was satisfied that none of his friend's companions were hurt. He thanked the Almighty God. He got down from his horse and started walking on foot by the side of the stretcher. He constantly wiped Sylvia's sad face with a wet handkerchief and checked her pulse. They had travelled approximately one mile when Sylvia faintly said, "Oh." The carriers immediately rested the stretcher on the ground. Sylvia sat up and said in very clear words, "Jack, my brother, where are you?"

Lord Lorimor asked, "Did you have a brother named Jack with you? Which place did you leave him?"

Sylvia pointed towards Fairfeld and started to cry.

Lord Lorimor asked, "Do you mean that your brother is in that part of the jungle?"

Sylvia said, "Yes, my brother is in the forest over there. Even if you people are dacoits, please take pity on me and earn the eternal gratitude of a helpless, orphaned girl by taking me to my brother. Or bring him here so that I may see his face and peacefully part with my life at his feet."

Lord Lorimor said, "We are not dacoits. I live in London and come from a highly respected family. The title of Lord was bestowed on us. Some dacoit was running away with you. I heard your cries and shouting. I chased that dacoit, killed him with my shot and rescued you. With the help of my companions we have safely brought you here. Please calm down and do not be afraid. You are very sick and upset right now. You are under my protection and no one can harm you any more. We were taking you to the hospital for medical attention and treatment. As long as you do not recover your full health, I will constantly remain with you. The work for which I was going can be postponed until such time that you recover your health. It is the tradition in my family that any work that we undertake, we stay with it till it is completed. Right now I will send two of my brave riders to look for your brother. Can you please tell us how he was dressed, and how he looked?"

Sylvia carefully analyzed the civilized and kind words of Lord Lorimor. She quietly placed her hand in his hand and looked at him with grateful eyes. After a few minutes she calmed down and said, "My brother is called Jack and he was wearing a coat like that of the workers here. He was fighting the dacoits to save me. Who knows what happened to him. Please bring him over here. For this kind deed the Almighty God will reward you."

Lord Lorimor called two of the riders and said, "If you can bring here the person named Jack, brother of this good hearted lady, I will reward you. I am sure you will find Jack near the place where you fought the other dacoits and killed them. Please hurry. We shall stay here till your return. The girl has now regained consciousness."

The two riders left immediately in the direction of Fairfeld. They searched all around and in the bushes that were on the sides. They kept their eyes on the surrounding areas and reached the spot where Nevlin Lane had shot down Tommy, the dacoit. The two riders looked at the dead body and assumed it was Jack. They turned over the body and searched the pockets of the coat. They found some bullets, a knife, a silver box of cigarettes along with matches. The coat appeared to be like that of a worker. After looking at everything the two riders were sure that this dead person was Jack and the dacoits must have shot him. They thought that carrying the dead body back would be time consuming and of no use at all. They decided to carry the coat back and thought that once the girl saw the coat she would recognize it and would be convinced of her brother having been killed in the fight with the dacoits. They removed the coat and the belt from the dead body and took these back to convince the girl of Jack's death.

What an irony and pity that Nevlin Lane was lying unconscious only a few feet from the place where they found the dead body of the dacoit. Neither of the two riders looked in his direction. If they had spotted and examined him, they would have realized that he was still alive. After reviving him, they could have found the truth about the dead body of the dacoit and his exchanging the coat with Nevlin Lane. But the riders assumed the dead body to be that of Jack and did not look any further. If they had looked around carefully, the whole truth would have been known. This would have avoided the great trouble that Sylvia would have to bear on recognizing the coat. But such is life and it is truly said:

> Whatever happens is as per God's Will
> We are only His agent as the boat in the hands of its rower.

Since such was to be the destiny, both the riders mistook the dead dacoit to be Jack. They returned with Jack's coat as a proof of his death. They saw the girl lying with her eyes closed and Lord Lorimor sitting by the side of her head. They gave the coat to Lord Lorimor and said, "We found Jack to be dead. He was shot by a bullet. We have brought his coat and belt as proof."

Lord Lorimor motioned to the two riders to be quiet by putting his finger on his lips. But it was no use. Sylvia had heard the two riders and the words sunk in her heart. She got up slightly and gave a loud shriek and fainted in the lap of Lord Lorimor.

Chapter 20

O Guru of glass maker, I pose you one question
Repairing a broken heart is indeed a unique art

Why are you worried to mend a broken heart
Remain within the mould of contentment, this is the real art.

When the riders returned back, Sylvia was conscious. She was lifted from the stretcher and gently placed on the soft grass to get some fresh air. Though her eyes were closed, she was conscious. When she heard from the riders the news about Jack's death and their bringing his coat and belt as a proof, she fainted again. When Lord Lorimor saw her in a state of deep unconsciousness, he thought he had lost her forever. However, as long as a person is breathing, there is always hope of recovery. With the help of Lord Gilmour, he laid her back on the stretcher. The riders picked up the stretcher and started walking towards the hospital.

When they had covered some distance, they met another traveller. He recognized Lord Gilmour and greeted him. He saw that everyone was walking on foot by the side of the stretcher and not riding their horses. He enquired from Lord Gilmour as to what had happened. Lord Gilmour told him the whole story about Sylvia's capture by the dacoits, their group's fight with these dacoits, the rescue of Sylvia from those dacoits, the presumed killing of Sylvia's brother Jack by the dacoits and Sylvia's fainting on receiving this news. He further mentioned that they were taking

Sylvia to the hospital at Lornehope Camp for treatment. On hearing this, the traveller said, "I go to Lornehope Camp every week from Fairfeld in connection with my business. I know very well that six days back a doctor from London has come here with all equipment and staff. He has established a camp here. He does not work at Lornehope camp but has his clinic about two furlongs from here by the roadside. He lives at this camp and also sees the patients and provides treatment at this clinic." Lord Lorimor asked him the directions to the doctor's camp and on his request the traveller joined them to show the way. They took the stretcher to the doctor's camp and Lord Lorimor met the doctor. He requested him to examine the patient.

The doctor was a resident of London. On a request from King of Austria, he had come to Lornehope camp to provide medical treatment to the people of this place. He was a very religious and pious person. He was an excellent doctor, who was highly experienced in his profession. He warmly greeted Lord Lorimor and Lord Gilmour. He carried the sick patient very carefully inside the camp. He laid her on a very comfortable, soft bed. After examining her, he took out a special medicine from his box to revive her and gave her a dose of the same. After fifteen minutes, the girl regained consciousness and shouted, "Oh Jack, Oh Jack, Jack my brother," and fainted again.

From Lord Lorimor's description, the doctor knew of the events that had led to the death of this girl's brother. When she regained consciousness, she shouted his name and fainted. The doctor gave her the same medicine again. From her pulse and general condition, he diagnosed that she was in a state of severe shock. He said to Lord Lorimor, "The patient will recover her health with my medicines. But she will need a full-time attendant to look after her. We should search for one soon." The wife of the doctor was also a very pious and kind-hearted woman. She returned from her morning walk just as the doctor was telling Lord Lorimor about finding a full time female attendant for the sick patient.

The doctor's wife inquired as to what had happened and learned that an orphaned, helpless girl, with no one to support her, had been brought there for treatment. The cause of her unconsciousness was her being captured by dacoits and her brother killed by those dacoits. On hearing all the details from Lord Lorimor, the wife of the doctor began to cry. In between sobs she said, "This girl deserves all our sympathy and kindness. Her innocent sweet looking face has moved me beyond words and I will personally attend to her with all my heart and ability. I shall attend to her needs day and night as I would for my own daughter." She sat down near the girl's head. With loving hands she started patting the girl's forehead. The doctor got busy in preparing medicines for the girl.

Lord Lorimor and Lord Gilmour along with their companions, established their camp just a few steps from the doctor's camp and ate the meals that they had brought with them. They spread their bedding on the floor and went to sleep. When they got up the next day, they met the doctor and enquired about the girl's condition. The doctor said, "She is going to be alright. She has regained consciousness but her mind is still not fully functional. All night she was very restless thinking of her brother, Jack. She kept calling her brother, in such a sorrowful tone, that my wife was deeply moved. My wife gave her the medicines all night and kept a constant vigil. Except for my wife she does not recognize anyone else and does not have strength to meet anyone."

The treatment of the patient went on for a week. In the meantime, both Lord Lorimor and Lord Gilmour went to Lornehope Camp every day. From morning till night, they visited workers and their homes. They tried to meet all the men and women and inquired about a person named Nevlin Lane. At the same time they also searched for a kind and experienced nurse to look after the girl. At every house they went to look for Nevlin Lane, the occupants expressed ignorance. Frustrated and dejected, they came back every evening and told the doctor about their fruitless search.

On the eighth day, the doctor said to Lord Lorimor, "The condition of the patient is much better now and her mind also is back to normal. Though she has not disclosed her past either to my wife or myself, we both feel that she is well educated and comes from a very civilized family. If you wish to speak with her, you can go and see her now."

Lord Lorimor went inside the camp. He saw the patient sitting on an easy chair resting against a cushion. There were dark shadows under her eyes, the cheeks were pressed in and her hands, feet and body looked pale and thin. She was the same Sylvia, who a week before, had big shiny eyes full of life and joy. Her cheeks had bloomed like roses and her hands, feet and body had looked healthy and strong. Today she was reduced to a thin and weak person grieving at the loss of her brother. Lord Lorimor could hardly recognize her and was sorry to see her in this state. He sat down beside the girl and asked in a very sympathetic and concerned tone as to how she was feeling. The patient took his hand and kissed it and tears came to her eyes.

Lord Lorimor said, "Please do not worry. The medicines have been effective and in a few days you will gain strength."

Sylvia said, "Do I really look better now? Yes I also think so. I had no hope left that I shall live. But your kindness and the excellent care and attention of the doctor and his wife have given me a new life. I have neither enough strength nor adequate words to express my gratitude to you for all you have done for me."

Lord Lorimor replied, "It is the duty of every human being to help his fellow beings in the time of their need. A person attains spiritual upliftment by good deeds. Otherwise people grow like wild flowers and grass that are simply destroyed and blown away by the wind. The person who does good and kind deeds, without expectation of any reward, is dear to God and rises spiritually. Eventually such a person attains spiritual peace. Our religious books teach the same thing. If you require any thing or if you have a relative where you would like to go for comfort and emotional support, please let me know. I will see that your wish is fulfilled. I am at your service."

Sylvia said, "Sir, I am an orphaned, helpless girl. My name is Sylvia Bond. There is no one left in this world now who is interested in my welfare. You have seen with your own eyes the trouble that I have faced and the condition that I am in at present.

I was captured by the dacoits. God sent a kind hearted and compassionate man like you to rescue me. You saved me from their cruelty with great bravery and courage, risking your own life. If all the hair on my body could speak like my tongue, even then I cannot thank you enough for what you have done."

Lord Lorimor interjected and said, "At this time you should not be thinking and speaking like this. You should completely forget what happened. Otherwise your recovery will be slow and the weakness will persist. I would like to see you get well and gain your strength soon."

Sylvia looked at Lord Lorimor with grateful eyes and said in a sweet and respectful tone, "Sir, you are indeed a very kind and compassionate person who believes in doing his duty. I have only one request and I will be grateful if you agree to it. Please let me have the coat and other belongings that your riders brought from the body of my dead brother, Jack."

Lord Lorimor replied in a very sympathetic tone, "I have given my word to fulfil your wish and I always keep my promise. I will certainly give you Jack's coat and other belongings. However, I am afraid it will refresh your pain and agony and you may become more sick than what you are now. It is not prudent to ask for something which will not serve any useful purpose."

Sylvia pleaded, "My dear Sir, it will not prove to be a useless emotional request, on the contrary it will be the means for my salvation. Looking at the things of my brother will give me peace. These things can become the reason for my living."

On hearing this, tears came to Lord Lorimor's eyes. He came out and went to his camp and took out the coat and other belongings of Jack from his suitcase. He gave them to Sylvia and stood outside beside the door.

With trembling hands, Sylvia picked up the coat and the belt and touched them with her eyes. She kissed them several times and cried to her heart's content. She searched the coat pockets and found Jack's pipe that he used to smoke. She recognized it at once. She also found two bullets for the gun and some ammunition and a knife. It was the same knife that Jack used for cleaning up meat at their house in Lornehope Camp. Once, while working in the kitchen, Sylvia had cut her finger with this same knife. On recognizing everything, Sylvia cried without control and began to shriek and shout, "Oh my Jack, my beloved Jack, oh Jack!"

On hearing Sylvia sob and shout, Lord Lorimor entered her camp and said in a very sad tone, "I should not have given you Jack's clothes. I unnecessarily gave you cause to refresh your grief and pain." He forcibly picked up the knife, the pipe, the bullets, the clothes etc. which were lying in Sylvia's lap and began to walk outside the camp. Sylvia shouted, "No! Please no. Please kind Sir, do not separate these things from me. These very things would provide me peace. I shall stop shouting and crying now and would read the last rites as per our religious book. I ask for peace for Jack's departed soul. Jack has gone to heaven. Oh, what a pity you did not see my Jack. He was very handsome, very brave and kind, had an excellent character and was very experienced. He deserved to be a lord. I have not come across any other man to match his high qualities of complete honesty and pure love. He looked after me with great love and affection. He endangered his life in protecting me. He faced the problems of the world calmly and with patience. For some reason he bid goodbye to his own profession and bravely took up the work of digging. He was constantly entertaining me. All his memories are engraved in my heart. I wish he was alive and a worthless person like me was killed. It would have been better if that dacoit had killed both of us, then we would have lived together in heaven and would have been grateful to our killer. Oh, it's my luck that he left me without any friend or support to cry for the rest of my life."

She continued, "He died alone. For the last one week, I see Jack everyday in my dreams. I see him sitting by my bedside and hear his sweet voice. I wake up and cry and shout, 'Jack, Jack'. I extend my hands to greet him but he disappears. Oh my, what shall I do now? How can I console myself? How can I bear the burdens of life without my Jack? How can I ever be happy in his absence? Oh Jack, how shall I ever forget your great honesty and love? If I had your body, I would have found peace by committing suicide beside you. How can I live now?"

Lord Lorimor could not bear this. Tears came to his eyes. He sat down beside Sylvia and said, "Dear sister, this world is transient. Everyone has to depart from this mortal, transitory world some day and face God. Death is by God's order and cannot be changed even by the most powerful emperor. Under these circumstances, everyone should accept and act as per the laws of nature. Please control yourself. Think positively about your future life. Prepare yourself to face the troubles and problems with courage and patience. Follow the path of kindness and compassion and God will be pleased. Try and leave a good name for yourself in this world. There is no better way to face God than following this path. I wish I had a sister from whom I could get the same kind of true love that you had for your brother, Jack. Such a person who has true love, is rare in this world. The type of kind and brave person, as your brother was, will be difficult to find. Do not think you are alone in grieving for him. I am sure that anyone who came in his contact and knew of his kindness and honesty, will also be very sorry to see him go. Please tell me who were his friends and other acquaintances in Lornehope Camp. Tell me how he looked and what he might have said to you about his past life and whether he was also known by any other name than Jack."

Sylvia said, "In Lornehope Camp there was no one else of the same calibre and intelligence. He did not have any relatives or friends living here. Though he used to meet everyone and assisted them in solving their problems, he never shared his thoughts with anyone else. He would readily and gladly give his things to others but would not take anyone's obligation. The persons in the office of Mr. McGregor, the contractor, used to call him Ian." She further said with a shyness in her tone that one or two persons used to call him Iain Herringdon. She began to cry again.

After listening to all this description and talk, Lord Lorimor assumed that Nevlin Lane had not come there. Because if he had come, he would have definitely met Sylvia. As the saying goes:

People of similar nature keep company
Birds of same feather flock together.

He thought that Jack and Sylvia were two civilized persons living in Lornehope Camp. If Nevlin Lane had come here, he would certainly have met these two persons and shared a few things of his past with them. They had the same kindly disposition and came from the same country. He thought he could not find anyone else here who would be more knowledgeable about the happenings in Lornehope Camp than Sylvia. Under these circumstances it was meaningless to search for Nevlin Lane there and it would be a waste of his precious time.

If Lord Lorimor had analyzed and thought calmly, he would have reached the conclusion that the qualities that Sylvia described in Jack and for whom she was grieving, were a clear indication that Jack was in fact the same Nevlin Lane in whose search he left his home. However, it is true, as the experienced and learned people have said that no one finds or gets anything in this world before the time set by God. Nothing moves without His command.

Lord Lorimor used to analyze everything in a rational manner and connected various events in a logical sequence. However, in this situation, he could not connect Jack's name to Nevlin Lane, because he was well aware that Nevlin Lane had only one brother, Jordan Lane, and no sister. Thus it never occurred to him that Jack and Nevlin Lane could be the same person. Moreover, Sylvia's built and features bore no resemblance at all to Jordan Lane. For this reason he considered it a waste of time to search for him further at Lornehope Camp. He looked at Sylvia and wanted to ask her a few more questions but realized that she had fainted. He got worried and called the doctor who rushed from his room and came where Sylvia was lying. He examined her and said, "She has fainted due to extreme grief. I shall give her a dose of my special medicine and that will revive her. However, it is important that she be moved away from Lornehope Camp as soon as possible because here she cannot get satisfactory rest and peace of mind. A change of climate will be good for her health. This place will constantly remind her of her brother. She should be taken to a cheerful city as soon as possible. Both my wife and myself have come to regard her as our own daughter. But we are helpless. Staying here will not be in her best interests and all our medicines and care will not help."

Lord Lorimor had developed a very special bond with Sylvia and was prepared to help her with all the resources at his disposal. With a little hesitation in his tone, he said to the doctor, "I had come from London in search of a person. And at this time I have a very important business to attend to. However, I consider it my duty to help Sylvia. The first priority is to find a suitable and qualified nurse to look after Sylvia and make arrangements for her comfort. After this is completed I will refocus my attention on my work. I shall take her to different cities and places to give her a change of climate."

The doctor expressed his great appreciation for Lord Lorimor's kindness and compassion. He said, "You are indeed a very kind person. First of all find a nurse to look after the patient."

Lord Lorimor said, "I will spend the whole day tomorrow in search of a suitable nurse."

Sylvia had recovered from her state of unconsciousness and listened to all the conversation that the doctor had with Lord Lorimor. After the evening dinner, Sylvia went to sleep. She had a bad dream and started to sob and woke up. She looked all around her and saw a middle aged woman sitting near the headboard of her bed. She was looking at Sylvia with loving and caring eyes. When she saw Sylvia getting up, she placed Sylvia's head in her lap and started to stroke her head gently. She said in a sympathetic voice, "Dear girl, there is no cause for fear at this place. Sometimes, if the hand rests on the chest during sleep, it triggers a bad dream. The doctor's wife instructed me to look after you. As per her orders I am sitting near your bed. I do not know why, but ever since you have come to this camp, I have felt attracted to you and have developed love for you in my heart. I feel like serving you day and night, all the twenty four hours of the day, with all my strength and attention." On hearing this Sylvia opened her eyes fully and looked more carefully at the person. She found a beautiful woman, lovingly stroking her head and looking at her fondly. Sylvia noticed that this woman was beautiful even though she appeared to be twice her own age. She seemed to be love personified. Sylvia felt comforted by her presence and asked in a calm voice, "What is your name?"

The woman hesitated a bit and her face looked pale but after a few moments she said, "My name is Mercie Fairflex."

Sylvia said, "Oh, you have a beautiful name. Are you a resident of Lornehope Camp or have you come from another city?"

Mercie Fairflex said, "The doctor brought me with him from London to serve his wife. Both the doctor and his wife are very happy with me. The doctor's wife may keep me in her service on a permanent basis or recommend me to one of their friends. My acquaintances in London spoke very highly of the doctor and his excellent qualities. That is why I accepted his offer to come here to serve his wife during the journey from London to this place. Now I will do whatever they wish me to do. Let us see where my luck tàkes me. Only God knows what is in store for us in the future, but my present condition is not good." When she finished saying this, tears came to her eyes and she lowered her head.

Sylvia said, "The doctor and his wife are indeed very pious and kind hearted persons. They provided accommodation to me, a helpless poor girl, in their special camp. They have looked after me with remarkable attention and care giving me the right medicines. I have no words to express my gratitude to them for all their kindness and compassion. I am very sorry that I asked you unnecessary questions and made you sad."

Merci Fairflex said, "Dear sister, this world is full of kind and selfless people. There are several men and women who help the helpless."

On hearing this Sylvia thought of the dacoit Lewryk and said, "This world also has many greedy, wicked and selfish people who destroy others for their own gain."

Merci Fairflex replied, "Yes there are lots of bad people also. God watches both good and bad persons and rewards or punishes them accordingly."

Sylvia asked, "Would you like to live in Lornehope Camp? From the way you talk you seem to be a well educated, civilized and well meaning woman. This jungle is not the right place for a person like you."

Merci Fairflex said, "When you are desperate and have no other alternative, you go wherever you find employment. God has made humans, who by nature seek pleasure and desire comfort and luxury. However, often the mistake that people make is to look for pleasure in worldly things which are transient and provide only physical pleasure. That's why instead of finding pleasure they become miserable. Anyway, I do not wish to engage you in this discussion. You are very weak and this will make your condition worse. If Dr. Langley or his wife happen to come here and find me having a discussion with you, they will be angry."

She straightened the sheets on the bed and asked Sylvia to take rest.

Sylvia said, with tears in eyes, "I feel like talking to you. When I close my eyes, the face of the kind person who is gone forever, comes before my eyes."

Merci Fairflex wiped Sylvia's tears with her handkerchief and said in a sympathetic voice, "Dear sister, our religious books instruct mankind to face the problems of the world with patience and courage. Faith and effort are the two most important things which should be practised constantly. Often I too get frightened in dreams. The faces of near and dear ones come before my eyes and in my thoughts. I have to make a constant effort and prayer to get rid of this. The sadness of being separated from my loved ones persists. The sayings of wise men and religious books cannot be wrong. I console myself by saying that I can have peace by praying to God rather than by artificial worldly things."

Sylvia felt very comforted by the wise and religious talk of Merci Fairflex. She closed her eyes and went to sleep. She slept soundly for three hours. When she woke up she found Merci Fairflex sitting by her bedside and looking after her.

Sylvia said, "Oh, you are still sitting by my side."

Merci Fairflex said, "Did you think that I will go and leave you alone? I love you from my heart and feel like keeping myself busy in serving you. If you wish to keep me with you, please let me know. I will go and tell Mrs. Langley that I do not want to return to London. I only want to serve patients. I will go wherever you go."

Sylvia said, "Certainly, you can tell Mrs. Langley. I would like you to be with me."

Merci Fairflex said, "I thank you from the bottom of my heart for your confidence in me. As promised, I will serve you faithfully. Now you try and get some more sleep."

Sylvia went to sleep again. She woke up several times in between. When she finally woke up in the morning, she found Merci Fairflex sitting by her side. Sylvia developed a special interest in the pale face and sad tone of Merci Fairflex's voice. Several times she thought of asking her the cause of her sadness but for some reason she kept quiet.

When a person meets another person in trouble, one forgets one's own problems and begins to show sympathy for the other person. Sylvia felt her own sadness and troubles diminish by looking at the sadness and pale face of Merci Fairflex. Her pulse became stable and she became better. For Sylvia, the company of Merci Fairflex proved more soothing and beneficial than any of the medicines.

Next morning, when Lord Lorimor came to see Sylvia, he found a woman in a black dress sitting beside her. He looked at her carefully. He wondered how Dr. Langley managed to find such a gentle and beautiful woman as a nurse. When Lord Lorimor's eyes met hers, she got up from the chair to greet him and out of respect bowed her head a little. In a very soft voice, she said, "Thank God that the condition of the patient is much better this morning. Last night Dr. Langley and his wife asked me to look after her. I am a qualified nurse from a London hospital and have considerable experience in nursing."

After saying this, she went out of the camp. After she left, Lord Lorimor shook Sylvia's hand and sat down on the chair beside her bed. He asked Sylvia: "Did you find a nurse? Is it true that you are feeling much better today?"

Sylvia said, "Yes Sir, My condition is much better today."

Lord Lorimor said, "Can I assume that you have the strength to answer my questions after considering all the implications?"

Sylvia hesitated a little and said, "Do I have to listen to some bad news? Please tell me, I will be able to bear it."

Lord Lorimor said in a sympathetic voice, "No, no. There is no bad news to upset you. On the contrary, I want to consult you on an important matter. Please feel free to give me your honest advice. Dr. Langley feels that a change of climate will be very beneficial for you. He has suggested that you leave this place as soon as possible."

Sylvia said, "The advice of the doctor is very good. I happily accept his recommendation."

Lord Lorimor said, "I have packed everything for the journey. I have purchased all the things for your comfort. Do you have any objection in travelling with me?"

On hearing this Sylvia lowered her head and became silent.

When Lord Lorimor saw Sylvia quiet and in deep thought, he said in a sympathetic voice, "Miss Sylvia, I do not wish to burden you with too many questions on this subject. The decision is entirely yours. Whatever we decide is to be with your full consent and should make you happy. If you feel like staying here, it is alright. Dr. Langley and his wife will look after all your needs. If you do not wish to stay here and hesitate to come with me, then you can stay at Lornehope Camp. I can provide everything for your comfort and support on a permanent basis. Let me know frankly, which one of these three alternatives, will make you happy. I left my home for a very important work and I have to travel to several cities to complete it."

Sylvia said, "I liked living at Lornehope Camp when Jack was there. Now I do not even want to look in that direction. I am very grateful to the doctor and his wife for their loving care and excellent hospitality. But I do not think I will find peace here. I will feel better in some cheerful place away from here."

Lord Lorimor said, "In these circumstances it is best if you come along with me. I will search for a good, gentle nurse at the next city. I will look after you and your safety with sincerity and with all the resources at my disposal. I will see to it that you have no problems or discomfort in travelling."

On hearing this, Sylvia held Lord Lorimor's hand and said with shyness in her eyes, "Why are you willing to take so much trouble and spend so much money for a helpless, useless girl like me?"

Lord Lorimor said, "I think you are very weak and cannot withstand any discomfort or hassles. If you know the address of any of your relatives, please tell me to correspond with them. I will go and inform him of your condition. If you wish to go to your relatives, I will personally escort you to their place."

Sylvia heaved a sigh and said, "Except for Jack, I had no one else in this world who is interested in my welfare and now . . ."

Lord Lorimor cut her sentence short and said, "Often people are not aware of their close relatives and family friends. Once you reach London, you may find out that you are not as much alone as you think you are at this time."

Sylvia said, "May be there is someone. However, to the best of my knowledge there is absolutely no one in London or anywhere else in this world who is my friend or well wisher."

Sylvia had hardly finished this sentence when Dr. Langley and his wife came there. Lord Lorimor got up from the chair to greet them and after shaking hands with them, said, "I have decided, after discussions with the patient, that we should leave this place for a change of climate and the patient's health. Please advise me when you consider it best for us to leave."

Dr. Langley said, "I think it will be alright for you to leave in one or two days."

After saying this the doctor came outside and Lord Lorimor followed him. Lord Lorimor said to the doctor, "In spite of very extensive search I have not been able to find any suitable woman here who can look after the patient. I need someone gentle and sympathetic who can look after her during the journey."

Dr. Langley said, "I think that for Sylvia's nursing, we need a mature woman. She should not be too young nor too old. The elderly women sometimes have difficulty in tending to the needs of a patient even though they can look after house pets."

Lord Lorimor said, "What you are saying is absolutely correct. However, such a mature and middle aged woman is impossible to find here."

The doctor just happened to look up and saw Merci Fairflex standing outside the camp with some knitting in her hands. The doctor said in a happy tone, "Look, that woman standing by the bamboo curtain, outside the camp, is just the right person to care for Sylvia, provided she accepts the job."

Lord Lorimor turned his head and saw the pale and sad face of Merci Fairflex.

Lord Lorimor said, "Doctor, please tell me, from where has this woman come. When I went to see Sylvia this morning she was sitting by her side."

Dr. Langley said, "I brought her with me from London as a companion for my wife. I do not know much about her past. However, I do know that she was a nurse at a London hospital. Several lady doctors at the hospital recommended her as efficient and conscientious. Whatever work is assigned to her she completes with diligence. I have found her to be kind and gentle. She is a good nurse who knows her work well."

On hearing this, Lord Lorimor thought carefully for a while and said, "What I do not understand is, why she would agree to leave a lively city like London and accept the job of roaming in foreign countries, and come to a desolate jungle like this. There is certainly some mystery behind all this."

Dr. Langley said, "I know that she is a widow and a very decent person. During the journey she looked after my wife and made her very comfortable. I can only say that she will be an excellent person to look after Sylvia. You will not find a more sincere and gentle woman."

Merci Fairflex could hear all this conversation while standing near the bamboo curtain. When the doctor finished this conversation she blushed and went inside the camp.

Lord Lorimor said, "I very much like the way this woman conducts herself and also her civilized manner of speaking. I would like to hire her as a nurse to look after the patient. I shall appreciate if you can please get her consent."

The doctor called Merci Fairflex by name. She came out of the camp and bowed her head slightly.

Dr. Langley said, "Listen Merci Fairflex, Lord Lorimor and myself were just now discussing about you."

Merci Fairflex straightened herself and said, "I overheard your conversation while I was knitting and standing near the curtain."

Dr. Langley said, "I do not want to part with you. Nor do I want to ask you to accept a job which involves travelling. However, I am honestly very concerned about the health of Sylvia. If you can look after her, it will be a great relief to me and make me happy. However, I do not want to force you into accepting this position."

In response, Merci Fairflex said in a low voice, "I shall be very happy to go with Sylvia Bond. I will serve her with all my heart and to the best of my ability until such time that she wants to keep me in her service. I do not know why, so suddenly, I have developed such sympathy and love for her." She thanked Dr. Langley for his kindness and consideration and went inside the camp.

Chapter 21

Love is fun when both are equally restless
The intensity of fire is equally intense on both sides

The shot fired by Lewryk had bruised Nevlin Lane in the leg, while Nevlin Lane's shot had killed the dacoit Tom. Nevlin Lane got up and tried to take support of the tree, but due to shock and pain, he fainted. The companions of Lord Gilmour had fought with the rest of the dacoits, killing five of them and leaving the others wounded. The two riders of Lord Lorimor had mistakenly assumed the dacoit Tom to be Jack. They took his coat and belt back, the same that dacoit Tom had earlier exchanged with Nevlin Lane.

The following day, Mr. Loket was out for his early morning walk with Sekhefer, a representative of workers. They happened to walk by the tree where Nevlin Lane was lying unconscious. Mr. Loket recognized him at once and said to his companion, "This person's name is Ian. He is a mine digger and works at our Camp. I cannot guess what business would make him leave his house to come here. He appears to be dead." After saying this, he sat down beside Ian. He kept one hand on his chest and with the other hand felt his pulse. He also examined the pupils of his eyes. He realized that Ian was alive. He looked at his legs and found a deep bullet wound in the left ankle. However, the bone was not fractured and appeared to be alright.

Mr. Loket said to his companion, "I am well acquainted with

this man. He is hard working, honest and always ready to help others. He had a very pleasant relationship with all the people here. He never argued with anyone and did not know the meaning of the word 'fight.' Wicked Lewryk was constantly harassing and troubling him. I think he must have chased Lewryk to this spot and got wounded by his bullet. This matter will be thoroughly investigated. However, for now I want to carry him back to his house. Please help me in arranging transport to take him from here as soon as possible."

At this request from Mr. Loket, Sekhefer climbed a tall tree and looked all around. He saw a horse carriage coming from the side of Fairfeld. He shouted in a loud voice, "Carriage driver, carriage driver" and motioned the carriage driver with his hand to come to him. When the carriage driver saw him, he thought that probably there was some danger ahead and some security guard was trying to warn him about it. He raced the horses and brought the carriage under the tree. A rich person was sitting in the carriage. He was going to Lornehope Camp to get medicine from the doctor there. Mr. Loket told the traveller about Ian being wounded and lying unconscious. He requested him to carry Ian in his carriage to Lornehope Camp. The traveller gladly agreed. Mr. Loket very gently lifted the wounded Ian with the help of the rich traveller, Sekhefer and the carriage driver and laid him down on a cushiony bed of blankets inside the carriage. The rest of them sat at the back and on the top of the carriage.

The carriage driver drove the carriage fast and reached the thatched house of Ian. The maid servant, Mathula, was there. Mr. Loket told her about Ian and the way he found him. Ian was carried to his bedroom and laid on his bed. The traveller left for his destination and Mr. Loket went with his companion to get the doctor. Mathula prepared some soup and forced open Ian's mouth with a spatula and fed him a little soup. After a short time, Ian's old friend, the doctor, came along with Mr. Loket, examined him thoroughly and carefully administered the necessary medicines. For full one day and night, both Mr. Loket and the doctor stayed with Ian to take care of him. They gave him various medicines, applied ointment and dressed his wound. On the third day, Ian regained consciousness and started to shout like a mad man, "Sylvia, Sylvia." The doctor whispered in the ear of Mr. Loket and Mathula not to talk to Ian and also not to inquire about his condition. He also asked them not to mention a word about Sylvia, under any circumstances. He gave Ian a strong sedative and Ian went off to sleep. Even in his sleep, he kept calling, "Sylvia, my dear Sylvia," off and on, throughout the night. Sometimes he would grind his teeth and shout, "Wicked Lewryk, where are you taking my dear Sylvia!" He constantly kept repeating these two things. He neither spoke to nor looked at anyone in the room. He also did not recognize anyone. For eight days his condition remained like this. On the ninth day, the medicines began to show effect and he regained full consciousness. He looked at the doctor and said in an angry voice, "Who are you? Where is my dear sister Sylvia? Bring her to me—I want to meet her. Arrest Lewryk and bring him in front of me. I will not rest till I take his life. How did he dare to run away with Sylvia?"

He kept on repeating the same thing over and over again. Both the doctor and Mr. Loket tried to talk to him in a calm and reassuring tone. But he would not listen to anyone and constantly kept repeating Sylvia's name in a loud voice. He would not say anything else. He tried to get up from the bed to run out. It was difficult to constrain him. On seeing his condition, the doctor, with the help of Mr. Loket, forced him back to bed and gently tied his waist, hands and feet to the bed with a soft rope and administered a strong dose of sedatives.

Mr. Loket suggested that Ian be transferred to the mental hospital but the doctor refused. He continued his constant vigil and treatment in the house. For one and a half week, Ian's condition remained the same and he acted like a mad person. The doctor, with great patience and care, tended to his wound and kept up the administration of medicines. The wound in the leg healed and the medicines had a very positive effect. Ian regained his normal way of thinking and behaviour. However, he had become remarkably weak. After two weeks of the incident, Ian opened his eyes, fully conscious and behaved in a normal way. He saw the doctor, who was sitting on a chair near the bed. Ian greeted him respectfully. He motioned him to come near and said, "Please, for God's sake, tell me any news that you may have about Sylvia. I am very restless and can get no peace without her."

The doctor, on the spot, fabricated a plausible story and said to Ian in a reassuring manner, "Ian, please keep your senses and mind in control. Do not get upset. Lewryk was running away with Sylvia but the police arrested him. Sylvia could not get proper rest and peace of mind at Lornehope Camp. Accordingly she has been sent to another place for a change of climate. Once you regain enough strength and are able to move around, Sylvia can be called back here."

Nevlin Lane was not convinced. He called the doctor a liar and started calling him bad names. He asked the doctor to bring back Sylvia immediately and to kill Lewryk. He just kept on repeating these two things again and again. The doctor gave him a dose of sedatives. Nevlin Lane once again fell asleep. In his sleep he would suddenly wake up and shout, "Sylvia, Sylvia" and fall asleep again.

The mad behaviour and condition of Nevlin Lane became a subject of discussion in all the houses of Lornehope Camp. The doctor urged all the households that if any one came to know the whereabouts of Sylvia, to please tell Ian about it. One day the doctor and the clerk Loket brought a traveller with them to Nevlin Lane's room. At that time Nevlin Lane was sitting on his bed and calling, "Sylvia, Sylvia." The traveller, on entering the room, said "Hello" to Nevlin Lane and said, "If you will calm down and are prepared to listen to me with patience, I can tell you all about Sylvia and her condition as I have seen it all with my own eyes. If you agree, I will narrate the entire episode from the beginning to the end."

Ian shouted with joy and said, "You are indeed an angel. Please be kind enough to tell me everything about Sylvia. I promise to be quiet and listen most attentively."

The traveller said, "On the invitation from the King of Austria and about three miles from here, Dr. Langley has set up a hospital to provide medical treatment to the people of Lornehope Camp and the surrounding areas. I saw Sylvia there under his treatment. I used to get an update of her condition as I used to go to the doctor daily for my medicines. A kind hearted and rich gentleman from London, who is visiting several cities for some personal work and is on his way to Lornehope Camp from Fairfeld, heard the cries of Sylvia in the jungle. He raced his horse and came to her aid. I also learned from his twelve strong companions that this nobleman killed the dacoit Lewryk and found Sylvia unconscious."

Nevlin Lane said in a grateful voice, "Yes, I can understand and accept this. All the events seem to tie up logically. So far people have told me stories that seemed illogical and my mind would not accept them. You appear to be an honest person. Please take me to the camp of Dr. Langley. If you cannot take me there then please tell me everything in detail."

Thet traveller said, "As I just told you, I used to go daily to Dr. Langley's camp to get medicines. I heard from the very reliable companions of Lord Gilmour, that a friend of Lord Gilmour, who belongs to London and has a title of 'Lord', had to come to Lornehope Camp for an important work. He was coming from the side of Fairfeld, along with his friend Lord Gilmour and his twelve strong companions, riding on horses. He felt concerned on listening to the cries of a woman in the jungle. He chased and shot dead the dacoit Lewryk and freed Sylvia from his grasp. The twelve companions of this dacoit attacked the party of Lord Gilmour, but the friends of Lord Gilmour fought back and killed five of the dacoits, four were badly injured and two ran away. They did not know what happened to the twelfth dacoit. The companion of Lord Gilmour also told me that when this Lord freed Sylvia, she was crying and shouting, 'Oh Jack, oh Jack' and then she fainted. These friends of Lord Gilmour made a stretcher and brought her to Dr. Langley's camp. When Sylvia regained consciousness, she requested this Lord to search for you. At her request, this gentleman sent two of the riders to look for you. Sylvia had told them that Jack was wearing the clothes usually worn by the workers here. These riders on their return told the Lord, in my presence, that Jack had been killed by the dacoits and as it was difficult to carry the body, they had brought back his coat and belt as proof and gave both the things to the Lord. Sylvia recognized all these things and grieved beyond words. Her grief was so great that all the persons present had tears in their eyes. She would shout, "Oh Jack, my brother Jack" and would faint, again and again. For two weeks the doctor gave Sylvia suitable medicines and advised the Lord that Sylvia be moved to another city for a change of climate. It was not possible for her to regain her health and happiness while living at Lornehope Camp. Accordingly Dr. Langley assigned a middle aged woman, who is a qualified nurse in a London hospital, to look after Sylvia. Her name is Merci Fairflex."

The traveller continued, "One day, when I was visiting the doctor to get my medicine, I heard this very civilized Lord, telling Sylvia, 'I will escort you to London comfortably and after full inquiries, hand you over to your legitimate relatives.' In response Sylvia said, 'Except for Jack, I have no relatives in London who can help me. Jack left for heaven and left me all alone to cry for the rest of my life.' The Lord cried after listening to Sylvia and tried to comfort her and said, 'Often times people are not aware of the existence of other relatives. I will search for your relatives after reaching London.' Mr. Ian, rest assured that Sylvia is very much alive and is under the care and protection of a very kind Lord of London. Though Sylvia had been very sick and had become weak because of the separation from you, Dr. Langley was confident that she would regain her normal health with the change of climate. I have learned that they have gone to another city. It is possible that Dr. Langley knows the name of this city. However, you are very weak and in no condition to go to Dr. Langley. Secondly, even if Dr. Langley knows the name of the city and you go there, what guarantee do you have that they have not moved to some other city? It is not advisable for you to travel from one place to another. This may also create complications in your recovery. It is better for you to first regain your full strength. Then you can do whatever you consider to be right. I also want to tell you that Sylvia is a very sensible and mature girl. Dr. Langley and his wife thought that Sylvia could not be the daughter of a worker here, that she came from a very civilized and cultured family as was evident from her behaviour. I have come to know that this Lord with whom Sylvia has gone, had some very important work to complete and will be visiting several cities in that connection. Seeing the behaviour of this Lord, I can also tell you that he is not only very kind and generous but also very systematic and thorough in his work. He takes great care of Sylvia. He considers it to be his duty to care for a person in need. In my presence he addressed Sylvia as his sister, and consoled and comforted her. You should ease your mind and be in peace from Sylvia's side, as she is under the excellent care of this kind Lord. You should take care of your own health and regain your strength."

When the traveller finished his narration, Ian thanked him. Both the doctor and Mr. Loket consoled Ian. He felt much better and looked cheerful. They all left him to take some rest.

Once Nevlin Lane was alone, he lay down on his bed and began to think about the events described by the stranger. They appeared to be true. No person, without being a witness, could describe the things in such detail and with so much confidence. There was no doubt that Sylvia was alive. This thought gave Nevlin Lane great relief and consolation. His mind became peaceful. Only the separation from Sylvia bothered him. He raised his hands towards the sky and prayed, "Oh Great God, You are very kind and merciful. In Your kindness You created circumstances that Sylvia was freed from the clutches of Lewryk and You sent this kind Lord just in time to protect her when she was in the midst of great trouble. You protected her from Lewryk's bad intentions and You did not let him succeed."

The story of Sylvia being safe and in good hands, proved to be a great tonic for Nevlin Lane. His strange behaviour disappeared. He gradually regained strength and started to move around. Within two weeks, he regained his normal health and strength. During Nevlin Lane's illness, all the people of Lornehope Camp and all the mine diggers and workers, men and women, came to his house to inquire about his condition. Everyone was very happy to see him back to his normal health. Neither Mr. Brown nor Miss Brown came to see him. However, sometimes, out of sympathy they did send cooked meat and a basket of fruits and flowers to his house. But neither the father nor his daughter came to his house to see him.

Nevlin Lane was relieved that Miss Brown did not come to see him. He used to frown at Miss Brown's shallow talk and behaviour. It was likely that if she had come during his illness, he might have said something to upset her and created unpleasantness. So it was just as well that she did not come.

Once Nevlin Lane fully recovered and regained his strength, he checked his digging tools and went back to his work. The gold that Nevlin Lane had packed in his coat pockets when they left their house, was never found. His coat and belt brought back by the two riders contained no gold at all. No one knew what had happened to that gold. It was never found. Nevlin Lane was not at all concerned with its disappearance and did not care as to who might have taken it. He never thought about it nor was sorry to lose it. Without Sylvia, he did not enjoy anything in this world, neither wealth nor other pleasures. He lost all ambition and desire to do anything. He became quite detached from the world. He did only minimum digging, enough to feed himself and Mathula and to take care of the daily expenses. The rest of the time he used to roam about in the jungle with his hands in his pockets, thinking of Sylvia all the time. His love for Sylvia increased by leaps and bounds every day. Her face was constantly in front of his eyes. He would recall the slow and gracious manner in which she used to walk, her bright face, her sweet voice and her expression of love in all her talk and actions. Such thoughts made him very restless. To forget all this, he considered taking up drinking but his upbringing would not allow him to do this.

Several times, the doctor and Mr. Loket informed Mr. McGregor, of Nevlin Lane's unusual condition and his roaming in the jungle aimlessly. However, the contractor ignored their reports. On the contrary he instructed them in writing to leave Nevlin Lane alone and said, "He is not a mad man but is suffering from the pain and loneliness caused by Sylvia's separation. No one should interfere with his way of life. He is a very useful member of our community and we stand to benefit a lot from his advice and experience."

The instructions of Mr. McGregor were circulated to all the workers and security guards. Accordingly, no one asked Ian any irrelevant questions or interfered with his personal life. They all treated him as if he was normal. Wherever Ian went, everyone greeted him cordially and with respect. Every one had a special affection for him.

For several months, Nevlin Lane roamed all around freely. He did not care to meet either Mr. Loket or the doctor. If he happened to meet them on the way or on the streets, he would greet them with respect and was polite to them.

One day, Nevlin Lane suddenly disappeared from Lornehope Camp. After one week of his disappearance, Mr. Loket made a formal report. On investigation, it was learned from Mathula that he had fully recovered his health. From the way he behaved it was obvious that he was planning for the future. The pain and setback from the separation of Sylvia was also much less and no longer obvious. Tired of poverty, he had left for some big city to look for a job in an office where he could use his reading and writing skills. He had bid goodbye to the job of digging forever. He did not leave any address. This information from Mathula was circulated to all the people at Lornehope Camp. The doctor corroborated this information from Mathula and expressed his satisfaction. He happily told Mr. McGregor that Ian's days of misery and poverty were over and that's the reason he thought of taking up a regular job. Wherever he would take up work, he would shine. Everyone would respect him.

All the people at Lornehope Camp respected the doctor and they all agreed with him. Everyone said that it was good that Ian left Lornehope Camp to seek a more rewarding job in some big city. However, no one knew which place Ian had decided to go.

Chapter 22

You are beautiful. You are heavenly.
You are wonderful. You are delicate.

I say honestly that earlier it was Laila
but now you are the most beautiful

Your beauty is unparalleled
The truth is that you are unique

The month of March is very pleasant in London. Every person appears to be full of new plans and hopes. In this context, Lady Marlow's party towards the end of March is worth mentioning where all kinds of people were invited. In the newspaper, *Morning Post*, were printed the names of the couples who were taking part in the dance. The decorations of the ballroom and the billiard room were done so lavishly, that it was a sight to behold. The chairs were upholstered with a fabric that had patterns of beautiful flowers. The dresses worn by the guests were of latest fashions, with bright colours. The dresses worn by the young girls enhanced their beauty. Their style of walking and conversation made the hearts of young men beat faster. With such beautiful ladies and the distinguished crowd, the party was most enjoyable for everyone. Even the older people said that they never had so much fun in any other party they had attended.

In this big party, the charm and beauty of Audrey Hope was

unique. She looked more beautiful than the other ladies at the party. The reason of her radiant beauty was that she was very happy. She was very excited about meeting her old friend Nevlin Lane and about her marriage to Lord Lorimor. Her friends, girls of her own age, took her out in the garden for a walk. They had great fun! Their laughs and giggles could be heard from a distance. Lord and Lady Marlow were happy and proud to see everyone admiring Audrey Hope. Their pride was justified because Audrey hope indeed was very beautiful and wise. Her behaviour towards everyone was pleasant and cordial. She had no ego or pride at all. This was the reason that her friends loved her and were happy on meeting her. Often people appreciated her very human approach.

The Prince of England, who had come to a nearby city to lay the foundation stone for a school building, was also invited. He was so impressed that he joined the party for two days. He spent considerable time in dancing with Audrey Hope. Seeing the attention that she received from the prince, some of the girls of rich families felt jealous of her. Outwardly they showed great friendship and cordial relations with her, but in reality they were envious of her. Some romantic types used to say that Audrey Hope had a heart made of stone. She did not know how to love anyone and had no romantic feelings. She did not even look at the eligible young men trying to woo her. If someone told her that he loved her, she ignored him and pretended that she did not care and made him feel embarrassed.

Lady Marlow had recommended several young men to Audrey Hope as worthy of her consideration. But she completely ignored her suggestions. Whenever Lady Marlow showed her anger and displeasure at her careless attitude, Audrey Hope lovingly put her arms round her neck and with her charm made her smile and brought her around to be her cheerful self.

One day, when the two of them were alone, Lady Marlow gave a stern lecture to Audrey Hope and said in an angry voice, "Girl, you have become too proud of your beauty and your ego is grown so much that you do not listen to anyone. Several rich and famous young men have proposed to you. You laughed at them and treated the whole thing as a joke. Poor Lord Lorimor was so depressed and angered by your careless attitude that he left. Only God knows where he has gone. I want to ask you what qualities you are looking for in a husband? Please tell me what is in your mind. I am worried and much concerned about your marriage. It is my desire to see you married and to see you living happily with your husband. I want to discharge my duty responsibly and spend the rest of my life peacefully. You run miles away when the topic of marriage is mentioned."

Audrey Hope replied, "Dear aunty, please consider me to be a foolish and disobedient girl. I consider you to be my most sincere and sympathetic adviser, just like my own mother. To this day, I have not done anything without your approval and blessings or against your wishes. However, in the matter of my marriage, I humbly request you, with folded hands, to leave this decision to me."

On hearing this, Lady Marlow frowned and said, "You have no experience of choosing a husband. If you go by your wishes, you will regret the outcome of your inexperience. You will end up marrying some wicked, manipulating and selfish person and suffer for the rest of your life."

Audrey Hope replied, "Yes, I will be entitled to all the suffering and troubles, provided I make such a mistake. No one can change one's destiny. Whatever has to happen will happen. No one can erase what is written in one's destiny."

Lady Marlow said, "If you marry someone against my advice, then you are surely asking for trouble. One makes or spoils one's destiny by one's own efforts. One who listens to the advice of elders and follows the path of righteousness, will always be happy in his life."

Lady and Lord Marlow and the other friends and acquaintances of Audrey Hope had absolutely no knowledge that she considered Lord Lorimor to be truly in love with her and in her heart she wanted to marry only him. She had accepted him as her future husband. She had not disclosed this to anyone and did not wish to tell anyone her secret until such time that Lord Lorimor was back. This was the reason that, in spite of Lady Marlow's insistence and her getting angry, she did not consider any other young man. However, she did not allow Lady Marlow to be angry for long and diverted her attention to other subjects and once again Lady Marlow was smiling and laughing.

Two years and five months had passed since Lord Lorimor made the promise to Audrey Hope. All this time she neither received a letter nor any other news from him about his journey or welfare. Nor had he returned back to London. For this reason, Audrey Hope looked a little worried and listless. She did not feel like doing anything. She constantly thought of different ways and means by which she might be able to get some news of Lord Lorimor. But she could not think of anything that would help.

At the end of the month of August, Lady Marlow had another party. She once again invited several people that included some very handsome young men from rich and famous families. One of the young men in the gathering was most handsome. He was an ambassador to a foreign country and appeared to be a fairly decent person to Audrey Hope. After a dance with her, he sat down on a chair next to her. He looked at her with loving eyes and admired her beauty. Audrey Hope was also laughing and enjoying, talking to him on several general topics. They had been talking for a short time when Sir Jordan Lane came there. He monopolised Audrey Hope's attention and began telling her about some dispute regarding one of his properties. Most of the people respected and admired Sir Jordan Lane and were aware that he was being considered for the position of a minister in the cabinet. Audrey Hope also knew that Sir Jordan Lane was soon going to be a minister and was aware of the fact that he was her neighbour. She listened attentively to what he was saying.

For the past two and a half years, Sir Jordan Lane had been planning and plotting to win over Audrey Hope. He did not love her. He was greedy and selfish and had resolved to get her money and property under his control. He had decided that once he gets her under his control he will humiliate her and destroy her self respect and then divorce her. He was constantly planning and plotting to achieve this goal. To gain her confidence, he had taken over the role of an adviser to her on various matters. He never expressed his love to her. On the contrary he would make a solemn and pitiable face to get her sympathy. Often he would stare at her with sly eyes and tried to guess if there was anyone else in this world who loved her. The close friends of Jordan Lane knew very well that his sincere style of talking and making a solemn and pitiable face was just an act and planned deceit. However, the persons who did not know him well were misled to believe that he was a true admirer and lover of Audrey Hope. They had also noticed that throughout the month of August, whenever there was a party at the house of a rich person, Jordan Lane was always present and on some pretext or the other monopolised the attention of Audrey Hope. At this party also when Audrey Hope was laughing and talking to the young man, Sir Jordan Lane came and took her away on the pretext of telling her about some property dispute. He requested her to walk with him towards the west side of the garden.

Sir Jordan Lane said to her, "Audrey Hope, please forgive me for interrupting the conversation with your ambassador friend but I would feel sorry if you were to lose in a dispute and for this reason I thought it important to discuss the details of this case. This is the reason I brought you away to a quiet place to talk so that I may tell you how to win in the dispute."

On hearing this, Audrey Hope smiled and fanned her face with her beautiful hand fan and said, "I was not much interested in the conversation of the ambassador anyway. For this reason I came with you on the pretext of going for a walk this way."

Sir Jordan Lane replied, "I am very well aware of the fact that you do not like to converse with young men and ignore their attention. You consider some people to be younger than you in age and some much older. In short, you find some fault with everyone and send them on their way. Listen Audrey Hope, generally the advice given by elders is true and sincere, and worth following. Their advice is given after much thought and consideration of the pros and cons. It does not matter to the elders if the young persons do not follow the advice. They neither get angry nor upset. They consider it their duty to give the right advice and are always there to show the right path. It is also worth remembering that older persons compared to the younger ones these days are more mature and far-sighted. They are wiser and have strong principles and values."

Jordan Lane continued and said, "Listen, if you care to walk with me to the gate, you will be able to see the people coming to this party and how much they are enjoying. At the same time you will benefit from the exercise and my discussion of this property dispute. My elders and myself have always wished you well. God has given you much wealth and wisdom and has also bestowed upon you great beauty and charm. I am not saying this to flatter you but because it is the truth. There is no other girl like you who is so kind and clever. This is the reason, Audrey, that I wish to warn you against the deceit and fraud in this world."

Audrey Hope was taken aback to hear Sir Jordan Lane call her by her first name but decided to ignore it. She kept on walking with him towards the gate talking about her property. When the guests were leaving the party, they saw the two of them walking together. They thought that Sir Jordan Lane had been able to get Audrey Hope's attention and would try his best to make her fall in love with him.

Chapter 23

When she learned the news of my status from a messenger
With anxiety she asked immediately, what happened and how

Sir Jordan Lane asked Audrey Hope to walk with him upto the gate to tell her about some property dispute. She neither accepted nor refused his suggestion. She simply covered her shoulders with a shawl and walked beside him towards the gate. The gate was lit up with artificial lights. The security guards were standing all along the driveway leading to the mansion. Some of the guests had taken seats in their carriages and were ready to leave while others were waiting for their carriages. Several men and women were walking on foot. There was only one exit gate. That is why the sentry at the gate had all the carriages lined up in a queue and was allowing only one carriage at a time to pass the gate. He was shouting for pedestrians to move aside and watch for the passing carriages.

Seeing all the commotion near the gate and without saying a word, Audrey Hope lifted herself up and sat down on the fence near the gate. Her feet were dangling by the fence and she was busy watching the guests leaving. Sir Jordan Lane positioned himself very close to her legs in such a way that his head reached upto her chest. He wanted to look into her eyes and propose to her. But he thought to himself, "Audrey Hope is fabulously rich and very beautiful and she has turned down very handsome and rich young men in high positions. She has even made a joke about their proposal and she may do the same with me and turn me down. I will feel humiliated for no reason." However, his selfish nature and ego overpowered such thoughts. He decided that this was a good opportunity to express his love for her, as there was no one else present to compete with him. He said to himself, "Lord Lorimor was in love with her, but he was so fed up with her indifference and attitude that he left for another place almost two and a half years ago. I am sure he will marry some other beautiful girl. I am sure there is no one else left who can claim to love her. I think she will now stop thinking about Nevlin Lane and marry me." He convinced himself that he was justified in expressing his love for Audrey Hope. He came closer to her and started to form sentences in his mind as to how best to approach the subject.

He said to Audrey Hope, "Listen Audrey, for the last fifteen minutes you have been just sitting here looking all around without uttering a single word. Are you thinking about some problem?"

Audrey Hope was feeling very offended by the way in which Sir Jordan Lane was standing so close to her. This was considered to be bad manners and was against civilized behaviour. Hearing him call her by her first name again, she was taken aback. Considering him to be her neighbour and an elder, she said with a smile, "At this time I was thinking that every human being, including the most intelligent people and the most dumb person, knows that this world is transient and one day everyone has to face God and defend his deeds. Even then people are not ashamed to do wicked deeds and act against good social behaviour. Rather than distancing themselves from selfishness, greed and fraud, they embrace unsocial behaviour and are not scared in the least of adopting the path of crime and dishonesty. In their heart they do not seem to have the fear of God. They bring a bad name to themselves. How can God ever forgive such persons?"

Sir Jordan Lane replied, "Only God knows when He is happy and when He is angry. Even the saints and most learned do not know the mysterious ways in which He works. How can an ordinary person understand Him. However, I am very happy that you are free of the vices you mentioned."

Audrey Hope said, "I do not count. I am just a foolish orphaned girl, good for nothing. God created me for no reason. To tell you the truth, it's a waste of a human body to have created me. I see all these men here, who are security guards or drivers driving carriages and I consider them to be much more useful than myself."

This sentence provided Sir Jordan Lane an opportunity to show his concern by consoling her and expressing sympathy. He pressed her body with his leg and looked into her eyes and said, "Do you recall what the people at the party, sitting on the chairs on the west side at the time of the dance, were saying about me?"

Audrey Hope replied, "All around people were saying all kinds of things. Several people were sitting close to me and talking about general things. I did not pay much attention. I cannot say if they were talking about anything worth mentioning."

Sir Jordan Lane said, "Audrey Hope, listen carefully. Several of my acquaintances in London, under the pretext of friendship, really act as my enemies. I consider them to be like a snake, foes under the cloak of friendship. If I do not invite them for lavish parties and entertain them with liquor and delicious food and do not go with them for gambling, they call me mean, selfish and greedy. If I try to maintain close relationship with these people then they think that I am foolish and insincere, and have some ulterior motive. If I refuse to lend money to some people who are not trustworthy and I issue a writ against the land which they do not own, they call me dishonest. If I point out their mistakes with a view to help them, then they call me arrogant. These people really do not know my kind and honest nature. They hold a grudge against me and go round criticizing me in the society. Listening to my so-called bad deeds from these persons, my friends have started to think that I am really a bad person and am ill-mannered. Listen, I am the type of person who respects a person who is honest and loves one without motive. Love of such a person should be considered true love. One should avoid a person who tries to win a poor girl by fraud and false pretence and the person who saves the girl from the clutches of such a person should be considered a true well wisher and a loyal friend. You just called yourself a useless person. I dare say that in my heart, I consider you to be a very useful person. Life is uncertain, but if a person follows the path of righteousness, then his or her life can be more valuable than the costliest treasures. Some people think that I am selfish and wicked but the rich and persons from decent civilized families consider me to be deserving of my wealth and the post of a cabinet minister. I will tell you that they are both wrong. They do not know what I like, what I think and what type of a person I am. As you are my neighbour and because I am your elder, I think you would be sympathetic and that's why I am confiding in you. I neither desire nor care for the ministership or the wealth. Since I am all alone and have no heir or any close relative as a dependent, what good is this wealth or the post of a minister to me? This will not make me happy. I have no need to be selfish. What can I possibly gain from it and for whom should I be selfish. However, if I had a wife then I would be very interested in worldly things and derive happiness from the same. The reason I did not get married so far is, that there is only one woman in this world, who is the kind of woman I like and want to marry. She is the lady I know from childhood. She is kind hearted, very civilized and sophisticated, very clever and very social. She is also an excellent hostess and well versed in duties of a housewife and she understands the government working and the business intricacies. For a long time I have observed and admired all these qualities in her. I am ready to serve her and please her in any way I can. But it is no use only my liking her. I do not find this lovely lady's attention and heart directed towards me at all. I fail to understand the reason behind her attitude and why she prefers another disloyal and untrustworthy person over me. What is it that she finds lacking in me? It is not possible for me to tear open my heart and let her see how I feel inside. I am only capable of telling her in words, how I love her. If she feels that it is just so much talk and means nothing then please tell me, Audrey Hope, how can I convince her?"

Audrey Hope said, "It is not possible that the one whom you

love does not have similar sentiments towards you. Nothing happens against the laws of Nature."

On hearing this Sir Jordan Lane felt bold enough to pursue the subject further and said, "People have believed in the laws of Nature since the creation of this world and would continue to believe till the end. But to understand them and act as per the laws of Nature is an altogether different matter. Well, it is written that 'Truth is God,' but I doubt it, as I find that telling the truth can lead to a serious fight." He wanted to say something further but Audrey Hope interrupted him. She said with a certain shyness, "Please stop your long lecture and the discussion about Nature. Leave this to some poet who can describe what Nature is. How about telling me some latest news of what is happening in the world?"

Sir Jordan Lane was enjoying this closeness to Audrey Hope very much. With a sad face he said, "I feel very ashamed to tell you the latest news. I never thought it possible and least expected that Lord Lorimor would do something so disgraceful. I consider it to be a crime to tell bad things about anyone behind his back. However, it is also not possible to hide from you the news about him. I have learned from very reliable sources that Lord Lorimor reached Paris after visiting several countries and cities. There he fell in love with a short statured, but beautiful girl, who is an employee of a theatre. She wins over the audience by her superb dance and music performances. This dancer has not told anyone her real name or her past. The theatre manager has given her the name of Senorita Estella. The rumour is that she has a very sweet voice and is very young and extremely beautiful. Because of her short height, the audience considers her to be in her teens. She has acquired such excellence in music and dancing that she has become the talk of the high society of Paris. They say that this singer's voice is very poignant and resounds like the sweet and enchanting voice of a bird. It appears that she belongs to our city of London. The respected Lord Lorimor is madly in love with this stage dancer. A formal engagement has been performed between Lord Lorimor and this stage singer. They are likely to get married within the next few days. I pray for the happiness of Lord Lorimor. I am trying to draft a letter of congratulations to the bridegroom and the bride at my London office."

On hearing this, Audrey Hope went into a state of great shock. She analyzed in her mind the words of Sir Jordan Lane and the serious nature in which he recited the news, and came to the conclusion that this news was wrong. This gave her some consolation and she felt better. She said to herself, "Lord Lorimor is not the type to marry a common stage singer. Upto the last minute before he was leaving, he told me that I was the most beautiful girl in the whole world. He solemnly promised that except for me he would not even look at another woman and I was the only woman in his heart. Even though it has been two years and six months since he made this promise, Lord Lorimor is an honest and completely trustworthy person. He would never marry a common stage girl and bring disgrace to his noble family and be a cause of shame to his respected elders." This thought completely eliminated the doubt, anxiety and turmoil in her mind.

She laughed and said, "The low class uncivilized people take pleasure in floating untrue rumours and defaming honest and decent people. It is quite likely that this news is wrong and has no basis. Some people, when they sit in a group, float rumours for fun. These rumours have no truth in them and surely this rumour has also originated in this manner."

Sir Jordan Lane realized that what Audrey Hope was saying was indirectly an insult to him and he felt uncomfortable. He put his hand in his pocket and hurriedly took out a cutting from a newspaper printed in Paris. He put this in the hands of Audrey Hope and said in a terse voice, "Please read this. You will find out for yourself that the news that I told you about Lord Lorimor is true. It is printed in this newspaper and supported by this article."

On hearing that the news is from the newspaper, Audrey Hope's heart began to beat faster and she began to hate Lord Lorimor. She felt ashamed and began to perspire. With trembling hands she opened the newspaper and tried to read the article but she could not bring herself to read it and considered it an insult to read it aloud. She handed the paper back to Sir Jordan Lane. To hide her curiosity and nervousness about the article, she began to wipe her face and eyes with the handkerchief. She said to Sir Jordan Lane, "I read several news in the newspapers that are not true and I get tired of reading long articles. So why don't you read it to me."

To oblige Audrey Hope, Sir Jordan Lane began to read, in a very emphatic voice, the following news article from the newspaper. He stressed each word as he read it·

Scene at the Paris Nom De Theatre

For the past few days Nom De theatre is entertaining unprecedented huge crowds such as never have been seen at any theatre before. If the tickets are not purchased a day earlier, it is almost impossible to get a ticket for the show. This theatre has hired a remarkable lady whose excellent singing, dancing and acting skills coupled with her very charming personality and beauty, have captured the hearts of everyone. The highly respected members of the society, the rich, the senior government officials and also the persons who usually do not go to a theatre, are willing and happy to pay even ten times the normal ticket price to get a seat in the theatre to watch her show. They feel very proud that they have been able to see the show and boast about it. It has not been possible to find the real name of this lady nor which country she belongs to, nor what religion or belief she follows. However, because she is so very beautiful and sings in such a sweet, melodious voice, people generally call her "the Silver Star." Truly she is the star of Paris. Lord Lorimor, a citizen of London, England, is on very intimate terms with this beautiful lady. He is a very handsome young man, kind hearted and very rich, belonging to the aristocratic and respected society of London. From his behaviour towards this beautiful actress, it appears that he loves her deeply and his mind is made up to marry her. We congratulate Lord Lorimor on his good luck to capture the heart of this actress and we convey our good wishes to both of them for their success and happiness.

On hearing the newspaper article, Audrey Hope lowered her

eyes and head with shame. She said to herself in a sad voice, "Men are very untrustworthy. God save me from such cunning men. Oh, Lord Lorimor, you turned out to be a real tormentor and cruel person. You promised me that you will search the world from one end to the other and find my lost friend, Nevlin Lane. I am so sorry that instead of finding him, you found yourself a woman. You tormentor, did it not occur to you that you gave a promise to an honest, decent, orphan unmarried girl not to marry for two years and that she is waiting for you! You unfaithful person, if you did find someone more able and with better qualities than myself, you should have at least informed me of your decision. What you have done is against your decent and honest nature, and the high family traditions. If I had known your unfaithful nature, I would not have given you my heart and made a fool of myself in front of other young men."

She placed her hand in the hands of Sir Jordan Lane. She also took the paper from him and kept it in her pocket to show it to Lady Marlow.

Sir Jordan Lane should have guessed that at this moment Audrey Hope's sad face and moist eyes reflected her frustration and hatred for Lord Lorimor, and that this was the perfect time for him to express his love and sympathy and propose to her. It was quite likely that she would have agreed to marry him and he would have been successful in his mission. However, his mind went blank and his lips were sealed and he could not say a word about marriage. He just stood there. At that moment Lady Marlow came there and the golden opportunity was lost.

Lady Marlow said, "Dear Audrey, what are you doing sitting here and watching the show? The prince has been waiting to have a dance with you. Only fifteen minutes are left for your scheduled dance with him."

Audrey Hope said, "Very well, I will come with you."

She said goodbye to Sir Jordan Lane and walked away with Lady Marlow, without even once looking back.

After she left, Sir Jordan Lane reproached himself, "Audrey Hope did not show any respect for either my high position in the society or my high reputation. She simply walked away from me. My lecture and advice did not seem to make the slightest impression on her. She completely ignored my show of love. The expression of love and other things that I said to her cloaked under hypothetical situation, I am sure, she has understood the true intent but pretended not to understand. Oh well, how long can she escape my plans—I will soon get her in my grip and humiliate her and bring her to her knees. She will curse her fate. The field is clear for me now. Lord Lorimor has fallen in love with a dancer in Paris and Nevlin Lane is gone and lost forever. There is no one else but myself left in the field."

Sir Jordan Lane carried on this chain of thought for a while and then he straightened himself, combed his hair and went inside with a happy face. He entered the dance hall. The dance was in progress and Audrey Hope was dancing with the prince. The people in the audience were admiring the beauty and charming face of Audrey Hope and the graceful manner in which she was dancing. Sir Jordan Lane sat down on a chair. He said to himself, "Audience, just wait and see. This angel like lady will soon be my wife. I will stop all her dancing and partying for ever. I will not allow her to go out of house."

His thoughts were interrupted by a person who greeted him in a respectful manner and said, "Sir, some very respected and rich persons from the surrounding areas have just arrived to join the party. They wish to meet you. They have sent me to request you to please come to the front sitting room." As requested, Sir Jordan Lane accompanied the person to the front room. He found there several rich landlords, business men, local magistrates, members of municipal committees and a few ladies from county Blough. As Sir Jordan Lane entered the room, they all got up and one by one came forward and shook his hand. They said, "When we were coming to attend the party we saw you near the gate talking with Audrey Hope and did not consider it appropriate to talk to you at that time. However, before going to the dance hall, we thought it would be better to meet you here. We all read, in the *Morning Star* newspaper, the text of the two speeches that you gave in the parliament yesterday. We congratulate you on your very able speeches and the points raised in them. We would like to thank you for the recommendations and proposals made in your speeches regarding prevention and termination of unfair practices concerning land taxes. These are just and right recommendations. These will prove very beneficial to our areas. We will support your proposals in the parliament session tomorrow."

Sir Jordan Lane expressed his thanks to his admirers. At this time he was informed that his carriage was ready and waiting outside. He took leave from the guests and left for his house. On the way the pedestrians and the shopkeepers greeted him. He acknowledged everyone's greetings by removing his hat and waving his hand. At one of the bends, the carriage stopped for a few moments, as the road was narrow and the bend had to be negotiated slowly. A handsome, young man was standing at this bend. He was wearing old and dirty clothes but appeared to be educated and seemed to belong to a civilized, decent family. As the carriage stopped, this young man looked and gazed intensely at Sir Jordan Lane. He moved forward and wanted to climb on the footboard in order to speak to Sir Jordan Lane. But the police constable on duty, who once got a gold sovereign as a bribe from Sir Jordan Lane after his meeting with Rachel, intervened and pushed the young man to one side and thus prevented him from climbing the footboard. The young man felt very angry and humiliated but in deference to the law he kept quiet and swallowed his pride. Before the constable could say any harsh words, he at once moved away. As the carriage passed in front of him, he looked at the fresh and well groomed face of Sir Jordan Lane and his expensive clothes of the latest design and fashion. This pedestrian then looked at his own dirty old clothes and laughed loudly.

This pedestrian was no other than the young, handsome, kind hearted Nevlin Lane, the step brother of Sir Jordan Lane! He was the one who used to dig the gold mines at Lornehope Camp and was known as Ian. Sylvia Bond called him brother Jack, and the priest and his daughter, Miss Brown, at Lornehope camp knew him as Iain Herringdon.

Chapter 24

A friend is a person who extends a helping hand
At times of anxiety and in times of need

Nevlin Lane stood at the same place for a few minutes thinking about the costly clothes of the latest design that his brother was wearing and the proud manner in which he was sitting in the couch. He felt content to see his brother doing well and in good health. He said to himself, "It was just as well that I did not speak with him at this time. I will not go and see him at the house for the time being, until I find out about his intentions towards me, his poor relative, and whether he has any kind thoughts for me. Generally most of the people judge others by outwardly appearances. They are glad to meet and are pleasant to persons who are well dressed. They respect and keep the company of people who seem to have a good standard of living and are outwardly surrounded by rich things. Such people ignore those who appear to be poor irrespective of their rich family background and ability. Just because they wear poor clothes, they look down upon them and treat them with contempt. There are indeed very few people in this world who are willing to help the poor and are sympathetic towards their problems. For this reason I will not go to see my brother till I find out about his frame of mind. It has been several years since we were separated. I hope he has improved and abandoned his wicked ways. I trust he has given up his cunning and deceitful ways and has left his habit of telling lies and blaming others with false accusations. I also hope he is no longer selfish and greedy and has stopped ruining the life of others for his personal gain. I hope he is following the path of religion, has stopped harassing poor people and is now an honest and straightforward gentleman. I will enter the house only after getting the proof of his being honest. After meeting him I will find a job in some office somewhere and spend the rest of my life in prayer to God. I will neither meet anyone nor visit anyone's house. I will adopt a life in pursuit of religious upliftment." With such thoughts going through his mind he lighted a cigarette and started walking on the pavement along with the other pedestrians.

He was the same Nevlin Lane, who only five years ago was the favourite and dear son of his late father Sir Gravlin Lane. By making false and baseless accusations, Sir Jordan Lane created a fight between Nevlin Lane and his father that forced their father to turn Nevlin Lane out of the house. Nevlin Lane was reduced to a state of starvation and complete frustration. He went to Austria in search of gold and began to dig at the mountains. There is no doubt that he found considerable amount of gold but he lost it all. The gold slab that he had found earlier, he used it for the purchase of Sylvia Bond at the auction. The gold that he found by the valley near the mountains was taken by the robbers. In short, Nevlin Lane was left penniless and starving. It is so ironic that in spite of all his hard labour, all that was left in his pocket at this time was one pound, seven shillings and six pence.

Nevlin Lane was not at all sorry at losing all the gold he acquired with his hard labour. However, he was very sad and his spirit was broken by the loss of Sylvia Bond. He wished Sylvia was with him at this time of his misery and poverty. If she was with him he would not have felt the pain of starvation, the thirst and loneliness that he had to endure along with other difficulties in his journey from Austria to London, which he covered mostly on foot. But Sylvia had disappeared from his life. Neither Sylvia knew the fate of her Jack nor did Nevlin Lane know the whereabouts of Sylvia. He only knew that she had gone away under the protection of a rich gentleman from London for a change of climate. But he had no knowledge as to which city she had gone to. He had a feeling in his mind that she might have come to London with the rich Lord and that is why he decided to come to London.

While walking on the sidewalk, Nevlin Lane thought, "To think about Sylvia at this time is of no use. The longing to meet her here is meaningless, because, even if she did come to London and suppose I saw her walking on the street at some place, she may not be friendly towards me. When you are in a state of poverty, then your own relatives try to avoid you and she is not even related to me. Moreover, she heard the news of my being killed by dacoits. She has probably consoled herself by now and is at peace with herself. She may have even developed a big ego being in the company of a rich Lord. She must be living in luxury and comfort." With this chain of thought, he said to himself that if he could only see her once, it would remove the pain of separation from his heart. He would also have the satisfaction that she was alright.

He kept on walking with thoughts like this when he heard two men talking to each other behind him. One of them said, "My friend, today's party at Lady Marlow's place was full of high class entertainment. Several young beautiful girls were at the party. They were all wearing the latest design clothes and costly jewellery and were showing off their youthful exuberance, stealing the hearts of young men. But believe me, they were no comparison to the beauty and charm of Audrey Hope. I am not alone in admiring her. Everyone at the party admired her radiant beauty, her kind nature and very pleasant manners. Let us see who the lucky person is to get her attention. I am really sorry that you were not successful in winning her heart. In my opinion that same able and famous man will succeed in winning her. He is very cunning and knows how to flatter. He is not only aspiring to be a cabinet minister but is also very rich. He has acquired the title of 'Sir.' It appears that Audrey Hope is also favourably inclined towards him."

In response his companion, Percy Heal said, "Friend, I understand that you are talking about Sir Jordan Lane. But your prediction is wrong. By God's grace, Audrey Hope is well educated, highly accomplished and intelligent. She can analyze things and judge others. In addition she is also foresighted. She can judge a person's honesty and character by just one look at him. She is not going to be fooled by the outwardly show and sweet talk of the greedy, wicked and mean Sir Jordan Lane. She will never allow him to win her over. You probably formed your opinion based on her friendly behaviour towards him for the past few days. It is likely that she is trying to test his real intentions. However, the day she finds out about the selfish and greedy nature of Sir Jordan Lane, she will stop listening to his sweet talk and lies and forget him forever. It is not difficult to find out the true nature of Sir Jordan Lane. Even his close friends know he is wicked and look down upon him. They like to avoid his company."

Lord Chester replied, "My friend, the fact is, these days Sir Jordan Lane is at the peak of his fame and popularity. The general public look at him with respect and awe. Wealth and money can hide all bad points of a person. In addition to being wealthy, he is also very cultured and highly educated. The members of parliament treat him with great respect. Soon he will be a senior cabinet minister and rule over you. He also has an impressive personality. He has mastered the art of giving a speech that completely hypnotizes every man and woman listening to him and draws them closer to him. Because of his high status, no one will dare expose his real nature to Audrey Hope. Any woman would easily fall prey to the charm and persuasion of a person like him in no time. I have seen with my own eyes that Audrey Hope was sitting on the fence near the gate and Sir Jordan Lane was standing close to her body. They were laughing and having a good time. She was answering him by looking straight in his eyes."

Percy Heal said, "Do you infer from all this that Audrey Hope will marry Sir Jordan Lane? I do not agree with you. In my opinion she will never marry the mean, wicked Jordan Lane. I will pray to God, who looks after honest and kind people, to give Audrey Hope the power to keep her guard and think right. Hopefully she will start hating Sir Jordan Lane. I will also pray that she marries a very able, highly civilized and wealthy man like you. If she marries you, she will be very happy all her life."

Lord Chester said, "I thank you from the bottom of my heart

for your kind words and sympathy. The fact is that I consider myself to be much more of a sinner than Sir Jordan Lane. I have not done any good deeds according to the religious teachings. I try to read religious books to uplift myself, find peace of mind and free myself of worldly worries. If I had done good deeds, then God would not have taken away my most loving, very pleasant and beautiful wife from me. I want to spend the rest of my life alone and even consider the thought of a second marriage a sin. I pray to God to give me true insight so that I may realize that all this gaiety and glitter of the world is a dream and I may be free of all worldly ties and realize God and see His presence in all things. I have promised to myself that I shall never marry again. I look upon all young girls as my daughters and regard all other women as my sisters or my mother."

The personal carriage of these two gentlemen was slowly following behind them. They stopped the carriage and sat inside. Nevlin Lane passed their carriage. Percy Heal, thinking him to be a beggar, extended his hand to give him a coin. Nevlin Lane did not take the coin but refused with the expression of his eyes by looking straight at him.

Nevlin Lane had overheard the conversation of these two gentlemen who had just climbed the carriage and had gone away. He refused the alms and walked ahead with a sigh.

He felt very happy to hear all the good things about his childhood friend, Audrey Hope. He said to himself, "Audrey Hope was very charming and beautiful in her childhood days and now that she has grown up to be a young girl, no doubt her beauty and charm is unique and unparallelled. I am very familiar with her high intelligence and her being exceptionally clever. Right from her childhood, she used to come out with such clever thoughts that I used to be amazed. I can never imagine that she would fall in love with my step brother. It is true that I do not consider my step brother to be so wicked and mean as those two gentlemen were describing him. I do not recall him committing a crime. In my time he was selfish and jealous. The reason he was so jealous of me was that he wanted the entire wealth and property of our father for himself. For this reason he accused me falsely and that made our father turn against me. This is the reason he turned me out of the house.

But why would he be mean to others? I wonder how he managed to do so well and rise so high in popularity, compared to his peers and other friends. I did not like to hear those two gentlemen saying bad things about him. After all, he is my brother and we have the same blood of our father. I feel bad that they used such harsh words against my brother. If they had carried on for a little longer and not climbed in the carriage, I am sure I would have put them straight and taught them a lesson for saying bad things about my brother. They would have forgotten all their pride and wealth." He thought of running after the carriage to tackle them but then thinking of London's social culture and the laws of the city, he refrained himself. Then he thought, "Maybe I should go and see Audrey Hope right now. I am confident that she will be very happy to see me alive and well and seeing my poor and destitute condition she will help me in all possible ways. She will make me rich by virtue of her wealth." His mind did an about turn and he said to himself, "I should not think like this as no one else can really turn my luck around. The wealth of my friends cannot change my destiny. It would be best for me to create my own resources. I will not meet either Audrey Hope or my brother at this stage."

With such thoughts, he reached the inn where he had rented a room for two days and went to his room. He laid down on the bed, tired, thirsty and hungry.

Nevlin Lane had some biscuits and a piece of cheese in his pocket. He also had enough money to go out and have a full meal. However, he did not feel like eating anything. The possibility of Audrey Hope marrying Sir Jordan Lane had upset him. He loved Audrey Hope as a sister and wanted somehow to go and warn her about the true character of his step brother. He could not sleep. He kept thinking about how he could warn Audrey Hope. To pass the time, he took out the newspaper from his pocket. He was short of money but had bought the newspaper on arrival in London to find out the latest news about his city and country. On the very front page, there was the text of the speech given by his brother in the parliament that day on the subject of the government helping the helpless and the orphans. He read the whole speech from the beginning to the end with great attention. In this speech, Sir Jordan Lane had expressed sympathy with the poor, the helpless and the orphans. He appealed to the citizens of London to help them. The language of the speech was simple and very effective and was written so as to stir emotions. There were quotes from famous poets and other learned persons making the speech very powerful in its impact.

Nevlin Lane should have felt proud of his step brother after reading the text of his wonderful speech. However, he began to dislike his brother even more because what he had heard indicated that his brother's actions were not in line with the text of the speech. He said to himself, "According to the elders, a person who professes sympathy outworldly but in reality tells lies and does the opposite, is a hypocrite, selfish and cruel person. His sayings have no impact. There is no sin greater than being a hypocrite." With this in mind, Nevlin Lane tore up the paper and threw it in the garbage. He tried to visualise the face of his brother, as he last saw it, when his brother was sitting in the carriage and passed him by. He came to the conclusion that the article in the paper regarding his brother's speech did not reflect what his brother was really like. What he wrote was all for show and did not mean a thing. It was not a speech written from an honest heart. It was likely that the author of the article was in fact exactly as Percy Heal was describing him, a cunning, manipulative and wicked person. Nevlin Lane wondered if this could be true.

This thought disturbed Nevlin Lane very much. He got up from the bed and paced the room up and down several times. He got tired and laid down on the bed and immediately fell fast asleep. In his dream he saw both Audrey Hope and Sylvia standing by his bedside and looking sad. He also saw his old home, the Greenwich mansion. It looked desolate and sad. He woke up startled by the dream. He got up from the bed and looked outside. He saw the morning star fading away and the scene of early dawn. He went through the morning routine and dressed up cleaning his old clothes of dirt with his hands. He decided he would go to the Greenwich mansion. He sat down on the chair for breakfast.

When Nevlin Lane had got down at the London Railway Station a few days back, he had learned from one of the porters about the death of his father. After hearing the news, Nevlin Lane had a strong desire to go and see his old home, the Court Lane. And also the sitting room of his father, where he died. He wanted to go there and pray for the peace of his father's soul. He also wanted to see the old favourite places of his childhood where he used to play with Audrey Hope. He took out all the money he had from his pocket and counted it. He realized that after paying for the rent at the inn and three days of meals, all he was left was six pence! After counting the money, he kept the balance of the change in his pocket. From his pocket he took out cheese and biscuits and ate them for breakfast. He had got used to eating stale and dry food because after leaving Lornehope Camp, on several occasions, he had to eat such food during his journey. That's why at this time he did not mind eating old dry bread, biscuits and cheese for breakfast. He finished it all and drank a cold glass of water and thanked God for the meal. He checked out of the inn and hired a cab for two pence to take him to the Court Lane house.

On way to his ancestral house, he saw posters on the walls of tall shops and houses, advertising the show at the theatre. He read the first line which was printed in very bold and big letters "Royal Italian Opera." The second line which was written in red ink, read "Senorita Estella in today's show will play the part of Margaret in a very elegant style and with great talent." As the carriage was going at fast pace, Nevlin Lane could read only these two lines. He could not read the rest nor was he really interested in reading the poster of a show. How could he have possibly known that his beloved Sylvia Bond had been given the name of Senorita Estella! And she was the one performing in the show in London. If he had known about it, he would have been saved this great anxiety and sadness.

The cab reached the populated area just outside the Court Lane mansion. Nevlin Lane recognized in one glance the various buildings, the trees and gardens with flowers. Dozens of people whom Nevlin Lane knew and recognized, were busy in shopping. Several people looked at him and he recognized them as persons living in his neighbourhood. As the carriage was going at a fast pace, no one recognized him. How could they recognize him anyway? All the inhabitants of the Court Lane, old and young people and children, knew Nevlin Lane as the favourite son of his wealthy father, who was always well dressed in costly clothes of the latest fashions, riding high bred horses or travelling in elegant carriages. They had seen him buying goods worth a lot of money and expensive merchandise from various shops. He always had several servants around him to serve him. So how could they even imagine that Nevlin Lane would be sitting in a hired cab, wearing old and dirty clothes. Nevlin Lane was trying to avoid looking directly at people, who knew him well. If anyone tried to stare at him, Nevlin Lane would bend his head down and look at the foot mat. This was the reason that none of the people on the street recognized him. In addition, no one was expecting that Nevlin Lane would return to London so suddenly and without prior information. Finally the cab reached near the gate of Court Lane after passing through the streets and market of Court Lane. He had the cab stopped in the shadow of a tree and paid the cab driver and asked him to go back. He started to walk on foot and reached the boundary of Court Lane. He felt very happy to see the old tall building that used to be his home, surrounded by big trees, fruit trees and the flower gardens. He spent the whole day roaming around the house. Whenever any one of the servants came out of the house, he hid by the side of the house or behind a big tree to avoid being seen. In the evening, he went to the big oak tree, where he used to play in his childhood the game of back riding with Audrey Hope. It was here that he would carry Audrey Hope on his back to his father's sitting room and at other times she had to carry him the same way. Standing under this big oak tree, Nevlin Lane looked in the north and happened to see the stairs which led directly to his father's sitting room. The room had a door leading to a balcony outside the room. Nevlin Lane felt as if the whole building looked very sad and all its walls looked pale as if wrapped in sorrow. Tears came to his eyes. Remembering his father, he cried uncontrollably to his heart's content.

He was about to wipe the tears from his face with his handkerchief when suddenly someone grabbed his waist from the back. Nevlin Lane jumped with such force and in a manner that the person who grabbed him from the back, fell flat on his face. The moment he fell, Nevlin Lane jumped and sat down on his chest and delivered a strong blow to his head and said, "Tell me at once who you are and why you grabbed my waist?" The fallen man recognized Nevlin Lane's face and his voice and said, "Oh my! You are my dear and near friend, Nevlin Lane, the Master of Court Lane!" Nevlin Lane also recognized the voice of the fallen man but could not exactly remember the face and his name right away. After all it had been nearly five years since he left this place and saw him last. Nevlin Lane was about to ask his name when the fallen man said, "Why, my dear Sir, you do not remember me! I am your childhood friend, Trail, now inspector of police. I am one of your old and most loyal servants and your reliable and trustworthy friend." On hearing this Nevlin Lane got up from his chest and helped him to get up. He shouted with great joy at meeting his old friend and shook his hand and hugged him and inquired about his well being.

Trail said, "I am just the same as I was when you were here. You tell me how you have been and the reason you are acting as a fugitive? What are you looking for? Where did you go away leaving us all behind here and why did you not inform me about your coming back to London? How long have you been back and why did you not come and see me straightaway as soon as you came here? Also whom are you waiting for standing here at this hour in the evening?"

Nevlin Lane said, "Oh my, Oh my! My friend, at meeting you I am reminded of our old association. I consider you my very sincere and true friend I am extremely happy to meet you."

On hearing this, Inspector Trail saluted him and bent his head to show respect and said, "Friend, please do pardon me. I grabbed your waist mistaking you for someone else."

Nevlin Lane said, "You must be expecting some robber? What else can be expected from you but to chase robbers."

Trail replied, "Kind Sir, I was watching you for nearly thirty minutes. Because of the trees, I could only see your feet and the sound made by your feet while you were standing here. I was waiting for an opportunity to arrest you because I have been in search of a famous dacoit who escaped from here. My informants told me that this dacoit named Banks, has been seen in this area. He was last spotted approaching Court Lane. I mistook you for him and grabbed your waist. Considering me to be your old loyal friend, please do pardon me for this outrage."

Nevlin Lane said, "You were concerned with the catching of this dacoit while I was watching my old home and the stairs leading to my father's sitting room. I was simply roaming around, crying. You may recall that this route of the stairs was constructed to allow easy access to my late father's sitting room. In my time this place used to be very lively but now it seems so desolate and abandoned."

Inspector Trail said, "Your sadness is justified. No one else would feel sad the same way as you would. In front of God, man and angels are both powerless and His will prevails. You know that there is nothing that could have been done. You must have patience and courage to face it. Now I want to know why you are wearing old and dirty clothes. For whose sake have you adopted this attire? Why do you look so nervous and confused? You should feel happy to be back home in good health. You should not mourn your father's death now. Let us go inside the house where you can pay proper homage to your father's memory by praying for peace to his departed soul. Since you left so suddenly, your old servants remember you everyday. They wait for the news of your coming back day and night and when they do not get any news, they cry. Come inside and console them. Go inside and pray for your father in his sitting room and do prayers as per the religious books. Make all your friends and servants happy once again by meeting them. The condition of your old servants is very bad. They are not able to work and constantly remember you. Not only human beings, but it seems, even the walls, all objects and the birds look sad because you went away. Whenever I meet any acquaintance on the road, after the usual greetings, they invariably ask about your whereabouts. All your friends and acquaintances miss you very much. Listen to my advice. Let us go inside the house. Meet your brother and make everyone happy."

Nevlin Lane said, "Listen buddy, do not fabricate tall stories. Even in our childhood you used to talk about such irrelevant things. You used to drive me crazy with too many questions. Before I tell you about the story of my travels, you tell me how you became a senior police inspector of our area from your background of playing marbles. No doubt you deserve this post because even in childhood you were good at making a capital case out of the most ordinary situations while playing hide and seek. You would win the round with your fast talking. Now to answer your question, I have put on this attire and appearance of poverty to test the love and loyalty of my old friends and relatives. There is a hidden reason behind all this. I want to see whether my old friends and relatives, who used to profess love and loyalty in the good old days, behave the same way and show true love when I appear to be poor and in need. You know well that from the very childhood I do not tell lies or pretend what I do not mean. I trust my friends and never hurt anyone. To tell you the truth I feel very proud and happy to see you as senior inspector and to meet you. It is as if I have found an old treasure."

Inspector Trail said, "My friend, it is because of your wise counsel that I have been able to achieve the rank of inspector. Your teachings gave me a special sense to judge a person. Just by looking at a person I can tell what he is really like. I arrested several well known dacoits and helped many people recover their lost belongings. This art that I have of judging a person has been instrumental in solving several big cases and my superiors have been very happy with my work. I discharge my duties with honesty and hard work.

I am always fair and just. All these qualities that I have are because of your teachings, otherwise, as you said, I used to play marbles and spent days in playing games. I am grateful to your late respected father. On his recommendation, I got a job in the police department and with your blessings, today I am the inspector in-charge of this area including Court Lane. You will see my work for yourself. These days I am in pursuit of a famous dacoit by the name of James Banks. I expect to arrest him any time in the near future. He is well known in the department and there is a prize for his arrest. The person who arrests him will get a big promotion. This dacoit used to live here and belongs to my area of Court Lane. He is often seen around your house at Court Lane. He disappeared about three years ago and has now come back."

Nevlin Lane said, "After listening from you about Banks, I now recall that he was very cunning and dangerous. I remember reading several articles about him in newspapers."

Inspector Trail said, "Certainly, you must have read about him. The newspapers are full of his description and exploits. This dacoit, who used to live with his kind and pious daughter at Stone Lake Street in Court Lane municipality, escaped from the prison here. His whereabouts are unknown for the past three years. In this three year period, twice there was news of his being seen in London. No doubt he must have come back here. Somehow I was misled and in spite of intensive surveillance, I have not been able to arrest him so far. I believe there is a very influential and powerful man behind him who assists him in escaping every time. I am also after this man who protects him. Today I got the information that he is here for a week and is hiding somewhere here in your house. This time he will not be able to escape my hands. I have closed all the surrounding roads and some very experienced officers are doing the surveillance. I will arrest him soon."

Nevlin Lane laughed and said, "You have indeed become an expert in capturing robbers and dacoits. I remember that I used to watch the daughter of Banks, about whom you just mentioned, going to school every day. She was known to be a very kind and gentle person."

Inspector Trail said, "For the past several months, she too has disappeared. I used to know this girl well from childhood. After the death of her mother, she used to live all alone in her house. Her mother was from a high class and very rich family. She was also very beautiful. However, she was very disturbed and sad at her husband's association with robbers and dacoits and was angry with her husband for the same. Eventually she died of this constant pain and suffering. This girl never co-operated with her father. She was beautiful, clever and of a good character. She did not want to see even her father's face and had nothing to do with him. You probably remember her face well—she often came to play with us and our other friends. She was so clever that she always came first in her school in all class examinations. But she is responsible for her own bad luck and for destroying her life. The rumour is that she got involved with some rich man who promised to marry her but left her after seducing her and destroying her pride. I only know this much. I have not seen her since then. I do not know which city she has moved to now. I have also not been able to find out the person who is responsible for destroying her life. Actually I did not make any effort to find him. She never told me about her condition and how she was managing. If she had requested my help I would have certainly made all efforts to find this man and would have at least made some arrangements for her comfortable living by negotiating for a proper allowance from this man who had destroyed her life. Oh well, let us leave this topic. One reaps as one sows. No one can change the way Nature works—no one has done it in the past nor can anyone do it in the future. Anyway, tell me why are you standing outside your own house and not going inside? And why have you not met your brother so far? You must meet him and read the will of your father along with your brother. I am sure your father must have left half of his property and wealth in your name. You must claim it."

Nevlin Lane said, "Listen friend, right now I do not wish to meet any person and also I do not want anyone to know about my return to London. I ask you to please refrain from mentioning it to anyone."

Inspector Trail said, "Alright. I understand what you mean and appreciate that you want to test your friends and relatives first and find out what has been going on in your home. You will meet your brother only after satisfying yourself. If this is your wish, it is alright with me. However, I would urge you to meet your old nanny, Mrs. Parson. From her you can know what has happened since you left. You may recall that Mrs. Parson used to referee the hide and seek game between Audrey Hope, yourself and me. She used to call you by your childhood name, Master Lane. I am telling you, without any hesitation, the absolute truth, that Mrs. Parson, your old nanny, loves you with a pure heart and has great respect for you. Six months after you disappeared, she left the employment of your brother and now she lives in Stone Lake Street. Come with me. I will show you her house. She is desperate to see your face again. She remembers you constantly and even cries remembering you. She will be overjoyed to see you. She must have asked about your whereabouts and your address a thousand times. Even though her house is small, she will do everything to make you feel most welcome. Audrey Hope is feeling the same way after being separated from you. These days she is not in her house at Court Lane. She is living in the house of Lady Marlow. If she was here, I would have informed her about your return right away, even if you had pleaded not to tell her a thousand times. In her grief of separation from you, she has given up her own pleasures and constantly remembers you like a crazy person. In every meeting she brings up your example of kindness and good nature. The moment she knows that you are here she will find you, even if you put yourself behind seven locks!"

Nevlin Lane said, "Please take me to Mrs. Parson. The news that she is alive and well has given my sad heart new energy and joy. I am not at all concerned about her small house. I have become accustomed to living in a very little space. She is my true well wisher from my childhood days and loves me with a sincere heart. I do not want to disturb you in your important work, just show me her house from a distance and I will go on my own. You can then go for your official work. However, you must meet me tomorrow evening and we can have dinner together. I have several matters to discuss with you and I can, at the same time, tell you about my experiences of travels abroad."

It is interesting to note that Nevlin Lane did not say anything to Inspector Trail about his poor condition. According to the elders and wise men, the persons who come from a poor family are always complaining about their monetary problems and are miserly even if they rise to big positions and become rich. Telling such people of your problems can be the basis of being looked down upon and being humiliated. This world is also full of kind and generous people. Persons from rich families and of rich disposition show respect to others who are less fortunate and are poor. They may suffer themselves but help the poor and needy. Remembering all this, Nevlin Lane did not say anything about his problems to his friend, Inspector Trail. He knew the family of Inspector Trail well. He came from a poor family and his parents were known to be miserly. He was bound to have inherited some family traits. Nevlin Lane ignored it that Inspector Trail neither invited him to his house nor offered to take him out for dinner, though he talked at length about his friendship and loyalty. On the contrary he directed Nevlin Lane to the house of his old nanny. Nevlin Lane knew that in comparison to Trail, Mrs. Parson was very compassionate and had a big heart. She used to pamper Nevlin Lane and looked after him with loving care and attention. She would often take Nevlin Lane to the market and buy him toys with her own money. She used to prepare his favourite dishes and fed him with great love and care. For this reason Nevlin Lane felt close to his old nanny and started to walk to her house with Inspector Trail. As Nevlin Lane was rich in his heart, he invited Trail for dinner the next day even though he did not have money for his own meals.

Chapter 25

The top and bottom are inseparable here
It is likely that small may ultimately become big

Lord Lorimor, on the instructions of Dr. Langley, had hired Merci Fairflex to look after and assist in the recovery of Sylvia Bond. He took Sylvia Bond with him to various places for a change of climate from Lornehope Camp. He travelled with her to many places ensuring that she was comfortable and well looked after. At all these places he entertained her by taking her to the various theatres.

Merci Fairflex looked after Sylvia, day and night, with complete devotion and dedication. Everyday Lord Lorimor did his best to console her. With the gentle and kind care of these two people, the change of climate and the excitement of visiting various places, Sylvia soon regained the radiance on her face. The effects of her trauma disappeared. She also gained some weight and her face and skin became as bright as a rose. Everyone who saw Sylvia could not help commenting on her very bright and beautiful features and how they suited her short stature. The religious minded people appreciated and admired the work of God when they looked at Sylvia and felt in awe of Him for creating such unparallelled beauty.

Sylvia was a very simple minded girl. She did not know how beautiful she was and did not care at all about her looks. She had no pride or ego. She was very humble by nature. She was constantly aware of the unqualified love, affection and very gentlemanly behaviour of Lord Lorimor and felt very grateful to him for all that he had done for her. Though outwardly she had recovered, in her heart she still missed Jack very much. Although she was convinced that Jack was killed, she saw his face in front of her eyes all the time. At times she got very restless and cried for Jack and did not want to see the face of any one else. Often in the night she would wake up crying, "Jack, Jack!" Sometimes she would sit at a quiet place in one position for hours, lost in his memory.

Lord Lorimor and Merci Fairflex tried their best to make her forget Jack, but it was of no avail. To keep her occupied and entertained, Lord Lorimor took her for walks by the river side, in the parks and other places. He also bought her beautiful dresses to wear when he took her to various theatres and shows. He took her to expensive restaurants to have delicious food. He talked to her on subjects which would give her peace of mind and console her. He read her the latest news from newspapers. However, nothing made her forget Jack.

One day Sylvia drew the attention of Merci Fairflex towards her and said, "Both you and respected Lord Lorimor have looked after and protected a lowly poor girl like me, with utmost kindness and care. You are doing this always with a smile. Even my real brother or sister would not have done as much as you have done for me. I do not have words to express my gratitude and indebtedness to both of you. If, during my illness, you had not looked after me with such dedication and loving care and if respected Lord had not spent so much money so lavishly to provide every possible comfort for me, I would not have survived and would have died. I pray to God everyday for respected Lord Lorimor's happiness, health and wealth. Except for prayers, I have nothing else to offer."

Merci Fairflex said, "Dear Sylvia, please do not think like this. I have carefully tested the kind and helping nature of Lord Lorimor. I can say, with full confidence, that he is the kind of person who helps the needy. He never expects anything in return for his kind deeds. He does not expect anyone to praise him or show him their gratefulness. He does all these good deeds without any self interest or any expectation of any kind in return."

Sylvia replied, "No doubt, whatever you are saying about him is correct. I think about him the same way. In this world no other person can be better than Lord Lorimor except for . . ."

On hearing the word, "except," Merci Fairflex cut short Sylvia's sentence and said, "By saying except, you are probably referring to your Jack."

Sylvia said, "Oh! Jack left this world before his time without any cause. In my eyes no one can equal Jack. God gave him a very kind nature and bestowed all the good qualities in him."

Merci Fairflex found Sylvia to be very clever, learned, skilled in several arts and one who had a very enchanting voice for singing. She had not met any other woman who was so pleasant and of such a loving nature. Lord Lorimor used to say similar things about Sylvia and his love for Sylvia was very sincere with no expectation. Though Sylvia was much more beautiful and accomplished than his beloved Audrey Hope, he never even once thought of Sylvia in any other way, except as a sister. He always called her "dear sister" and behaved like a brother towards her. He had eyes only for Audrey Hope and spent all his time thinking about her. He continued searching for Nevlin Lane in all the cities he travelled, as per the request of Audrey Hope.

After searching for Nevlin Lane in all the cities of Austria, Lord Lorimor went to other cities of Europe. He planned to look for Nevlin Lane in London itself and felt that the climate of London would also suit Sylvia. For this reason he talked to Sylvia about London, its environment and its attractions. He began to read to Sylvia the important news and articles about London from the newspapers. He promised to take her to various theatres and the magic shows of London. However, whenever the topic of London came up, Sylvia would frown and her face would become tense and pale. It was obvious she did not like the city of London.

Merci Fairflex noticed Sylvia's reaction and very tactfully said to Lord Lorimor, "Sylvia will not like the environment of London. The memory of her brother Jack, which is gradually fading away, will once again begin to surface. In my humble opinion, it will be better if we try and find a suitable place for her to live somewhere around here."

Lord Lorimor seriously thought about this. He went to Sylvia and spoke to her in a very soft and gentle voice, "If you would like to stay in Italy for a little longer period, it is possible it may do some good to your grieving mind. The refreshing and natural environment of Italy is very healing to even the most seriously ill patients and they get better. You should know that I am on a mission to search for a person on the request of a friend. Because of this commitment I cannot stay at one place for too long. However, I will be happy to arrange for a house and provide all other things for your comfort whether you live in Italy or any other city of your choice. With the money I have, I can provide for anything that you need for your comfort, in no time. I can look after your safety myself when I am here and make arrangements for your safety when I am away. I will not let you be inconvenienced or face any problems. I consider it my duty to spend money for your comfort, as I look upon you as my sister."

Sylvia thanked Lord Lorimor very sincerely and said in a very polite and respectful voice, "I have read about Florence in books, and I understand it is a very nice and beautiful place. I would very much like to live there."

Both Lord Lorimor and Merci Fairflex fully concurred with Sylvia's choice of living in Florence—a city located in the centre of Italy. They made all the arrangements for her to move to Florence. Lord Lorimor escorted Sylvia, and they reached Florence with all her belongings. He made appropriate arrangements for her to stay at the guest house in the Women's College. After settling her, he left in search of Nevlin Lane in the nearby cities.

After Lord Lorimor left, Merci Fairflex took Sylvia to various famous buildings and beautiful sites of Florence. She also began to read books to Sylvia, on various interesting subjects. This kept her occupied and entertained. One day both Sylvia and Merci Fairflex went to the Florence Church, for prayers. In the church, girls, of the same age as Sylvia, were singing hymns and other religious songs on the organ, in their melodious voices. Sylvia liked the church building, the service and the atmosphere very much. She also felt very happy to meet the girls. She listened to their music and spent considerable time talking to them and finally returned to her room at the guest house. After dinner, she started to sing the hymns that she had heard the girls sing at the church, with great devotion in her melodious voice. She felt happy singing the song. Though the door of Sylvia's room was closed, her enchanting and melodious voice could be heard by people staying there. They were mesmerized by the sweetness of her voice. Merci Fairflex was working in the adjoining room. When she heard Sylvia singing, she rushed to Sylvia's room and found the door of her room closed. She peeped through the window and asked Sylvia, "Is that you singing there, Sylvia Bond?" Sylvia stopped singing, opened the door for Merci Fairflex and said, "Yes, I was trying to remember the words of the song I heard at the church."

Merci Fairflex said, "Well done Sylvia! Very good, Sylvia! I felt as if an angel from above had come down on earth to sing with her melodious voice. I had read in the books about the very beautiful angel who lives in heaven and sings with a loud and most enchanting voice. What I have read, I now hear in your singing. I regret that you never sang any song in the presence of Lord Lorimor. He would have been so happy to hear you sing."

Sylvia replied, "Do you really think that Lord Lorimor would have liked my singing? If I knew this before I would have sung for you and Lord Lorimor every day. To tell you the truth, I sang only to entertain myself today, after a very long time. The person who really liked my song is no longer alive." Her eyes filled with tears as she said this and she could not speak any further.

Four days after this incident Sylvia bought a piano of her choice. She started to sing songs of separation and other hymns, regularly. She sang with great emotion in the memory of her Jack and to please Merci Fairflex, who enjoyed her singing.

Near the women's college guest house there was a hotel, the doors of which were adjacent to Sylvia's rooms. Several prominent persons, travelling in Italy, were staying at this hotel. One of these persons was a famous singer from London, who had come to meet someone in Florence. On hearing Sylvia's melodious voice, he went to her room and quietly entered it without informing her or knocking at the door. He stood near the piano and said to Sylvia, "Child, you sing very well. God has given you a very sweet and melodious voice. A good melodious voice is a gift from God. Please pardon me for entering your room without your permission. On hearing your beautiful voice and singing I just could not resist myself."

Sylvia got up from her chair and respectfully greeted the old singer. The Old Man said "Child, may God give you a long life. Please tell me who taught you to sing in such style?"

Sylvia said, "Sir, my late father taught me to sing like this. He made me learn different kinds of songs. Since his death, I just sing once in a while to take my mind off other things."

The Old Man said, "If your father taught you to sing like this, then he must be a highly cultured and educated person who enjoyed life. Child, please don't be shy and do not consider my praise, flattering. I am a singer myself and by God's grace, I have made money by my knowledge of music. I have no children. From the very childhood I have been devoted to music and singing. Now I like to teach music to people with gifted voices and those who like music. At this stage, I very much enjoy passing on my knowledge to men and women who have the potential to excel in music. These days, without charging any money, I teach talented young people the art of singing, dancing and acting and see them rise to the top in their selected field. Now please sing the same song again from the beginning and I will point out to you the areas where you have made a mistake. My only wish is that my students rise to the highest level of perfection in music so that even after I am gone I am remembered in this world."

As per the request of the old man Sylvia sang the same song that had brought the old man to her room. He said to Sylvia, "Very good, very well sung. If you would like me to teach you the various pitches, intricacies, the theory of music and train your voice, come with me to the Government Academy of Music. At this institute, talented girls are taught music, free of charge. I teach there on a regular basis. It will be my pleasure to teach you everything about the theory and I will also train your voice for good classical music within forty days. You will learn music in such a way that anyone who hears you will be ecstatic. By virtue of your excellent voice, within these forty days you will learn everything that one needs to know about music. Anyone who knows even a little bit about music will admire your song. The common folks will be happy listening to your enchanting voice and you yourself will enjoy your music much more and will be lost in your own melodious songs." After saying this, he left Sylvia's room without waiting for an answer.

After the old singer left the room, Merci Fairflex asked Sylvia, "Sylvia, do you really want to go to the academy of music to learn music?"

Sylvia thought for a few minutes and asked, "Did the old singer mean that I learn music to earn money?"

Merci Fairflex said, "How do I know as to what he meant? But I can only say that music is a good art and it does not imply that people who learn music necessarily do so to earn money. Many boys and girls learn it for the sake of the art and for their own pleasure and satisfaction. They may sing at a party only, to please their friends and relatives. In my opinion, learning the art of music will prove to be very good for you. It will not only keep you occupied but it may also turn out to be the right medicine to make your sorrow become light and bearable."

Sylvia said, "You are my true and sincere friend and my well wisher. I would like to share my thoughts with you. For the past few months I have been thinking that I should acquire some skill that would enable me to earn a living for the rest of my life. Due to the kindness and generosity of respected Lord Lorimor, I have all possible comforts and luxuries. He is spending a considerable amount of money on my health, welfare and protection. He has not placed any restrictions on my spending money on any thing that I want. In fact, at the time that he was leaving for his trip, he left a large sum of money with me and asked me to buy anything I want and not to be inconvenienced in any way. If you ask my true feeling, I consider this, at best, a kind of charity. I have been thinking day and night, for a long time, that somehow I should be able to earn my own living with my own efforts. So far I could not think of any skill that I have that would enable me to earn a living. Now if this old man can teach me the art of music that would enable me to earn an honest living. I would prefer that rather than being dependant on Lord Lorimor. I will definitely learn music from this old man and inquire if there is a way for me to earn money from my knowledge of music. If he suggests something which is to my liking and suits my temperament, then I will not hesitate to accept his advice."

Merci Fairflex fully agreed with her. She went to the hotel where the old man was staying and requested him to teach music to Sylvia in a formal manner. The old singer agreed to her request.

Next day both Sylvia and Merci Fairflex accompanied the old man to the Government Academy of Music. Sylvia developed great interest in music. For three months she went to the Academy every day with Merci Fairflex. As Sylvia was an exceptionally talented and clever girl, the old man, as per his promise, made her a master of music within forty days. She stood first amongst the students at the academy in all areas of music. Thanks to the help and teachings of the old man, Sylvia, in addition also learned the art of acting, and became very accomplished at this also. All this made Sylvia very relaxed and she was now always smiling and happy.

Lord Lorimor did not find Nevlin Lane in the cities of Europe and returned back. He found Sylvia to be twice more beautiful and charming since he had left her a few months back. She had accomplished a high degree of excellence in singing and music. She was no longer restless and depressed. Her youth was blooming all over her small body.

To convey his thanks to the old man, Lord Lorimor went to his room at the hotel. After the initial exchange of greetings, he learned that Sylvia in addition to mastering the art of music, had also done very well in the art of acting. He said, "She acts her parts with such perfection that the characters she portrays seem real. She has a natural God given gift of a very melodious and sweet voice. I have spent all my life in this field of music and acting and have seen hundreds of talented singers and actors. But

Sylvia is the best amongst them all. I have never come across anyone like her. I have also come to know that she lives under your guardianship. She does not like to do anything without first discussing it with you and taking your permission. If you want Sylvia to make a name for herself, I suggest you get her a job with one of the renowned theatres. I know of four such theatres, where the proprietors and managers have great respect for the professional singers and dancers. They come from very respected and rich families and are perfect gentlemen. They have built theatres to make money. To maintain the reputation and integrity of their theatres, they have laid down very strict guidelines and rules of behaviour. I rarely see such strict rules in the best of families. The owners and managers of these theatres are very selective as to whom they employ and are very strict in enforcing their rules. With the result no boy or girl with a loose character can work there. It is true that the owners of these theatres do not make as much money as some of the other theatres, but they prefer to make less money and have a good reputation. If you agree, then I can try and get Sylvia a job at one of these theatres."

Lord Lorimor did not express any opinion. He took leave of the old man and came back to where Sylvia was living. He said to Sylvia, "The old singer was full of admiration for you. He also praised the owners of four theatres and their rules and guidelines for the employees. From his discussion I understand that you too would like to work in a theatre and are thinking of a job in one of them. I took you under my protection because you were at the time helpless with no friend or relative to look after you. I did whatever I could to assist you in settling down. People in several cities now know that you are under my protection and guidance. If any one of your relatives, acquaintances or close family members comes to know that you have taken up an employment in a theatre for singing and dancing, they would look down upon on me and I would be very embarrassed for no reason."

Sylvia said, "Sir, as I mentioned to you before I have no one in this world who knows me or is interested in my welfare, nor have I any relatives or friends to look after me. I am all alone.

Even if we suppose that some relative or friend does suddenly appear from somewhere, why would he feel bad in my working at an honest and decent job in a theatre?"

Lord Lorimor sensed that Sylvia's mind was made up. He willingly gave his consent. He went with Merci Fairflex to the old singer's room and accompanied him to meet the manager of Theatre Florence. He informed the manager of Sylvia's desire to work in his theatre. On hearing Sylvia's excellent accomplishments, the manager went to meet Sylvia at the guest house. On obtaining Lord Lorimor's permission, Sylvia sang a song for the manager and demonstrated her skills in music and singing. The manager was very happy with her performance and offered her a job on the spot that paid one hundred pounds per month. Sylvia accepted the offer and the manager drew up the contract. Sylvia promised to come to the theatre at the time that was agreed upon.

After dinner in the evening, Sylvia said to Merci Fairflex, "If you like and approve of my job as a singer and agree to stay with me just as we are living now, I would like to keep you with me forever. I will look after you like a daughter taking care of her mother. Please tell me if you are willing to stay with me."

Merci Fairflex hugged Sylvia and with tears in her eyes she said, "I do not want to be separated from you even for a moment, until such time that you yourself tell me that you do not need my services any more. I will be proud to serve you day and night, to the best of my ability."

Sylvia was very happy to hear this from Merci Fairflex and thanked her profoundly for agreeing to stay with her.

At her first meeting with the manager of the Florence Theatre, she presented him, in writing, with the conditions of her working at the theatre. These were, "I will come to the theatre only fifteen minutes before the show time and immediately after the show I will return to my place. I will not meet any men or women even if they are recommended by you. I would like to be informed of the part that I have to play at the theatre, at least two hours in advance, at my place of residence. Since I can read and write, I can practise on my own. I will not come for practice and for rehearsals. I shall gladly perform any part given to me, be it old or new, to the best of my ability. I will not give anyone any reason to criticize my work. Merci Fairflex will always accompany me except when I am on stage."

The manager of Florence Theatre gladly agreed to Sylvia's terms and conditions. On the contract he wrote, "Agreed," and then he signed the document. He suggested that Sylvia take the name Senorita Estella for the theatre work. To this she agreed.

The posters, in which the name of the new famous lead singer Senorita Estella was printed, were pasted all over the city. Big advertisements were given in the newspapers of the forthcoming performances of Senorita Estella. The people of Florence were impressed by the advertisements and wanted to see this new singer cum actor, who was said to perform her part in a unique manner. On the day of the show, four thousand tickets were sold by early morning and by the time the show was to start, the theatre was full to the limit. There was not even standing room left. Sylvia reached the theatre fifteen minutes before the show, as per her contract and promise. Seeing the huge crowd, she became nervous and was overwhelmed by the multitude of people. She hugged Merci Fairflex and with tears in her eyes, she said, "If my Jack was alive, he would have been so very proud of me today."

Merci Fairflex wiped Sylvia's tears with her handkerchief and said, "The theatre bell is ringing. Take courage and compose yourself. Now go and perform your part with confidence and grace." Sylvia pulled herself together and went to her assigned place for the start of the show. She performed her part very gracefully and sang her songs with such a melodious and enchanting voice that the crowd was completely mesmerized by her singing and acting. They applauded like they had never done before. From all sides people shouted their appreciation. She became an instant favourite and a smashing hit with the crowd. Because of Sylvia, Florence theatre became world famous and its owners made huge profits and became very rich within a short period of time.

Chapter 26

What a pleasure when a stranger finds out about you
The magic in it keeps the suspense till the end.

Sylvia, alias Senorita Estella, became extremely popular in Florence. The Florence World Theatre got such huge crowds that the normal ten pence ticket was resold for fifty cents. Some folks, who were willing to pay ten times that price could not get a ticket even for that price. All tickets were sold well in advance. There was not even standing room available at the theatre. Several people had to go back disappointed because they were unable to get a ticket. God's gift of a very melodious and sweet voice, combined with excellent acting that made the characters look real, made Sylvia the craze of the town.

The newspapers' pages were filled with praise of her extraordinary performances, her singing and acting. Newspapers made up stories about Sylvia's life. One famous journalist wrote in his article, "According to me the famous singer and actress, Senorita Estella, is from London. She is very beautiful and at this young age sings and acts like a professional. She comes from a very rich and highly cultured family, but due to some family problems she has accepted a job with the World Theatre. However, her knowledge and mastery of music and acting deserves the highest acclaim."

Another journalist wrote in a famous newspaper, "Senorita Estella comes from a highly respected family and is the daughter of a very rich and highly placed officer. For some reason her parents asked her to leave the house. She ended up in Florence and found refuge at the World Theatre and started singing and dancing to support herself."

Another newspaper article speculated, "Senorita Estella is in fact the beloved girl friend of Lord Lorimor, a very rich, well known gentleman of London. The Lord is madly in love with her. It is rumoured that the engagement of Senorita Estella with Lord Lorimor will be announced shortly. This is the reason that the famous singer neither grants any interviews, nor talks to any one. She is not flattered by praise and all the attention she gets, and has no greed for money. It is likely that very soon she will leave the profession of singing and dancing and marry Lord Lorimor."

People all over the city were gossiping and guessing about the life of Senorita Estella. Newspapers speculated to satisfy the public's curiosity, adding their own theories about the subject. Every day, the tickets for the special and first class seats of the Theatre were sold by the morning. For the lower class seats, the line up for the tickets used to start two hours before the show and all the tickets were sold much before the show time. People who came just before the show, were not able to get a ticket at any price. The immense popularity of Senorita Estella was evident from the great applause by the audience, from all parts of the theatre. The people sitting in special, first and second class seats, in the front rows of the theatre, would shower the stage with flower bouquets for Senorita Estella. Some people who thought they were in love with her, would enclose a letter in the bouquet requesting a date. Some rich and high ranking officers would enclose currency notes and throw them with such good aim that the bouquets would land at Senorita Estella's feet. Sylvia would thank all the persons for their bouquets and would pick them all up with grace. She would then bow to the audience and leave the stage. On reaching home, she would take out the letters and currency from the bouquets and the next morning return them to the sender with a note saying, "Returned with thanks." She would put them in an envelope and give them to Merci Fairflex to post at the Florence post office.

The ones that did not have a return address, she would shred and throw in the waste paper basket.

Sylvia was now over seventeen. Her face looked bright and full of life, and reflected her kind nature, her very graceful manners, and her good qualities. The men and women of good families, by simply looking at her face could tell that she was a girl of a very good moral character and was not the type of girl who usually worked in theatres. In spite of all their efforts and investigation, they were unable to find out anything about her background, or the secret of her working at the Florence World Theatre. She was the talk of the town and subject of every household conversation. Everyone knew that this great singer was neither interested in money nor in visiting other places for entertainment and fun. Even when she went out for a stroll, she was never alone and she neither looked at anyone nor talked to anybody. From her face she looked intelligent and far-sighted and she was ever so beautiful—no one could be compared to her. People praised her without any hesitation. The truth is, that a man or woman develops a reputation which fits one's actions. If one tries to say untrue things about a decent person, that person does not become notorious. The one who says such things becomes a suspect, just like a person who tries to throw dust towards the moon, has the dust flying back in his own eyes instead of going towards the moon, and the moon keeps shining as usual!

Except for Lord Lorimor, Sylvia never spoke to any other man or woman. Even when a woman would request to speak with her, Sylvia would firmly refuse. She was very simple by nature. She would always wear clean, simple but decent clothes and hated make up and other beauty aids. She was not interested in money at all and regarded it as an essential nuisance. One fourth of her salary used to be deposited with Merci Fairflex to buy the daily groceries and the other things for the house. She would personally send one fourth of her salary to charitable organizations, the poor and the needy. Half of her salary was deposited in the banks in her own name for taking care of the future and the unforeseen requirements. She managed her affairs and money well. She dealt with all her responsibilities and duties in an efficient manner. Overall she began to lead a very comfortable life, living like a rich person. She rented a very elegant carriage to go for a daily ride and outing. Merci Fairflex was always by her side, whether she was in the house or outside. Whenever the fans greeted her on her way to the theatre or when she went out for a ride, she always acknowledged the greetings in a polite manner by bowing and waving her hand. People from all walks of life were very impressed by her radiant beauty and charm. She had such an air of elegance and aloofness about her that nobody dared come forward to shake her hand or to speak with her.

Sylvia was a very hard working and intelligent girl. She was fortunate to have found an excellent teacher in the old singer. He made her an expert in both music and acting in a very short period of time, without charging any money. Music became her obsession. She wanted to learn more so that she could acquire the highest possible standard. She began reading novels and other classics by famous authors. She obtained permission, in writing, from the publishers for converting their novels into plays for the theatre. She would work hard with the other actors and actresses of the theatre to help them practise their parts. She perfected the art of direction and production and was able to have a new play ready to be shown at the theatre at the start of each month. This earned her a great honour and reputation. The authors and publishers of the novels thanked her for playing their novels because not only the plays, but their books also became popular and earned them considerable revenues. Because of Sylvia, alias Senorita Estella, the owners of the theatre became very rich too and so did Sylvia.

During his stay at Florence, Lord Lorimor used to go to World Theatre every single day. He enjoyed watching Sylvia sing and act in a most captivating and professional manner. He marvelled at her art of making the characters from the novels come alive on stage. He appreciated her talent and was very proud of the fame and honour bestowed upon her. He very much admired her radiant beauty and her accomplishments. He often used to think whether she was the same Sylvia that he rescued from the grip of the wicked dacoit when she was lying alone and helpless with no friends in the jungle. She was now very famous and everyone admired and praised her! He used to say to himself, "God is Great, He alone looks after everyone and helps them as He sees fit:

> He bestows respect on those He wants to favour
> He gives humiliation to those He wants to punish."

Lord Lorimor used to say nice things to Sylvia. He used to tell her how much he appreciated her singing and acting and was very proud of her. Outwardly Sylvia appeared to be very happy and content. However, Lord Lorimor had noticed that when she was alone, she would invariably take Jack's name and mourn at his passing away.

One day Lord Lorimor said to himself, "Sylvia remembers her brother Jack constantly. She is a very loving person. God has created women like that. Once they love someone, all their actions are dedicated to him and they love that person whole-heartedly. I should also bid goodbye to my roaming around in foreign lands and go back to my beloved Audrey Hope and see how she is doing. Is she still in love with me and is waiting for my return or has she forgotten me? I have to search for Nevlin Lane only in the northern part of Europe. That is the only part left. I will search for him there for a month. If I find him I shall escort him to London otherwise I will return back to London and tell Audrey Hope, the whole story of my search from the beginning to the end. I am sure, when she listens to the great inconvenience and troubles I had to face during the journey, and the sincerity of my search, she will overlook the fact that I could not find her friend Nevlin Lane. My whole life depends on her marrying me. I cannot look at another woman. In fact I consider it to be a sin to even think of any other woman. I love only Audrey Hope and she is the only one for me."

With these kinds of thoughts going through his mind, he walked to the room of Sylvia and found both Sylvia and Merci Fairflex looking very happy and reading a letter. On seeing Lord Lorimor, they both expressed their joy. Sylvia handed the letter to Lord Lorimor and requested his advice regarding the subject matter. Lord Lorimor read the letter and shouted with joy and said, "Why, this is excellent, who could ask for anything more? The famous theatre in London has requested the World Theatre management to come to London with their whole cast to perform in London and they assure them of handsome revenues. Furthermore the management of World Theatre is requesting you to accompany them and have undertaken to pay all your expenses. They are committing in writing to give you one eighth of the daily revenues from the show, in addition to your pay. My dear sister, Sylvia, congratulations on this big promotion. May God bless you. Hard and sincere work is never wasted. You worked very hard in learning music and acting and you also worked honestly and with loyalty. The result is that you have now acquired such perfection the like of which I have not seen anywhere. May I ask you what you are going to do with the amount of money that you will earn? You will now become fabulously rich."

On hearing this, Sylvia first laughed heartily, then with tears in her eyes she said, "If my Jack was alive, probably you would not be asking this question because he would have taken care of everything. I would have given him all the money and asked him to distribute it amongst poor and helpless people. Now this is what I have in mind. I will use all the money I have saved in the bank, in the name of my admired and respected guardian, Lord Lorimor. I will build a big and tall church with a beautiful garden and landscape around it, with Lord Lorimor's statue in the front. Under the statue I will arrange for an inscription in big bold letters, 'This is the statue of that person whose motto from the very childhood has been: "Do kind deeds without expectation of any return."' This will be my way of saying 'thank you' in a small way for all the kindness and affection you have showered upon me."

She wanted to say more but Merci Fairflex interjected in between and said, "Respected Lord Lorimor, I would like to tell you today about the kind and simple nature of Sylvia Bond. She is neither interested in eating rich and delicious food, nor in wearing expensive clothes, nor in buying or using luxurious things. She has absolutely no ego or a 'show off' attitude. She has a simple, saintly nature. She sends a part of her salary to an orphanage in Paris. If, during her walks, she sees any poor or helpless man or woman, or learns about someone in need of help, she helps them without any hesitation. Though I live with her day and night, even I do not know all the poor people she is helping. I go and mail her letters at the post office and that's how I come to know of the people she is helping. She herself has never said a word about it."

Merci Fairflex wanted to say more but Sylvia motioned to her, with the expression in her eyes, to stop and asked her in a soft and polite voice, to keep quiet. Sylvia kept her hand on the shoulder of Lord Lorimor and said with her eyes looking down, "Sir, I have never done anything or taken any decision on my own, without your advice and permission, until now. If you ask me not to accept this offer then I will inform the theatre management accordingly and take up any other job that you may advise me to do. If you advise me to go to London as the theatre management has requested, I will go to London. I will not take any steps against your advice."

Lord Lorimor listened to Sylvia and after thinking for a few minutes said, "During the parties in London, I have met hundreds of girls. Except for one or two of them, no one can even come close to you for being so kind, gentle and honest natured. To have this kind of attitude is rare. My dear sister, I think you should go to London with the World Theatre. The fame, respect and great profits that the Florence World Theatre is enjoying is all because of you. The owners have made a lot of money because of the several new plays produced and directed by you. They are looking forward to similar growth in future. This is the reason that the owners are requesting you, in such a polite and respectful manner, to accompany them to London and are providing you with excellent benefits. I think, to disappoint them and turn down their offer will not be the right thing to do. This is also a unique opportunity for you to gain fame in London. You will also profit and make a lot of money from the London shows as will the owners of the theatre. All my friends in London will be very happy to see your art and to meet you. You will be honoured and will become extremely popular and famous in London."

Sylvia responded in a polite voice and said, "I really do not care for fame or honour. I have absolutely no interest in becoming rich. All my desires and ambitions are buried in the coffin alongside my dearest Jack. I only want to follow your directions and act as you may advise me to do. With your blessings, I will also be able to see London. I left the city at such a young age that my recollections of London are just like a hazy dream."

Lord Lorimor said, "Did you and your brother go straight to Lornehope Camp after leaving London? What was the purpose and need to go to Lornehope Camp?"

Since Sylvia did not want to share her past life with anyone at this stage, she changed the subject and said, "Respected Sir, I do want to tell you the details of my past, but please excuse me at this time." She started to cry.

Lord Lorimor said, "My dear sister, Sylvia, look at me. I certainly do not want to see you crying and being sad. I take my question back. I am sorry I made you sad by asking useless questions. This was not my intention. I gladly urge you to accept this offer and go to London. I will pray for your success and safety even when I am travelling abroad."

On hearing this, Sylvia was startled and asked in an anxious voice, "Do you mean you will not accompany me to London?"

Lord Lorimor replied, "Right now I cannot come to London with you under any circumstances. For the next few days it is important that I search for a person in the eastern towns and jungles of this continent. However, God willing, I do expect to be able to come to London after four or five weeks."

Sylvia said, "Seemingly you have not had enough of searching for this man living in some wilderness!"

Lord Lorimor replied, "You are right. I still have one more area left to search for this man."

Sylvia said, "I wish I could also assist you. I would like to take over the full responsibility of your travel mission and spend all my time and energy in completing it. If you do not consider me fit for this mission then please tell me if I can do anything in London to assist you. If you wish to write a letter to someone in London, I will be glad to deliver it as you instruct me to and carry out any assignment you wish me to."

Lord Lorimor blushed and said, "There is only one person in London to whom I can write a letter." He said it in such a low voice that Merci Fairflex could not hear it. She left the room and went to the other room to sew some lace on Sylvia's dress.

When Merci Fairflex left the room, Sylvia asked Lord Lorimor with a smile on her face, "Is this person a lady by any chance?"

Lord Lorimor replied, "Your guess is absolutely right. Yes, she is a lady."

Sylvia said, "A ha. Now I understand—she is the person in whose memory you are sad at times. Please do tell me, is this lady very beautiful? I am sure she must be exceedingly charming and good looking."

Lord Lorimor lowered his head and said, "Yes, she is beautiful and she is also kind. I have been in love with her for a long time. For me, there is no other woman more beautiful than her."

As he finished the sentence, tears came to his eyes.

Sylvia wiped his tears with her scented handkerchief and said in a joking tone, "I feel sad and happy at the same time knowing what you have just said. I am happy to know that you love this lady. I am sad that in spite of the fact that this lady is so beautiful and you care for her so much and love her deeply, you left her to roam around in jungles with no result. This I do not understand. Kindly do tell me the meaning of all this."

Lord Lorimor said, "It is on the instructions of this lady that I am roaming abroad. She requested me to search for her very dear childhood friend. She promised to remain single and not to marry anyone for two years. In spite of a very intensive search and doing everything in my power, I have not been able to find this person. It is now over six months past the two year period but I have had no luck. I have also not corresponded with her in all this period."

Sylvia asked, "Respected Sir, why did you not go back to

her after the two year period ended and why did you not keep the correspondence going all this time?"

Lord Lorimor replied, "I take it that your questions are based on your inexperience and lack of understanding of the situation. Dear sister, first of all try to understand the reason as to why I did not go to see her after the completion of the two year period and why I did not write to her all this time. I will tell you the logic behind it. Suppose I went to see her after the two year period ended, empty handed and without her lost friend, would she not take me to be a liar and doubt my story as an excuse for not completing the task? If I wrote to her and told her of my fruitless efforts and the great inconvenience and hardships of the journey, would she not consider this to be a ploy to get her sympathy and my inability to complete the given task?"

Sylvia listened to Lord Lorimor's reasoning, lifted her hands in sorrow and rubbed them hard. Then she shouted in a loud anguished voice, "Sir, I am sorry to say that your thinking is absolutely absurd and makes no sense. She would have married you straightaway on seeing you back and would not care whether you found her friend or not. This kind lady is apparently very wise and far-sighted. Such childish thoughts that you describe, would have never crossed her mind for a person that she was going to marry and have as her husband. She would never entertain such foolish thoughts for the person she loved so dearly. It seems to me that you are not sure yourself and do not know if she really loves you or not."

Lord Lorimor said, "You are talking like a child—how can I know how much she loves me when she has never made a promise to marry me or given me any other indication of her love towards me?"

Sylvia countered, "I am not a child. I am an experienced woman. Sometimes men, inadvertently, act very innocently. Most of the men do not understand love. You men folk cannot understand the depth of a woman's love. Please think seriously. If this lady did not love you whole-heartedly, would she assign you such a meaningless and foolish task? The request to search for her friend was only an excuse. The real reason was to test your love for her."

On hearing this, Lord Lorimor took a deep breath and looked at Sylvia with a surprised look and said, "You are probably right."

Sylvia said, "What do you mean probably—I am convinced that I am right. I am telling the truth. This lady loves you very dearly with all her heart. She is passionately in love with you. She does not care for anyone else except you. She has given her heart to you. She loves you more than you love her. You are unnecessarily wandering all over because you do not understand her love. It is a waste of time and effort. It is so unfortunate that you did not consider returning back to her immediately after the two year time period. Tell me how many letters have you written to her after this two year time period expired?"

Lord Lorimor replied, "As long as I could not find her lost friend, I did not have the courage or any grounds to write to her. However, before starting for Lornehope Camp, I wrote her a letter with the full intentions of mailing it myself at the post office. But somehow I forgot to mail it and since then it has been in my pocket. I did not consider it appropriate to mail it from another city because I was not sure if I will be successful in finding the lost person in that city. Moreover, there was nothing to write except that I love her with all my heart and soul. I have personally told her this several times. However, this lady has never expressed her love or sentiments in any way to indicate to me that she cares."

Sylvia said, "Oh well, Sir, You have given me another example of your lack of understanding. Please keep in mind that unlike men, women do not go around broadcasting their love. Can you not see and understand her love by her actions, her way of talking and the expression in her eyes? The truth is that a man howsoever clever and highly educated he may be, cannot understand the inner feelings and love of a woman. Because of his preoccupation with his own thinking, he ignores all the meanings of a woman's words."

Lord Lorimor said, "Listening to you and reflecting on your comments, I feel as if I am talking to this lady face to face."

Sylvia said, "All women, who are kind and balanced, think

alike. You are surprised because your thinking on this subject is not clear and you are confused."

Lord Lorimor asked, "Should I go and see her right away?"

Sylvia replied, "Most definitely—if there is a faster means then right away, go by that, fly if you can, go on a flying horse—you should see her without any further delay. I am confident that you will be able to win her over when you see her. God knows, how much this lady has suffered and what problems she may be facing because of your delay. It is all so unfortunate. All kinds of thoughts and doubts must be going through her mind and she must be feeling very sad."

On hearing all this from Sylvia, Lord Lorimor was speechless. Tears came to his eyes and he began to choke. His heart started to beat very fast and his face turned red. He lowered his head and just kept quiet. His face became sad and he looked very depressed.

When Sylvia saw Lord Lorimor feeling so sad, she kept her hand on his shoulder in a friendly manner and looking into his eyes lovingly, she said in a soothing sweet voice, "My kind Sir, because I have great sympathy for you, I took the liberty to say a lot of things which I should not have said to you and I may have been disrespectful. I apologize for my behaviour. It was never my intention to make you sad. Please pardon me for my disrespectful behaviour. You are aware that I do not even know this lady. Just because we are both women, I looked at the situation from her viewpoint and for some reason I suddenly developed a great sympathy for her in my heart. This is not an excuse for my disrespectful behaviour. I have said a lot of things which I should not have said. Now I have controlled my emotions and with folded hands I would like to say: 'Whatever you did was correct. I am only a woman and do not have brains to think. I am sure you will forgive me for my rudeness considering that I am only a woman.'"

Lord Lorimor said, "I consider you not only as my own real sister but also a friend whose love for me is true and sincere and who is genuinely sympathetic. Between a brother and sister, the word forgiveness should never be mentioned. Your words of sound counselling have been very effective and I am deeply impressed by what you have said. I believe your advice is like a voice from above and I accept it. I just want to make one last attempt to find the lost one and am planning to start right away. Around this city, and in this country there is great activity in building and laying new railway tracks. I want to search for him there. I understand the railway head office is just a few miles from here. There is work going on, on a very large scale, in constructing railway stations and laying miles of railway tracks. Several Englishmen from all walks of life are working there in various positions. Some are holding senior positions, some are in clerical positions and some are workers in construction and in laying tracks. It is likely that the friend of my beloved is working there in some capacity. I shall search for him for exactly one month and not a minute more. From there I shall go to London directly and meet my beloved. I shall tell her about my journey and the details of my efforts to search for her friend. I am sure I will be able to convince her that I spared no efforts. If, as you said, she really loves me, she will marry me. Otherwise I shall spend the rest of my life in her memory in some corner of the world, because there is no place in my heart for any other woman."

Lord Lorimor said goodbye to Sylvia and went into the room of Merci Fairflex. He asked Merci Fairflex to listen to him and said, "Please accompany Sylvia to London and look after her comfort and safety with love and devotion in the same way that you have looked after her so far. Please ensure that she is comfortable in every way and serve her well. Please never separate from her under any circumstances." After giving these instructions. Lord Lorimor left the house in search of the lost person.

Sylvia and Merci Fairflex also left for London the next day as per the arrangements made with the theatre. On reaching London and on the advice and guidance of Merci Fairflex, Sylvia rented a nice big house in St. James Street and they both settled down there. The equipment for the theatre had still to arrive and other arrangements for the new show had to be finalized. This gave both of them time to spend in seeing the famous places of London.

Sylvia was happy and fascinated to see the famous parks of

London. Not only was the environment of the park fresh and pleasant, the place was full of people from all walks of life. She saw women and young girls wearing fine jewellery and dressed in latest fashions, young men dressed smartly, young children and older people, all talking while having a stroll in the park and enjoying themselves. What surprised her most was that everyone was looking at her. Her simple but elegant dress, her calm style of walking, combined with her beautiful and bashful eyes was the reason that everyone was looking at her, especially the young men who were drawn towards her beauty.

One afternoon when Sylvia was walking in the park with Merci Fairflex, she turned her head to say something to Merci Fairflex and noticed that Merci Fairflex's face was turning pale, she was trembling all over and looked sick. Merci Fairflex could hardly stand, she gave a shriek and sat down on the ground. Sylvia asked, "Why Merci—what happened? What is the reason for you to look so frightened and concerned. Why are you trembling like this?"

Merci Fairflex replied, "Nothing, my dear nothing happened. I was reminded, for some reason, of my young days."

With these words she stood up. Sylvia looked all around to see what may have frightened her, but she could not see anyone or anything that could have scared her. She only saw a pale looking, tall man who was sitting with his head down in a yellow coloured carriage and the carriage was coming towards them. His carriage passed by them. Except for him there was no other person or any other carriage or riders on horses. Sylvia satisfied herself by saying to herself that there was nothing there to frighten Merci Fairflex.

Sylvia turned to face Merci Fairflex and held both her hands with great warmth and affection and asked her in a loving voice, "Merci dear, how are you feeling now? What made you turn so pale that you almost fainted? I pray to God that you have not contracted any disease or infection after coming to London."

Merci Fairflex replied, "Please do not worry yourself unnecessarily on my account. I am fine and thank God I am not sick or ill. I just felt tired and exhausted because of the heat. Now by standing up and with the fresh air I feel quite normal."

On hearing this Sylvia was satisfied. They both walked back through the market and reached their house safely.

After two weeks, the World Theatre was ready for its opening night. Fifteen minutes before the show, Merci Fairflex assisted Sylvia with her dress and jewellery for the show. Just before the show started, Sylvia peeked through the curtains and saw that every seat in all classes of tickets was taken and the theatre was jam packed. There was not even standing room anywhere. Sylvia felt nervous looking at the huge crowd, her heart began to beat faster and she started to tremble. Merci Fairflex put her hand on Sylvia's head to calm her and said in a loving voice, "My dear Sylvia you look pale and nervous—what's the matter? Are you feeling alright?"

Sylvia said, "I do not know why I have a choking sensation in my throat and my heart is beating so fast. I feel that some strange thing is about to happen."

Merci Fairflex replied, "The strange thing that you will see is that the men and women in all classes of the theatre are going to admire your performance immensely and will clap for a long time to show their appreciation like never before. You should not be scared of this crowd of spectators. You should perform with confidence and in a professional manner."

Sylvia said, "I am not scared of the crowd. But I feel that a new chapter in my life is about to begin. Because of this I have this choking feeling. It is possible that my own thoughts are making me depressed. Therefore I am going to push all my thoughts to one side and get ready to go for my performance."

Sylvia had hardly finished the sentence when the stage manager came and standing at the door said to Sylvia, "Please go and stand beside the entrance to the stage near the curtain as there is only one minute left for the curtains to open."

On hearing this Sylvia went to the stage and stood beside the curtain. She had hardly positioned herself, when the curtain opened. Sylvia started her music and dance performance. The audience liked her singing very much and from all sides of the house, the audience shouted and showed their appreciation for her sweet enchanting voice by the prolonged clapping of hands and by giving her a standing ovation. After finishing her part, Sylvia returned to her dressing room where Merci Fairflex was waiting for her. Merci Fairflex said, "Well done, very well done, congratulations. Your performance was superb. You sang your songs in a most delightful manner and the audience liked your performance so much that they are still talking about it. I have never heard you sing in such a delightful way before—it looked as if the goddess of music was personified in you."

Sylvia replied, "I thank you very much for appreciating my performance. Please tell me who is the young and very beautiful girl sitting in the first class section in the VIP row of chairs in the front? What is her name? I wonder what is the reason for her staring at me with hatred in her eyes. She did not take her eyes off me till my performance ended. She was quietly moaning and looked sad. Please tell me what's her name and who she is—you belong to London and you must know her."

Merci Fairflex replied, "I did not see any girl or woman staring at you. However, when I looked at the audience, I only saw them trying to get a better look at you by inching up in their chairs. Moreover, all my attention was concentrated in watching your performance and I did not feel the need to look at anyone else."

After listening to Merci Fairflex, she took her near the curtain and lifted a little corner of the curtain and whispered to Merci Fairflex, "Look at the first class row on the right hand side, after the first two chairs, on the third chair. There is a very beautiful lady sitting on it. She is so pretty and charming, is dressed in such beautiful and expensive jewellery and is wearing the latest fashion clothes. Somehow her lovely and charming face is attracting me towards her. See for yourself how beautiful she looks. This lady kept a steady gaze on me from the moment I started my performance. When I looked towards her, she frowned and turned her face away. She kept looking at me, all throughout my dance and music performance, with a look as if she hates me. She is so beautiful that I believe she is the ultimate in beauty."

Merci Fairflex said, "Oh my! God forbid. Sylvia do you think you alone have the monopoly on judging beauty? Just looking at her face you consider her to be the goddess of beauty and also assume that she was constantly staring at you with disdain! Your thinking is meaningless. To me it appears that there are several very pretty ladies in the audience here."

Sylvia said, "Yes, but the girl I am referring to is quite unique in her beauty and charm. There is no comparison to her in beauty and elegance. The elderly lady sitting next to her is probably her mother. I do not know why my heart is drawn towards this girl. I have this desire to meet her and ask her why she is looking at me with hatred. To me she appears to be the most beautiful of ladies and while dancing and singing I felt that my show was just for her. She also kept her eyes focused on me. From my experience I know that the stare of this lady has some special meaning. At times she looked at me with anger in her eyes and at other times she looked with contempt."

Merci Fairflex said, "I cannot understand how you develop such thoughts in your mind. It is not fair to entertain such thoughts regarding a spectator in the audience."

Sylvia said, "Oh well, never mind. In my opinion this girl is definitely angry with me. I wish somehow I could find her name and address. Maybe you can find this out from one of your acquaintances living in London."

After requesting for the information from Merci Fairflex, Sylvia left her to get ready for her next dance and singing performance on the stage.

Merci Fairflex gathered other actors and actresses and lifted a little corner of the curtain and pointed out to them the lady sitting in first class in the VIP area on the third chair from the side and asked them if they knew who she was and what was her name. They all said that they did not know her. However, the assistant manager, who was newly hired and was busy supervising the opening and closing of curtains, said, "Yes I know her. Her name is Audrey Hope and the lady sitting on the next chair is her aunt, Lady Marlow. They are both very rich people of London. They come from noble families and are well known in London's elite circle."

Merci Fairflex thanked him for providing the information. When Sylvia came off the stage after her performance, she told her the lady's name and the other details.

On learning that Audrey Hope and her aunt Lady Marlow were very rich and famous, Sylvia lost the desire to meet them. She thought that the rich people generally have a big ego and do not like to socialize with actors and singers who perform on the stage. Therefore, it was not surprising that the young lady was staring at her with contempt in her eyes. These rich people have very little sympathy for the poor and they look down upon everyone.

With this thought, Sylvia gave up the idea of meeting the young lady and ignored her perception that the lady was staring at her with hatred in her eyes and got busy with her performance and other work at the theatre.

Chapter 27

Look the murderer has arrived
He has come to kill me

On seeing the name of Senorita Estella in the lead role on posters of the World Theatre, Sir Jordan Lane had reserved theatre seats in the first class VIP area. He had read the news of Senorita Estella's engagement to Lord Lorimor, in the Paris newspapers. He did not care whether the news was correct or not. All he wanted to do was to turn Audrey Hope's attention away from Lord Lorimor.

From the text of the Paris newspaper article, Sir Jordan Lane guessed that the news of the engagement may not be correct. But he was sure of one thing. There had to be some connection between Senorita Estella and Lord Lorimor. For this reason, he wanted to plan the things in such a manner that Audrey Hope would be forced to marry him, before the return of Lord Lorimor, and not get an opportunity to meet Lord Lorimor on his return to London. To fulfil this plan he decided to visit the theatre every day and had accordingly reserved four seats for the show for the next several days. He was sure that after seeing Senorita Estella on stage, Audrey Hope would become jealous of her and start hating Lord Lorimor. This would help her to drive him out of her mind forever. This way, he figured she would marry him before Lord Lorimor returned to London.

With these thoughts in mind, he kept two theatre tickets in

his pocket and went to Audrey Hope's house. He joked and chatted with Audrey Hope on general topics. After a short time, Lady Marlow also came to the room. Sir Jordan Lane greeted her with respect and inquired about her health. After a while he brought up the topic of the new show at the theatre and asked her, "Are you ladies going to the World Theatre today to see the new show starring Senorita Estella?"

Lady Marlow replied, "We were planning to go and I sent a note to the theatre manager requesting him for two tickets for the first class special seats. However, the manager returned the money with a note saying that all the seats were completely sold out and there was not a single ticket available in any class. Thus we had to cancel our plans of going to the theatre.

Sir Jordan Lane said, "I have reserved two seats in the first class VIP section for the next two months by paying thirty pounds in advance. I am afraid I will not be able to go today. Why don't you take these tickets and go to the theatre today?"

Lady Marlow looked at Audrey Hope and asked her, "Would you like to go to the theatre and see the show?

Audrey Hope had started hating Senorita Estella for taking Lord Lorimor away from her. But she was also keen to meet her in the hope of getting some news about Lord Lorimor. She had been to the show two or three times but was hoping that she would get an opportunity of meeting Senorita Estella and with this in mind she said to Lady Marlow, "If you are going, I will certainly join you."

Sir Jordan Lane took out the two tickets from his pocket and handed them to Lady Marlow. He said, "Please accept these with my compliments. I neither have time nor any particular liking for the theatre. I will be happy if you use these tickets." After handing over the tickets, he left for his house.

After lunch, Audrey Hope went to her room and laid down on her bed. She started to think as to how she could arrange to meet Senorita Estella and get some news of Lord Lorimor to verify the truth of the newspaper article. However, she could not think of any excuse to meet her. She kept on thinking about this until the evening and when the bell rang for dinner, she came and went to the dining room. After dinner she went to dress up for the evening. She put on expensive jewellery and one of her finest, most elegant dresses of the latest fashion and combed her hair nicely. As she came out of her room, Lord Marlow called her and said in a happy voice, "Audrey, today you have dressed up very nicely and you are looking extremely charming. May God keep you safe from the evil eyes of others. Tell me, who is the lucky man with whom you are going out?"

Audrey Hope smiled and said, "Today I am going to the theatre with my fabulous looking, respected and dear aunt."

Lord Marlow said, "Oh yes! Now I understand—you ladies are going to listen to the enchanting songs of Senorita Estella. Some of the ladies have been to her show four times, but still are not satisfied. They want to go and see her lovely face and listen to her enchanting music again and again. It is no wonder that men like to go and see her show every day. It is the fifth time that you are going with your dear aunt. I have a feeling that you would like to go and see her show every day and perchance if there is a second show in the afternoon, you would want to go to that too. Oh well, we can go on talking like this forever, but in all seriousness, the truth is that I have never seen such a gentle and beautiful singer with so much charm and such a sweet, melodious voice. I get very angry with people who say uncharitable things about others without a reason. Newspapers in Paris have published articles that Senorita Estella is engaged to Lord Lorimor. This is absolute nonsense. In my opinion the article was published without investigating the facts. If she was engaged to him, would you not think that he would have come with her? He is not with her."

Lady Marlow motioned to her husband to drop the subject. Lord Marlow complied and said, "Oh well, some people just like to gossip for no rhyme or reason. It really does not concern Audrey or us and we have no need to analyze it."

Lady Marlow wanted Audrey Hope to marry Sir Jordan Lane and was trying her best to see it happen. For this reason she was looking for some way to prove that the newspaper article about the engagement of Senorita Estella and Lord Lorimor was true. With this in mind, Lady Marlow said, "If the editor of a reliable newspaper has published this news about the engagement of Lord Lorimor to Senorita Estella, how can we dispute that it is against logic and is not true? Is it not true that this singer is highly accomplished and very beautiful? This girl is definitely not a singer by profession. From her innocent eyes and the grace and charm on her face, even a dumb woman can see that she comes from a civilized and rich family. Probably, due to mistreatment at home, she has run away and started singing in a theatre to earn a living. It is quite possible that Lord Lorimor fell in love with her."

Lord Marlow said, "The reason why I think that this news in the paper is speculative is that Lord Lorimor is a wise and mature person. It does not matter how beautiful and decent this singer is, he is not going to associate with a girl who sings in a theatre. It is against his nature. The people who think that he is engaged to this singer are foolish. If Lord Lorimor was looking for a beautiful girl there was no need for him to roam around the jungles. There are plenty of beautiful girls in London, right here."

Lady Marlow made a face that showed her frustration due to the argument with Lord Marlow, and then she turned her face away. She took Audrey Hope's hand and went towards the carriage. They asked the driver to take them to the theatre.

Throughout the drive, Audrey Hope sat with a sad face pondering at the last sentence of Lord Marlow. When the carriage reached the theatre, she brushed aside her thoughts, checked her seat number and sat down on the chair next to her aunt, Lady Marlow. She looked around and saw Sir Jordan Lane and Lord Marlow sitting on two chairs in the row behind hers. Sir Jordan Lane had lied to Lady Marlow when he said that he had reserved two seats. He had actually reserved four seats. He gave two tickets to Lady Marlow and kept the other two tickets for himself. He took Lord Marlow with him to the show. The theatre was exceptionally crowded that day. Lady Marlow started to talk to her acquaintances sitting on the nearby chairs. Audrey Hope's eyes were fixed at the theatre curtain. At last, exactly at 9 p.m., the curtain opened and the show started. There was a complete silence in the theatre. All the eyes were fixed at the beautiful Senorita Estella. At her appearance on the stage, the audience shouted with glee and clapped.

Looking at the face of Senorita Estella, Audrey Hope felt very jealous and started to stare at her. She sat listening, mesmerized by the very melodious singing. Whenever their eyes met, she hid her face behind the hand fan, otherwise she kept looking at Senorita Estella with hatred and disdain.

Lady Marlow said, "Look dear Audrey, this girl has such a melodious and sweet voice. She is also so beautiful. The angel of beauty is supposed to be the most beautiful of all. Now I have seen myself that she looks like an angel and is beauty personified."

Audrey Hope said, "No doubt she is par excellence. If her character is equally good, I shall have no hesitation in bestowing upon her the title, 'Angel of beauty.' Her face has a dazzling radiance and brightness. I see dozens of young unmarried girls in the audience. None of them can be compared to her in beauty." She silently said to herself, "God knows how Lord Lorimor, after being engaged to her, can keep himself away from her! He should be with her like a shadow and should get her to quit this profession." Audrey Hope repeated this sentence in her mind several times and began to choke. Tears started flowing from her eyes and she began to cry.

It is worth mentioning that Audrey Hope's tears were not only caused by her envy of Senorita Estella but also by the manner in which she played the part of Margaret, in the drama being played on the stage, and the way she sang with great emotion and feeling. There was hardly anyone in the audience whose eyes were not filled with tears.

The curtain came down as soon as Act 1 finished. Several persons from the audience went to the theatre lobby for a drink or for a cigarette. Several others got up from their seats and walked over to socialize with their friends. In the audience, sitting in the first class section, were Sir Jordan Lane, Lord Marlow, Lady Marlow and Audrey Hope. During their conversation they said that all the nice things published in the London newspapers regarding

Senorita Estella were true. She really had a very sweet and enchanting voice and sang like a nightingale. She was also very beautiful. After all she belonged to their city of London and that was why she was so highly accomplished in her art.

Audrey Hope said, "She is exquisitely beautiful, just like an angel and she is also very graceful."

Lord Marlow replied, "Audrey, you have given her the best compliment. I have often heard menfolk use such high praise for other women by calling them an angel of beauty. But coming from you, it shows that you have developed a special affection for this lovely singer. This is probably the reason that you are staring at her without even blinking. The fact is that we are biased and praise persons from our own country and women have special sentiments for women from their own country. It is no wonder that you Audrey, call her the angel of beauty. However, no one knows her country of domicile and in which country she lives now, or about her real background."

Sir Jordan Lane interjected and said, "I know this much about this great singer, that she is engaged to Lord Lorimor."

Audrey Hope looked at Sir Jordan Lane with anger in her eyes, and to avoid any discussion she started looking at the stage curtain. Lord Marlow said, "I do not understand why people spread such cheap gossip. I am very familiar with Lord Lorimor's excellent character and his kind nature. I have known him from his childhood. He used to come to me for his lessons. I have never ever, to this day, seen him do anything bad or wrong. I know well that he has never even looked at the stage dancers and singers."

Audrey Hope did not feel it was necessary to carry on this conversation. So she kept quiet. She began to think about this great singer. Other persons who had come to say hello to Lady Marlow began to discuss the drama on stage and how well this singer was playing her part. They expressed their individual opinions. Amongst this gathering there was also Lord Chester. He looked at Lady Marlow and said, "In all my life, I have never seen, even in a dream, such a beautiful young girl, who sings with such a sweet enchanting voice. At this young age this girl has acquired such a high degree of perfection in singing and acting. Everyone has become a fan of hers. Several people here estimate her age to be around seventeen. Her face is so radiant and she looks to be very intelligent. Audrey Hope, in your opinion is she a highly skilled professional?"

Audrey Hope replied, "In my opinion, she is not only a highly skilled professional but also very attractive."

Lord Chester added, "You are right, she appears to have everyone under a magic spell."

As he was speaking, the curtain began to rise. All returned to their seats and there was complete silence in the theatre.

Sylvia started her performance of dance and music. Throughout her singing, she kept looking at Audrey Hope in a special way and with a sparkle in her eyes. Both these women began to feel a special bond that seemed to be pulling them together. The interesting part was that neither of them knew the reason for this special bonding. Sylvia thought, "This girl sometimes looks at me with love and affection and at other times I detect anger and jealousy in her eyes and then she hides her face from me. What could be the reason for this?" Similarly, Audrey Hope was thinking, "Why does Senora Estella look at me with love and affection and why does she dance looking at me all the time with that special look in her eyes?" In short they were both absorbed in their own thoughts and were keen to meet each other. Audrey Hope wanted to ask Senorita Estella about Lord Lorimor and Sylvia wanted to ask Audrey Hope the reason for her apparent hatred for her.

As the last line of the song, sung by Senorita Estella was about to finish, Audrey hope threw a beautiful bouquet of flowers towards the stage for her. As her hands were shaking, the bouquet fell short of stage and landed on the floor. The manager of the theatre picked it up and gave it to Senorita Estella, who kissed it and touched it with her eyes to show her appreciation to Audrey Hope and left the stage thanking Audrey Hope with her eyes. The play had finished and Sylvia went inside.

As the play was over, Sir Jordan Lane picked up Audrey Hope's coat, slung it on his shoulders and took her hand to escort her to her carriage outside. He felt Audrey Hope's hands shaking.

Instead of inquiring the reason for this, he tried to please her by saying, "The majority of women were looking at Senorita Estella with contempt in their eyes. But you continuously looked at her with compassion in your eyes. This is because of your kind nature. There appears to be some mystery about this."

Audrey Hope said, "Sir, I do not know why you find everything mysterious! I appreciate her excellent singing and am a fan of hers. However, when menfolk try hard to get her attention, then we women certainly find it offensive."

Sir Jordan Lane replied, "By nature you are kind, compassionate and trusting. You never think badly about others. There are thousands of different types of people and God has made each one with an individual face and characteristic. I always look down upon persons who are not loyal and change their mind at the slightest excuse. I do not like to meet them or talk to them. You look at my determination and steadfastness. In spite of your indifference and anger towards me, I keep on loving you with all my heart and am never discouraged. I constantly pray for your welfare and happiness. I consider your happiness to be the source of my happiness. Do you think there will ever be a place for me in your thoughts? I am confident that one day you will find a place for me in your heart. I only want to hear one word from your sweet lips. That will be the foundation for my life!" After saying this, he squeezed the soft and delicate hand of Audrey Hope.

Audrey Hope was filled with jealousy because Senorita Estella had taken away Lord Lorimor from her. She had read in the newspaper herself that Lord Lorimor was deeply in love with this singer. For this reason Audrey Hope considered Senorita Estella to be in competition with her for Lord Lorimor's love. She began to think of Lord Lorimor as a man with no principles or character. Her emotions overruled her judgement and rational thinking. She became blind with jealousy and said to herself, "It is certain that Senorita Estella will marry Lord Lorimor. Why should I let this opportunity slip away from me? I have already turned away several young men who wanted to marry me. Why should I not agree to get engaged to Sir Jordan Lane?" With this in mind, she also squeezed the hand of Sir Jordan Lane.

Sir Jordan Lane was ecstatic with joy at Audrey Hope's squeezing back his hand in response. He kissed her hand several times and wanted to hug her but saw Lady Marlow approaching, so he held back. He greeted Lady Marlow and escorted them to their carriage. He opened the carriage door and helped them climb inside the carriage. Their carriage left and he went looking for his own carriage.

On the way, the carriage of Senorita Estella passed by the carriage of Audrey Hope. Audrey Hope had a quick glance at the faces of Senorita Estella and Merci Fairflex before their carriage took a turn for a different road. Throughout the journey, Audrey Hope sat with her eyes closed and looking sad. She did not even speak to Lady Marlow. As soon as they reached the house she went straight to her room and lay down on her bed.

Lady Marlow, after changing her clothes, went to the room of Audrey Hope and was surprised to see her lying on her bed with her eyes closed. She sat down on the bed beside Audrey Hope and placed her head on her lap. Audrey Hope held both the hands of her aunt on her chest and began to breathe deeply.

Lady Marlow said, "My dear girl, how are you feeling? I overheard the conversation that you were having with Sir Jordan Lane. It is obvious that he loves you very much and is a great admirer of yours. He has been waiting very patiently for a considerable time to win you over. He is a very capable person who is also fabulously rich. In addition, he is also a member of the parliament. He is a mature and sensible person. I pray to God that you two marry and wish you both great happiness."

On hearing the word "happiness," Audrey Hope began to cry and her voice choked. She could not speak a word. Lady Marlow assumed that she was very tired and sleepy and she left after bidding her good night. Audrey Hope eventually fell asleep.

Next morning, after breakfast, Sir Jordan Lane went to the London publishing firm which published several good books in addition to the daily national newspaper, *London Times* and other local newspapers. This popular newspaper was read by persons from all walks of life. This was also the favourite newspaper of army personnel. The persons who could afford to buy the paper would buy it while the others read it by borrowing from friends or reading it at the public library or at the school.

Sir Jordan Lane figured out that if the engagement of Lord Lorimor with Senorita Estella was published in one newspaper, then it was important that the news of his engagement with Audrey Hope was also published in all the newspapers. He also thought that he would gain advantage on two other points. For this reason, he got the incentive to publish the news of his engagement. He thought, "Firstly, when Audrey Hope reads the news, she will become my slave forever. She will consider it to be very embarrassing and insulting to deny the news and would not dare to publish a counter statement that would contradict the news of our engagement. She will stop ignoring me and will be more pleasant towards me. She will also consider this not to be a mean plot on my part because she, on her own free will, pressed my hand indicating her consent. To my statement of love for her, she neither became angry nor changed the subject. For this reason she cannot say anything against my interpretation of her consent and will be forced to accept me. It is likely that she will try to delay the marriage with one excuse or the other but surely she will agree to a formal engagement ceremony. I will be able to control all her extensive real estate and vast wealth. Even if my step brother Nevlin Lane returns alive and launches a court case against me to get half of our father's property and wins it, I shall still be very rich with Audrey Hope's property under my control."

With such thoughts in mind, Sir Jordan Lane went to the manager's office and wrote out the text for the notice to be published about his engagement. He requested the manager to publish it in *The Times* and other newspapers. He paid the charges for the notice and left the manager's office.

In the morning edition of *The Times*, one news item read, "Audrey Hope is engaged to Right Honourable, Sir Jordan Lane, JP and Member Parliament."

The previous night, at the theatre, the public had showed their appreciation of Senorita Estella's performance by a standing ovation and she acknowledged it by bowing her head. After the show finished, Senorita Estella went to her dressing room. She kept the flower bouquet given by Audrey Hope in front of her on the table and began to look at it intently. Merci Fairflex, while helping her to change her stage clothes, said, "Sylvia dear, you should not have any doubt at all about your immense popularity and great success. You have created such an impression in London that every one is mesmerized by you. All the men and women only talk about you and praise you. In my memory I have never seen anyone being so immensely popular in the city—every household in the city is talking about you only.

Sylvia said, "I am really not interested in anyone's praise and it does not make me any happier. Look at this flower bouquet. All its flowers are beautiful and bloom like the cheeks of Audrey Hope. I still visualize the elegant manner in which she threw this at me and I will never forget that moment. By the way, I wanted to ask you, who was that tall gentleman who was holding her hand and escorting her from the theatre with her coat over his shoulder? From my experience I can say that this man is not an honest and reliable person. He also appeared to be selfish. Can you suggest any plan whereby I can meet Audrey Hope and get an opportunity to talk to her alone? To me it appears that though it is not impossible, it is highly improbable that I will get an opportunity to meet her. There is usually a big chasm between the rich ladies sitting in first class section and the artists who sing and dance on the stage. I do not think it will be possible for her to come to the show everyday, as the people in high society do not have time to take their families to the theatre everyday. It is against the society standards. They also think it is going to have adverse effect on their children. Oh well it does not matter whether she comes everyday or not, I am going to keep this flower bouquet in front of me on the table till all the flowers wither away."

Merci Fairflex said, "You talk like a crazy girl as if you have fallen in love with this bouquet!"

Sylvia replied, "You have spoken the truth, yes I am in love with this bouquet and am very keen to meet the lady who threw this bouquet to me."

Merci Fairflex said, "So far you have returned back hundreds of bouquets with thousands of pounds, and bank cheques, from rich and handsome young men without even looking at them. What is so special about this bouquet of flowers that you want to keep it in front of you all the time, and why are you so anxious to meet this lady? I cannot understand your love for a bouquet thrown by another woman."

Sylvia replied, "Honestly, I have never felt so happy to receive a bouquet as I feel now. There must be some special bond between this lady and myself."

Merci Fairflex said, "Alright, do not worry. You get all excited. I will soon arrange for you to meet this lady, Audrey Hope."

Sylvia replied, "Very good, I will be patient, even though it appears that it will be very difficult to arrange a meeting with her."

While Sylvia was saying this, her mind drifted to the days at Lornehope Camp and in particular to the place where she first got the news of Jack's death. However, because of the kind words of Merci Fairflex and her concern for Sylvia's happiness, she soon forgot about that image that had flashed on her mind. She once again became happy at her success and popularity. She began to smile.

Sylvia and Merci Fairflex came out of the theatre to get their carriage and return home. After a few steps, Sylvia said to Merci Fairflex, "I pray to God and hope everything is alright tonight. I do not know why I am suddenly gripped with fear and my heart is pounding as if something bad is about to happen."

Merci Fairflex held Sylvia's hand and said several soothing things to calm her. Several actors and actresses who worked with Sylvia at the theatre passed them by and they all greeted Sylvia and bowed their heads with respect. Just as Sylvia was about to board her carriage there was suddenly a big surge of the crowd from the back and her hand got separated from the hand of Merci Fairflex. It became impossible to board her carriage as she was pushed to a side by the force of the crowd's pressure. Feeling helpless, she just moved to one side to let the crowd pass. She saw an ugly looking, big tall man, coming from the opposite direction, walking very fast and then he disappeared from her sight behind some trees and bushes further down the road. The moment Sylvia saw this man she began to shake with fear. In the meanwhile Merci Fairflex managed to come beside Sylvia by pushing the crowd with her hands and saw Sylvia shaking, and gripped with fear. She held Sylvia's hand tightly and asked her what had happened. Sylvia was almost hysterical and between sobbing, said, "I just saw a man who crossed in front of me and vanished behind the trees on the west side. This man is the wicked dacoit Lewryk. He is the person who shot and killed my dearest brother Jack, and kidnapped me. Surely he is Lewryk. He did not die even after Lord Lorimor shot him and has now come here to kill me."

Merci Fairflex said, "This is all figment of your imagination. It is impossible for Lewryk to come to London."

Sylvia was shaking with fear so much that she could not reply. She began to feel very cold. She covered herself from head to foot with her cloak and held the hand of Merci Fairflex tightly. Merci Fairflex called their carriage driver and they both embarked it and asked the driver to drive fast to their house. On the way, Sylvia said to Merci Fairflex: "See I was right. I knew that something bad was going to happen. I saw Lewryk. He will not rest till he kills me. Merci, believe me that man was the wicked dacoit Lewryk." Merci Fairflex did not say anything.

Chapter 28

The heart is changing under the celestial dome
The light of the Sun is cleansing all the malice.

On reaching their house, Merci Fairflex hugged Sylvia and like a child coaxed her to sleep. She sat beside Sylvia's bed to keep vigil. Twice or thrice during the night, Sylvia got up with an uneasy feeling. She had a very restless night. Everytime she got up, Merci Fairflex consoled her. However, Sylvia was still very upset. Merci Fairflex said, "My dear Sylvia, you are very scared by the thought of Lewryk coming back. I assure you he can never dare to step on this soil and come near this place. It is likely that you have seen someone else who had a close resemblance to him."

Sylvia said, "No, it was no one else but him. I am certain it was him. Since you do not know him and have never seen him, you would not recognize him and are doubting me. But I tell you honestly that I am very familiar with his face and his character. He has tried three or four times to take me under his control, but because of Jack, I was saved. Since he has killed Jack, he has traced me here and has come to kill me also."

It is worth mentioning that Merci Fairflex had also seen wicked Lewryk. She saw him walking at a very fast pace towards the trees on the side lane. However, she did not mention it to Sylvia. In fact the real name of Merci Fairflex was Rachel and she was the daughter of Lewryk. She was the girl who was seduced by Sir

Jordan Lane with a promise of marriage and later abandoned by him. Since Rachel was a girl with very high morals and had an excellent character, she left the house after the death of her mother. She hated her father and his wicked life style. She did not even want to see his face. She knew that persons who adopt the line of dacoity generally spend al! their life in prison and eventually die there. After Sir Jordan Lane left her, she took up the profession of nursing at the London hospital to get away from her past and to avoid any rumours or scandal that would give her a bad name. From the hospital job, she went with Dr. Langley to Lornehope Camp and accepted the offer of serving Sylvia by looking after her. She did not want to tell Sylvia about her real self and her past and for this reason she did not want to meet anyone in London. She was very much scared of her past being exposed, and the shame it would bring. She was still very much in love with Sir Jordan Lane but was hurt by his attitude and the manner in which he humiliated her. She suffered in silence because of his leaving her. For a long time she knew that her father was known by the name Lewryk, even though his real name was Banks.

Merci Fairflex was extremely attached to Sylvia. She was also her very sincere friend and well wisher. Seeing Sylvia so terrified, she kept her hand on Sylvia's head, stroked her hair and said in a very loving voice, "Alright, I accept that you indeed saw Lewryk and recognized him. But you should not be so scared of him now. Listen dear, this is the city of London and not Lornehope Camp. We live together in a safe and well guarded house. There is constant police guard, in front of our house. There are proper courts to deal with a person like him. We live in a fairly busy area and there is constant traffic on the road in front of the house. At the slightest provocation, hundreds of people will gather around to help. The police station is very close to the house. The guard is always at our door and at his whistle several policemen from the police station will come to help within no time. We are both very safe here. Under these circumstances, why are you so scared of Lewryk? Before anyone can even touch you, they will have to kill me. I am a brave woman who is not scared of anyone and if need arises,

I will kill before anyone dares to attack us."

Sylvia said, "What you are saying is true and logic says the same. Somehow, the very thought of Lewryk makes me sick. He used to look at me with hatred. He had become a bitter enemy of Jack and was bent upon killing him. I saw Lewryk firing a bullet at Jack. I saw Jack's face as he fell on the ground. My mind has captured that look on Jack's face and I am constantly reminded of the same. What can I do about it? I am unable to find peace in my heart." She became hysterical and began to cry.

Merci Fairflex hugged Sylvia and wiped her tears and asked in a very soft and sympathetic voice, "In the morning, should I go to our neighbours and solicit their help? I could also send a written request to the police station to arrest Lewryk?"

Sylvia replied, "No, please no. I do not wish to take revenge on any one. Everyone in this world has to answer to God for his deeds, good or bad, and is punished by Him. I am sure that Lewryk will not be able to stay in this well governed city for long. If he commits any crime here, he will be arrested quickly and punished by the authorities. As you said, he cannot harm me in any way while living in this city." This kind of talk reassured Sylvia and she fell asleep. She slept very soundly for at least a couple of hours.

In the morning, Sylvia got up and dressed up as usual and had her breakfast. She felt fully refreshed. As she sat down to read a book, she got a letter from the manager of the theatre. It read, "Every ticket, from first class to the lowest class, is already sold out for today's show. A very rich person has taken over the contract for the entire show tickets for today and has paid the money for the same. He will be responsible for the management of the show today. I have received numerous letters from the public. Some are willing to pay any price for the show tickets and some are asking for special seats to be placed for them. I have sent letters to all of them refusing their requests. I have also informed all the theatre employees and the artists not to recommend any of their friends for tickets or special consideration in obtaining tickets for the show. Trust this arrangement is satisfactory to you." In the end he inquired about Sylvia's health and wished her a good day.

In addition to the letter from the theatre's manager, Sylvia also received approximately two hundred other letters in the morning mail. Most of the letters were from well known, rich young men expressing their admiration and love for Sylvia and requesting for an opportunity to meet her. Some invited her for dinner and some even offered her two hundred pounds for a two minute interview! As usual, Sylvia just glanced through the letters and burned them in the fireplace. She only kept the letter of the theatre manager and wrote a brief reply to him. She said in her letter that she was well. In the next paragraph she said that she did not want to recommend anyone for tickets and had never done so in the past. She said that she did not know anyone in London and did not wish to meet anyone. She wished to lead her own quiet, private life. She signed the letter and asked Merci Fairflex to have it delivered to the theatre manager.

After finishing her morning routine, around noon time, she sat down for lunch at the dinner table with Merci Fairflex. As they were about to start eating, the maid delivered a letter from Radel, a famous photographer, who she said was waiting outside for a reply. In his letter Radel said that he had taken the liberty to come to her residence with a request that she grant him permission to take her photograph at her convenience. He said that he was willing to share half of the profit he made from her picture.

Sylvia got up and invited Radel in the sitting room. She met him with Merci Fairflex at her side. She politely thanked Radel for coming to her house and giving her the opportunity to have her photograph taken. She said to him, "I am not interested in the photograph or any money. I am sorry that you took all this trouble to visit me and am sorry to disappoint you."

On hearing this the photographer looked at Sylvia intently and said, "I am in the business of taking professional photographs for the last two years. The actors and actresses at the theatre have requested me, on their own, to come to their house and take their pictures. They dress up in all kinds of fancy clothes and jewellery and have their pictures taken in different poses. I have also been invited by the rich and high society ladies and gentlemen to come to their mansions and take their pictures with different clothes and in different places. I have sold hundreds of these pictures and have made good money. I also have some pictures which I have not sold to anyone. In this business I have made a lot of money and the actresses at the theatre have also made good money. It is very surprising that you are not interested in having your picture taken and in making some extra money."

Sylvia replied, "I am afraid I have absolutely no interest in getting my picture taken. I have neither any need for money nor am I greedy. In our World Theatre, there are several actors and actresses and you may wish to approach them for their pictures. Trust you will understand and excuse me." She ended the conversation by getting up and saying goodbye to the photographer.

After finishing their lunch, she went to her room and spent the time talking to Merci Fairflex. In the evening she dressed up and went to the theatre at the appropriate time. She changed into her stage dress and when the curtain opened she went on the stage and started her performance. The hall was jam packed and the audience was clapping at her performance. However, Sylvia noticed that in the front row in the first class section, there were two empty seats where Audrey Hope and Lady Marlow normally used to sit. They were both not there. After the first act, Sylvia returned to her dressing room and the other artists went on the stage to perform. On reaching her room, Sylvia said to Merci Fairflex, "You know, the two ladies who sit in the front row in the first class section are not there today. I wonder why they have not come?"

Merci Fairflex asked, "Who are these two women whom you are missing so much?"

Sylvia replied, "Oh my dear, you certainly ask these questions to tease me. I mean Audrey Hope. I like her very much and my heart is aching to meet her. The song that I was going to sing today would have changed her attitude towards me and instead of looking at me with contempt, she would have admired me."

Merci Fairflex said, "Tell me. Do you sing so happily everyday because of Audrey Hope? Is she the only one who understands your music? Are the others in the audience not capable of understanding your music and great talent? Do they just come to the theatre to listen to your songs? You know Sylvia, sometimes I find your opinions and thinking very strange."

Sylvia said, "You just watch—today I will not be able to sing with the same enthusiasm and my voice will have only half of its normal pitch."

Merci Fairflex did not think it was any use carrying on this conversation. She helped Sylvia dress, put on her jewellery for the next part in the show and went to the other room. Sylvia peeked through the side of the curtain and she saw Audrey Hope and Lady Marlow sitting on the two seats that were empty before. Sylvia was very happy to see them. She returned back to her dressing room and said to Merci Fairflex, "Audrey Hope has arrived. I believe there is some special reason behind her late arrival today."

Merci Fairflex said, "Your thinking and talk is beyond my understanding. People come to the theatre when they are free from other things. What is so special in her being late for the theatre?"

Sylvia said, "I am really not concerned about others. My interest is only in Audrey Hope and my thoughts are confined to her."

As it happened there was a special reason for Audrey Hope's being late for the show. Lady Marlow had to go to Lady Girvin's place for a dinner and dance party that night. Sir Jordan Lane was also imploring Audrey Hope to accompany him to the same party where he too was invited. However, Audrey Hope was very keen to go to the World Theatre to see the show. This all resulted in some discussion as to what they wanted to do. Audrey Hope insisted that she would rather go to the theatre than to Lady Girvin's party. In the end they decided that Audrey Hope and Lady Marlow would go the theatre and Sir Jordan Lane would go to the dance party and join them later at the theatre.

Sir Jordan Lane had started calling Audrey Hope by her first name. But when he did that, there was no trace of love or affection as one would expect from a newly engaged man. Anyway, Audrey Hope eventually reached the theatre late, just as Act 2 was about to begin. Soon after they had taken their seats, the curtain opened and Senorita Estella came on the stage. She started her dance and music performance. Her performance today was really par excel-lence. She had so much grace and charm that everyone in the audi-ence marvelled at her performance. Throughout the performance, Audrey Hope and Senorita Estella kept looking at each other. Though today Audrey Hope did not have any flower bouquet to throw, she looked at Sylvia with such respect and love that only Sylvia could understand her gesture.

After the show finished, Sylvia returned to her dressing room and changed from her stage dress to her normal, well designed clothes. She came out of the theatre with Merci Fairflex to go the her carriage. However, her carriage was not at the place that was reserved for her. The street was full of carriages lined up one after the other. The police officer controlling the traffic was allowing only one carriage at a time to pass through, in front of the theatre. The reason for this was that the road was under construction and only one lane was open for traffic. Only one carriage was able to pass at a time for the fear of complete traffic jam. For this reason, Sylvia's carriage was not parked by the theatre. Sylvia found it difficult to find her carriage in this great line of other carriages, and the general confusion created by everyone trying to locate their own carriages. She wanted to get back inside the theatre till this confusion eased off. Just as she turned to go inside, she and Merci Fairflex were pushed forward by the huge crowd going in the other direction. It became difficult to walk either way. Sylvia and Merci Fairflex held each other's hand tightly so as not to lose each other in the crowd. The pressure of the crowd was such that Sylvia could hardly keep her foot on the ground and was forced towards the carriage in the front, that was waiting to let the pedestrians cross the road. Her body struck the side door of the carriage. Sylvia was not hurt at all but at the impact Sylvia said softly, "Oh, oh." Merci Fairflex rushed and immediately supported Sylvia by her hand and probably saved her from falling. She said to Sylvia, "In a crowd like this, it is inevitable for one to be pushed around a little. Gather your cloak tightly around you so that it may not get caught in the wheels of the carriage and trip you."

Suddenly, from the carriage door a hand came out and rested on Sylvia's shoulder. Though the touch of the hand was as soft as satin, Sylvia at once jumped because of the impact of the hand. As Sylvia turned her head, she saw Audrey Hope sitting inside the carriage who asked very politely, "Are you hurt anywhere? Are you alright?" Sylvia, with nervous hands, loosened her grip on the cloak and said in a very pleasant manner with a smile on her face, "Yes Madam, I am fine. I was just waiting for my carriage when suddenly the force of the crowd pushed me and my head struck your carriage." Audrey Hope's face turned red. She looked very surprised and was overcome with sympathy. She could see Sylvia's face as the cloak slipped from her face. Audrey Hope exclaimed, "Oh my, you are the famous and respected Senorita Estella! Please tell me the truth. Are you alright and is your head hurting?" Without any hesitation, Audrey Hope opened the carriage door and said sympathetically, "The crowd is heavy, please come inside the carriage and sit down here so that the impact of the crowd does not hurt you." Sylvia was surprised to hear this from Audrey Hope and as she looked up, Audrey Hope bent down and helped Sylvia up the carriage step and pulled her inside the carriage by her shoulders. Merci Fairflex followed Sylvia and they both sat down in the carriage.

Sylvia said, "I am very grateful to you for your kindness and sympathy and for offering us a seat in your carriage without any hesitation. I once again assure you that I am not hurt anywhere and am perfectly alright. I am sorry, that because of us, there is less space for you, and you have to sit cramped in your carriage."

Audrey Hope said, "Oh no, there is plenty of space in the carriage. I apologise that in my anxiety to assist you I pulled your arm. I am sorry and I sincerely hope you are not angry with me."

Sylvia replied, "Audrey Hope, you are indeed very kind to show so much sympathy towards an ordinary person like me. I am so happy and relieved to see that you are so kind, full of sympathy and so soft spoken. I can never thank you enough for your compassion in accommodating us in your carriage."

Audrey Hope asked, "How did you come to know my name?"

Sylvia replied, "The very first time on the first day, when I went on the stage, I happened to see you, in the middle of all the clapping and noise from the audience. You were sitting very gracefully in the front row of the first class section and I noticed that sometimes you looked at me with what I perceived to be hatred in your eyes. This made me curious and I inquired from my fellow singers and artists if they knew your name. The assistant manager, who was hired locally by the management of the theatre on reaching London, knew you. He told me your name, who you were and where you lived. I must also tell you that during my performances, hundreds of people have thrown beautiful flower bouquets on the stage for me. By nature, I am very detached and have all these bouquets either distributed to others, or thrown away. However, your beautiful flower bouquet meant a lot to me and I got so much attached to it that I always kept it on my table in front of me. I will not part with it until it has completely withered away."

Audrey Hope was much touched by Sylvia's sweet voice, and her honest and straightforward answer. Audrey Hope was no ordinary girl herself. She was highly intelligent. She told Sylvia that she was much impressed by Sylvia's honest and straightforward answer. She also told Sylvia that she liked her very much. As she said this, she took Sylvia's hand and held it tightly in her hand as a sign of warmth and happiness in meeting her. Both the girls sat silently admiring each other.

Lady Marlow greeted Merci Fairflex by shaking her hand and said to her, "Your companion has become very famous in this city at a fairly young age."

Merci Fairflex replied, "Yes Madam. Senorita Estella, in addition to being highly educated and very good at housework, has also learned the art of music and acting with great enthusiasm, diligence and hard work. I am also amazed that she has acquired such perfection at this young age "

Lady Marlow said, "In addition to being such an excellent artist she is also very beautiful."

Merci Fairflex replied, "She is kind hearted too."

Lady Marlow added, "I am sure Senorita Estella is also very

honest and of high character. It is natural for a person to fall in love with her at first sight. Tell me, are you related to her?"

Merci Fairflex replied, "No Madam. I am her sincere servant, her well wisher and a close friend."

Lady Marlow said, "I think you also love her."

Merci Fairflex replied, "I am not the only one. Anyone who is fortunate enough to talk to her, falls in love with her. She is so charming and likeable."

Lady Marlow looked at the two girls and saw them talking softly and intimately. She said to Merci Fairflex in a low voice, "Look, these two girls just happened to meet by chance, right in front of my eyes and they are already talking like old friends."

The coachman got clearance in the line and slowly began to move forward. When Senorita Estella noticed the carriage moving, she asked, "Where are we going? We better get down."

Audrey Hope said, "Please tell us your address and we will drop you."

Sylvia replied, "We live on Berry Street, house no. 2. However, I would not like you to go out of your way just to drop us."

Audrey Hope said, "We live on Grosvenor Street. Berry Street is on our way home." She called the coach driver and ordered him to stop the carriage at house no. 2 on Berry Street. After instructing the driver, Audrey Hope turned towards Sylvia and said, "Can I come and see you at your house sometime tomorrow?"

Sylvia, with happiness and excitement in her voice, said, "Would you really come tomorrow?"

Audrey Hope replied, "I want to talk to you about several things and this wayside meeting is really not enough to get to know each other. I would come at noon tomorrow, if you are free. I do appreciate that a person of your fame and status would have several visitors coming to meet you in the morning and you may not be free. In that case please tell me what other time will be convenient for you."

Sylvia said, "Except for one person, I never meet with any other person socially, irrespective of his wealth or status in society. I have followed this practice for a long time now. For this reason, no one dares approach me for a meeting, be he a king or a beggar. With the manager and the management of the World Theatre, I only deal by correspondence."

On hearing this Audrey Hope thought that the only person that she was talking about must be Lord Lorimor. This thought made her sad and she felt jealous of Sylvia. Her face became pale. She controlled herself as another thought crossed her mind and she said in a shaky voice, "I will definitely come to your house at twelve noon tomorrow." She had hardly finished the last sentence when the coachman stopped the carriage in front of no. 2 Berry Street. They shook hands and Sylvia and Merci Fairflex got down from the carriage and went inside their house.

Once the carriage moved again, Lady Marlow said, "Audrey, you have become very independent. You have also become very headstrong. If Sir Jordan Lane comes to know that we met Senorita Estella, and, not only did we give her a lift in our carriage but are also planning to socialize with her, what do you think he will say? He will certainly blame me for your behaviour."

Audrey Hope replied, "He will neither say anything nor blame you. He should have no concern about my meeting her. Mature people trust others and moreover, I am not his subordinate that he can boss over me. Did you not notice that Senorita Estella is such an honest and straightforward person and she talks so sweetly. Actually, I found that her talking voice is much more soft and appealing than her singing voice in the show at the theatre. In my opinion, Senorita Estella is a very respectable, fine, honest, charming and highly skilled person. It is a pleasure to know her."

Lady Marlow said, "There is no doubt that Senorita Estella appears to be a very respectable girl. Generally the dancers and singers of the theatre do not have such innocent and graceful faces. They are not shy like normal ladies. But Senorita Estella does not appear to be a regular stage girl. However, we should not develop too much intimacy and socialize with a girl who dances and sings on stage. It is better for us to keep our distance from such girls."

Audrey Hope replied, "If you do not want me to be seen socializing with Senorita Estella and ask me to keep my distance from her, I will ask uncle Marlow and request Senorita Estella to come to our countryhouse."

Lady Marlow said in an angry voice, "Oh my girl, this a new thing you have come up with. Girl, I give up on you. You are getting out of my control. Once I put you in the hands of Sir Jordan Lane, you can do what you want and it will be his responsibility. In my old age I do not want to be sneered at by my peers and become a laughing stock of society."

Lady Marlow was in the middle of her sentence when the carriage stopped in front of their house. As they entered the house they saw Sir Jordan Lane sitting in the living room, waiting for them. As they entered the room, he got up from the chair and greeted them. He took Audrey Hope's hand and squeezed it. She freed her hand with a jerk and looked at him as if she did not care for him. Seeing Audrey Hope in such bad mood, Sir Jordan Lane did not have the courage to kiss her hand or say anything. He thought that it had been only four days since the notice of their engagement was published in the newspaper. He should give her some more time. With this in mind he quietly sat down on the chair.

Lady Marlow said, "Let me tell you the latest news about our family. Today, when Senorita Estella came out of the theatre after the show, she was pushed against our carriage by the massive crowd outside the theatre. We thought she might have been hurt, so we invited her to our carriage and dropped her at her house on Berry Street. On the way, Audrey Hope and Senorita Estella got to know each other and had a pleasant conversation. Tomorrow, at twelve noon, Audrey Hope is going to her house to meet her."

On hearing this Sir Jordan Lane became angry and upset but did not say anything. He started thinking that if Audrey Hope starts to socialize with Senorita Estella, there was a possibility that she would meet Lord Lorimor at her house and this may revive her old love for him. She might change her mind about marrying him. On second thoughts, according to the news in the newspapers, Lord Lorimor was already engaged to Senorita Estella and was due to marry her in the near future. Therefore he would have no interest in Audrey Hope. Under these circumstances it does not seem wise to stop Audrey Hope from seeing Senorita Estella. Moreover, Audrey Hope is known to be very strong willed and does what she considers to be right. If he asked her not to see Senorita Estella, she would do just the opposite and go and see her. Since he did not love Audrey Hope he had no need to be jealous. As far as he was concerned his whole plan was to get her under his control by marrying her and then grab all her wealth as soon as possible. Once she married him, he would destroy all her pride and ego and she would be his slave and do exactly what he wanted her to do. With these thoughts in his mind, he did not show any anger, nor did he say anything negative about her seeing Senorita Estella. On the contrary he said with a smile, "I too wish I could meet her. She has a great charm about her. I have learned from reliable sources that several rich men and high officers have thrown thousands of pounds at her in flower bouquets, with requests for interviews, invitations for dinner and letters expressing their love for her. She has such high morals and good manners that I understand she returned all the money back to the senders, and has burned all other letters and ignored all requests. She neither talks to anyone nor grants any interviews. The famous photographer Radel approached her to take her photograph and offered to share half of the profits with her. But she refused to let her photograph be taken. She is not greedy for money. She turned down his proposal. She has chosen to live in seclusion. I think Audrey Hope is lucky that Senorita Estella has agreed to meet her and in my opinion Audrey Hope should go alone. If anyone goes with her, the girls will not be able to talk freely. Moreover, I have some important work at my house in Court Lane and it will be necessary for me to stay there for two or three days. For this reason I will have to postpone my meeting with Senorita Estella for a later time." Sir Jordan Lane bid Lady Marlow goodnight and left for his house.

Chapter 29

She has come to our house it is God's miracle
Sometimes I look at the house and sometimes at her

Next morning, Sylvia was so absorbed at the thought of Audrey Hope coming to her house that she completely forgot that she had seen wicked Lewryk the other night. She kept smiling while repeating Audrey Hope's conversation in her mind. She kept on thinking about the sweetness and charm of Audrey Hope and her voice.

When Merci Fairflex noticed that Sylvia was smiling and talking to herself, she inquired, "Sylvia, dear girl, please tell me what you are thinking and smiling about?"

Sylvia said, "I am very happy at the thought of Audrey Hope coming to our house today. Do you think she will come at twelve noon sharp to meet me? Is it likely that she was just trying to be polite and did not really mean that she would come? Maybe her other relatives will prevent her from coming because the rich and high society people do not really want to socialize with singers and dancers."

Merci Fairflex smiled and said, "I do not think so. I am sure Audrey Hope will come as she promised. She is also very keen to meet you. That girl seems to be the kind of a person who keeps her word and is of a very independent nature. You probably did not notice that she opened the carriage door without the slightest hesitation and without asking her aunt's permission. She pulled you up and offered you the seat beside her. If she was not interested in knowing you, she would not have bothered to be so kind as to inquire about your condition and your health."

Sylvia said, "I will always remember her sympathy and kindness."

Merci Fairflex was right. Exactly at twelve noon Audrey Hope came to Sylvia's house, and she was alone. She entered the house unannounced. She came to the drawing room, but it was empty. Both Sylvia and Merci Fairflex were busy in the kitchen and did not hear her enter the house. She had an opportunity to browse around. She found everything absolutely neat and clean and kept at its proper place. The whole house was decorated in a very elegant and tasteful fashion. The flowers in the vases were well arranged and the vases were very pretty. She thought that this reflected Senorita's character. She was a girl of good upbringing and knew how to keep her house looking so good. Audrey Hope liked the way the furniture and furnishings were arranged. Audrey Hope wanted to take this opportunity to see how the house was kept and get an idea as to what type of a person Sylvia was. A woman is known by the way she keeps her house.

Sylvia came to the drawing room from the verandah. She was dressed in her long dress with a shawl on her shoulders. She saw Audrey Hope standing in the drawing room. She shouted with glee and extended her hand to shake Audrey Hope's hand. Audrey Hope shook her hand but hesitated for a few seconds. Sylvia looked like a small girl in her long dress and Audrey Hope was not sure if she was really Senorita Estella. On the stage Senorita Estella looked so different—dressed in stage clothes and jewellery, she looked like a fully grown up woman. For this reason Audrey Hope just stood there for a few seconds, with a surprised look on her face, looking at Senorita Estella. Once she realized that she was Senorita Estella, she took her hand and shook it with great warmth. Sylvia invited her to sit down and sat on the chair beside her.

For the first ten minutes they were both shy and looked at each other without saying very much. But after the initial hesitation, they started to talk freely. To find out about Senorita Estella's job,

Audrey Hope began by saying, "Senorita Estella, you are excellent in your profession. But you seem to be very young. Looking at you one can never imagine that you are the same Senorita Estella who sings so beautifully on the stage. You have earned our great admiration and have cast a spell on all of us."

Sylvia replied, "Yes, I am sorry that I am not big and tall. But trust me, I am working on it every day."

Audrey Hope laughed and said, "You appear to be very mature and wise for your young age. I guess that you must have acquired this confidence and poise by working on the stage for a number of years."

Sylvia replied, "I have started this profession only for the last few months to keep myself busy. If someone had asked me to sing and dance at a theatre, just six months back, I would have called him mad and dumb. I would have laughed at the very suggestion and ran back to Austria." As she spoke, her eyes filled with tears.

Audrey Hope said in a sympathetic voice, "You seem to have suffered in the past."

Sylvia replied, "Yes. I am left to live without any friends or well wishers in my life. If two persons had not taken pity on me and looked after me, I would have died long back. One of these two persons is a lady by the name Merci Fairflex, the one who was sitting beside Lady Marlow in the carriage. She looked after me day and night with great devotion and dedication. Her behaviour towards me has been like a mother. The other person is an Englishman, who is a thorough gentleman, very reliable and kind hearted. He comes from a very rich family in London. Because of the kindness of these two people, my life has been saved."

Audrey Hope thought, "This gentleman must be Lord Lorimor. I should really hate Senorita Estella for taking him away from me and not show any affection or friendship towards her." At this thought she drew her hand away from Sylvia's hand and moved her chair a little further from her chair. She asked in a hurt voice, "What is the name of this gentleman? Maybe I know him."

Sylvia ignored the look of contempt in Audrey Hope's eyes.

Keeping in mind her simple and trusting nature, she said, "Yes I am sure you know him. He is kindness personified, very brave and mature. He is from the aristocratic society of London."

Audrey Hope looked straight in the eyes of Sylvia and asked, "Is he in London at present?"

Sylvia said, "He is not here. But I am expecting him any day now. He should be here tomorrow. I had insisted and implored that he return back to London without delay. He has been travelling for the past two and a half years and that seems to occupy all his attention. He said he was searching for some person in the wilderness."

Audrey Hope asked shyly, "Is he still travelling around? Did he give you any details of his mission?"

Sylvia replied, "He did tell me a lot of things, but I am afraid I am not at liberty to discuss the same. Even though I know that it is not in his nature to be angry with anyone, it would upset him if I discussed his private life with someone else. I have never even once seen him angry. Though he is so rich and comes from a noble family with a title, he is very simple in his tastes and behaviour. I consider you to be my true well wisher and a trustworthy friend. I believe you will not divulge his private life to anyone else. He has given his heart to a very beautiful and kind hearted young lady. He loves her dearly and is prepared to do anything for her. He told me in great detail how well mannered, beautiful and wonderful this girl is. He loves her with all his heart."

Audrey Hope shivered and asked hurriedly, "What is the name of this girl?"

Sylvia replied, "This girl, who sent him to search for this unknown person in the jungles and cities all over the world, had a friend whom she lost in her childhood. She sent him in search of him to test his love. Though I asked him the name, he did not tell me. He had promised her to return within two years with her lost friend. The promised two years have passed but he is still busy searching for this person as I was very angry with him. I asked him why he did not go back to her beloved after the expiry of this two year period. He said it was humiliating for him to go back and face his beloved without finding her lost friend. He also thought that if he wrote to this girl explaining his efforts to find her friend, she would take it to be a bunch of excuses. To carry out her wishes, he has roamed all over the world. He is now concentrating his search in an area around Florence. They are constructing a new railway line there. It is rumoured that thousands of workers from the surrounding areas and England have gone there to work. He said that he will search for the lost friend of his beloved, in all these workshops and offices for another four weeks and then he will return to London. The name of this kind gentleman is, Lord Lorimor. In my opinion the girl, who sent such a wonderful kind and gentle person to search for her friend in the various cities and jungles and put him to so much hardship and inconvenience, must be a proud, inconsiderate and ignorant woman. The girl who truly loves a person can find thousands of other means to test his love. I am sure you agree with me."

On hearing all this, Audrey Hope began to shiver and felt very ashamed of herself. She said, "Yes I agree. In addition, in my opinion, this girl is also cruel and hard hearted. Perhaps this girl will have to pay a heavy price for her stupid and inconsiderate behaviour and will have to suffer all her life. I notice that you are so proud of Lord Lorimor. A book can be written about all the praises you have showered upon him. I do not think that you have left out any word in praise of him. If there were any new words found in a dictionary, you would have used them too!"

Sylvia showed impatience and said, "You are making fun of me. This is not fair. Whatever I have said about Lord Lorimor is true. It is alright, if in his praise, a book can be filled. However, I have reserved utmost praise for another person, provided he is still alive. In my life I have come across only two people who are worthy of such praise. Except for these two, I do not consider anyone else deserving of my confidence and my deep respect." Sylvia wanted to say something more but tears came in her eyes and she choked. She regained her composure and said to Audrey Hope, "Lord Lorimor will be coming here in a day or two and I will introduce him to you. You will see for yourself that everything that I have said about him is true."

Audrey Hope smiled and said, "From your extensive description of Lord Lorimor it appears to me that you are in love with him. He probably loves you also in the same manner."

Sylvia looked at Audrey Hope directly in the eyes and said boldly, "What did you say, that he has fallen in love with me? It is a pity that you are unable to appreciate the fine and pure intentions of a person. By accusing him of being in love with me, you have done a great injustice to this kind and wonderful person. My dear, you do not know this gentleman. He only has one heart and he has given that heart to this girl for whom he is travelling all over the world. He keeps her picture in his heart all the time and almost worships her. For her sake, he has endured numerous hardships and has also risked his life a few times. How can he possibly love any other girl when he has committed all the love in his heart, to this girl? I look at him as a brother and he treats me like his sister. I know him well and have also tested his friendship and what I say is from my personal experience."

On hearing this, Audrey Hope laughed heartily and held Sylvia's hand with warmth and enthusiasm and said, "Let us make a pact like school girls by crossing our heart, that we shall be friends forever and our friendship will be based on honesty. We shall share the joys and sorrows of each other. We will discuss our problems with each other, without any hesitation and nothing will come between us. Please tell me if this is acceptable to you."

Sylvia said, "Every individual knows in his heart as to what his true feelings are. You can judge others based on your experiences with them. I do not know what force has drawn me so close to you. From the very first day I saw you, I knew that you were going to be my closest and true friend. In fact, I love you more than a real sister. If anyone asks me the reason for this special bond between us, I honestly will not be able to tell them. Out of thousands of spectators in the audience, I do not know why I was attracted towards you alone. Well I have told you how I feel and I will know more how you feel as we get to know each other."

Audrey Hope replied, "I too feel the same way. In spite of

the fact that several close friends advised me against my coming, I was restless to meet you and could not resist coming here. What else can I say to prove my love and friendship for you. I came alone to meet you. I am myself surprised that after talking with each other for just ten minutes, we are feeling so close. From today please call me by my first name. Dear Senorita, when you look at me during your performance on the stage and smile, I am sure that some people in the audience will guess that we are friends. Wherever I go, people will point at me and envy me because I am your friend and will request me to introduce them to you. They will inquire about you. It is likely that a crowd will gather at my house. At that time I will feel so proud that I am your friend. I cannot tell you how happy I will be."

Sylvia said, "I think, rather than being proud of your friendship with me, you may be embarrassed. People may say things that would make you regret that you became my friend. What you are saying about our friendship now, is in the heat of emotion and enthusiasm but when you will think calmly you may not cherish the idea of your friendship with a stage singer and dancer."

Audrey Hope replied, "This is not a thing that would fade with time or circumstance. This friendship is for ever. I am a very independent person and whatever I say or do, I do after full consideration of its outcome. I am not afraid of gossip mongers and what other people say and am not swayed by them. I have one shortcoming. If any one of my friends or well wishers tells me something with authenticity and insists on proving the statement, I generally trust him and accept what he is saying. But if he is wrong I get very angry. However, from today I have made a resolution that I will not accept anything that my friends or well wishers say unless I thoroughly investigate it and prove it myself. I will not believe in hearsay or the versions of others. I will also try to be calm and not get angry at others. Within the next few days, you will see the change in my attitude for you, and you will know me and understand me better. Since I consider you to be more educated and mature than myself, from now on, I shall consult you and take your advice regarding my problems."

Audrey Hope moved closer to Sylvia and said in a soft tone, "Let us discuss our future plans and chart a course of action as a guide for our decisions. First you tell me what your plans are for the future and what steps you are taking to ensure a financially worry free life."

Sylvia was feeling very happy sitting next to Audrey Hope and listening to her frank and sympathetic talk. Considering Audrey Hope as a sincere and true friend, she said, "Dear Audrey, from the very childhood I have only seen misery and suffering in my home. A very rich and famous man of London, who was very influential, had become a bitter enemy of my parents. My father never told me the name of this person or the reason for his animosity. This person had vowed to ruin their lives. With the result that wherever my father got a job based on his excellent qualifications and experience, this person contacted his superiors, levelled false accusations against my father and ensured that he was fired from the job. My mother died when I was very young due to the constant harassment and suffering at the hands of this influential person. My father, because of his very gentle and decent nature, did not take any action against this enemy. He began to live outside London because he was afraid of the influence this person had in London. He spent all his money in providing for me until his funds were completely exhausted. He provided me with the best of education and training. In addition, he taught me the art of cooking, sewing, knitting and other house running skills. He taught me music and other arts. My father had to bear untold hardships and suffering and finally he died in a remote jungle, leaving me without a penny or a friend. Because of the turn of events I too had to face considerable suffering and pain. To be independent and to feed myself, I accepted this offer of singing and dancing at the theatre. I used to consider this profession to be very bad but I would rather earn my own living than to be dependent on someone else. I do not work under any pressure and have established very clear rules that no one can meet me. I neither talk to nor meet anyone. I am neither greedy for money nor care for fame and admiration. Whatever I have earned at the theatre as a result of my honest and hard work is enough to provide me with a reasonable, decent living. I propose to quit the work of dancing and singing very soon. I am planning to buy a small farmland near London, where I will keep poultry and cows. I will build a small house on the farm and spend my time in gardening, growing vegetables and fruits. The profits that I earn from the sale of my farm products will be enough for my living and I will spend the rest of my life with Merci Fairflex, happy and content with what I have. I notice Audrey that you are smiling at my plans for a future life."

Audrey Hope said, "The reason I am smiling is that suppose in the near future you meet some third person in addition to Merci Fairflex, who may have different ideas about your future, then all your planning will mean nothing."

Sylvia said, "Aha, Aha. I know what you mean. Dear Audrey, I am never going to marry. I am going to remain single all my life. However, there was a very kind person named Jack, who, in Lornehope Camp, came to my rescue when I was absolutely helpless and without friends. He looked after my welfare and protected me without any selfish motive and saved my life. In my assessment he is a degree higher than Lord Lorimor. In trying to protect me he fell on the ground right in front of my eyes from a bullet shot by a dacoit. If by God's Grace, he is still alive and comes to London in the near future and expresses his love for me, I will certainly marry him. Otherwise I will spend the rest of my life in remembrance of my Jack. I will stay with Merci Fairflex and do gardening and farming for the rest of my life."

Audrey Hope said, "I hope that you will have a room for your friend in your beautiful house on the farm."

In response Sylvia said, "Of course, I am going to build a very nice room for you. I will decorate it with my own hands with the finest drapery, furnishings, and colourful wall paper on the walls. I will have laced curtains and hang them in a fashion that will enhance the decor of the room. You will like it."

They spent a few more minutes talking in general and laughing. Audrey Hope then got up from her chair and bid Sylvia good bye. Sylvia came to the door to see her off. Audrey Hope asked the carriage driver to take her to the central park instead of going directly to home. She went and sat down on a bench in a quiet corner of the park. She covered her face with both her hands and cried. She cursed herself and kept on saying to herself, "What have I done. My beloved Lord Lorimor is roaming in the jungles for my sake, and here I have agreed to be engaged to Sir Jordan Lane. I have ruined my life. I am so sorry that I fell for Sir Jordan Lane's trap and meaningless talk and squeezed his hand, which he took to be my consent to be engaged to him. Worse still, I did not protest when he published the news in the paper without my consent. God, why did I falter in my faith in Lord Lorimor? Why did I allow Jordan Lane to take such liberty with me? Why did I create such a mess? Everyone in our society must have read the news about my engagement with Sir Jordan Lane and the news must be all over the place by now. He tricked me. Even if I beg him and implore him to forget about the engagement, he is not going to leave me alone. He is a person with a mean heart. I cannot think of any plan or strategy to free myself from him. It is a pity that Lord Lorimor delayed so much and did not contact me. Even if he had written one word, I would have waited for him. This would have been enough for me to convince myself of his true love and I would never have wavered in my decision."

The innocent and kind hearted Audrey Hope was tricked by Sir Jordan Lane. He ruined her present and future happiness. But the persons who want to harm others for their own benefit, in the end, harm themselves. Their wicked plans prove to be their own destruction. They do not know that God is always just and on the side of kind and noble people. The other name of God is the "Causer of causes," in other words He creates circumstances whereby the wicked and bad persons weave their own destruction. His justice is fair and exact and is beyond the comprehension of mortal human beings. The noble and honest people are awarded salvation while the wicked and bad people are punished by Him.

Chapter 30

You are cruel, you create suffering and you torment
After plucking the wings, you ask the bird to fly away

Any sensible person would be unhappy by the outwardly show of friendship and enthusiastic praise from other persons who may express happiness at his promotions but do not mean it in their heart. They do not want to give the impression that they consider such a person to be selfish and self-centred. Sir Jordan Lane, however did not care if people hated him and considered him selfish. He was happy with the outwardly praise of people. He was satisfied that with his crafty manipulation and planning, he had managed to trick Audrey Hope and gained control over her. He ignored the great age difference between them. His sole motive was to take control of Audrey Hope's wealth and property by tricking her to marry him, and prevent her from marrying the rich, wise and handsome Lord Lorimor. He left no stone unturned in his planning and even published the news of their engagement in the newspaper. His close friends, colleagues at the office, his peers, his neighbours and local shopkeepers all considered him to be mean and selfish. The girls who had come in contact with him at one time or another also hated him. None of them was happy at the prospect of Audrey Hope's wedding with him. However, Sir Jordan Lane ignored the negative comments from everyone and pursued his goal of getting Audrey Hope to marry him.

Lady Marlow had informed Sir Jordan Lane that Audrey Hope

was going to visit Senorita Estella. However, knowing that Audrey Hope was a very determined girl and would do as she wished, he did not object to her going and in fact praised Senorita Estella and said he would have also liked to meet her sometime. He did not consider the consequences of Audrey Hope's friendship with Senorita Estella and gave his permission for her to go. After leaving Lady Marlow's place, he decided to walk back to his house. On his way back, he began to think that he should plan the wedding with Audrey Hope as soon as possible. He said to himself, "I am going to make Audrey Hope stay with me at my mansion in Court Lane, in the portion where my father died. That has not been cleaned since his death. I am going to demolish the existing building and construct four distinct portions in its place. In one portion I will ask the architects and engineers to design a spacious living area. In the second portion I will construct a special stable for the horses. Audrey Hope is very fond of horses. I will buy fast and expensive horses of good pedigree for her and have them in her stable. This stable will be at the place where my father's bedroom and study is at present. I will demolish that completely. This way I will not be reminded of my late father and feel guilty that I have not carried out his wishes. In the third portion I will build a bird house for the pleasure of Audrey Hope. In the last and fourth portion I will build a big hall for dances and parties. I will throw big dance parties and invite all the young men who wanted to marry Audrey Hope and her other friends who dislike me. I will thoroughly enjoy the expression of jealousy on their faces when they see Audrey Hope sitting by my side. When they realize that I control all her wealth, they will probably have fits of jealousy and curse their luck. I will enjoy dancing with Audrey Hope." He kept himself busy with such thoughts till he entered his house.

It is interesting to note that Sir Jordan Lane was determined to dismantle the house so lovingly built by his father. He wanted to erase the memories connected with his father. In civilized, decent families, the sons generally do everything to preserve and perpetuate the memory of their parents. Some create a trust in memory of their father for the education of poor students. Some erect a monument in their memory and some start libraries. Only people with no morals think of erasing the memory of their parents. It was too much for Sir Jordan Lane to keep the place of his father's death lighted and have prayers for the peace of the departed soul. He did not even have his father's bedroom and sitting room cleaned. In fact he was planning to demolish the whole portion. The laws of Nature are well defined. They punish such persons. Jordan Lane was building his own destruction with such mean and obscene thoughts. The evil deeds of such people form the basis of their inevitable destruction and severe punishment by Nature. As the saying goes such persons suffer in the fire of hell.

Sir Jordan Lane strolled in the gardens of his mansion, absorbed in pleasant thoughts of future. The bell rang for dinner and he entered his house and went to the dining room. On the front wall of the dining room pictures of his late father and his step brother Nevlin Lane were hanging. Sir Jordan Lane looked at them and felt uncomfortable. He thought about his step brother being the favourite son of his father. Now Nevlin Lane was roaming somewhere in the world, whereas he was enjoying the luxuries of material wealth. This was the result of his careful planning and his controlling his father to become the sole beneficiary of his wealth and property. He looked at the picture of Nevlin Lane as if to say, "Audrey Hope who was your close friend and whom you admired so much at one time, is now going to be mine." He sat down to eat dinner. However, as his mind was full of thoughts of hatred towards his brother, he did not enjoy the delicious food. He finished dinner in a hurry and went to the living room. He glanced at the day's mail, replied a couple of urgent letters and came out on the verandah. He began to pace up and down. On the side of the stairs he saw the shadow of a man. He looked carefully all around but did not see anyone. He still had doubts that someone was lurking near the stairs and he began to pace faster. The thought of the lurking shadow kept nagging him. However, since he could not see anyone, he thought it was just his imagination and he went inside the room. He lighted a candle and went to his late father's sitting cum bedroom. This was the room in which his father had died. Everything in the sitting room was covered with dust as the room had not been cleaned since the day his father died. He started looking for the piece of paper that he had searched for several times earlier also. He seriously began to shift things to look under them for this lost piece of paper. He opened the cabinet near his father's bed and searched it thoroughly. He did not find the paper there. With great disappointment he approached the passage near the room to go out. But just at that moment the candle that he was using, extinguished. He was nonplussed by the sudden darkness and wanted to light a match to light the candle. But as he took out the match, he heard a rattling and shuffling sound from the roof of the room. He became nervous and began to shake with fear. He looked up at the window of the room and in the moonlight saw a hand outside the window. He began to sweat with fear. He sat down on the floor. After a few seconds, he regained his confidence and said to himself, "It appeared to be the hand of a man. Why should I be scared of it. I better investigate and challenge the person outside to find out what he wants. I better have the whole place searched and arrest the intruder."

Sir Jordan Lane, with a feeling of guilt, got up and wanted to walk to the balcony outside. But he was scared stiff and his feet would not move. After a few minutes and still scared, he began to think, "Maybe my step brother Nevlin Lane has returned and has come here in the night to take revenge on me for turning our late father against him by fabricating false accusations. He must have come to know of our father's death. He has now found an opportunity to come back and kill me. Except for Nevlin Lane no other person can come to this side of the living room. No one else knows this back entrance to the house. He must have come by the back garden and jumped through the window to enter the living room. He must be trying to scare me by showing his hand and is now ready to kill me."

These negative thoughts of Sir Jordan Lane for his step brother Nevlin Lane were a reflection of his own crooked way of thinking. Nevlin Lane was a very kind and mature person and never had such thoughts about his brother. In fact he defended his brother whenever anybody tried to say anuthing against him. Nevlin Lane suffered to live in poverty in a far away country, rather than challenge his brother and claim his rightful share. He loved his father dearly and used to cry in his memory.

Sir Jordan Lane controlled himself and looked carefully at the window again. The hand he had seen previously seemed to disappear outside. Someone shook the panels of the window. Jordan Lane wanted to get up and open the window and catch the intruder. However, both the panels of the window opened suddenly. He saw the light from a lantern and someone shouted in a mocking voice, "My, oh my, why, Sir Jordan Lane, you got so scared of me." While Sir Jordan Lane tried hard to recognize the voice of the intruder, an ugly looking man jumped through the window and came and stood facing Jordan Lane. He could hardly speak because of fear and with a shaky voice said, "Oh, it is you, Banks!"

The dacoit Banks, also known as Lewryk, took his time and kept the lantern on the table. Now both of them could see each other's face more clearly. Sir Jordan Lane regained his composure and adopting an attitude of authority he asked Banks in a firm voice, "How dare you come to see me at this time of the night by jumping through the window?"

Banks said, "I came to see you at your house but I thought that the servants must be asleep and I did not want to wake them up to inform you about my desire to see you. So I went to the other side door and saw a light in your late father's sitting room at the back of the house. I came to the sitting room by the back garden and looked through the window. I saw you searching for something by turning over things in the cabinet near your late father's bed. I am pretty good at jumping and there was no problem for me to jump through the sitting room window. Moreover, I had once before, opened the window's latch from outside and jumped through the window to enter this room. Today I present myself before you in connection with my last visit here. Probably you were in the middle of cleaning up the dust in this room."

Sir Jordan Lane kept his hand on the bell for summoning the servants and said to Banks, "If you do not leave this room within two minutes, I will ring the bell and my servants will come immediately. You will not be able to leave quietly once they arrive."

Banks said, "I am your old friend. Today I have come to discuss something that will prove to be of great benefit to you. If you so wish, please go ahead and ring the bell and call the servants. It would be nice if they also hear what I have to say."

On hearing this, Sir Jordan Lane remembered how greedy Banks had been in the past and his hands began to shake. He removed his hand from the bell. He said, "What can you possibly tell me that will be of any benefit to me. Be frank. You are in need of money and you have come to ask me for the same. Right?"

Banks said, "Aha, since you mentioned money, it reminds me Sir, that you promised to give me a considerable sum of money for killing a certain person. Because of your own mistake and the wrong information provided by you, the job could not be done, though I was determined to carry out the assignment. I was not at fault at all. I was entitled to the money promised by you but you postponed giving me the money at that time and promised to give it at a later date. I believe that you would still hesitate to give me the promised money."

On hearing this Jordan Lane lunged towards the dacoit to hit him but Banks held him back by one hand and pulled his gun out of his pocket by the other hand. He aimed the gun at Sir Jordan Lane and said. "Spit out your anger, it will not help you. Do not even think of fighting me. Do not be proud of your strength because it is no match for my strength. I am quite familiar with your double talk and your habit of forgetting your promises and for this reason I brought the gun as an added precaution. I sincerely hope that you will not force me to use it. Though I am well aware of the fact that you are a very wicked person, I also know that you are a person with foresight. Now calm down and listen carefully to what I have to say and after that you can do as you please."

Sir Jordan Lane said, "Why do you call me wicked and say that I forget my promises. I gave you a task to kill a certain person. Since you did not complete the job you have no right to ask for the money. Are you thinking that I am scared of our secret being leaked out by you and would agree to your demands? Are you not aware of my power, status and high position? There are several charges pending against you in the court. Out of these, three crimes committed by you are of very serious nature. I can get you arrested right now on a charge of robbery and you will be jailed for life."

Banks said, "Alright, have it your own way and satisfy your whim. Go ahead, call the police and get me arrested. But remember you cannot stop me from telling the police everything about you. If you are bent upon destroying yourself then in God's name, please call the police. I look forward to tell them everything. It will implicate you in such a manner that you will lose all your high position and status and probably spend the rest of your life in prison. Once the public knows the truth about you, you will have no alternative but to commit suicide."

On hearing Banks speak in such a threatening tone, Sir Jordan Lane became very nervous and said in a soft and conciliatory tone, "Oh well, never mind. We shall talk about this later. Now tell me why did you come to see me at this time of the night."

Banks kept the gun back in his pocket and said, "Listen carefully with a cool and calm mind, to what I have to say. Right now I did not come to ask you for money. I am not in need of money at this time. I came purely to inform you of something that would be of great benefit to you. I risked my life in a foreign country to meet you here. I am sure you must be wondering about how a rich person of such a high status like you, can benefit from a lowly person and a common dacoit like me. But rest assured, that my interest in coming here tonight is to help you as a friend and to see you benefit immensely."

Sir Jordan Lane said, "What service can you possibly provide me? I still think you want to shoot me with your gun and then rob me and my house and run away."

Banks said, "Oh no, Sir! Get such thoughts out of your mind. I have, as such, enough charges against me and the police here is after me like a bunch of hounds chasing a rabbit. I considered your house to be the safest place for my meeting with you."

Sir Jordan Lane said, "I am not in the least interested in your meaningless talk. Please do not waste any more of my time and tell me what you have in mind for my benefit."

Banks said, "Alright, listen. Do you recall the day and time when your father died? You were in his bedroom standing near the headrest of your father's bed and your father was moments away from breathing his last breath. At that time I was standing outside this same window and had opened the window door very slightly. By chance the direction of the wind was towards my side and I could clearly hear your father's faint voice and what he was saying. He was desperately remembering his other son Nevlin Lane. He was asking you to help him in every way. He kept on saying, 'Oh my dear son Nevlin. Nevlin please come back.' He was saying to you, 'Son, you made false accusations against your brother and made me so angry that I asked Nevlin Lane to leave the house. I learned of the truth after he left the house. He is absolutely innocent. He is a very wise and loving son of whom I am very proud. It is your duty to search for him and ask him to return back to his home as soon as possible. If he returns after my death then tell him that his father was very sorry and begged for his forgiveness.' I will only continue further if you agree, that whatever I have said about Nevlin Lane so far is correct."

In response, Sir Jordan Lane said, "It does not mean anything. I made great efforts to search for Nevlin Lane and am still searching for him."

Banks continued, "After your father expressed his pain at the separation from Nevlin Lane, he said another thing. He said, 'I was in love with a girl who was my classmate. However, she refused to marry me and married another person. I was completely consumed by jealousy and caused this lady and her husband great suffering and harassment. They were completely destroyed because of my relentless persecution of them. This lady died leaving a small girl behind her. Her husband fled to some other country with this baby girl.' After narrating this story, your father asked you to find out about this girl and arrange for her to come here. He further said, 'Always look after her needs and protect her.' He also emphasized that in his original will he divided his property, wealth and jewellery in three parts. One part was for Nevlin Lane, the second part for you and the third part for this girl. He further told you that his original will was the real one. He wrote this of his free will and in the right frame of mind and this will did justice to everyone concerned. He asked you to promise him that you will help and protect the other two in his will. He further asked you to make a solemn pledge to him to act as per his wishes. He said, 'Since you wanted to inherit all the property, you forced me, under duress, to write the second will in your favour. Promise me that you will be fair and regard my original will as my real will. If you act contrary to your promise to me then you will not benefit from my wealth and property.'"

Banks continued, "To humour your father you promised him that you will do as he wished. This appeared to satisfy him. He started to have difficulty in breathing. You covered your father's face with the sheet and opened the night table drawer beside his bed. You took out two papers from the drawer. These two papers were the two wills your father had mentioned. One was the real will in which your father distributed his assets to your brother Nevlin Lane, yourself and the girl. The second paper was the invalid will in which he left everything to you and was written under duress. You had taken out both these wills. I saw both these papers in your hand from the window. You were on the point of leaving the bedroom when someone knocked at the sitting room door. You became disoriented and very nervous. While running to open the door, you tried to keep both these papers in your inside coat pocket. The real will which your father wrote in his sound mind, in a calm and cool atmosphere and also had a witness, dropped on the floor as your hands were shaking while you were trying to put it in your pocket. The other invalid will that your father had written with a shaky hand and under duress, leaving everything to you, remained in your pocket. The person knocking at the door was Mrs. Parson, your nanny. When you opened the door, she came inside the room and you told her about the deterioration in your father's condition. Within two minutes the family doctor and four of your servants also came in the room. You were pacing the room in a very agitated manner. Your father had expired and the doctor certified the same.

After the doctor left, Mrs. Parson also left the room crying. After she left the other four servants also left the room. You began to search your pocket and could only find the invalid will, the one written with a shaky hand. On not finding the real will in your pocket, you looked distraught and concerned. You began to search for the real will all over the room. From your worried look and frenzied search I gathered that the paper that fell from your hand while you were trying to put it in your pocket, was probably the real will. Sir, please tell me what I have said is true."

Jordan Lane looked at Banks with raised eyebrows and said, "I have heard enough of your funny story. If you want to save yourself, I suggest you run for your life right now. Oh yes, get this out of your mind that those papers were the wills of my father. There is only one signed will of my father in which he left the entire property and wealth in my name and that will is with me. I am not in the least bothered by the story that you have fabricated. You may tell the whole world your story. No one will believe a convicted dacoit like you. I am a respected member of the parliament. All the government and police officers in this county work under me. At my orders they will arrest you in no time and because of your crimes in the past, you will be jailed for the rest of your life. However, at this time I do not want to send you to prison. Somehow I always had a soft heart for persons who come to my house. Therefore count your blessings and take my advice. Get out of here and go to some distant country where no one knows you, otherwise be prepared to spend the rest of your life in the prison here."

Banks said, "I may be guilty of crimes and am a dacoit but I am certainly not a liar nor do I defraud others by dishonest and wicked means. I keep my word and am firm in keeping my promises like a true dacoit. On the contrary you pretend to be civilized and a decent gentleman. But under this cloak you defraud people by dishonest and cunning tactics. Now listen to me. The real will exists and is not lost. It was written in the presence of your nanny Mrs. Parson and it is properly signed by her. Mrs. Parson is still alive and lives nearby. She spends her whole day in the memory of her favourite master, Nevlin Lane. She misses him very much. In the near future, the real will is going to be presented in the court for execution in London. Mrs. Parson, the old loyal servant of your father and your nanny will testify to its authenticity. Because of your dishonesty and greed for wealth, you will lose two thirds of what you have and above all you will come out looking so mean that you will wish you were dead."

Sir Jordan Lane felt ashamed. He lowered his head and said in a soft voice, "Alright, I admit that my father wrote two wills. However, my respected father destroyed the first will right in front of my eyes and threw it in the garbage. The second will is in my possession."

Banks said, "Why do you keep on lying like this! This is why I say that under the pretence of a civilized gentleman, you are a crooked and dishonest robber. Your father never destroyed and burned the real will, though your intentions were to burn it. But God is Great and Just. By His Grace, He created circumstances to safeguard the real will."

Sir Jordan Lane said, "What proof do you have that the real will exists? Without proof I am not going to be intimidated by a dacoit like you. If the real will exists then tell me where it is and who has its custody."

Banks said, "The real will dropped from your hand on the floor of your father's bedroom. I found it and it is with me. I have kept it with great care in a very safe place."

Chapter 31

The enemy is prepared to destroy your very existence
For God's sake wake up from your deep slumber, look out

Everyone was far behind you but they are now marching on
Observe your pace and compare it to their speed, look out

If the person lost in the morning returns in the evening
Why call him lost he is the one who suffered, look out

This is no time to waste in sweet sleep
It is time to get ready to fight for your rights, look out

Rt. Hon. Sir Jordan Lane, Member of Parliament, belonging to the British aristocratic class, fabulously rich and powerful, considered himself a master in the art of deceit and fraud. He boasted of his cleverness in administration and public affairs. Unfortunately, he had to listen to the private details and the truth about his family from the dacoit Banks who had also humiliated him and called him names. As a result of all this, he felt lost and ashamed. He felt nervous and was at a loss for words. He lowered his head and his face turned red. His heartbeat became fast and he asked Banks in a voice that was full of anxiety, "Is it true that you have the real will of my respected father with you?"

Banks smiled and said, "Yes Sir, it is with me. When you

heard the knock at the door and were leaving the room to open the door for Mrs. Parson, you tried to put both the wills in your pocket. But as your hands were shaking, the real will slipped from your hand and fell on the floor. In your hurry and nervousness you did not realize this. You kept on thinking that both the wills were in your pocket. As I was hiding behind the window and had listened to all the conversation, the moment you turned to open the door, I slipped gently into the bedroom of your father. I dashed towards the bed and picked up the paper which was lying against the leg of the cabinet. I ran back and jumped from the window in the garden below. I examined the paper on reaching home and realized it was the real will with the signatures of your respected father Sir Gravelin Lane. Since you are too clever for your own good, you never even suspected me, though I knew that you had seen me jumping from the window. To this day, you have been searching for the real will in the bedroom. So as not to interfere with your search, you never got the room dusted and cleaned. The whole house looks so depressing. If you had called me at that time, it was very likely that I would have confessed that I took the real will and ran with it. As a matter of fact you should have suspected me because you saw me and you knew who I was and how I operate."

On hearing all this from Banks, Sir Jordan Lane felt sick and dizzy. His mind went blank. He sat down on a chair and held his head in his hands. He began to think of how to deal with this un nerving situation.

The selfish Sir Jordan Lane could not bear the thought th the real will was in the hands of another person and that he migl be forced to share his father's property with his step brother Nevl Lane and the daughter of his father's girl friend. He was determin not to share his father's property with anyone. He decided to ta back the possession of the real will from this dacoit at all cc and thus eliminate all the worry about a legal challenge in courts. He said to himself, "I can then relax in peace forev

Sir Jordan Lane was quite familiar with the greedy na of Banks. He also thought that this will could not be of any to this dacoit. All he could do was to search for the other beneficiaries named in the will and sell the will to them and create problems for him. It was much better that he bargain with him and tempt him with an offer of giving him money, and get back the real will from him. Once he accepted the money from him, he would forget about the others and save himself the trouble of finding the others named in the will. He thought that before he bargained with him, it was important to find out from him if he had been able to locate the others named in the will. If he had been able to locate them, he could ask for a ridiculous amount of money. If he had not, he could get the will back from him for very little money. In that case he could bribe him and even threaten him and force him to give the will back to him. With these thoughts in his mind, he felt better and more confident. He got up and sat down on an easy chair. He looked at Banks directly and invited him to sit down beside him.

Sir Jordan Lane said to Banks, "From what you have told me, it is obvious that you stole the real will. This will is of no use to you. You may as well give it back to me."

Banks said, "How can you say that this will is of no use to me?"

Sir Jordan Lane replied, "Of course, it can never be of any use to you, because you will not dare to present this will to anyone who has any authority. There are several very serious charges against you. The police all over the country is looking for you. The moment any police officer sees you, he will arrest you. Secondly, after your arrest if you show this will to any officer and tell the same story in the court of law, they will not believe it. All London courts are under my jurisdiction. I have the means, and it is a very simple matter for me to prove you to be a liar and the will to be a forgery. Since I have the other will of my father with me, I can hire any number of lawyers to prove that the will in my possession is the real will. On the other hand, if you want to give this real will to my step brother, Nevlin Lane, forget about it. You can never benefit from it. Nevlin Lane died a long time back. I doubt if you would even find his bones in the grave. For a moment, let us assume that he is alive somewhere, you will surely not think of benefitting him at my cost because I am your old friend. You have already taken advantage of my friendship several times in the past. You may recall that I have helped you to escape police custody, twice in the past. I gave you my clothes and helped you to change your appearance. You tricked the police and ran away to save your life. Several times I have helped you by giving you money. You have a great obligation to me for all that I have done to help you. Because of these obligations I am sure you realize that your loyalty and duty is first towards me as compared to Nevlin Lane. To say that Mrs. Parson will testify in the court is nonsense. I am sure she does not wish to be dragged in the courts just to prove that a piece of paper is the real will. I am aware of the fact that Mrs. Parson, as Nevlin Lane's nanny, has looked after him from childhood and that she loves him very much. Suppose, because of this love for Nevlin Lane, she agrees to testify in court, their combined testimony will be no match for my money and power. They are both poor and without any resources. No one can even have a say in the courts without enough money to pay the expensive lawyers. Lastly, about this girl whom my father wanted to marry, I have learned from reliable sources that she died a long time back and her husband ran away to France with this little girl. They both must have died by now from sheer starvation. All these factors are in my favour. I am sure you will see that it is absolutely useless for you to pick up a fight with me. You can do no harm to me. On the contrary I can send you to jail for the rest of your life."

Banks smiled and said, "Kind Sir, the girl who is named beneficiary of one third of the property is alive and well."

Sir Jordan Lane replied, "Even if I agree that you are telling the truth, it will be impossible for you to prove that she is the same girl whose parents were harassed by my father."

Banks said, "Oh, give up all your wishful thinking and face the facts. I do not say things that I do not mean. I think my goal is now straightforward. I will find this girl and hand over the real will to her. As a foreign citizen, I will sue you in court, on her behalf, for her rightful share of one third of your property. I know several rich people. There is no shortage of people who will spend money to see justice being done. You will be found guilty of grabbing the share of a helpless girl and she will get her rightful share."

Sir Jordan Lane asked, "Where will you find a person who will testify to the parentage and true identity of this girl?"

Banks said, "The girl herself has the proof of her birth and parentage. I was present at the time when her father died. Before dying, he told her the name and address of the person who was responsible for the tremendous suffering that her parents had to face, along with the other details. The papers of her birth, duly signed by the bishop of London, were enclosed in a locket. He gave her that locket to wear. He instructed the girl to safeguard the locket with her life. He further asked her to open the locket when she was eighteen years old and told her that the papers inside the locket would establish her identity. Consequently the girl wore the locket around her neck right in front of my eyes."

Sir Jordan Lane said, "Listen, I am telling you once again that you can do me no harm. Even after searching for this girl for years around the world, you may still not find her. In the end you will be either trapped by the police and arrested or you will be killed by some wild animal in the jungles. As a remote possibility, even if you succeed in bringing the girl here and sue me, all that can happen is that you may drag me and my family's reputation in the courts and nothing more. I am not going to part with any of my property as long as I live. The lawyers are good at finding dozens of loopholes in any case they are working on, and they are good at proving the guilty innocent and the innocent guilty. A better alternative in your favour is, that we decide on a mutually satisfactory arrangement, provided you have the real will with you. You will be better off by taking some money from me in exchange for the real will. Now it is upto you as to what you want to do next. I have nothing to fear and I really do not care what you decide. Oh yes, I almost forget that we have been engrossed in deep discussions for over an hour and have not eaten supper. I am hungry. We both need some snacks to refresh ourselves before we continue further."

Sir Jordan Lane got up and went to the room near the kitchen and brought back two plates with ten or twelve boiled eggs, some biscuits, bread and a bottle of liquor. He invited Banks to come and sit at the table. Bank had a weakness for drinking and was very happy to see the bottle of liquor. He filled up a glass and raised it to his lips to drink. However, as he was about to drink he smelled a pungent smell from the glass. He at once removed the glass from his mouth and pushed it to the lips of Sir Jordan Lane and said, "You drink from this glass first and then I will drink the rest."

Sir Jordan Lane said, "Wait, please wait. What are you doing! Don't you know that I have not touched any liquor for years now? I do keep a few bottles in the wine cabinet for guests like you. This whole bottle is for you. Go ahead and enjoy it but excuse me for not joining you."

On hearing this, Banks became angry and said, "People who try to deceive their friends are people with no morals. You are no match for me in spotting deceit and trickery. I am quite capable of mixing several types of poison in the wine without sacrificing its taste or smell and guarantee that no one can detect it. I have taken practically every type of liquor and wine produced so far and am familiar with the taste and smell of each one of them. I also know the different types of poison that can be mixed with wine. Since you are an amateur crook, you mixed the poison in such a quantity that I could detect it right away, even without taking a sip." Banks forced the glass of liquor to the lips of Sir Jordan Lane and said in an angry voice, "You are not only wicked but also the worst type of a crook. You have no morals and you have just failed to deceive and kill your friend. You want to kill me by mixing poison in the wine. The right punishment for you is that you are forced to drink this glass of wine yourself. Hurry up otherwise I will slit open your mouth and force all the wine down your throat."

Sir Jordan Lane requested, "Remove it. Please remove the glass of wine from my mouth. This is pure wine. What would I gain by mixing poison in this wine."

On hearing this, Banks forced the glass against Sir Jordan's lips and said in a very angry tone, "Go ahead and drink it right now, otherwise I will take my revenge by killing you with my gun right here. If you drink this wine, I will be convinced that this is pure wine and no poison is mixed in it."

Sir Jordan Lane pushed the glass away from his mouth with such great force that the glass fell on the floor and broke in several pieces. Accidentally, his body struck the table leg and the liquor bottle also fell on the floor and broke. The whole floor was soaked with the wine. He faced Banks and said, "Look if you do not want to drink because of your suspicions, then do not drink. But you have no right to force me to drink and break my promise of not drinking liquor. Listen to me. Sit down and with a calm mind discuss the business at hand. Neither you drink, nor force me to drink. Now hand over the real will of my father to me for a reasonable price. The reason for my wanting to have this will back is that I am on the verge of becoming a minister in the cabinet. At this stage I do not want any scandal about my family to be brought up in the public and I do not wish to spend my time in attending various court hearings. It is certain that this will spoil my reputation and I will be humiliated. However, there is no doubt that I shall eventually win the case. The public opinion is sure to be divided. Some will side with me and others will think that I am wrong. For this reason I am anxious to quietly settle this with you in the house here."

Banks said, "Since you are my old friend and have done me some favours in the past, I do not want to drag your name and reputation in the courts. Give me five thousand pounds and take the will from me. You can then rest in peace."

Sir Jordan Lane said, "What a fancy thought! Seemingly you have no control on your tongue. How can I give you such a huge amount for a useless piece of paper? Get out of my sight and my house. In one of my unguarded moments, I consented to sit down and talk with you. I should have got you arrested by the police the moment you entered the room. I should not have wasted my valuable time in discussing a deal with you."

On hearing this, Banks got up from his chair and buttoned his coat and said, "I give you time till tomorrow evening to think it over. Please weigh carefully all the benefits and harm that can come to you from this deal. If you are convinced, then bring me five thousand pounds in a small bag, otherwise let me know that you are not interested. I have some work in London now which I expect to finish by tomorrow evening. I can meet you at any place of your choice tomorrow night. And remember I am not scared of any of your threats. You can ring the bell and call your servants or send for the police. You are the one who is a coward."

Banks did not give Sir Jordan Lane a chance to reply. He dashed to the window, jumped to the ground and disappeared. He did not even turn back his head to look at Sir Jordan Lane.

Chapter 32

By nature he is mischievous and unjust
He is constantly finding means to hurt

Though he preaches morals but has no morals
His planning is always wrong and lopsided

Like a wasp he hovers above inflicting pain
First he bites and drinks and then stings

After Banks left, Sir Jordan Lane stretched on the chair and covered his face with both hands realizing that the dacoit had jumped through the window without any fear and had taken the upper hand in the dealings. Since his father's death, he had no peace of mind. He thought of all the problems before him. First, the worry and concern at the loss of the real will of his father. Secondly, the fear of Banks's return to London and the possibility of his exposing him and blackmailing him. Thirdly, the fear that Rachel, the girl he had seduced and jilted and whose heart he had broken, may come back any time to take revenge. Lastly, the constant worry about his step brother, Nevlin Lane, who could return anyday to claim his share. The guilty feeling he had and all these problems had been weighing heavily on his mind for the past years and making him very restless and uneasy. He hardly enjoyed the food and could never sleep soundly because of these worries. He said to himself. "Now this sudden and unexpected meeting with Banks has created another serious problem." The thought of parting with the large sum of five thousand pounds made him forget everything else. This was now weighing heavily on his mind. He forgot all cunning ways. He realized that Banks not only knew the exact wordings of his father's will but he also had the will in his possession. Everything he had said seemed to fit together like the parts of a puzzle. He said to himself, 'If I can get the real will for five thousand pounds then it is not a bad deal. I shall be marrying Audrey Hope in the near future. Then I will control all her wealth. If I do not go along with the deal with Banks or get him arrested, then this rascal is sure to create a bigger problem for me. I will not be surprised if he defames me and ruins my reputation in public. It is also quite likely that once Audrey Hope hears of all the charges against me, she may refuse to marry me. All my future plans and happiness will be jeopardised if I pick up a fight with Banks at this time. However, I feel very bad in parting with five thousand pounds but there seems to be no other alternative. Right now I have to think a way to resolve this problem. One problem that has to be sorted out is whether my step brother Nevlin Lane and this girl named in the will by my father, can under any circumstances, contest the will in court. Supposing that Nevlin Lane, who has been away for such a long period, has perchance died, then I will get his share automatically. This will only leave the girl, whose parents were harassed by my father, to deal with. Banks says that this girl is alive and he threatened to sue me in court on her behalf. In my view, this dacoit will never be able to prove the real identity of this girl in the court of law. Moreover, neither the girl nor the dacoit can possibly know what I have inherited in clothes, jewellery and expensive paintings because they do not have the list of such items. If the court even issues a verdict whereby the girl is given one third of the share of my wealth, she will not be able to realize even a penny from me as long as I live. I will involve her in such complicated and lengthy court battles that it will become exceedingly difficult for her to get anything from me."

Sir Jordan Lane satisfied himself that this was a feasible solution as far as the girl was concerned. He began to think as to how he could get rid of Banks. The first thought that came to his mind was to have him killed. He considered it and realized that this would be very difficult and not feasible. He then thought that maybe he could shoot the dacoit himself. He felt that he did not have enough courage to do this. He was well aware that this dacoit was very alert and clever and could easily fathom the intentions of others. His plan would not succeed in front of him. This dacoit could at once detect that there was poison in the liquor the moment he brought the drink near his mouth. He was always very alert and swift and could guess your move just by looking at you. He always carried a gun in his pocket. He came to the conclusion that there was no alternative but to give the dacoit five thousand pounds in exchange for the real will. No other trick or plan would work. He then started thinking, 'Supposing that the dacoit takes his five thousand pounds and then refuses to hand over the will. What will I do then?' This thought once again made him very uneasy. He became dizzy and nervous. When Banks had held his neck tightly to force the drink down his mouth, his fingers had left deep marks on his neck and now his neck also began to hurt. In spite of this condition a thought came to his mind that gave him relief and he gained confidence in handling the situation. He got up and gathered all the broken pieces of the wine glass and bottle from the floor and threw them outside. He locked the window and slowly walked to his bedroom. He looked at his face in the mirror and noticed that he looked tired and his face was very pale. He cursed the dacoit in his heart for making him go through this agony. He wished that the dacoit had been killed while jumping out from the window.

It is interesting to note the selfish and mean nature of Sir Jordan Lane. He wished for the death of Banks and even contemplated killing him. To avoid sharing the inheritance with the innocent girl and his step brother, he hoped that his brother was dead. He planned to harass and intimidate the girl in court battles till she agreed to give up on her share. To satisfy his greed for money, he was prepared to commit a murder. He was determined to kill the dacoit. So he took out his special gun from the locked cabinet in his room. The gun was capable of firing twenty shots at one time. He loaded it with twelve cartridges and kept it on the table in his room, ready for use. He consoled himself that this gun was far superior to anything that the dacoit might have and had sufficient ammunition to kill him. He thought to himself, "I can threaten him with this gun and force him to hand over the real will. My top priority right now is to get the real will back, so that this problem will not nag me anymore and would be eliminated forever." With this determination he went to bed but could not sleep and kept turning and tossing for a long time. Finally around three in the morning, he fell asleep.

When he woke up the next morning, he was very restless. His whole body was aching and he felt lethargic. His feet felt heavy and he could not bring himself to get out of his bed. He also felt dizzy and sick. His mind was blank due to all the thoughts and plans that he kept making the previous night. He could hardly think straight. His face was pale and the deep finger marks of the dacoit on his neck were now very visible and painful. When it was late in the morning, the servant knocked at the door. He did not feel like getting up to open the door and told the servant that he was not feeling well and wanted to rest. He said he will come out at noon. On receiving this message, the servant left. Sir Jordan Lane closed his eyes and tried to sleep again. Because of his current problems, he completely forgot that today was the day that he was supposed to do several things. He had arranged a meeting with the architects that morning to discuss the demolition of his father's bedroom and sitting room area and the construction of a bird house, a stable for horses and a dance hall in its place. He was also planning to meet his friends to invite them at the engagement ceremony. He had some shopping to do from the market. Above all, he was planning to meet Audrey Hope to discuss the arrangements for their engagement party and fix up a date for their wedding. He had forgotten all this. Finally, after great effort, he got up from the bed around eleven o'clock. After the morning routine he came out of the room. He ordered breakfast. After finishing his breakfast he sat down at his desk and wrote the following letter to Audrey Hope:

My dear Audrey,

You are more precious to me than my heart. Today I have a meeting at my old house to settle a few things with the farmers who work on my lands. For this reason I will not be able to come and see you. You are probably aware that I consider it my duty to look after the welfare and interests of my farmers. I feel proud to provide my farmers with material comforts and other benefits for their happiness. Since looking after the farm workers is also part of a landlord's responsibility, I have to, single-handedly, bear the whole burden of managing the farms. However, I am sure that a wife like you, who is clever and an excellent administrator, would be of great help in solving all my problems. I will be able to relax and enjoy the worldly pleasures once again. Dear Audrey, my only wish now is that we get married as soon as possible. I was going to mention this to you when we last met but I thought at that time that this may annoy you and I kept quiet. I should be free from my work here in two or three days and I look forward to come and hear the sweet word of consent for a wedding date from your lips. I am sure you will make me very happy by sharing your life with me.

I remain, longing for your love,
Jordan Lane

Sir Jordan Lane kept the letter in an envelope and sealed it. He rang the bell for the servant and asked him to go and mail the letter. He went to his room and dressed up for the day. He tied a scarf round his neck to hide the finger marks of the dacoit. He opened the door of his room and came out. The servants, who seemed to be busy in their work, noticed the scarf around his neck and expressed their concern. They enquired as to how he was feeling and suggested that they go and fetch the doctor. He said to them, "Oh, it is nothing serious. Just a little sore throat due to a cold and I do not require any medicine. Two of you go and wait at the main gate outside and be alert. I am expecting a person to come and see me today. I have to discuss important official business with him. As soon as he arrives, bring him to my bedroom as I do not feel like climbing down the stairs to come to the drawing room."

The servants were surprised to get these instructions from their master. They went to their room and speculated as to the cause of their master's sudden illness. One said that the master was fine till last night. The second servant said that he was very surprised at this sudden illness. The third one suggested that he was really not sick but some very serious problem must have surfaced overnight and it was this problem that was bothering him and making him look so worried. While the servants were gossiping in their room, Sir Jordan Lane went to his bedroom and began to look at the day's mail. He had hardly read a couple of letters when the pressure and stress on his mind overcame his concentration. He just closed his eyes and stretched on the chair. He started thinking of the sad turn of events and was soon lost in deep thought. In the evening the servant came and lit the lamp in the room and brought the evening tea and kept it on the table.

As he picked up the cup of tea he heard the sound of a carriage pulling in front of the house. He looked from the window and saw a middle aged man with a long beard and wearing glasses getting down from the carriage. He was wearing clean white dress. He greeted the servants waiting at the gate. The servant said to him, "You are probably the gentleman who has come to discuss some official business with our master. He told us about your coming and is waiting for you in his bedroom. We will escort you to his room."

On hearing this from the servants, Banks thought that it was a good thing that he had dressed up as a lawyer because Jordan Lane had seemingly informed his servants about his coming. He said in a tone of authority, "Yes, I am that person. Please take me to your master."

The servant informed Sir Jordan Lane about the arrival of the expected guest, who they understood was the official who was to come to discuss business. On his instructions, the servant escorted Banks to their master's room.

Sir Jordan Lane motioned to him with his hand to sit on the

chair. Banks greeted Jordan Lane and sat down on the chair. The servants left the room and were in the process of closing the door when Sir Jordan Lane asked them to lock the door behind them. The guest at once interjected and said in a very sharp voice, "Please do not lock the door as I am expecting my servant in ten minutes. When he comes, please let me know, without opening the door. None of you should enter the room without our calling you and make sure that no one else enters the room without your first informing us." Sir Jordan Lane did not say a word against these instructions of Banks and the servant took it to be his wish as well. The servant closed the door behind him and left. After the servant left, Banks pulled his chair nearer Sir Jordan Lane's chair and said in a low voice. "Please tell me Sir, what have you decided about our conversation yesterday? You want to fight or accept the deal?"

Sir Jordan Lane said, "It is a waste of time to talk about a fight or a deal. Let us calmly talk about the important matter at hand. There is no danger of any kind here and you are completely safe. None of the servants here know your name or have any knowledge about the subject of our talk tonight."

Dacoit Banks said, "I am always apprehensive of the danger here because of your dishonest and crooked nature. Kindly let us move our chairs towards the door near the gallery as Inspector Trail and his detectives often peek through the front windows of the room. Our chairs are visible from that window and it is not safe to sit here. I can then finish our talk in a couple of minutes and be on my way out."

Since it was very important for Sir Jordan Lane to get the real will from Banks, he did what Banks had requested him to do. The dacoit also moved his chair and sat down, facing him.

Banks said, "Now, please tell me your decision about the proposal I made to you yesterday."

Sir Jordan Lane replied, "The truth is that your profession is robbery. You are not afraid to commit a crime. You do not care for the police and you laugh in their face. You have a habit of appearing and disappearing in seconds. The respected people hesitate in talking to you and you rob and harass the rich people. You are an expert in pulling several tricks and in deceiving other people. Knowing all this, it will be foolish on my part to trust you. Therefore, I would first like to see my father's will and inspect it carefully. If I am satisfied, I will put five thousand pounds in your pocket as demanded by you. I am afraid that unless I inspect the will, you may run away with the money without giving me the will or hand me a forged and useless document."

Banks said, "I thank you for the kind words you spoke regarding my expertise in my line of work. But, as compared to me, you are far more crooked and wicked. I know you well. I have heard from several people in London about your selfish, cunning and deceitful nature. You are notorious in London society. I have experienced myself your deceit in your dealings with me. Under these circumstances what assurance do I have that you will quietly and honestly hand over the money to me on receiving the will. Because of our mutual mistrust of each other, tell me a solution that is workable and acceptable and we can both have what we want. I never imagined in God's name, that I could get such a large sum of money in exchange for the real will. It is the fault of your own nature that made me ask you for this amount. Regarding people in my kind of business, remember that we are known for honesty in our dealings and keeping our promises. You will not find an honest person like me in thousands of rich and highly placed officials in London. If you trust me with a clear conscience, then I will also trust you. I swear in the name of God that I will not defraud you and I will hand over the real will to you. I will not even count the five thousand pounds notes that you give to me. If we deal in good faith and with honesty, neither you nor I will have any cause for worry afterwards. You should know and understand that no business in this world can be carried out without mutual trust. Persons who do not trust and always try to look for faults, can never get very far in this world. They always regret their actions in hindsight. For you this amount of five thousand pounds is not a big sum and does not mean much. Suppose for a minute that I take your five thousand pounds and in exchange give you a forged useless document. You will not be any worse off by the loss of five thousand pounds. By God's grace you have plenty of everything. However, on the contrary, I will be living in constant fear whether I am in a faraway city or jungle or anywhere else. At this time I have taken the liberty to come to London because of you. I roam around here knowing that you will protect me and help me to escape the police. If I deceive you, I cannot stay in London even for a minute nor can I hide myself in your house like I do now. Same way if you deceive me, you will not have peace of mind even for a minute. You will not be able to sleep peacefully because you will be scared that I may take revenge anytime. Thus it is binding on both of us to be honest. I do not give you forged papers and you do not give me forged money. It will benefit both of us to deal in good faith and honesty. We will both be losers if we try to deceive the other." Banks continued, "In my opinion and if you agree, the best solution to carry out the transaction, is this: This Friday, exactly at ten o'clock in the night, you bring five thousand pounds in cash to the side garden of Stonelake at your house. I will be sitting on a branch of the big oak tree. On seeing you, I will immediately take out the tin container from the hollow of the tree in which the real will is kept and stored for safekeeping. With one hand I will hand over this container to you and with the other hand you hand over the five thousand pounds to me. Both the transactions will be completed simultaneously. In my opinion there is no better way of completing our transaction."

Sir Jordan Lane said, "This method seems alright to me. I agree to your suggestion. But why wait till Friday? Why not complete the transaction tonight? It appears to me that the will is in the possession of someone else and you have to get it from him."

Banks replied, "I know that the will is dear to you but it is far more valuable to me. I am protecting it like my own life and I have kept it at a safe place with my own hands. I cannot get it from that place before Friday. Now I will leave. It is upto you whether you come on Friday with five thousand pounds or bring inspector Trail to arrest me. I will come prepared for both the situations."

Sir Jordan Lane said, "I will come with the bundle of notes. Since we are both in need of something that the other has, you should have complete trust in me."

Sir Jordan Lane got up from his chair and moved towards the table to ring the bell for the servants. Banks stopped him and said, "Now that we both have reached an understanding and have agreed to trust each other, I want to ask you a favour. If you know anything about my daughter Rachel, please tell me. Do you know where she lives and what she is doing? You are also the district magistrate of this area and you get all the news and information about everyone in your jurisdiction. You are aware of all the rich and poor in this area. You must know about Rachel. You are well aware that both my wife and I come from very well to do families. Our daughter Rachel was very dear to us. She studied in the same school located in your area. She was a good student and completed her education at the school. She was clever and very intelligent. Her mother also trained her in all the housework and gave her religious training. I was not able to get any government job in spite of my trying very hard. There were just no jobs available. I learned several trades in the hope of getting a job but was unable to find any job. We were almost on the verge of starvation. I had to beg for our daily food. On one of my rounds in search for a job, I happened to meet a person who appeared to be rich and well to do, but was in fact a dacoit by profession. I happened to fall under his influence and against my better judgement and my wishes I was forced to join a group of dacoits. My wife was of a very pious and decent nature. She did her best to dissuade me from joining this group, but I ignored her pleas and went to the jungle and distant places with this group of dacoits. I left my wife and daughter in our house at Stonelake. While living in the jungles, I often used to remember my daughter and wife and missed them badly. I came to London to see them but they were not at the Stonelake house. On inquiring, I learned that my wife was very sad and grieved at my becoming a dacoit and she passed away because of this shock and sadness in her heart. Rachel was left alone without any parental control and guidance. I understand she got involved with some rich boy in her school who deceived her and after ruining her life, ran away. He promised to marry her but then turned her down. He has probably left town to escape the scandal. My blood boils when I think of this man who ruined my daughter's life. If I can find his name, I will take my revenge for Rachel's humiliation by killing him with my bare hands. Not even a hundred policemen or jails will be able to stop me from killing this man. If you know Rachel's address, please tell me so that I can find out the name of this person who ruined her life and then take revenge on her behalf. It does not matter if Rachel has decided to lead a low life on streets, I still want to meet her. It is not her fault that she had to do this. The fault is mine. I did not provide her the security of a family life and a model to follow. Helpless and without any friends she may have fallen into bad ways to sustain herself. She is my blood and it is necessary for me to make amends for her. If you know her address please tell me, I shall be very grateful to you forever."

On hearing Banks speak like this, Sir Jordan Lane began to perspire with shame. He began to think as to how best he could handle this situation and turn it to his advantage. As per his nature of dishonesty and deceit, he fabricated a story that was not true. He said to Banks, "About six months back your daughter Rachel met me on the street. I advised her to give up the street life and adopt a decent and respectable living. Since she lived in my district, I had sympathy and a certain responsibility towards her and for this reason I took considerable pain to reason with her and gave her the right advice. However, instead of listening to my advice, she turned and laughed at me. Now that I have heard your story and see how desperate you are, I feel great sympathy for you. For this reason I will share the family secret with you. One of the major reasons behind my father asking Nevlin Lane to leave the house was this very situation. He began to like Rachel very much when he was at school, and was after her all the time. My father came to know of it and tried his best to persuade Nevlin Lane to mend his ways and leave the girl alone but he refused. He got into the company of some crooks and began to live a life of shame and reckless behaviour. My father asked him repeatedly to marry Rachel. But he refused point blank and said he would never marry Rachel, but he kept her as his mistress and servant. My father was a wise man and he could see that Nevlin Lane would never mend his ways and was going to spend all money on drinking, chasing women and other bad habits. For this reason, as a punishment, he ordered him to leave the house. He thought that if he got away from his bad company here for a while, he would realize his mistake and come back on the right track. He would give up his bad habits and corrupt lifestyle. For this reason, after Nevlin Lane left, he bequeathed all his wealth and property to me. He left instructions for me to look for Nevlin Lane and if he came back to a sober life of decent habits, to help him settle down. You also heard my father say the same thing. Since you also belong to my area, you must know Nevlin Lane well. For goodness sake do not kill him, after all he is my step brother." Sir Jordan Lane made this last statement to show that he cared for his brother, though in his heart he did not care what happened to Nevlin Lane. Sir Jordan Lane continued, "You are hot tempered and you may feel like killing him for humiliating Rachel, but do not carry out your threat. I did not tell you the name of the person who destroyed Rachel's life for you to take revenge and turn your anger against my own family by killing my step brother Nevlin Lane."

He continued, "Now regarding your daughter Rachel, I know that she took up a government job as a nurse at the Central London Hospital. About four or five months back, she left for Austria with the wife of a doctor as her companion. This doctor was going to set up a hospital a little further south from Fairfeld at Lornehope Camp. I believe this employment with the doctor was just a cover up. Her true aim was to find Nevlin Lane. Someone told her that Nevlin Lane had gone to Austria and I think that she has gone there to find him and live with him as his mistress. The doctor's name and exact address can be easily found from the London Hospital."

Banks said in a very angry voice, "I had never seen your brother Nevlin Lane come near our house anytime. I am also not familiar with his face. I never saw him with you and whenever

I came to meet you he was not present. Thus I do not recognize him. But if I am convinced that he is the one who humiliated my daughter Rachel, I promise that I will hunt him out wherever he maybe. It is not difficult for me to locate him in and around Austria. I am very familiar with that region of the country. I will appreciate if you kindly show me some proof of the truth of this story that you have just narrated. I am sure that you must have some proof to substantiate the story of your brother's exploits as you would never make up such a convincing story without some concrete proof with you. Whether the proof is in writing or some article, please show it to me so that I may go to Austria immediately and start the search for Nevlin Lane and satisfy the fire burning inside me by killing him."

Sir Jordan Lane said, "I have got the written proof with me but I am afraid that you will kill my step brother Nevlin Lane. However, since you appear to be very restless to meet your daughter Rachel, I do not feel justified in keeping the proof with me. I will give you the letter written by your daughter to Nevlin Lane on one condition, that instead of killing Nevlin Lane, you bring him back here and hand him over to me. I will make him see the right from wrong and persuade him to marry Rachel. I will give them a suitable regular allowance so that they may both live a happy and carefree life. Your daughter will get back her lost respect and place in the society."

Banks shook Sir Jordan Lane's hand with great warmth and happiness and said in a flattering tone, "Please show me that letter. Who knows what the future holds. Man proposes, God disposes. In these circumstances I can neither say yes or no. I will be eternally under your debt. Please show me that letter. Please give it to me."

The wicked, greedy and big liar, Sir Jordan Lane, got up and went to his cabinet. He took out a bundle of letters from the drawer. He turned them over one by one and pulled out one letter from it. The top part of the letter with the date and name of the addressee was partly burned. The rest of the letter was intact and written in neat handwriting. At the end it was clearly signed, Rachel. He handed the letter to Banks.

This was the same letter that Rachel had written to Sir Jordan Lane and a mention of the same was made previously in the conversation that took place between Rachel and Sir Jordan Lane when they met last on the street as he was returning from a party at Lady Marlow's house. Rachel had called him wicked, dishonest and untrustworthy at his face. She had cursed him for his disloyalty and deceit and told him that after humiliating her and not keeping the promise of marriage, he had left her high and dry. She told him to keep the meagre sum of money he was offering her because she would never accept anything from him. She also told him that she would die rather than live with him as his mistress. She had written the same kind of things in the letter that she had sent to him.

Banks recognized the signature and handwriting of his daughter. He asked in a surprised tone, "How did this letter of Rachel written in her hand come to be in your possession?"

Sir Jordan Lane, who was master of fabricating false stories, said, "When my late father turned Nevlin Lane out of the house, I went to Nevlin Lane's room to sort out his things. I found a big pile of burned letters. I stood there and in my presence I got the servants clean up the mess of those burned letters and papers. In that pile, there were several letters which were only partially burned. Some letters had the bottom text burned and this letter had some of the top part burned. I looked at this letter and noticed that the part that said 'Nevlin Lane' was burned in such a manner that only the word Lane could be identified. The first part and date was burned. I kept this letter safely along with my other papers with the intention of returning it back to Rachel. Since then I did not have any opportunity to meet her and thus I could not return her letter. You are at liberty to keep this letter with you and give it back to Rachel when you meet her. If I may suggest, you should burn this letter yourself rather than returning it back to Rachel because that will only reopen her past wounds and sad memories. Also by keeping this letter with you, you are likely to get more and more angry and do something that you may later regret."

Banks kept the letter in his pocket. He was shaking with anger. He began to curse Nevlin Lane and called him bad names. He could hardly control himself. When he sobered down a little, he said to Sir Jordan Lane, "I shall remain eternally grateful to you. Whatever problems I might have faced in searching for the person who spoiled the life of my daughter are now all gone, thanks to you. I will find both Nevlin Lane and Rachel wherever they are—in the deserts or cities of Austria. I will search for Nevlin Lane in every corner of that country. Now he cannot hide from me!" Banks got up and left the room.

Chapter 33

We can say today in front of your picture
Oh yes, yes it is no match to your real face

Oh wise one your teachings are of no value
I am with you but my heart is not

The promise of true friendship that Audrey Hope had made with Senorita Estella at her house blossomed and strengthened as each day passed. Audrey Hope felt restless unless she was able to meet Senorita Estella, at least once everyday. Audrey Hope considered Sylvia to be her sincere friend because Sylvia was unselfish and did not say things to unduly flatter her. The jealousy and hatred that she felt towards Senorita Estella, after she had read the newspaper article shown to her by Sir Jordan Lane, had completely vanished and she now respected and admired her very much. On the third day after their meeting, Audrey Hope came to Sylvia's house in her special carriage. With great enthusiasm she invited Sylvia and insisted that she come to her house. She herself escorted Sylvia to her uncle, Lord Marlow's house. Initially, Lady Marlow greeted and welcomed Sylvia with some restraint and hesitation taking her to be a stage singer. However, very soon she was completely won over by Sylvia's great charm, beauty and intelligence. Lord Marlow also came to join them for the evening tea and Audrey Hope introduced Sylvia to him. He too was much impressed by her intelligent talk.

He began to treat her like his own daughter. After carefully watching her way of talking, her manners at the table and her general poise, he was convinced that Senorita Estella was very simple by nature. From all her actions and the way she ate and talked, she appeared to belong to a very decent family. She did not seem to have any ego about her great beauty, her earning such a high salary or her great popularity. Within a short while all the men and women and the servants in Audrey Hope's house, came to meet the famous Senorita Estella and were won over by her beauty and charm. Lord Marlow began to talk with Sylvia freely, in the same way as he spoke with Audrey Hope. Lady Marlow took Lord Marlow to one side and asked him why he was treating Senorita Estella thus. He said, "I have a feeling that I saw her in the arms of a very rich and decent lady as a baby, but in spite of my trying hard to recall who this lady was, I cannot place her. I will tell you the name of this lady when I remember it." He continued talking with both the girls for a long time after the tea was over. When the two girls left for a walk in the garden, Lord Marlow said to his wife, "Senorita Estella's face is very attractive and charming. I have not seen such a well mannered and beautiful girl anywhere in my county before. Audrey Hope's time spent with her is time well spent and she should spend more time in her company. I am very surprised at how she managed to acquire such great skill and expertise in her profession at such a young age. Her popularity amongst the public in London is phenomenal. However, I believe there is some mystery in her past."

Lady Marlow said, "What mystery can there be? She is a stage singer and has taken up the profession of singing and dancing like anyone else in her line of work."

Lord Marlow replied, "I think you are wrong. This girl belongs to some rich and well to do family. She has taken up stage singing and dancing to support herself."

Lady Marlow said, "Men folk have a funny way of judging other people. They are very opinionated. If they consider someone to be good or bad, they stick to it all the time without any logic. We really have no need to analyze her situation. It is enough for us that she is a stage singer and dancer. It is not good for Audrey Hope to be friendly with this girl. We can all get a bad reputation from this association. Sir Jordan Lane has advertised well the news of their engagement and Audrey Hope herself has not contradicted it. In another few days they will be married, he will be her legal husband. Then it is upto him whether he wants her to keep on meeting Senorita Estella or impose some restrictions on her. He can decide what he wants to do."

Lord Marlow said, "I do not think Jordan Lane should exert any pressure, even after the legal marriage has taken place. There should be no interference in the friendship of these two girls. By the way, tell me where is Jordan Lane? Why has he not come here for the past few days?"

Lady Marlow responded, "Jordan Lane has gone to his ancestral home at Court Lane. He is planning to make a few changes to his house. He is also buying costly furniture and furnishings to redecorate the house. Because of his wealth, he is planning a big and magnificent wedding, full of pomp and show. He is also converting his mansion into a palace."

Lord Marlow said, "This will befit his pride and status. After all he is marrying a very beautiful and highly accomplished girl who is known for her expensive, royal tastes and habits."

Senorita Estella and Audrey Hope walked in the garden, hand in hand and continued their walk in the Central Park of London. When the general public saw them talking and laughing like close friends, they realized that these two girls had become good friends.

The men and women, hoping to get a chance to meet these very beautiful girls, sent several letters to Audrey Hope. After few days Audrey Hope came to Senorita Estella's house with all these letters. Sylvia was surprised to see so many letters. Audrey Hope laughed and said, "My dear friend, you see these letters sprinkled with perfume are from people belonging to rich families and in high positions. These have been sent to my house over the past few days. All the letters that are addressed to me have an invitation for you as well. I want to tell you that hundreds of young men and women in London are completely mesmerized by your beauty and charm. All the newspapers are full of praise and admiration for you. You have become very, very popular. This world is such a big place and full of wonderful things and if you so wish, you can plunge into it and enjoy life."

Sylvia said, "Leave this poor girl to live a quiet life. I have absolutely no desire to get involved in worldly life. I like to lead a quiet life and in my spare time pray to God. I have read in books that God has made human beings in His image. He has given us intelligence to try and be like Him. In my mind, I have adopted you as God's image and whenever I pray to God, I keep your face before me. Living in this world, I see life's ups and downs every day. To survive I have to work as well. I wear rich or ordinary clothes to suit the occasion. I have to speak and mix with people from all walks of life. But inside me, I always have a feeling that this is all a dream. In the theatre, I sometimes act as king, queen or a princess. Or as a poor person or a beggar. At other times I sing songs of happiness or of sadness. At the time I play these roles, I do not feel happy to be a queen or feel sorry or sad to be a beggar. However, at the time, it becomes absolutely essential to act and behave like the person whose role I am playing. Similarly living in this world, I have to perform my duty. It does not make me happy or sad. Only my meeting with you has created a desire in me to be with you all the time. This seems to be a reality for me. I want to be with you, whether you are sitting in a party, or in a church, or in a garden. I will be there with you. I will also enjoy things in this world with you. However, do not expect me to get seriously involved in anything. I want to see all this as a spectator, just like a swan who lives in the water, but when she comes out of water, her wings are dry. Similarly, I want to be unattached to this world, while living in it."

Audrey Hope said, "Alright. From now onwards I will also try and follow the views expressed by you. However, living in this world you have to follow some traditions. If you can perform these duties without getting attached to people and things, then that is the best attitude towards life. As long as you live in this world, you have to go and meet others and invite them to your place and do some socializing. As it happens I am invited to a party today, by one of the princesses closely related to the royal family. It is essential and important for me to attend this party. As you know, I do not feel happy when I am away from you. What do you say that we both go to this party together tonight?"

Sylvia smiled and said, "O.K. I will go with you. But you know that I have clothes and jewellery that I wear at the theatre."

Audrey Hope said, "The theatre jewellery is all artificial and the theatre dresses have imitation work on it. There is no need for you to wear these dresses. I will arrange for something more appropriate right here."

Sylvia said, "I am grateful to you for your kindness. However, I just remembered that I will not be able to go to the party tonight because Merci Fairflex is not well. When I was coming to your house she was compiaining of a headache. I made her lie down on the bed and promised to come back soon. Her face looked flushed and pale. I have to look after her and give her the medicine. I am sorry I cannot come with you today. Please forgive me."

Audrey Hope took Sylvia's hand in her hands and said in a pleading tone, "I must take you to the party, I must. I will not let you go back to your house. A headache is not a serious illness and no medicine is required. A good night's sleep will make her fresh and perfectly normal in the morning. If you go and disturb her, the headache is surely going to get worse."

Audrey Hope got up and brought her jewellery box and took out some studded diamond jewellery for Sylvia. She also brought a beautiful dress from her wardrobe and requested Sylvia to get dressed. Sylvia thanked Audrey Hope for her generosity and returned her jewellery and dress and said, "This costly jewellery and these dresses befit rich people like you. I am being frank with you. These will not suit me. I have never gone out anywhere in my theatre clothes and jewellery. But I have something that I can wear." Sylvia asked Audrey Hope's personal servant to fetch her silk and velvet black dress with real lace work, from her house. She got dressed in it.

They both reached the royal princess's party. The palace

where the party was being held was huge and very magnificent. It was furnished with costly furniture and lit by fancy chandeliers of all shapes and sizes. People were dressed in clothes of the latest fashion and as per their personal taste. They were enjoying the party in their own way. Several people were talking about the close friendship between Audrey Hope and Senorita Estella. They admired the simple but elegant dress of Senorita Estella and her soft spoken and charming personality. Sylvia remained by the side of Audrey Hope like a shadow throughout the party, and also through the dinner and dance while Audrey Hope socialized with the various people. She did not leave her even for a minute. After the function they both decided to walk, hand in hand, back to their house. Lady Marlow was walking just behind these two girls. On the way Audrey Hope asked Senorita Estella, "Well dear, how did you like the party?"

Sylvia said, "It was a magnificent party and there were lots of people but . . ."

Lady Marlow who was walking just behind them, asked, "But what?"

Sylvia replied, "You see Audrey Hope belongs here. She knows most of these rich and famous people from her childhood. The young girls were admiring her beauty and charming personality and she was very popular. But what surprised me was, that wherever I looked, I found people staring at me. Several times I felt like addressing them and telling them that Senorita Estella was a poor, insignificant girl from Lornehope Camp and at one time had no cap on her head and no shoes on her feet. She was a runaway from Austria who had no friends. It is my feeling that if I had addressed them like that, they would not only have stopped staring at me but would not even stand facing me. People are generally fascinated by the glitter and popularity and flock around rich and famous people like the insects around a light. There are very few people who sympathize with poor without any motive."

Lady Marlow said, "If you had narrated this story, that you have just told us, people would have been surprised."

Sylvia took a deep breath and said, "I really do not care if people had been surprised, nor do I care for their praise. People come to the theatre to watch me act and dance and listen to my songs. They really do not care about my background."

Sylvia turned her face away from Lady Marlow and spoke to Audrey Hope, "Today there is no show at the theatre but tomorrow's show is worth watching. Please, you must come."

Audrey Hope said, "I will definitely come to your house tomorrow at noon provided you invite me to join you for a cup of tea. After tea we can go to the theatre together."

Sylvia gladly accepted Audrey Hope's suggestion and took leave of Audrey Hope and Lady Marlow. When she entered her house, she found Merci Fairflex lying in bed. She asked her maid servant to go and get the doctor who lived nearby. She wanted to get proper medical treatment for Merci Fairflex. However, Merci Fairflex interjected and asked the maid servant not to fetch the doctor. She said to Sylvia, "There is no need for any medicine. My headache is much better. A good night's sleep is all that I need and I will be back to normal by morning. Now tell me how was the party and the food?"

Sylvia took off her dress and sat down beside Merci Fairflex on her bed. With a little moaning sound to show her boredom at the party, she said, "This was my first opportunity to go to a party at the palace of a royal princess. I have decided that I shall not go to any such parties in the future. Audrey Hope, you and me, the three of us, will have parties of our own. We will not invite any fourth person. The idea of a party is to enjoy and I enjoy Audrey Hope's and your company the most. I feel somewhat shy in the presence of a fourth person and resent the same. I do not know why I have become so attached to Audrey Hope and love her so much."

Merci Fairflex said, "Dear Sylvia, life is a puzzle and it is not easy for everyone to understand it. The majority of people want to enjoy life as much as they can. They do not realize that this life is also full of problems and sadness. In this world the pleasures are short lived, grief and sadness are prolonged. Joy, sadness, pleasure and grief are all mixed in this life and everyone is dealt a share of each. I am very happy about the fact that your acquaintance with Audrey Hope has blossomed into a friendship and is strengthened as each day passes. Your lucky star has arrived. All your past grief and problems are now over. From now onwards you will have joy and happiness. God bless you."

Sylvia sighed and said, "Probably you are right. However, I doubt if my friendship with Audrey Hope can make me forget the sadness and grief I have suffered in the past." She began to cry. She said goodnight to Merci Fairflex and went to her room and lay down on her bed. After a while she fell asleep.

The next day, Audrey Hope came to Sylvia's house in the afternoon as she had promised. Both the girls sat down and had their tea while talking and laughing together. At six'o clock, Audrey Hope got up to get dressed in her lovely and gorgeous theatre dress.

Sylvia took both the hands of Audrey Hope and sat her down in front of the mirror at her dressing table. She picked up a small mirror from the table and looked at Audrey Hope's face in her small mirror. She praised Audrey Hope's lovely dress and jewellery. She began to admire Audrey Hope's facial features and the grace on her face. She kept repeating how beautiful Audrey Hope looked and imitated her. Audrey Hope blushed and moved the small mirror held by Sylvia. Sylvia teased her by bringing the mirror back in position so that she could see Audrey Hope's face in it again. Audrey Hope moved the mirror away again. They were having fun teasing each other. In the meanwhile the maid servant entered the room to announce that someone was waiting outside to meet Sylvia. In their enjoyment both the girls ignored her and hardly listened to what she was saying. Suddenly, Audrey Hope removed the mirror and shouted in surprise as she sat down on the floor. Sylvia asked in a worried tone as to what had happened. Audrey Hope was hardly able to answer. Sylvia turned and saw a tall, very handsome gentleman standing at the door of the room. Sylvia at once threw the mirror on the table and ran with both arms extended and shouted with joy, "Oh! Lord Lorimor . . ."

Lord Lorimor took both the hands of Sylvia to greet her but his eyes were glued on Audrey Hope.

Chapter 34

Died for you and turned to dust and even dust is destroyed
Now tell me oh mirror in front of me what is the reality.

The tired and sad face of Lord Lorimor beamed with happiness on seeing Audrey Hope. He jumped with joy and said excitedly, "Audrey, Miss Hope, are you really here or is it my imagination?"

Audrey Hope looked at Lord Lorimor shyly and joyfully. She looked at him with a partly surprised and partly ecstatic look, as if she was seeing him in her dream. She said in a hurry with a very soft voice, "Lord Lorimor, good evening Sir."

Sylvia noticed the happiness in the eyes of both of them and at once guessed as to what was happening. She said with a smile, "Yes, yes she is Audrey Hope, my very close friend. She came to meet me here. I see that you already know my dear friend."

Audrey Hope was taken by surprise and was at a loss for words. She got up and with her head lowered, very shyly she shook the hand of Lord Lorimor but did not say a thing.

Lord Lorimor sat down on an easy chair. Audrey Hope sat down on the carpet on his right side of him and Sylvia sat on the left. Sylvia started asking Lord Lorimor all sorts of questions.

Sylvia said, "Lord Lorimor, why did you not inform me about your coming to London and why did you delay it so much?"

Lord Lorimor's entire concentration was on the lovely face of Audrey Hope. He had seen his beloved after a very long time.

All kinds of desires and hopes were going through his mind and he was basking in the satisfaction of his love for her. He was admiring her quietly in his heart. When Sylvia asked the question the second time, he came out of his trance and said, "Oh, Sylvia Bond, did you ask me something?"

On hearing this, Audrey Hope looked at Lord Lorimor, smiled and realized that he was lost in her love. Sylvia guessed that Audrey Hope was the lady because of whom Lord Lorimor had searched all the cities and jungles to find the lost person. On realizing this, Sylvia giggled and said in a special way, "Respected Sir, this servant of yours was asking why you took more time than what you had promised and why did you not inform me about your arrival with a letter or a telegram."

Since Lord Lorimor's whole attention was towards Audrey Hope, he felt confused, looked at Audrey Hope and said, "Is it your voice that I am hearing?" He brushed his hair with his hand and said, "Oh, this voice is from the left side. It must be Sylvia Bond asking me the reason for the delay in my coming back. Listen my dear sister, how could I inform you. I did not know till last evening that I would be able to leave for London in the morning. It was two days back that I found out from the senior railway officials that there was no Englishman working in the railway offices. They said there were a lot of unskilled and uneducated labourers from several distant countries. The contractor and his supervisors were looking after these labourers, but no formal railway office had been opened to look after the routine office paper work. They said the amount of paper work did not justify hiring any paid office staff at that time. After this information I went to the site myself and saw each worker to satisfy myself and make sure that no one resembled the person I was searching. A thought came to my mind. There might be a possibility that he may have someone special in London, whom he loved very much, and he may have returned to London and that is why I couldn't find him anywhere. With this thought I decided to return. Throughout the journey I thought that since I have searched for him in all the cities and in all the jungles, I should now go and start looking for him at Stonelake, the place that he belonged to." After giving this explanation, he looked lovingly at Audrey Hope and asked her about Lord and Lady Marlow's welfare.

Audrey Hope could tell, from the look on Lord Lorimor's face, as to how much he loved her and what was going through his mind. However, noticing how happy Sylvia looked and how she laughed and talked with Lord Lorimor, she once again began to doubt their true relationship. The pleasure she was getting from listening to Lord Lorimor turned to a feeling of uneasiness. However, with tact and foresight she controlled herself and replied to his question, with some coldness in her voice, "Yes Sir, with the grace of God they are doing well and are in good health."

Lord Lorimor noticed the coldness in Audrey Hope's tone and did not like it. He turned towards Sylvia and said, "As soon as I entered London, I came to know that you have won the hearts of thousands of men and women here with your excellent acting and singing. At the railway station I happened to meet a person who is the assistant manager at the theatre. He gave me your address. Everyone here seems to be praising you, and the skills you have in your profession."

Sylvia said, "I am surprised myself why people appreciate my dancing and singing so much. Personally I do not care for their praise or criticism, I just do my best. However, I consider myself very lucky and am proud that soon after coming here, I met dear Audrey Hope who is very honest and beautiful. We have become very close friends and enjoy each other's company immensely. You must be wondering how Audrey Hope, who is from such a rich and noble family and belongs to the elite society of London and I, a stage dancer and singer, became such close friends."

Lord Lorimor said, "From everything you have said, I find that you are not only her close friend but are very proud of it as well. Yes I am surprised at your friendship but at the same time I am also very happy. Tell me what brought you together and how did you two meet?"

Sylvia said, "The way and how we met is a long story. Someday I will get Audrey Hope to tell you the complete story. In brief, when I was performing at the stage, our eyes met and from then onwards, we both had a strong desire to meet each other. Some great force arranged for us to meet in the most peculiar circumstances. However, please tell us about your travels. Have you given up the search for this lost person or are you still planning to go back to the jungles again?" At Sylvia's remark, Audrey Hope and Lord Lorimor looked at each other and lowered their heads in shame.

Sylvia said, "Why are you hesitating? Please go ahead and tell us all the details of your travel. I don't care if Audrey Hope listens to it. I am interested in knowing all the details."

Lord Lorimor thought, "If I start telling her every detail then Sylvia will know that this lady sitting here is the one for which I undertook this travel and faced numerous troubles and great inconvenience. I will also have to tell about the rescue of Sylvia and my sympathy for her condition. This too will not be appropriate to tell in front of Audrey Hope." So he said with some hesitation, "The tale of my travel extends over two years and six months and if I start giving all the details, then it may take at least three days for me to narrate it. Very briefly, I am coming here directly from Switzerland."

He had hardly finished the sentence when Sylvia's maid servant came and said to Sylvia, "Merci Fairflex sends her regards and would like to inform you that the time for the final theatre preparations is approaching and a quick rehearsal is required for the new play. She asked if you could please come to the theatre now."

In response Sylvia said, "Please get my carriage ready. I am coming in a minute." Sylvia turned towards Lord Lorimor and said. "Merci Fairflex, whom you hired for looking after me, has been with me since then. She is a wonderful and kind person. She stays with me all twenty hours of the day and looks after me with love and devotion. Right now she is at the theatre, busy making arrangements at the stage, for tonight's show. If she was at the house she would have been delighted to see you come back. I too have to go to the theatre now. Please do excuse me at this time. Also please do come to the theatre this evening for the show."

Sylvia rushed towards the door and as she was leaving, Audrey Hope called her in loud voice and said, "Sylvia Bond, please wait. I am also going to join you."

Lord Lorimor interjected and said, "Audrey Hope, can you please stay for a few more minutes as I have a few things to talk with you." Sylvia also stopped at the door and said to Audrey Hope, "Yes, I think it will be better if you come to the theatre after a little while. I am also afraid that Lord Lorimor may once again be possessed by the desire to travel and vanish in some corner of the world, in some jungle or city. Why don't you entertain him with your sweet talk for a while. I shall be back within an hour, after making the final arrangements at the theatre." After saying this Sylvia ran to the carriage.

After Sylvia left, Lord Lorimor got up from the easy chair and sat down beside Audrey Hope on the floor. He said in loving voice, "Dear Audrey, I have come to London only to see you. As it happened, I met you here. I trust you are not angry with me for sitting beside you and would give me permission to give a report of my travels in search of your friend." He suddenly stopped as he realized that Audrey Hope's face had turned pale. She was perspiring all over with a feeling of shame and guilt. He thought that she did not like to talk in privacy, and was perplexed. However, Audrey Hope said in a carefree and cold voice, "I am happy to see you back."

Lord Lorimor said, "How can you be happy when I did not carry out your wish? Please believe me, I searched for your friend, Nevlin Lane, in every country and did not leave any stone unturned in search of him. I am very sorry that I did not find him anywhere and did not even get any news about him from any source. The knowledgeable people say that Europe is a small continent in comparison to the others. But it seems to be far bigger than the earth to hide Nevlin Lane. It seems that Nevlin Lane is hiding underground and that makes it almost impossible to trace him."

Audrey Hope said in a low but cold voice. "This is very surprising."

It is interesting to note that if there was any other person in place of Lord Lorimor, he would have been very upset and heart broken. After all the hardships and trouble he went through for his beloved, Audrey Hope did not even say a polite "Thank you." Her behaviour was cold and not very congenial. However, Lord Lorimor's love was true. He was thinking that Audrey Hope's behaviour reflects her pride and was secretly admiring her. He kept on telling her about his efforts and said, "Dear Audrey Hope, God is my witness. The reason I did not write to you was that I felt that you may think that I am just making excuses. Even after the two year period expired, I kept myself busy in search of Nevlin Lane, with full determination and hope."

While talking, he looked down at Audrey Hope's feet and like an innocent young boy said shyly, "Tell me Audrey Hope, is there any hope left for me? I do not want to sound as if I am bargaining and asking you this favour, in exchange for my troubles. I am truly in love with you and even in my travels in the deserts and jungles, your face was always before me and gave me the inspiration to continue. My heart was always sad at my separation from you. If what I desire can be realized by finding Nevlin Lane, then I am willing to go back and continue the search. I would only like to know from you, if there is still hope for me. I will immediately leave for the distant countries again. Your happiness is my priority. If you had given me more time I would not have returned to London at this time. I would have continued my search everywhere, till I found Nevlin Lane and brought him back with me. I love you very much. In the past two and a half years, I searched for your childhood friend in snow covered mountains, in valleys, in deserts, in jungles, in cities everywhere. Wherever I went, your face was always in front of me. Several times I dreamt that you were sitting by my side holding my hands. Several mornings I would get up and your sweet voice would sound in my ears. When I would wake up in the morning and realize that you were not there and that it was only a dream, I used to cry a lot. I felt like packing up and come running back to you. But my promise to you held me back and I continued with my search."

On hearing Lord Lorimor speak like this, Audrey Hope's eyes filled with tears and she began to cry. Her tears dropped on her own hands. The voice of her true love, Lord Lorimor, sounded to her as if an angel from above was speaking to her. She had a choking sensation because of all the emotions building up inside her. She kept sitting quietly and intently listening to all the experiences of Lord Lorimor. Her eyes were fixed at his face.

Lord Lorimor continued and said, "In my dream I once saw you getting angry at me and calling me disloyal. You were going to marry someone else. This dream bothered me so much that, for one full day and night I could not eat any food. When Sylvia saw my condition, she insisted upon knowing the reason for my concern. Reluctantly, I only told her that, 'I love a lady with all my heart and I have been seeing her in my dreams for the last few days. She asked me to search for her lost childhood friend and gave me a limit of two years to find him. This time limit expired some months back but my conscience did not permit me to go back to her without completing the mission that I undertook.' On hearing this Sylvia was really angry with me, gave me a lecture and advised me in these terms, 'The lady who sent you on this wild goose chase to find her friend loves you with all her heart. She asked you for this task just to test your love. You should have gone back to her a day before the expiry of the two year period. Men generally do not understand the indicators given by women to show their love, and invariably never understand a woman's love. Men also tend to form wrong opinions based on outwardly appearances. They do not know the reality. In spite of being very intelligent and highly educated they do not understand a women's nature. Although you have not told me the name of this lady in spite of my inquiring several times, I have great sympathy for her as one woman to another. Since my sympathy is for her, I tell you as a woman, that a woman does not go around speaking of her love all the time. All of us women who are honest and come from decent families are the same. Love is manifested in our looks and not in our talk. Therefore, I say to you with full confidence that this lady loves you very much. I can bet on it. You made a very serious mistake by ignoring the promise of the two year time limit. You also did not write to her. It is best if you go to her right now without a moment's delay.' I trusted Sylvia's advice and have come back now. Dear Audrey please say something. Look at me. If, according to Sylvia, you do love me, will you marry me and be my wife?" He took both her hands and pulled her towards him, trying to hug her. Audrey Hope immediately pulled her hands away and said in a soft and shy voice, "No, please no!"

Lord Lorimor said, "Is your 'No' a response to my question? Alright, I should not be shocked and pained by your reply. I am sorry I wasted so much of your time by my meaningless talk. I am now convinced that you do not love me at all."

In response, Audrey Hope again said softly, crying all the time, "No, please no. You do not understand."

Lord Lorimor, instead of trying to seek clarification, got lost in the emotions of grief and sadness at losing his battle of love. He said with grief in his voice, "I sensed your coldness the moment I came here but because of my true love for you I was hopeful of receiving mercy from you. I lived with this hope buried in my heart all these years. This hope which was with me throughout my travels, is shattered today."

Audrey Hope once again began to cry. On seeing her cry so much, Lord Lorimor felt ashamed. He began to regret what he had said. He said to Audrey Hope, "Please do not cry. I am sorry if my words hurt you. Please don't be angry or sad at what I have said. I would rather kill all my hopes and ambitions than tolerate to see you sad. I will bid you and all my hopes for the future goodbye and let them go to hell. You be happy and enjoy yourself. Please congratulate Sylvia Bond on my behalf for her fame and great success. Please also say my last goodbye to her. I hope and pray that the lucky man who marries you, will always keep you happy. I have only one question left in my mind. Tell me honestly who is the person who has won your heart?"

Audrey Hope lowered her head in shame and between sobs, said to Lord Lorimor, "The news of my engagement with Sir Jordan Lane has been published in the daily newspapers."

On hearing this, Lord Lorimor went into a fit of uncontrollable rage. His body began to shake with anger and jealousy. His face became red. His eyes had the appearance of blood in them. He began to pace the room and shout like a mad man, "That wicked Jordan Lane is going to marry the honest and kind hearted Audrey Hope! Are there no decent men left in this world to marry Audrey Hope. Oh my, Oh my, he is a fraud, he is cunning, he is disloyal, he is greedy, he is dishonest, he cheats other people. Many people are familiar with Jordan Lane's mean and wicked nature. His step brother Nevlin Lane, Percy Heel, Lord Chester and several other people I know, are well aware of his nature. They have first hand experience of his wicked and dishonest behaviour and think of him as most untrustworthy and a liar. How could he possibly manage to entice a fair and loyal girl like you to marry him?"

Lord Lorimor just kept shouting angry statements without addressing anyone in particular. He began to run towards the door to leave the house. Just then, Sylvia entered the house after completing the preparations for the new play. With his hands shaking, Lord Lorimor held Sylvia by her shoulders and pinned her against the wall like a doll. Sylvia could not understand what was happening and just moaned, "Oh, Oh!" Sylvia was about to say something when Lord Lorimor spoke in a very agitated voice, "Sylvia Bond, please excuse me for this mad and unbecoming behaviour. I bid you my final goodbye, I am leaving for good."

Sylvia could see that Lord Lorimor's face was red with rage and he was very upset, and she could guess that the kind Lord was not quite himself. She asked him in a very worried voice, "Where are you going? Why are you behaving like a mad man and a person not able to control himself? What made you so upset and frustrated. Please control yourself and tell me where you are going? I have a right to know."

Lord Lorimor said, "Except for hell, there is no other place left for me to go to. Please accept my last farewell. Please, please save this lady!" After saying this he ran out of the door and could be seen running on the street. Within seconds he was out of sight.

Sylvia entered the room feeling dazed and concerned. She saw

Audrey Hope lying on the floor with her face down, crying and sobbing uncontrollably. Sylvia, with her hands shaking, helped her to sit up. She wiped her tears and straightened her hair a bit with her hands. Sylvia asked in a soft voice, "What is going on? What did Lord Lorimor say to you in my absence and what did you say to him? I have never seen him behaving in such an inappropriate manner and acting like a mad person ever before. Please tell me honestly what happened."

Audrey Hope said, "Like a glass broken into pieces, I broke his heart with my careless remarks."

Sylvia said, "Why did you do that?"

Audrey Hope said, "Did you not guess by now that I am that very miserable, stupid woman who sent Lord Lorimor to the deserts and jungles?"

Sylvia looked very surprised and asked, "Are you the lady who sent Lord Lorimor to search for her lost friend?"

Audrey Hope replied, "Yes, I sent Lord Lorimor to search for my lost childhood friend."

Sylvia said, "Oh dear! how could I have known that you are the unnamed lady. I must apologise for saying several things which were not very complimentary to you. I am very sorry."

Audrey Hope's eyes filled with tears and she said, "My dear friend, please do not even think about it. I deserve to be called worse. The fact is that I crushed all his hopes. Due to my stupidity I behaved towards him in a cold manner. Before I could calm him down and explain, he rushed out of here. Men generally are very rash and act fast. Lord Lorimor is a step ahead of others."

Sylvia thought that if Lord Lorimor was not so fast acting, how could he have saved her from the clutches of wicked Lewryk. Sylvia smiled and said, "Sometimes a fast acting man can be a great boon for us women folk. Oh well let us leave this subject, it will not get us anywhere. Tell me, are you angry with Lord Lorimor for not being successful in finding your friend Nevlin Lane and bringing him back here?"

Audrey Hope replied, "Oh no. Not at all. I really do not care whether he found the lost person or not."

Sylvia said, "Yes, I understand. You devised all this to test the true love of Lord Lorimor. What I do not understand is this. Now that Lord Lorimor has come back here, what is the cause for all this immense grief and sadness?"

Audrey Hope said, "It would have been better if Lord Lorimor had not met me here. The news of my engagement to Sir Jordan Lane has been published in all the newspapers."

Sylvia was taken by surprise on hearing this news. Her eyes filled with tears and she said, "I can see that poor Lord Lorimor must have been deeply shocked by this news. Now I can understand his behaviour. Tell me who is this Sir Jordan Lane. What is his status and what type of a person is he?"

Audrey Hope said, "Sir Jordan Lane is the step brother of the person in whose search I sent Lord Lorimor. He is the one who published the news of my engagement with him. I am now tied to him."

Sylvia said, "Dear Audrey, there is nothing wrong with this. If you have fallen in love with him then it is not your fault."

On hearing this Audrey Hope began to cry once again and between sobbing, said, "No, the fault is entirely mine. I am disloyal, untrustworthy and very dumb. As you also said before, I will have to suffer all my life because of my shortcomings and faults. I deserve all the punishment that I may get." Audrey Hope had hardly finished the sentence when her maid came with the carriage and informed her that her carriage was ready and waiting at the door for her. At the same time Sylvia's maid also came and informed Sylvia that it was now time for her to leave for the theatre and her carriage was also waiting at the door.

Sylvia had a lot of work to do at the stage for that day's show. She got up at once and requested Audrey Hope to come to the show. "Today we are going to stage a new play at the theatre. Please, you must come to see it."

Audrey Hope wiped her tears and said, "I cannot say no to you. However, when I come to the theatre I will still be in a sad mood. I will be the most miserable and unhappy person in the theatre tonight."

Sylvia climbed into her carriage and drove away. She did not have time to respond to Audrey Hope properly. On the way to the theatre, Sylvia remembered the time when Jack was killed by the dacoit. His coat was brought back by the servants of Lord Lorimor. The coat was given to her and was lying on her lap. She recalled how she was completely heart broken. Remembering her own experience, she felt great sympathy for Lord Lorimor. His last words spoken with great emotion began to haunt her: "Please, please save this lady." She wondered what the respected Lord meant by this. How was it possible to change her heart if she already loved someone else? She decided that she will have to question Audrey Hope further to get to the bottom of this. She wondered how far she could intervene and help them, when Audrey Hope loved this other person. She thought that to question Audrey Hope further would only result in making her more miserable. She felt very sorry for Lord Lorimor. She was absorbed in these thoughts as the carriage reached the theatre. Once she reached there she got busy in the preparations for the show.

Chapter 35

By continuously expanding our horizon of search
We shall find you wherever you may be.

There was a man named Parson, who was a resident of London. He was employed as a servant at the house of late Sir Gravlin Lane. His wife was also employed at the house to look after the children. Even after the death of her husband she kept on working at the house. She served as a nanny to the children of Sir Gravlin Lane and discharged her duties with great love and diligence. Nevlin Lane was looked after by this same nanny from the day he was born. Her love for Nevlin Lane was no less than that of his own mother. From the very childhood, Nevlin Lane used to create new games to play with other children. He used to gather all the neighbourhood children and teach them these new games. That is why Mrs. Parson, the nanny, used to call him Master Lane. After the death of Sir Gravlin Lane, she could not tolerate the nit picking, nagging and the angry attitude of Jordan Lane. She resigned and left his employment. She began to live alone in a house in an area known as Grosvenor Borough. She had managed to save a good sum of money during her employment and was able to live comfortably on the interest she earned from this money. She was a quiet natured person and did not like to talk much. She never socialized with other servants in the house. She spent most of her time reading religious books. She was an honest and straightforward person. She never indulged in gossip related to the happenings in the house nor did she ever complain against her employer in front of others. She was a very loyal servant. She thought she would make God angry if she was disloyal to her employer. Sir Jordan Lane, due to his cunning ways, grabbed everything after the death of his father and became the sole owner of all the property and wealth. Mrs. Parson knew him to be a liar and a cheat from his childhood. She knew he was very jealous type. She also knew that he seduced Rachel, the daughter of dacoit Banks and left her after making all kinds of false promises. She also knew that he made false and serious, baseless accusations against Nevlin Lane to their father and made him so angry that he turned Nevlin Lane out of the house. She was aware that after Nevlin Lane left the house, he had lied to his father by promising to help Nevlin Lane. He had forced his father to write a new will leaving everything in his name. His father did this under duress. This was the reason that Jordan Lane was always angry with her and humiliated her in front of other servants. He did not want to fire her because he knew that Nevlin Lane was very close to her and she loved Nevlin Lane very much. He was well aware that she knew all that had happened in the past and was involved in all the family matters. He was afraid that if one of these days Nevlin Lane returned back to London, she would tell him all his secrets and cunning schemes. However, he made her life very miserable and difficult, hoping she would resign and leave on her own. Mrs. Parson eventually decided that she could not serve in such humiliating conditions. She was getting no respect from Jordan Lane. She got fed up of daily bickering and shouting. She left the employment of Jordan Lane and bought a house in the nearby area and began to live there.

The true friend of Nevlin Lane, inspector Trail, had shown him the house of his old nanny Mrs. Parson from a distance and had left for his office work. Nevlin Lane entered the house without knocking at the door. Mrs. Parson recognized him immediately, and ran to him, saying, "Master Lane, Master Lane." She hugged him and kissed his forehead and eyes. Nevlin Lane greeted her respectfully and kissed her forehead. He went towards one of the chairs in the room and sat down. He said in a kind voice, "I do not know how to thank you for your love and affection. You recognized me at once and gave me a very warm welcome. You may also remember that in my childhood days, you used to make special biscuits for me and fed me with your own hands. You always looked after me. You used to let me buy the food and toys that I liked from the market. You used to cradle me in your lap when I was young. I am your very same Nevlin Lane. My love and admiration for you has not diminished one bit."

Mrs. Parson affectionately kissed his hands several times and said with a big smile, "Yes I remember all your childhood things very well. Do you remember you used to jump and skip in front of me and like a monkey you would climb trees leaping from one branch to another. You also taught Audrey Hope naughty pranks and several new games. Just like me, she too will be overwhelmed and filled with joy on seeing you here. She misses you very much. About two weeks back she came to see me and for a long time we talked about you and prayed for your welfare. She kept asking me if I knew your address. I did not know where you were or how you were doing. So I could not tell her anything. Dear Nevlin Lane, Audrey Hope is now a mature, young woman. She is very wise, beautiful and well trained. She is a very loving girl. She constantly remembers you and is very upset at her separation from you." She left for the kitchen across the central courtyard in the house to prepare some food for Nevlin Lane to eat and continued talking from the kitchen. "Dear Nevlin Lane, you may have already heard that she is about to be married to your step brother Jordan Lane. Have you been to see your brother? How long has it been since you came back to London? Tell me everything. Where were you all this time? How did you manage? Where were you living, which place? What were you doing in a foreign country?"

Nevlin Lane sighed deeply and said in a sad tone, "My story is very long and complicated. I will tell you at a later date. First of all you tell me as to how you are managing? Since when have you been living alone? Have you left my brother's service permanently? I have come directly to your house. I have only met inspector Trail so far. No, I have not been to see my brother, nor have I met any other of my acquaintances. I also do not intend to meet anyone else at this stage. First I want to know about everyone from you. Tell me about my brother. How is he doing and how is he keeping? How is his behaviour towards others?"

Mrs. Parson said, "You know me very well. It is not in my nature to fight with anyone. I do not go visiting other people's houses, nor do I listen to or spread any gossip. I do not believe in rumours, whether they are true or false. As you know I have been employed in your family ever since I was young. I have been a loyal servant and have never said a single word about your family to anyone because I consider it to be disloyal. However, it is different with you. I have cared for you since you were born. It is your family and you are a part of it. I have absolutely no hesitation at all in talking to you about your own family. There is no disloyalty in talking to you. I tell you, Jordan Lane made my life miserable. After you left, he started to mistreat me. There was bickering daily and he would create a scene. I was driven to complete frustration and I could not take it anymore. Finally I resigned and left his employment for good. He still hates me. What to talk of respect or consideration, he does not even like to talk to me while passing in front of my house, though I call him and say hello. Now he is a big officer and very rich too. But for me he is still the same old child that I cared for. I also used to give him a bath and dress him every morning and kept his toys and other things neatly arranged. But he does not respect me at all. He has become so proud of himself and his ego is so bloated that he considers everyone else much inferior to him. It is not in his nature to be kind. I spent forty years in the service of your family and not even once did anyone speak to me harshly or in a demeaning way. As soon as Jordan Lane took over, he began to make my life so miserable that it became impossible to stay in the house even for a minute. He began to find fault in everything I did, and I was hardly able to finish one task when he would ask me to do another job. He would not give me sufficient time to complete the task. In short, he considered me to be his enemy. I think one of the main reasons for this was that he considered me to be loyal to you and he knew very well that I love you like my own son. I know all the cunning schemes of Jordan Lane and other confidential family matters. However, I do not wish to backbite nor do I want to plead my case in front of you. I am sure when you meet him, you will find for yourself, how he is behaving towards others. You will eventually come to know of everything that has been going on in your house."

Nevlin Lane said, "I do not wish to meet my brother at this time. Right now I want to meet your sister's son, your nephew. He was my close friend and was also my class fellow. He is my childhood friend. He is very clever and mature and I know he is sincerely interested in my welfare. When he comes here, please tell him right away about my return to London and my desire to see him. First I would like to consult you and your nephew on several matters and only after that I will plan to meet my other friends and relatives."

Mrs. Parson said with tears in her eyes, "My nephew left for a sea voyage long time back. The rumour is that he drowned in the sea. I have not mentioned this to anyone so far. I have kept quiet about this tragedy. Only inspector Trail knows about his drowning. I am grateful to the all merciful God that He has sent you in place of my nephew. Though I am your servant, my feelings for you are that of a mother and I expect the same from you. I insist that you now stay with me in this house and eat the food that I cook for you. Trust me, I am not going to let you go out of my sight anymore, not even for a minute. You are my master and now with your presence in the house I will not feel lonely anymore. I can live the rest of my life knowing that you are with me. You may go out to meet others or for a walk but you must come back by meal time because I am not going to eat till I have fed you."

Nevlin Lane was very happy at hearing this from his nanny and to see such affection and sincerity. He readily agreed to the request. He enjoyed the meals lovingly prepared by Mrs. Parson. After lunch he went to the drawing room and looked at the various books in the cabinet. Mrs. Parson spent the whole afternoon getting the room ready for Nevlin Lane and in the evening he shifted in this room which was so tastefully decorated for him. After dinner he retired to his room and relaxed. That night, after a long time, he had a very sound sleep. Though the room was small, it was very neat and clean. It had a little thatched verandah in front that gave it shade. Nevlin Lane could detect the smell of Lavender perfume in the room and found the room very pleasant and nicely furnished. He could see that Mrs. Parson had decorated the room with her loving hands and had taken great pains to make it comfortable. Nevlin Lane settled down in this room and made a routine to go out for a walk in the morning and evenings. During the day, he spent his time in gardening. There was a small garden in front of his room and he enjoyed working there, planting flowers. Sometimes in the evening, when he was tired of working in the garden, he would go for a walk in the gardens of his old house, Lane Court, carefully avoiding being seen by any servants. He would entertain himself by visiting the favourite spots of his carefree childhood days, where he used to play with inspector Trail, Audrey Hope and other neighbourhood children. He spent considerable time looking at these places.

One evening Mrs. Parson spent considerable effort and time in preparing some special dishes for Nevlin Lane. She laid the dinner table very nicely and invited Nevlin Lane to come and have dinner. She talked to him in a very affectionate and kind manner about the old days. She served him every dish personally. The food was delicious and Nevlin Lane took time to enjoy every dish and relish each bite. The dinner took a long time to finish because they were talking and eating leisurely. After dinner Nevlin Lane got up from his chair to go for an evening walk. As he was getting up, Mrs. Parson said, "Listen son, today is Friday and every Friday I read the Bible. By the time I am finished, it gets rather late in the night. Therefore, when you return from your walk, please go to your room directly without wishing me goodnight, and have a good sleep. I will see you in the morning." Nevlin Lane said goodnight to his nanny and went to his room.

Nevlin Lane took out his revolver and kept it in his pocket. He decided to visit that portion of his old house, Court Lane, where the big and very dense old oak tree used to be. He used to play under this tree with Audrey Hope. He remembered that he used to hide in the thick branches of the tree while playing hide and seek with her.

He started walking leisurely towards his old house. On the way his thoughts turned to Audrey Hope and his friend at Lornehope Camp, Sylvia Bond. He wondered where Sylvia was now, what she was doing and how she was passing her time? He had heard that she was under the care of a rich and kind Lord from London and hoped that she was happy under his protection. He thought, "By living in luxury with this rich Lord, I will not be surprised if she has forgotten me. It is a fact that when a person is dead for some time, even his closest friends and relatives tend to forget him and their pain and sorrow gradually diminishes with the passing of time. Eventually the dead person is forgotten. They carry on their work in the world according to their own ability and experience without missing the dead person. This is a fact of life. I am so sad that Sylvia has been separated from me. I remember fondly the time when Sylvia, cook Mathula and I used to live a carefree life at Lornehope Camp. It was so peaceful and we all lived very happily. Sylvia's hair were as smooth as silk. I miss her innocent and charming face and her sweet talk. She had a very good voice and she sang very well. I loved to hear her sing. I used to carry on with my job of digging, with the picture of her soft face in front of me. She was always with me. As it happens, my love for her has increased so much since our separation that her sweet face is now always in front of my eyes. Who knows, God may arrange for us to meet again some day. Only God knows what is in store for us in the future. I think that the rich Lord must be busy with his friends and his social circle. Sylvia too would be enjoying herself and having a good time under his care and guidance. In her enjoyment, singing, dancing and partying in London, she will not have any time to remember a poor man like me. There was a time when she used to call me Jack and look after me with such tender loving care. My condition is much worse now than it was before and it is a fact that even the closest relatives of a person, who is poor, do not like to talk to him. The possibility of my getting out of this condition of poverty is very unlikely, though not impossible." He suddenly decided that after visiting his old house in Court Lane tonight, he would say goodbye to it forever and leave London to go back to Austria the next day, or day after at the latest. He said to himself, "I will once again try my luck at digging. I have no more desire left to get rich by digging gold. All my ambitions for money and getting rich have been destroyed by Sylvia's separation. But somehow I have to feed myself."

The chain of thought was interrupted by the voice of inspector Trail calling him from behind. He caught up with Nevlin Lane by taking a couple of fast steps.

Inspector Trail said, "My friend Nevlin Lane! Where are you going?"

Nevlin Lane replied, "I came out for an evening walk from the house of my nanny and did not realize how far I have walked. After walking a little further I shall return back to her house."

Inspector Trail said, "I would have joined you for the walk but I have a very important work at the railway station. I have learned that these days your step brother, Sir Jordan Lane is residing at your old house Court Lane."

Nevlin Lane was surprised to hear this and asked Inspector Trail, "Can you tell me for how many days my elder brother has been here?"

Inspector Trail replied, "I generally keep myself informed of his coming and going from here. I have been hearing about his coming for over a week. But, all of a sudden, two days back he came here. I hear he is not keeping well. Probably you are on your way to see him at this time."

Nevlin Lane said, "Oh no. No, I have no intentions at all of meeting him at this time. I had just come out for a walk and would return back shortly. Tell me what's the latest news of the town?"

Inspector Trail said, "It is surprising that you have not met your brother so far. I have learned from reliable sources that your brother is planning some extensive renovations to your old house. He is planning to stay at the Court Lane house after his marriage to Audrey Hope. He is planning to convert one portion of the house into a heavenly place for entertainment. In this respect I will talk to you in more detail tomorrow morning when there is more time. I also want to consult you and seek your advice about something on my mind regarding this proposed marriage of Audrey Hope. You know I consider Audrey Hope to be like my sister. We all used to play together and grew up together. We have love and affection for each other like brothers and sisters, in fact more. However, right now I have an extremely urgent matter to take care of and I shall discuss all this at a more leisurely time."

Nevlin Lane said, "I may not be able to see you after today. I have already decided to leave London tomorrow."

Inspector Trail said, "For goodness sake, do not do any such rash thing."

Nevlin Lane replied, "I have made up my mind to leave London tomorrow. I have already seen my old house Court Lane, where you, Audrey Hope and I used to play and enjoy in our childhood days. There is only one more area left which I want to visit. After that I will be satisfied. I have only two true and sincere friends here. One of them is you. No words can convey the feeling of happiness that I have experienced after meeting you. I find you just the same old sincere friend as you were in our childhood days, truly interested in my well being. The other friend is Audrey Hope. I often remember her. I have already learned all the news about her. Everyone has told me how beautiful, kind hearted and wise she has become. I am anxious to see her once. I am hoping to see her face somewhere during my walk. Except for you two, I have no desire to meet anyone else in London. In this situation there is no point in my staying here any longer. If not tomorrow, I shall certainly leave London the day after."

Inspector Trail said, "Even at this age, you seem to be very determined. I remember, that in our childhood days too, you had a certain rash trend and would do exactly what you had decided to do in your mind without considering the outcome. I find you the same determined person at this age also. My kind friend, listen, I have still got thousands of things to talk over with you. Moreover I am not satisfied with the time we have spent together. Please promise me that you will not leave or go anywhere without first meeting me. Right now I have this extremely important assignment. I have to arrest someone near the railway station otherwise I would have insisted that you come with me to my house. I am going to inform all my police department right now of your intention to leave London. Unless you decide to grow wings and fly over London, my men will catch you the moment you try to leave and will bring you to my house! It will be futile for you to attempt to try and go away." He shook Nevlin Lane's hand with warmth and affection and walked away with a fast pace towards his mission.

Nevlin Lane put both his hands in his trouser pockets and kept walking towards the big oak tree located by the side gardens of his old house at Court Lane. He was very happy to see this old tree. He jumped and climbed on one of the branches of the tree and said to himself, "I used to hide from Audrey Hope in the thick leaves of this tree. This branch is still the same, loaded with thick green leaves. We used to hide in this branch of the tree and our other friends, the boys and girls from neighbouring houses would go crazy looking for us all over the place and finally we had to help them by shouting their names. We preferred this area for playing hide and seek as compared to other areas of the Court Lane house. If Sylvia Bond had come back safely to London with me, I would have introduced her to Audrey Hope. These two girls would have been good friends. I would have played hide and seek with her at this very location. I love this sport and I am still fond of it." This thought suddenly brought back the memory that there used to be small ants and insects on the branches of this tree. With this thought he started shaking his clothes vigorously in case ants and other insects might have come on his clothes. In a few seconds when he realized what he was doing he laughed heartily. He hugged the tree trunk and kissed it and spoke to the tree in a loud voice, "My dear friend, it is after ages that I have climbed your branches.

It is my love for you that has brought me here at this time." After this he took out his pipe to smoke and looked for the matches in his coat pocket. He searched all his pockets but could not locate the box of matches. He thought that it had probably fallen from his pocket while he was climbing the tree. He wanted to get down from the tree and look for the box of matches on the ground, but the moon was not fully over the sky and the light of the stars was not sufficient to clearly see the ground. In spite of this, Nevlin Lane tried to locate the matches on the ground from his position up in the branch. Suddenly he heard footsteps in the distance and he could see a man coming from the front. As the leaves were dense and dangling in front of his eyes, he could not clearly see the face of the man. He thought that probably his mind was playing tricks on him because nobody would come to Stonelake at this late hour in the night. When the sound of the steps became louder, then Nevlin Lane thought that it must be a robber who was coming to rob his brother's mansion. He thought of getting down from the tree and confronting this man but noticed that this man stopped under the big oak tree on which he was sitting. In the dim moonlight, he could barely make out the features of the man but noticed that the man was dressed in neat looking clothes. Nevlin Lane thought that maybe this man was drunk and had lost his way and has just stopped to rest under the tree. Once again he thought of getting down to find out from the man as to what he was doing there. But he noticed that the man was now sitting at the base of the tree. He was measuring the ground with his hand. Nevlin Lane did not get down from his perch on the tree but kept sitting absolutely motionless and quiet to find out what the man was doing there. The man took out a candle from his pocket and lighted it. He looked all around. With the light from the candle, Nevlin Lane could see clearly that the man was dressed in a suit and wearing a turkish style cap and expensive shoes. He was wearing golden rim glasses and a gown like that worn by lawyers. His hair and moustache were white. He looked a little apprehensive and was nervously looking all around with a candle in his hand. He waited for about five minutes and then he kept the lighted candle on the ground. He started in the north direction measuring with the palm of his hand. He measured eleven full palm lengths. He took out a small but sharp shovel from his coat pocket and measured one more palm length and marked this twelve palm length spot with the shovel. He went back to the base of the tree and once again measured twelve palm lengths and came to the same spot he had marked before and assured himself that he had the right spot. He kept the candle near the spot and with the small shovel began to dig at that spot. A bird flew from the opposite tree where he was digging and he stopped digging and carefully watched the bird. The bird settled in a nearby small tree and he resumed digging. He kept an eye on the surrounding area constantly. In about ten minutes he dug up a fair size hole. He deposited the excavated soil near his side. He bent down and pulled a long and broad thing from the hole. He examined it carefully turning it from side to side. After examining it, he held it under his feet and filled the hole back and levelled it with the excavated earth.

Nevlin Lane who was watching this man with full concentration, thought that this person, who was dressed as a lawyer, appeared to be interested in making medicines. He must have buried some dead animal or some metal for seasoning and had come back to dig it up when the temperature had cooled down. He was now going to go away to prepare some special medicine. Nevlin Lane was interested in knowing as to what this man would do next. With this intention, he kept sitting in his place very quietly. He kept his eyes on this person and could see his every movement in the candle light.

Chapter 36

Ask Moses about God's Grace
Went to pray and found spiritual guidance.

Nevlin Lane noticed that this man, who appeared to be a lawyer by the clothes he was wearing, brought the candle and kept it at the base of the oak tree. He began to examine carefully the article that he had dug out. Nevlin Lane could now clearly see the article and realized it was a metallic cylinder and not a herb or dead animal as he had initially thought. Looking at the metallic cylinder Nevlin Lane thought that he was probably a very rich man and had hidden gold coins and jewellery to safeguard them from his relatives. As he was imagining various possibilities, the man took out a knife from his pocket and loosened the lid of the cylinder by scrapping its edges all around. He took out a piece of paper from the metallic cylinder. The paper was also rolled up in a cylindrical shape. He examined the paper, folded it and carefully kept it in the inside pocket of his coat. He dug another hole a few inches from the tree base and buried the empty metallic cylinder in it. He again levelled this hole with the excavated earth and leaves. He took out a cigar from his pocket and began smoking it. The smoke from cigar filled the surrounding air. After finishing the cigar he took his time to take out that paper from his pocket and looked all around. He jumped on one of the lower branches of the same tree. He tried to catch the thick stem of the branch above him by stretching himself a few times, like